'Deaver has produced an exciting cyberthriller'
Sunday Telegraph

'Once again displays his penchants for multiple false
endings . . . This is the most ambitious attempt yet to
turn computer crime into fiction . . . Deaver's customary
brilliant plotting'
The Sunday Times

'Jeffery Deaver's story, set in California, sets out to
dazzle and bewilder reader with all manner of cyber-clues
and deceptions . . . a classic detective yarn'
Gerald Kaufman, *Scotsman*

'Slick, pacey and jam-packed with action'
Yorkshire Evening Post

'He has pulled off the considerable coup of introducing
two distinctive new heroes . . . Recently, authors such as
Patricia Cornwell have come adrift when trying to create
a fresh formula for their books, but Deaver writes as if
the prose in *The Blue Nowhere* had been his house style
all along. Working against the considerable disadvantage
of an online villain – Deaver really has to work hard to
make him truly sinister – he has created a high-tech
thriller that suggests he need never go back to his
Lincoln Rhyme books. But he probably will'
Publishing News

The Blue Nowhere

Jeffery Deaver

CORONET BOOKS
Hodder & Stoughton

Copyright © 2001 by Jeffery Deaver

First published in Great Britain in 2001
by Hodder and Stoughton
A division of Hodder Headline

The right of Jeffery Deaver to be identified as the
Author of the Work has been asserted by him in accordance
with the Copyright, Designs and Patents Act 1988.

A Coronet paperback

20 19 18

A CIP catalogue record for this title
is available from the British Library.

ISBN 0 340 76751 0

Printed and bound in Great Britain by
Clays Ltd, St Ives plc

Hodder and Stoughton
A division of Hodder Headline
338 Euston Road
London NW1 3BH

[W]hen I say that the brain is a machine, it is meant not as an insult to the mind but as an acknowledgment of the potential of a machine. I do not believe that a human mind is less than what we imagine it to be, but rather that a machine can be much, much more.

– W. Daniel Hillis, *The Pattern on the Stone*

GLOSSARY

Bot (from robot): A software program that, operating on its own, assists users or other programs. Also referred to as an agent.

Bug: An error in software that prevents or interferes with the operation of the program.

Chip-jock: A computer worker who specializes in hardware development or sales.

Civilians: Those individuals not involved in the computer industry.

Code: Software.

Code cruncher: An unimaginative software programmer who performs simple or mundane programming tasks.

Codeslinger: A talented software programmer, whose work is considered innovative. Also referred to as a samurai.

Crack: To illicitly break into a computer, usually to steal or destroy data or to prevent others from using the system.

Demon (or daemon): An unobtrusive, often hidden, software program that isn't specifically activated by a user command but that operates autonomously. It usually becomes active when certain conditions within the computer where it resides occur.

Firewall: A computer security system that prevents unwanted data from entering the computer it's intended to guard.

Freeware: Software made available by its developers at no charge.

Guru: A brilliant computer expert, a *WIZARD*.

Hack: Originally this word meant to quickly write a software program for a limited purpose though it evolved to mean the study and writing of innovative software programs. Increasingly the term is used by *CIVILIANS* to mean breaking into computer systems for malicious purposes – a practice more properly referred to as *CRACKING*. The word is also used as a noun to mean a clever piece of programming.

ICQ (I seek you): A subnetwork of the Internet similar to the *IRC* but devoted to private conversations. Similar to instant messaging.

IRC (Internet Relay Chat): A popular subnetwork of the Internet, in which a number of participants can have real-time conversations in online chat rooms devoted to specific interests.

.jpg (or .jpeg, for joint photographers experts group): A format for digitizing, compressing and storing pictures on computers. Pictures in such formats are designated by the extension .jpg after the file name.

Kludge: A quickly written, often improvised, software program that serves a particular purpose, often intended to fix a *BUG* or remedy some other setback in computer operations.

Machine: A computer.

MUD (Multiuser Domain, Multiuser Dimension or Multiuser Dungeons): A subnetwork related to the *IRC* in which participants play real-time games or engage in simulated activities.

MUDhead: One who participates in *MUD*s.

Packet: A small string of digitized data. All information transmitted over the Internet – e-mail, text, music, pictures, graphics, sounds – is broken down into packets, which are then reassembled at the recipient's end into a usable form.

Packet-Sniffer: A program loaded on a computer *ROUTER, SERVER* or individual computer to divert *PACKETS* to a third-party's computer, usually for the purpose of illicitly reading a user's messages or learning passcodes and other information.

Phishing: Searching the Internet for information about someone.

Phreak: To break into telephone systems primarily for the purpose of placing free calls, eavesdropping or disrupting service. The word is also used to describe one who engages in this practice.

Root: In the *UNIX* operating system the word refers to the *SYSADMIN* or other individual in charge of a computer or network. It can also describe that control itself, as in "seizing root", which means taking over a computer.

Router: A computer that directs *PACKETS* through the Internet to their desired destination.

Script: Software.

Server: A large, fast computer on a network – such as the Internet – on which are stored data, Web sites and files, which users can access.

Shareware: Software made available by its developers at a nominal charge or for limited uses.

Source Code: The form in which a programmer writes software, using letters, numbers and typographic symbols in one of a number of programming languages. The source code is then converted into machine code, which is what actually runs on the computer. The source code is usually kept secret and is highly guarded by its developer or owner.

Sysadmin (for systems administrator): The individual in charge of the computer operation and/or network for an organization.

Unix: A sophisticated computer operating system, like Windows. It is the operating system most of computers on the Internet use.

Warez: Illegally copied commercial software.

.wav (for waveform): A format for digitizing and storing sounds on computers. Sounds in such format are designated by the extension .wav after the file name.

Wizard: A brilliant computer expert, a *GURU*.

THE BLUE NOWHERE

I
THE WIZARD

It is possible . . . to commit nearly any
crime by computer. You could even kill a
person using a computer.
                    – *a Los Angeles Police Department officer*

CHAPTER 00000001 / ONE

—◦◦◦—

The battered white van had made her uneasy.

Lara Gibson sat at the bar of Vesta's Grill on De Anza in Cupertino, California, gripping the cold stem of her martini glass and ignoring the two young chip-jocks standing nearby, casting flirtatious glances at her.

She looked outside again, into the overcast drizzle, and saw no sign of the windowless Econoline that, she believed, had followed her from her house, a few miles away, to the restaurant. Lara slid off the bar stool and walked to the window, glanced outside. The van wasn't in the restaurant's parking lot. Nor was it across the street in the Apple Computer lot or the one next to it, belonging to Sun Microsystems. Either of those lots would've been a logical place to park to keep an eye on her – if the driver had in fact been stalking her.

No, the van was just a coincidence, she decided – a coincidence aggravated by a splinter of paranoia.

She returned to the bar and glanced at the two young men who were alternately ignoring her and offering subtle smiles.

Like nearly all the young men here for happy hour they were in casual slacks and tie-less dress shirts and wore the ubiquitous insignia of Silicon Valley – corporate identification badges on thin canvas lanyard around their necks. These two sported the blue cards of Sun Microsystems. Other squadrons represented here were Compaq, Hewlett-Packard and Apple, not to mention a slew of new kids on the block, start-up Internet companies, which were held in some disdain by the venerable Valley regulars.

At thirty-two, Lara Gibson was probably five years older than her two admirers. And as a self-employed business-woman who wasn't a geek – connected with a computer company – she was easily five times poorer. But that didn't matter to these two men, who were already captivated by her exotic, intense face surrounded by a tangle of raven hair, her ankle boots, a red-and-orange gypsy skirt and a black sleeveless top that showed off hard-earned biceps.

She figured that it would be two minutes before one of these boys approached her and she missed that estimate by only ten seconds.

The young man gave her a variation of a line she'd heard a dozen times before: *Excuse me don't mean to interrupt but hey would you like me to break your boyfriend's leg for making a beautiful woman wait alone in a bar and by the way can I buy you a drink while you decide which kneecap?*

Another woman might have gotten mad, another woman might have stammered and blushed and looked uneasy or might have flirted back and let him buy her an unwanted drink because she didn't have the wherewithal to handle the situation. But those would be women weaker than she. Lara Gibson was "the queen of urban protection," as the *San Francisco Chronicle* had once dubbed her. She fixed her eyes on the man's, gave a formal smile and said, "I don't care for any company right now."

Simple as that. End of conversation.

He blinked at her frankness, avoided her staunch eyes and returned to his friend.

Power . . . it was all about power.

She sipped her drink.

In fact, that damn white van had brought to mind all the rules she'd developed as someone who taught women to protect themselves in today's society. Several times on the way to the restaurant she'd glanced into her rearview mirror and noticed the van thirty or forty feet behind. It had been driven by some kid. He was white but his hair was knotted into messy brown dreadlocks. He wore combat fatigues and, despite the overcast and misty rain, sunglasses. This was, of course, Silicon Valley, home of slackers and hackers, and it wasn't unusual to stop in Starbucks for a vente skim latte and be waited on by a polite teenager with a dozen body piercings, a shaved head and an outfit like inner-city gangsta's. Still, the driver had seemed to stare at her with an eerie hostility.

Lara found herself absently fondling the can of pepper spray she kept in her purse.

Another glance out the window. No van. Only fancy cars bought with dot-com money.

A look around the room. Only harmless geeks.

Relax, she told herself and sipped her potent martini.

She glanced at the wall clock. Quarter after seven. Sandy was fifteen minutes late. Not like her. Lara pulled out her cell phone but the display read NO SERVICE.

She was about to find the pay phone when she glanced up and saw a young man enter the bar and wave at her. She knew him from somewhere but couldn't quite place him. His trim but long blond hair and the goatee had stuck in her mind. He wore white jeans and a rumpled blue work shirt. His concession to the fact he was part of corporate America was a tie; as befit a Silicon Valley businessman, though, the design wasn't stripes or Jerry Garcia flowers but a cartoon Tweety Bird.

"Hey, Lara." He walked up and shook her hand, leaned against the bar. "Remember me? I'm Will Randolph. Sandy's cousin? Cheryl and I met you on Nantucket – at Fred and Mary's wedding."

Right, *that's* where she recognized him from. He and his pregnant wife sat at the same table with Lara and her boyfriend, Hank. "Sure. How you doing?"

"Good. Busy. But who isn't around here?"

His plastic neckwear read *Xerox Corporation PARC*. She was impressed. Even nongeeks knew about Xerox's legendary Palo Alto Research Center five or six miles north of here.

Will flagged down the bartender and ordered a light beer. "How's Hank?" he asked. "Sandy said he was trying to get a job at Wells Fargo."

"Oh, yeah, that came through. He's at orientation down in L.A. right now."

The beer came and Will sipped. "Congratulations."

A flash of white in the parking lot.

Lara looked toward it quickly, alarmed. But the vehicle turned out to be a white Ford Explorer with a young couple inside.

Her eyes focused past the Ford and scanned the street and the parking lots again, recalling that, on the way here, she'd glanced at the side of the van as it passed her when she'd turned into the restaurant's parking lot. There'd been a smear of something dark and reddish on the side; probably mud but she'd thought it almost looked like blood.

"You okay?" Will asked.

"Sure. Sorry." She turned back to Will, glad she had an ally. Another of her urban protection rules: Two people are always better than one. Lara now modified that by adding, Even if one of them is a skinny geek who can't be more than five feet, ten inches tall and is wearing a cartoon tie.

Will continued, "Sandy called me on my way home and asked if I'd stop by and give you a message. She tried to call you but couldn't get through on your cell. She's running late and asked if you could meet her at that place next to her office where you went last month, Ciro's? In Mountain View. She made a reservation at eight."

"You didn't have to come by. She could've called the bartender."

"She wanted me to give you the pictures I took at the wedding. You two can look at 'em tonight and tell me if you want any copies."

Will noticed a friend across the bar and waved – Silicon Valley may contain hundreds of square miles but it's really just a small town. He said to Lara, "Cheryl and I *were* going to bring the pictures this weekend – to Sandy's place in Santa Barbara. . . ."

"Yeah, we're going down on Friday."

Will paused and smiled as if he had a huge secret to share. He pulled his wallet out and flipped it open to a picture of himself, his wife and a very tiny, ruddy baby. "Last week," he said proudly. "Claire."

"Oh, adorable," Lara whispered.

"So we'll be staying pretty close to home for a while."

"How's Cheryl?"

"Fine. Baby's fine. There's nothing like it. . . . But, I'll tell you, being a father totally changes your life."

"I'm sure it does."

Lara glanced at the clock again. Seven-thirty. It was a half-hour drive to Ciro's this time of night. "I better get going."

Then, with a thud of alarm, she thought again about the van and the driver.

The dreadlocks.

The rusty smear on the battered door. . . .

Will gestured for the check and paid.

"You don't have to do that," she said. "I'll get it."

He laughed. "You already did."

"What?"

"That mutual fund you told me about at the wedding. The one you'd just bought?"

Lara remembered shamelessly bragging about a biotech fund that had zoomed up 60 percent last year.

"I got home from Nantucket and bought a shitload of it. . . . So . . . thanks." He tipped the beer toward her. Then he stood. "You all set?"

"You bet." Lara stared uneasily at the door as they walked toward it.

It was just paranoia, she told herself. She thought momentarily, as she did from time to time, that she should get a real job, like all of these people in the bar. She shouldn't dwell so much on the world of violence.

Sure, just paranoia . . .

But, if so, then why had the dreadlocked kid sped off so fast when she'd pulled into the parking lot here and glanced at him?

Will stepped outside and opened his umbrella. He held it up for both of them to use.

Lara recalled another rule of urban protection: Never feel too embarrassed or proud to ask for help.

And yet as Lara was about to ask Will Randolph to walk her to her car after they got the snapshots she had a thought:

If the kid in the van really *was* a threat, wasn't it selfish of her to ask him to endanger himself? Here he was a husband and new father, with other people to depend on him. It seemed unfair to—

"Something wrong?" Will asked.

"Not really."

"You sure?" he persisted.

"Well, I think somebody followed me here to the restaurant. Some kid."

Will looked around. "You see him?"

"Not now."

He asked, "You have that Web site, right? About how women can protect themselves."

"That's right."

"You think he knows about it? Maybe he's harassing you."

"Could be. You'd be surprised at the hate mail I get."

He reached for his cell phone. "You want to call the police?"

She debated.

Never feel too embarrassed or proud to ask for help.

"No, no. Just . . . would you mind, after we get the pictures, walking me to my car?"

Will smiled. "Of course not. I don't exactly know karate but I can yell for help with the best of them."

She laughed. "Thanks."

They walked along the sidewalk in front of the restaurant and she checked out the cars. As in every parking lot in Silicon Valley there were dozens of Saabs, BMWs and Lexuses. No vans, though. No kids. No bloody smears.

Will nodded toward where he'd parked, in the back lot. He said, "You see him?"

"No."

They walked past a stand of juniper and toward his car, a spotless silver Jaguar.

Jesus, did *everybody* in Silicon Valley have money except her?

He dug the keys out of his pocket. They walked to the trunk. "I only took two rolls at the wedding. But some of them are pretty good." He opened the trunk and paused and then looked around the parking lot. She did too. It was completely deserted. His was the only car there.

Will glanced at her. "You were probably wondering about the dreads."

"Dreads?"

"Yeah," he said. "The dreadlocks." His voice was different, flatter, distracted. He was still smiling but his face was different now. It seemed hungry.

"What do you mean?" she asked calmly but fear was detonating inside her. She noticed a chain was blocking the entrance to the back parking lot. And she knew he'd hooked it after he'd pulled in – to make sure nobody else could park there.

"It was a wig."

Oh, Jesus, my Lord, thought Lara Gibson, who hadn't prayed in twenty years.

He looked into her eyes, recording her fear. "I parked the Jag here a while ago then stole the van and followed you from home. With the combat jacket and wig on. You know, just so you'd get edgy and paranoid and want me to stay close. . . . I know all your rules – that urban protection stuff. Never go into a deserted parking lot with a man. Married men with children are safer than single men. And my family portrait? In my wallet? I hacked it together from a picture in *Parents* magazine."

She whispered hopelessly, "You're not . . .?"

"Sandy's cousin? Don't even know him. I picked Will Randolph because he's somebody you *sort of* know, who *sort of* looks like me. I mean, there's no way in the world I could've gotten you out here alone if you hadn't known me – or thought you did. Oh, you can take your hand out of your purse." He held up the canister of pepper spray. "I got it when we were walking outside."

"But . . ." Sobbing now, shoulders slumped in hopelessness. "Who *are* you? You don't even know me. . . ."

"Not true, Lara," he whispered, studying her anguish the way an imperious chess master examines his defeated opponent's face. "I know everything about you. Everything in the world."

CHAPTER 00000010 / TWO

———◆◆◆———

Slowly, slowly . . .

Don't damage them, don't break them.

One by one the tiny screws eased from the black plastic housing of the small radio and fell into the young man's long, exceedingly muscular fingers. Once, he nearly stripped the minuscule threads of one screw and had to stop, sit back in his chair and gaze out his small window at the overcast sky blanketing Santa Clara County until he'd relaxed. The time was eight A.M. and he'd been at this arduous task for over two hours.

Finally all twelve screws securing the radio housing were removed and placed on the sticky side of a yellow Post-it. Wyatt Gillette removed the chassis of the Samsung and studied it.

His curiosity, as always, plunged forward like a race-horse. He wondered why the designers had allowed this amount of space between the boards, why the tuner used string of this particular gauge, what the proportion of metals in the solder was.

Maybe this was the optimal design but maybe not.

Maybe the engineers had been lazy or distracted.

Was there a better way to build the radio?

He continued dismantling it, unscrewing the circuit boards themselves.

Slowly, slowly . . .

At twenty-nine Wyatt Gillette had the hollow face of a man who was six feet, one inch tall and weighed 154 pounds, a man about whom people were always thinking, Somebody should fatten him up. His hair was dark, nearly black, and hadn't been recently trimmed or washed. On his right arm was a clumsy tattoo of a seagull flying over a palm tree. Faded blue jeans and a gray work shirt hung loosely on him.

He shivered in the chill spring air. A tremor made his fingers jerk and he stripped the slot in the head of one tiny screw. He sighed in frustration. As talented mechanically as Gillette was, without the proper equipment you can only do so much and he was now using a screwdriver he'd made from a paper clip. He had no tools other than it and his fingernails. Even a razor blade would have been more efficient but that was something not to be found here, in Gillette's temporary home, the medium-security Federal Men's Correctional Facility in San Jose, California.

Slowly, slowly . . .

Once the circuit board was dismantled he located the holy grail he'd been after – a small gray transistor – and he bent its tiny wires until they fatigued. He then mounted the transistor to the small circuit board he'd been working on for months, carefully twining together the wire leads.

Just as he finished, a door slammed nearby and footsteps sounded in the corridor. Gillette looked up, alarmed.

Someone was coming to his cell. Oh, Christ, no, he thought.

The footsteps were about twenty feet away. He slipped the circuit board he'd been working on into a copy of *Wired* magazine and shoved the components back into the housing of the radio. He set it against the wall.

He lay back on the cot and began flipping through another magazine, *2600,* the hacking journal, praying to the general-purpose god that even atheist prisoners start bargaining with soon after they land in jail: Please let them not roust me. And if they do, please let them not find the circuit board.

The guard looked through the peephole and said, "Position, Gillette."

The inmate stood and stepped to the back of the room, hands on his head.

The guard entered the small, dim cell. But this wasn't,

as it turned out, a roust. The man didn't even look around the cell; he silently shackled Gillette's hands in front of him and led him out the door.

At the intersection of hallways where the administrative seclusion wing ran into the general population wing the guard turned and led his prisoner down a corridor that wasn't familiar to Gillette. The sounds of music and shouts from the exercise yard faded and in a few minutes he was directed into a small room furnished with a table and two benches, both bolted to the floor. There were rings on the table for an inmate's shackles though the guard didn't hook Gillette's to them.

"Sit down."

Gillette did.

The guard left and the door slammed, leaving Gillette alone with his curiosity and itchy desire to get back to his circuit board. He sat shivering in the windowless room, which seemed to be less a place in the Real World than a scene from a computer game, one set in medieval times. This cell, he decided, was the chamber where the bodies of heretics broken on the rack were left to await the high executioner's axe.

Thomas Frederick Anderson was a man of many names.

Tom or Tommy in his grade school days.

A dozen handles like Stealth and CryptO when he'd been a high school student in Menlo Park, California, running bulletin boards and hacking on Trash-80s and Commodores and Apples.

He'd been T.F. when he'd worked for the security departments of AT&T and Sprint and Cellular One, tracking down hackers and phone phreaks and call jackers. The initials, colleagues decided, stood for "Tenacious Fucker," in light of his 97 percent success record in helping the cops catch the perps.

As a young police detective in San Jose he'd had another series of names – he'd been known as Courtney 334 or Lonelygirl or BrittanyT in online chat rooms, where in the personas of fourteen-year-old girls he'd written awkward messages to pedophiles, who would e-mail seductive propositions to these fictional dream girls and then drive to suburban shopping malls for romantic liaisons, only to find that their dates were in fact a half-dozen cops armed with a warrant and guns.

Nowadays he was usually called either Dr. Anderson – when introduced at computer conferences – or just plain Andy. In official records, though, he was Lieutenant Thomas F. Anderson, chief of the California State Police Computer Crimes Unit.

The lanky man, forty-five years old, with thinning curly brown hair, now walked down a chill, damp corridor beside the pudgy warden of the San Jose Correctional Facility – San Ho, as it was called by perps and cops alike. A solidly built Latino guard accompanied them.

They continued down the hallway until they came to a door. The warden nodded. The guard opened it and Anderson stepped inside, eyeing the prisoner.

Wyatt Gillette was very pale – he had a "hacker tan," as the pallor was ironically called – and quite thin. His hair was filthy, as were his fingernails. Gillette apparently hadn't showered or shaved in days.

The cop noticed an odd look in Gillette's dark brown eyes; he was blinking in recognition. He asked, "You're . . . are you Andy Anderson?"

"That's *Detective* Anderson," the warden corrected, his voice a whip crack.

"You run the state's computer crimes division," Gillette said.

"You know me?"

"I heard you lecture at Comsec a couple of years ago."

The Comsec conference on computer and network security was limited to documented security professionals and law enforcers; it was closed to outsiders. Anderson knew it was a national pastime for young hackers to try to crack into the registration computer and issue themselves admission badges. Only two or three had ever been able to do so in the history of the conference.

"How'd you get in?"

Gillette shrugged. "I found a badge somebody dropped."

Anderson nodded skeptically. "What'd you think of my lecture?"

"I agree with you: silicon chips'll be outmoded faster than most people think. Computers'll be running on molecular electronics. And that means users'll have to start looking at a whole new way to protect themselves against hackers."

"Nobody else felt that way at the conference."

"They heckled you," Gillette recalled.

"But you didn't?"

"No. I took notes."

The warden leaned against the wall while the cop sat down across from Gillette and said, "You've got one year left on a three-year sentence under the federal Computer Fraud and Abuse Act. You cracked Western Software's machines and stole the source codes for most of their programs, right?"

Gillette nodded.

The source code is the brains and heart of software, fiercely guarded by its owner. Stealing it lets the thief easily strip out identification and security codes then repackage the software and sell it under his own name. Western Software's source codes for the company's games, business applications and utilities were its main assets. If an unscrupulous hacker had stolen the codes he might have put the billion-dollar company out of business.

Gillette pointed out: "I didn't do anything with the codes. I erased them after I downloaded them."

"Then why'd you crack their systems?"

The hacker shrugged. "I saw the head of the company on CNN or something. He said nobody could get into their network. Their security systems were foolproof. I wanted to see if that was true."

"Were they?"

"As a matter of fact, yeah, they were foolproof. The problem is that you don't have to protect yourself against fools. You have to protect yourself against people like me."

"Well, once you'd broken in why didn't you tell the company about the security flaws? Do a white hat?"

White hats were hackers who cracked into computer systems and then pointed out the security flaws to their victims. Sometimes for the glory of it, sometimes for money.

Sometimes even because they thought it was the right thing to do.

Gillette shrugged. "It's their problem. That guy said that it couldn't be done. I just wanted to see if I could."

"Why?"

Another shrug. "Curious."

"Why'd the feds come down on you so hard?" Anderson asked. If a hacker doesn't disrupt business or try to sell what he steals the FBI rarely even investigates, let alone refers a case to the U.S. attorney.

It was the warden who answered. "The reason is the DoD."

"Department of Defense?" Anderson asked, glancing at a gaudy tattoo on Gillette's arm. Was that an airplane? No, it was a bird of some kind.

"It's bogus," Gillette muttered. "Complete bullshit."

The cop looked at the warden, who explained, "The Pentagon thinks he wrote some program or something that cracked the DoD's latest encryption software."

"Their Standard 12?" Anderson gave a laugh. "You'd need a dozen supercomputers running full time for six months to crack a single e-mail."

Standard 12 had recently replaced DES – the Defense Encryption Standard – as the state-of-the-art encryption software for the government. It was used to encrypt secret data and messages. The encryption program was so important to national security that it was considered a munition under the export laws and couldn't be transferred overseas without military approval.

Anderson continued, "But even if he *did* crack something encoded with Standard 12, so what? *Everybody* tries to crack encryptions."

There was nothing illegal about this as long as the encrypted document wasn't classified or stolen. In fact, many software manufacturers dare people to try to break documents encrypted with their programs and offer prizes to anybody who can do so.

"No," Gillette explained. "The DoD's saying that I cracked into their computer, found out something about how Standard 12 works and then wrote some script that decrypts the document. It can do it in seconds."

"Impossible," Anderson said, laughing. "Can't be done."

Gillette said, "That's what I told them. They didn't believe me."

Yet as Anderson studied the man's quick eyes, hollow beneath dark brows, hands fidgeting impatiently in front of him, he wondered if maybe the hacker actually *had* written a magic program like this. Anderson himself couldn't have done it; he didn't know *anybody* who could. But after all, the cop was here now, hat in hand, because Gillette was a wizard, the term used by hackers to describe those among them who've reached the highest levels of skill in the Machine World.

There was a knock on the door and the guard let two men inside. The first one, fortyish, had a lean face, dark blond hair swept back and frozen in place with hairspray. Honest-to-God sideburns too. He wore a cheap gray suit. His overwashed white shirt was far too big for him and was halfway untucked. He glanced at Gillette without a splinter of interest. "Sir," he said to the warden in a flat voice. "I'm Detective Frank Bishop, state police Homicide." He nodded an anemic greeting to Anderson and fell silent.

The second man, a little younger, much heavier, shook the warden's hand then Anderson's. "Detective Bob Shelton." His face was pockmarked from childhood acne.

Anderson didn't know anything about Shelton but he'd talked to Bishop and had mixed feelings concerning his involvement in the case Anderson was here about. Bishop was supposedly a wizard in his own right though *his* expertise lay in tracking down killers and rapists in hard-scrabble neighborhoods like the Oakland waterfront, Haight-Ashbury and the infamous San Francisco Tenderloin. Computer Crimes wasn't authorized – or equipped – to run a homicide like this one without some-body from the Violent Crimes detail but, after several brief phone discussions with Bishop, Anderson was not impressed. The homicide cop seemed humorless and distracted and, more troubling, knew zero about computers.

Anderson had also heard that Bishop himself didn't even want to be working with Computer Crimes. He'd been lobbying for the MARINKILL case – so named by the FBI for the site of the crime: Several days ago three bank robbers had murdered two bystanders and a cop at a Bank of America branch in Sausalito in Marin County and had been seen headed east, which meant they might very well turn south toward Bishop's present turf, the San Jose area.

Now, in fact, the first thing Bishop did was to check the screen of his cell phone, presumably to see if he had a page or message about a reassignment.

Anderson said to the detectives, "You gentlemen want to sit down?" Nodding at the benches around the metal table.

Bishop shook his head and remained standing. He tucked his shirt in then crossed his arms. Shelton sat down next to Gillette. Then the bulky cop looked distastefully at the prisoner and got up, sat on the other side of the table. To Gillette he muttered, "You might want to wash up sometime."

The convict retorted, "You might want to ask the warden why I only get one shower a week."

"Because, Wyatt," the warden said patiently, "you broke the prison rules. That's why you're in administrative seclusion."

Anderson didn't have the patience or time for squabbles. He said to Gillette, "We've got a problem and we're hoping you'll help us with it." He glanced at Bishop and asked, "You want to brief him?"

According to state police protocol, Frank Bishop was technically in charge of the case. But the detective shook his head. "No, sir, you can go ahead."

"Last night a woman was abducted from a restaurant in Cupertino. She was murdered and her body found in Portola Valley. She'd been stabbed to death. She wasn't sexually molested and there's no apparent motive.

"Now, the victim, Lara Gibson, ran this Web site about how women can protect themselves and gave lectures on the subject around the country. She'd been in the press a lot and was on *Larry King*. Well, what happens is, she's in a bar and this guy comes in who seems to know her. He gives his name as Will Randolph, the bartender said. That's the name of the cousin of the woman the victim was going to meet for dinner last night. Randolph wasn't involved – he's been in New York for a week – but we found a digital picture of him on the victim's computer and they look alike, the suspect and Randolph. We think that's why the perp picked him to impersonate.

"So, he knows all this information about her. Friends, where she's traveled, what she does, what stocks she owns, who her boyfriend is. It even looked like he waved to somebody in the bar but Homicide canvassed most of the patrons who were there last night and didn't find anybody who knew him. So we think he was faking – you know, to put her at ease, making it look like he was a regular."

"He social engineered her," Gillette offered.

"How's that?" Shelton asked.

Anderson knew the term but he deferred to Gillette, who said, "It means conning somebody, pretending you're somebody you're not. Hackers do it to get access to databases and phone lines and passcodes. The more facts about somebody you can feed back to them, the more they believe you and the more they'll do what you want them to."

"Now, the girlfriend Lara was supposed to meet – Sandra Hardwick – said she got a call from somebody claiming to be Lara's boyfriend canceling the dinner plans. She tried to call Lara but her phone was out."

Gillette nodded. "He crashed her mobile phone." Then he frowned. "No, probably the whole cell."

Anderson nodded. "Mobile America reported an outage in cell 850 for exactly forty-five minutes. Somebody loaded code that shut the switch down then turned it back on."

Gillette's eyes narrowed. The detective could see he was growing interested.

"So," the hacker mused, "he turned himself into somebody she'd trust and then he killed her. And he did it with information he got from her computer."

"Exactly."

"Did she have an online service?"

"Horizon On-Line."

Gillette laughed. "Jesus, you know how secure that is? He hacked into one of their routers and read her e-mails." Then he shook his head, studied Anderson's face. "But that's kindergarten stuff. *Anybody* could do that. There's more, isn't there?"

"Right," Anderson continued. "We talked to her boyfriend

and went through her computer. Half the information the bartender heard the killer tell her *wasn't* in her e-mails. It was in the machine itself."

"Maybe he went Dumpster diving and got the information that way."

Anderson explained to Bishop and Shelton, "He means going digging through trash bins to get information that'll help you hack – discarded company manuals, printouts, bills, receipts, things like that." But he said to Gillette, "I doubt it – everything he knew was stored on her machine."

"What about hard access?" Gillette asked. Hard access is when a hacker breaks into somebody's house or office and goes through the victim's machine itself. Soft access is breaking into somebody's computer online from a remote location.

But Anderson responded, "It had to be soft access. I talked to the friend Lara was supposed to meet, Sandra. She said the only time they talked about getting together that night was in an instant message that afternoon and she was home all day. The killer *had* to be in a different location."

"This's interesting," Gillette whispered.

"I thought so too," Anderson said. "The bottom line is that we think there's some kind of new virus the killer used to get inside her machine. The thing is, Computer Crimes can't find it. We're hoping you'd take a look."

Gillette nodded, squinting as he looked up at the grimy ceiling. Anderson noticed the young man's fingers were moving in tiny, rapid taps. At first the cop thought Gillette had palsy or some nervous twitch. But then he realized what the hacker was doing. He was unconsciously typing on an invisible keyboard – a nervous habit, it seemed.

The hacker lowered his eyes to Anderson. "What'd you use to examine her drive?"

"Norton Commander, Vi-Scan 5.0, the FBI's forensic detection package, Restore8 and the DoD's Partition and File Allocation Analyzer 6.2. We even tried Surface-Scour."

Gillette gave a confused laugh. "All that and you didn't find *anything?*"

"Nope."

"How'm I going to find something you couldn't?"

"I've looked at some of the software you've written – there're only three or four people in the *world* who could write script like that. You've gotta have code that's better than ours – or could hack some together."

Gillette asked Anderson, "So what's in it for me?"

"What?" Bob Shelton asked, wrinkling up his pocked face and staring at the hacker.

"If I help you what do I get?"

"You little prick," Shelton snapped. "A girl got murdered. Don't you give a shit?"

"I'm sorry about her," Gillette shot back. "But the deal is if I help you I want something in return."

Anderson asked, "Such as?"

"I want a machine."

"No computers," the warden snapped. "No way." To Anderson he said, "That's why he's in seclusion. We caught him at the computer in the library – on the Internet. The judge issued an order as part of his sentence that he can't go online."

"I won't go online," Gillette said. "I'll stay on E wing, where I am now. I won't have access to a phone line."

The warden scoffed. "You'd rather stay in administrative seclusion—"

"Solitary confinement," Gillette corrected.

"—just to have a computer?"

"Yes."

Anderson asked, "If he was to stay in seclusion, so there was no chance of going online, would that be okay?"

"I guess," the warden said.

The cop then said to Gillette, "It's a deal. We'll get you a laptop."

"You're going to bargain with him?" Shelton asked Anderson in disbelief. He glanced at Bishop for support but the lean cop brushed at his anachronistic sideburns and studied his cell phone again, waiting for his reprieve.

Anderson didn't respond to Shelton. He added to Gillette, "But you get your machine only *after* you analyze the Gibson woman's computer and give us a complete report."

"Absolutely," the prisoner said, eyes glowing with excitement.

"Her machine's an IBM clone, off the shelf. We'll get it over here in the next hour. We've got all her disks and software and—"

"No, no, no," Gillette said firmly. "I can't do it here."

"Why?"

"I'll need access to a mainframe – maybe a supercomputer. I'll need tech manuals, software."

Anderson looked at Bishop, who didn't seem to be listening to any of this.

"No fucking way," said Shelton, the more talkative of the homicide partners, even if he had a distinctly limited vocabulary.

Anderson was debating with himself when the warden asked, "Can I see you gentlemen up the hall for a minute?"

CHAPTER 00000011 / THREE

———◆◆◆———

It had been a fun hack.

But not as challenging as he would've liked.

Phate – his screen name, spelled in the best hacker tradition with a *ph* and not an *f* – now drove to his house in Los Altos, in the heart of Silicon Valley.

He'd been busy this morning: He'd abandoned the blood-smeared white van that he'd used to light the fires of paranoia within Lara Gibson yesterday. And he'd ditched the disguises – the dreadlock wig, combat jacket and sunglasses of the stalker *and* the squeaky-clean chip-jockey costume of Will Randolph, Sandy Hardwick's accommodating cousin.

He was now someone entirely different. Not his real name or identity, of course – Jon Patrick Holloway, who'd been born twenty-seven years ago in Upper Saddle River, New Jersey. No, he was at the moment one of six or seven fictional characters he'd created recently. They were like a group of friends to him and came complete with driver's licenses, employee ID cards, social security cards and all the telltale documentation that is so indispensable nowadays. He'd even endowed his cast with different accents and mannerisms, which he practiced religiously.

Who do you want to be?

Phate's answer to this question was: pretty much anybody in the world.

Reflecting now on the Lara Gibson hack, he decided it'd been just a bit too easy to get close to someone who prided herself on being the queen of urban protection.

And so it was time to notch the game up a bit.

Phate's Jaguar moved slowly through morning rush-hour traffic along Interstate 280, the Junípero Serra Highway. To the west the Santa Cruz mountains rose into the specters of fog slipping toward the San Francisco Bay. In recent years droughts had plagued the Valley but much of this spring – like today, for instance – had been rainy and the flora was a rich green. Phate, however, paid the expansive scenery no mind. He was listening to a play on his CD player – *Death of a Salesman*. It was one of his favorites. Occasionally his mouth would move to the words (he knew all the parts).

Ten minutes later, at 8:45, he was pulling up into the garage of his large, detached house in the Stonecrest development off El Monte Road in Los Altos.

He parked in the garage, closed the door. He noticed a drop of Lara Gibson's blood in the shape of a sloppy comma on the otherwise immaculate floor. Careless to miss it earlier, he chided himself. He cleaned the stain then went inside, closed and locked the door.

The house was new, only about six months old, and smelled of carpet glue and sweet paint.

If neighbors were to come a-calling to welcome him to the neighborhood and stand in the front hallway, glancing into the living room, they'd see evidence of an upper-middle-class family living the comfortable life that chip money has provided for so many people here in the Valley.

Hey, nice to meet you. . . . Yeah, that's right – just moved in last month. . . . I'm with a dot-com start-up over in Palo Alto. They brought me and half the furniture out from Austin early, before Kathy and the kids – they'll be moving here in June after school's over. . . . That's them. Took that one on vacation in Florida in January. Troy and Brittany. He's seven. She's going to be five next month.

On the mantel and on the expensive end tables and coffee tables were dozens of pictures of Phate and a blond woman, posing at the beach, horseback riding, hugging each other atop a mountain at a ski resort, dancing at their wedding. Other pictures showed the couple with their two children. Vacations, soccer practice, Christmas, Easter.

You know, I'd ask you over for dinner or something but

this new company's got me working like crazy. . . . Probably better to wait till after the family gets here anyway, you know. Kathy's really the social director. . . . And a lot better cook than me. Okay, you take care now.

And the neighbors would pass him the welcoming wine or cookies or begonias and return home, never guessing that, in the best spirit of creative social engineering, the entire scene had been as fake as a movie set.

Like the pictures he'd shown Lara Gibson these snapshots had been created on his computer: his face had replaced a male model's, Kathy's was a generic female face, morphed from a model in *Self.* The kids had come from a *Vogue Bambini.* The house itself was a facade too; the living room and hall were the only fully furnished rooms – and that had been done exclusively to fool people who came to the door. In the bedroom was a cot and lamp. In the dining room – Phate's office – were a table, lamp, two laptop computers and an office chair. In the basement . . . well, the basement contained a few other things – but they definitely weren't for public view.

If need be, and he knew it was a possibility, he could walk out the door immediately and leave everything behind. All his important possessions – his serious hardware, the computer antiquities he collected, his ID card machine, the supercomputer parts he bought and sold to make his living – were in a warehouse miles away. And there was nothing here that would lead police to that location.

He now walked into the dining room and sat down at the table. He turned on a laptop.

The screen came to life, a C: prompt flashed on the screen and, with the appearance of that blinking symbol, Phate rose from the dead.

Who do you want to be?

Well, at the moment, he was no longer John Patrick Holloway or Will Randolph or Warren Gregg or James L. Seymour or any of the other characters he'd created. He was now Phate. No longer the blond, five-foot-ten character of slight build, floating aimlessly among three-dimensional houses and office buildings and stores and airplanes and concrete ribbons of highway and brown lawns chain-link fences semiconductor plants strip malls pets people people people people as numerous as flies. . . .

This was his reality, the world inside his monitor.

He keyed some commands and with an excited churning in his groin he heard the rising and falling whistle of his modem's sensual electronic handshake (most real hackers would never use dog-slow modems and telephone lines like this, rather than a direct connection, to get online. But Phate had to compromise; speed was far less important than being able to stay mobile and hide his tracks through millions of miles of telephone lines around the world).

After he was connected to the Net he checked his e-mail. He would have opened any letters from Shawn right away but there were none; the others he'd read later. He exited the mail reader and then keyed in another command. A menu popped up on his screen.

When he and Shawn had written the software for Trapdoor last year he'd decided that, even though no one else would be using it, he'd make the menu user-friendly – simply because this is what you did when you were a brilliant codeslinger, when you were a wizard.

Trapdoor

Main Menu

1. Do you want to continue a prior session?

2. Do you want to create/open/edit a background file?

3. Do you want to find a new target?

4. Do you want to decode/decrypt a password or text?

5. Do you want to exit to the system?

He scrolled down to 3 and hit the ENTER key.

A moment later the Trapdoor program politely asked:

Please enter the e-mail address of the target.

From memory he typed a screen name and hit ENTER. Within ten seconds he was connected to someone else's machine – in effect, looking over the unsuspecting user's shoulder. He read for a few moments then started jotting notes.

Lara Gibson had been a fun hack, but this one would be better.

"He made this," the warden told them.

The cops stood in a storage room in San Ho. Lining the shelves were drug paraphernalia, Nazi decorations and Nation of Islam banners, handmade weapons – clubs and knives and knuckle-dusters, even a few guns. This was the confiscation room and these grim items had been taken away from the prison's difficult residents over the past several years.

What the warden was now pointing out, though, was nothing so clearly inflammatory or deadly. It was a wooden box about two by three feet, filled with a hundred strips of bell wire, which connected dozens of electronic components.

"What is it?" Bob Shelton asked in his gravelly voice.

Andy Anderson laughed and whispered, "Jesus, it's a computer. It's a homemade computer." He leaned forward, studying the simplicity of the wiring, the perfect twisting of the solderless connections, the efficient use of space. It was rudimentary and yet it was astonishingly elegant.

"I didn't know you could make a computer," Shelton offered. Thin Frank Bishop said nothing.

The warden said, "Gillette's the worst addict I've ever seen – and we get guys in here've been on smack for years. Only what *he's* addicted to are these – computers. I guarantee you he'll do anything he can to get online. And he's capable of hurting people to do it. I mean, hurting them bad. He built this just to get on the Internet."

"It's got a modem built in?" Anderson asked, still awed by the device. "Wait, there it is, yeah."

"So I'd think twice about getting him out."

"We can control him," Anderson said, reluctantly looking away from Gillette's creation.

"You *think* you can," the warden said, shrugging. "People

like him'll say whatever they have to so they can get online. Just like alcoholics. You know about his wife?"

"He's married?" Anderson asked.

"*Was*. He tried to stop hacking after he got married but couldn't. Then he got arrested and they lost everything paying the lawyer and court fine. She divorced him a couple years ago. I was here when he got the papers. He didn't even care."

The door opened and a guard entered with a battered recycled manila folder. He handed it to the warden, who in turned passed it to Anderson. "Here's the file we've got on him. Might help you decide whether you really want him or not."

Anderson flipped through the file. The prisoner had a record going back years. The juvenile detention time, though, wasn't for anything serious: Gillette had called Pacific Bell's main office from a pay phone – what hackers call fortress phones – and programmed it to let him make free long-distance calls. Fortress phones are considered elementary schools for young hackers, who use them to break into phone company switches, which are nothing more than huge computer systems. The art of cracking into the phone company to make free calls or just for the challenge of it is known as phreaking. The notes in the file indicated that Gillette had placed stolen calls to the time and temperature numbers in Paris, Athens, Frankfurt, Tokyo and Ankara. Which suggested that he'd broken into the system just because he was curious to see if he could do it. He wasn't after money.

Anderson kept flipping through the young man's file. There was clearly something to what the warden had said; Gillette's behavior *was* addictive. He'd been questioned in connection with twelve major hacking incidents over the past eight years. In his sentencing for the Western Software hack the prosecutor had borrowed a phrase from the judge who'd sentenced the famous hacker Kevin Mitnick, saying that Gillette was "dangerous when armed with a keyboard."

The hacker's behavior regarding computers wasn't, however, exclusively felonious, Anderson also learned. He'd worked for a number of Silicon Valley companies and invariably had gotten glowing reports on his programming skills – at least until he was fired for missing work or falling asleep on the job because he'd been up all night hacking. He'd also written a lot of brilliant freeware and shareware – software programs given away to anyone who wants them – and had lectured at conferences about new developments in computer programming languages and security.

Then Anderson did a double take and gave a surprised laugh. He was looking at a reprint of an article that Wyatt Gillette had written for *On-Line* magazine several years ago. The article was well known and Anderson recalled reading it when it first came out but had paid no attention to who the author was. The title was "Life in the Blue Nowhere." Its theme was that computers are the first technological invention in history that affect *every* aspect of human life, from psychology to entertainment to intelligence to material comfort to evil, and that, because of this, humans and machines will continue to grow closer together. There are many benefits to this but also many dangers. The phrase "Blue Nowhere," which was replacing the term "cyberspace," meant the world of computers, or, as it was also called, the Machine World. In Gillette's coined phrase, "Blue" referred to the electricity that made computers work. "Nowhere" meant that it was an intangible place.

Andy Anderson also found some photocopies of documents from Gillette's most recent trial. He saw dozens of letters that had been sent to the judge, requesting leniency in sentencing. The hacker's mother had passed away – an unexpected heart attack when the woman was in her fifties – but it sounded like the young man and his father had an enviable relationship. Gillette's father, an American engineer working in Saudi Arabia, had e-mailed several heartfelt pleas to the judge for a reduced sentence. The hacker's brother, Rick, a government employee in Montana had come to his sibling's aid with several faxed letters to the court, also urging leniency. Rick Gillette even touchingly suggested that his brother could come live with him and his wife "in a rugged and pristine mountain setting," as if clean air and physical labor could cure the hacker of his criminal ways.

Anderson was touched by this but surprised as well; most of the hackers that Anderson had arrested came from dysfunctional families.

He closed the file and handed it to Bishop, who read through it absently, seemingly bewildered by the technical references to machines. The detective muttered, "The Blue Nowhere?" A moment later he gave up and passed the folder to his partner.

"What's the timetable for release?" Shelton asked, flipping through the file.

Anderson replied, "We've got the paperwork waiting at the courthouse now. As soon as we can get a federal magistrate to sign it Gillette's ours."

"I'm just giving you fair warning," the warden said ominously. He nodded at the homemade computer. "If you want to go ahead with a release, be my guest. Only you gotta pretend he's a junkie who's been off the needle for two weeks."

Shelton said, "I think we ought to call the bureau. We could use some feds anyway on this one. And there'd be more bodies to keep an eye on him."

But Anderson shook his head. "If we tell them then the DoD'll hear about it and have a stroke about us releasing the man who cracked their Standard 12. Gillette'll be back inside in a half hour. No, we've got to keep it quiet. The release order'll be under a John Doe."

Anderson looked toward Bishop, caught in the act of checking out his silent cell phone once again. "What do you think, Frank?"

The lean detective tucked in his shirt again and finally put together several complete sentences. "Well, sir, I think we should get him out and the sooner the better. That killer probably isn't sitting around talking. Like us."

CHAPTER 00000100 / FOUR

◆━◆━◆

For a terrible half hour Wyatt Gillette had sat in the cold, medieval dungeon, refusing to speculate if it would really happen – if he'd be released. He wouldn't allow himself even a wisp of hope; in prison, expectations are the first to die.

Then, with a nearly silent click, the door opened and the cops returned.

Gillette looked up and happened to notice in Anderson's left lobe a tiny brown dot of an earring hole that had closed up long ago. "A magistrate's signed a temporary release order," the cop said.

Gillette realized that he'd been sitting with his teeth clenched and shoulders drawn into a fierce knot. With this news he exhaled in relief. Thank you, thank you. . . .

"Now, you have a choice. Either you'll be shackled the whole time you're out or you wear an electronic tracking anklet."

The hacker considered this. "Anklet."

"It's a new variety," Anderson said. "Titanium. You can only get it on and off with a special key. Nobody's ever slipped out of one."

"Well, one guy did," Bob Shelton said cheerfully. "But he had to cut his foot off to do it. He only got a mile before he bled to death."

Gillette by now disliked the burly cop as much as Shelton, for some reason, seemed to hate him.

"It tracks you for sixty miles and broadcasts through metal," Anderson continued.

"You made your point," Gillette said. To the warden he said, "I need some things from my cell."

"What things?" the man grumbled. "You aren't gonna be away that long, Gillette. You don't need to pack."

Gillette said to Anderson, "I need some of my books and notebooks. And I've got a lot of printouts that'll be helpful – from things like *Wired* and *2600*."

The CCU cop said to the warden, "It's okay."

A loud electronic braying came from nearby. Gillette jumped at the noise. It took a minute to recognize the sound, one that he'd never heard in San Ho. Frank Bishop answered his cell phone. The gaunt cop took the call, listened for a moment, flicking at a sideburn, then answered, "Yessir, Captain. . . . And?" There was a long pause, during which the corner of his mouth tightened very slightly. "You can't do anything? . . . Okay, sir."

He hung up.

Anderson cocked an eyebrow at him. The homicide detective said evenly, "That was Captain Bernstein. There was another report on the wire about the MARINKILL case. The perps were spotted near Walnut Creek. Probably headed in this direction." He glanced quickly at Gillette as if he were a stain on the bench and then said to Anderson, "I should tell you – I requested to be removed from this case and put on that one. They said no. Captain Bernstein thought I'd be more helpful here."

"Thanks for telling me," Anderson said. To Gillette, though, the CCU cop didn't seem particularly grateful for the confirmation that the detective was only halfheartedly involved in the case. Anderson asked Shelton, "Did you want MARINKILL too?"

"No. I wanted this one. The girl was killed pretty much in my backyard. I want to make sure it doesn't happen again."

Anderson glanced at his watch. It was 9:15. "We should get back to CCU."

The warden summoned the huge guard and instructions were given. The man led Gillette back down the corridor to his cell. Five minutes later he'd collected what he needed, used the toilet and pulled on his jacket. He preceded the guard into the central part of San Ho.

Out one door, out another, past the visitors' area, where he'd see a friend once a month or so, and the lawyer–client rooms, where he'd spent so many hours working on the futile appeal with the man who'd taken every penny that he and Ellie had.

Finally, breathing fast now as the excitement flooded into him, Gillette stepped through the second-to-the-last doorway – into the area of offices and the guards' locker rooms. The cops were waiting for him there.

Anderson nodded to the guard, who undid the wrist shackles. For the first time in two years Gillette was no longer under the physical domination of the prison system. He'd attained a freedom of sorts.

He rubbed the skin on his wrists as they walked toward the exit – two wooden doors with latticed fireglass in them, through which Gillette could see the gray sky. "We'll put the anklet on outside," Anderson said.

Shelton stepped brusquely up to the hacker and whispered, "I want to say one thing, Gillette. Maybe you're thinking you'll be in striking distance of some weapon or another, what with your hands free. Well, if you even get an itchy look that I don't like you're going to get hurt bad. Follow me? I won't hesitate to take you out."

"I broke into a computer," the hacker said, exasperated. "That's all I did. I've never hurt anyone."

"Just remember what I said."

Gillette sped up slightly so that he was walking next to Anderson. "Where're we going?"

"The state police Computer Crimes Unit office is in San Jose. It's a separate facility. We—"

An alarm went off and a red light blinked on the metal detector they were walking through. Since they were leaving, not entering, the prison the guard manning the security station shut the buzzer off and nodded at them to continue.

But just as Anderson put his hand on the front door to push it open a voice called, "Excuse me." It was Frank Bishop and he was pointing at Gillette. "Scan him."

Gillette laughed. "That's crazy. I'm going out, not coming *in*. Who's going to smuggle something *out* of prison?"

Anderson said nothing but Bishop gestured the guard forward. He ran a metal-detecting wand over Gillette's body. The wand got to his right slacks pocket and emitted a piercing squeal.

The guard reached into the pocket and pulled out a circuit board, sprouting wires.

"What the fuck's that?" Shelton snapped.

Anderson examined it closely. "A red box?" he asked Gillette, who glanced at the ceiling in frustration. "Yeah."

The detective said to Bishop and Shelton, "There're dozens of circuit boxes that phone phreaks used to use to cheat the phone company – to get free service, tap somebody's line, cut out wiretaps. . . . They're known by colors. You don't see many of them anymore except this one – a red box. It mimics the sound of coins in a pay phone. You can call anywhere in the world and just keep punching the coin-drop-tone button enough times to pay for the call." He looked at Gillette. "What were you going to do with this?"

"Figured I might get lost and need to phone somebody."

"You could also sell a red box on the street for, I don't know, a couple of hundred bucks, to a phone phreak. If, say, you were to escape and needed some money."

"I guess *somebody* could. But I'm not going to do that."

Anderson looked the board over. "Nice wiring."

"Thanks."

"You missed having a soldering iron, right?"

Gillette nodded. "I sure did."

"You pull something like that again and you'll be back inside as soon as I can get a patrol car to bring you in. Got it?"

"Got it."

"Nice try," Bob Shelton whispered. "But, fuck, life's just one big disappointment, don't you think?"

No, Wyatt Gillette thought. Life's just one big hack.

On the eastern edge of Silicon Valley a pudgy fifteen-year-old student pounded furiously on a keyboard as he peered through thick glasses at a monitor in the computer room at St. Francis Academy, an old, private boy's school in San Jose.

The name of the room wasn't quite right, though. Yeah, it had computers in it. But the "room" part was a little dicey, the students thought. Stuck away down in the basement, bars on the windows, it looked like a cell. It may actually have been one once; this part of the building was 250 years old and the rumor was that the famous missionary in old California, Father Junípero Serra, had spread the gospel in this particular room by stripping Native Americans to the waist and flogging them until they accepted Jesus. Some of these unfortunates, the older students happily told the younger, never survived their conversion and their ghosts continued to hang out in cells, well, *rooms,* like this one.

Jamie Turner, the youngster who was presently ignoring spirits and keying at the speed of light, was a gawky, dark-haired sophomore. He'd never gotten a grade below a 92 and, even though there were two months to go until the end of term, had completed the required reading – and most of the assignments – for all of his classes. He owned more books than any two students at St. Francis and had read the Harry Potter books five times each, *Lord of the Rings* eight times and every single word written by computer/science-fiction visionary William Gibson more often than he could remember.

Like muted machine-gun fire the sound of his keying filled the small room. He heard a creak behind him. Looked around fast. Nothing.

Then a snap. Silence. Now the sound of the wind.

Damn ghosts. . . . Fuck 'em. Get back to work.

Jamie Turner shoved his heavy glasses up on his nose and returned to his task. Gray light from the misty day was bleeding through the barred windows. Outside on the soccer field his classmates were shouting, laughing, scoring goals, racing back and forth. The 9:30 physical ed period had just started. Jamie was supposed to be with them and Booty wouldn't like him hiding out here.

But Booty didn't know.

Not that Jamie disliked the principal of the boarding school. Not at all, really. It was hard to dislike somebody who *cared* about him. (Unlike, say, for instance, hellll-ohhh, Jamie's parents. "See you on the twenty-third, son. . . . Oh, wait, no. Your mother and I'll be out of town. We'll be here on first or the seventh. Definitely then. Love you, bye.") It was just that Booty's paranoia was a major pain. It meant lockdowns at night, all those damn alarms and the security, his checking up on the students all the time.

And, for instance, refusing to let the boys go to harmless rock concerts with their older and way responsible brothers unless their parents had signed a permission slip, when who knew where the hell your parents even *were,* let alone getting them to spend a few minutes to sign something and fax it back to you in time, no matter *how* important it was.

Love you, bye. . . .

But now Jamie was taking matters into his own hands. His brother, Mark, a sound engineer at an Oakland concert venue, had told Jamie that if he could escape from St. Francis that night he'd get the boy into the Santana concert and could probably get his hands on a couple of unlimited-access backstage passes. But if he wasn't out of the school by six-thirty his brother'd have to leave to get to work on time. And meeting that deadline was a problem. Because getting out of St. Francis wasn't like sliding down a bedsheet rope, the way kids in old movies snuck out for the night. St. Francis may have *looked* like an old Spanish castle but its security was totally high-tech.

Jamie could get out of his room, of course; that wasn't locked, even at night (St. Francis wasn't *exactly* a prison). And he could get out of the building proper through the fire door – provided he could disable the fire alarm. But that would only get him onto the school grounds. And *they* were surrounded by a twelve-foot-high stone wall, topped with barbed wire. And there was no way to get over that – at least no way for *him,* a chubby geek who hated heights – unless he cracked the passcode to one of the gates that opened onto the street. Which is why he was now cracking the passcode file of Herr Mein Fuhrer Booty, excuse me, Dr. Willem C. Boethe, M.Ed., Ph.D.

So far he'd easily hacked into Booty's computer and downloaded the file containing the passcode (conveniently named, "security passcodes." Hey, *way* subtle, Booty!).

What was stored in the file was, of course, an encrypted version of the password and would have to be decrypted before Jamie could use it. But Jamie's puny clone computer would take days to crack the code and so the boy was presently hacking into a nearby computer site to find a machine powerful enough to crack it in time for the magic deadline.

Jamie knew that the Internet had been started as a largely academic network to *facilitate* the exchange of research, not keep information secret. The first organizations to be linked via the Net – universities – had far poorer security than the government agencies and corporations that had more recently come online.

He now figuratively knocked on the door of Northern California Tech and Engineering College's computer lab and was greeted with this:

Username?

Jamie answered: *User.*

Passcode?

His response: *User.*

And the message popped up:

Welcome, User.

Hm, how 'bout an F minus for security, Jamie thought wryly and began to browse through the machine's root directory – the main one – until he found what would be a very large supercomputer, probably an old Cray, on the school's network. At the moment the machine was calculating the age of the universe. Interesting, but not as cool as Santana. Jamie nudged aside the astronomy project and uploaded a program he himself had written, called Crack-er, which started its sweat labor to extract the English-language password from Booty's files. He—

"Oh, hell shit," he said in very un-Booty language. His computer had frozen up again.

This had occurred several times recently and it pissed him off that he couldn't figure out why. He knew computers cold and he could find no reason for this sort of jamming. He had no time for crashes, not today, with his 6:30 deadline. Still, the boy jotted the occurrence in his hacker's notebook, as any diligent codeslinger would do, and restarted the system then logged back online.

He checked on the Cray and found that the college's computer had kept working away, running Crack-er on Booty's password file, even while he'd been offline.

He could—

"Mr. Turner, Mr. Turner," came a nearby voice. "What are we up to here?"

The words scared the absolute hell out of Jamie. But he wasn't so startled that he failed to hit ALT-F6 on his computer just before Principal Booty padded up to the computer terminal on his crepe-soled shoes.

A screen containing an essay about the plight of the rain forest replaced the status report from his illegal cracking program.

"Hi, Mr. Boethe," Jamie said.

"Ah." The tall, thin man bent down, peering at the screen. "Thought you might be looking at nasty pictures, Mr. Turner."

"No, sir," Jamie said. "I wouldn't do that."

"Studying the environment, concerned about what we've done to poor Mother Nature, are we? Good for you, good for you. But I can't help but notice that this is your physical education period. You should be *experiencing* Mother Nature firsthand. Out in the sports fields. Inhaling that good California air. Running and kicking goals."

"Isn't it raining?" Jamie asked.

"Misting, I'd call it. Besides, playing soccer in the rain builds character. Now, out we go, Mr. Turner. The greens are down one player. Mr. Lochnell turned left and his ankle turned right. Go to their aid. Your team needs you."

"I just have to shut down the system, sir. It'll take a few minutes."

The principal walked to the door, calling, "I expect to see you out there in full gear in fifteen minutes."

"Yessir," responded Jamie Turner, not revealing his huge disappointment at forsaking his machine for a muddy patch of grass and a dozen stupid students.

Alt-F6ing out of the rain forest window, Jamie started to type a status request to see how his Crack-er program was doing on the passcode file. Then he paused, squinted at the screen and noticed something odd. The type on the monitor seemed slightly fuzzier than normal. The letters seemed to flicker too.

And something else: the keys were a little sluggish under his touch.

This was way weird. He wondered what the problem might be. Jamie had written a couple of diagnostic programs and he decided he'd run one or two of them after he'd extracted the passcode. They might tell him what was wrong.

He guessed the trouble was a bug in the system folder, maybe a graphics accelerator problem. He'd check that first.

But for a brief instant Jamie Turner had a ridiculous thought: that the unclear letters and slow response times of the keys weren't a problem with his operating system at all. They were due to the ghost of a long-dead Indian, floating in between Jamie and his machine, angry at the human presence as the spirit's cold, spectral fingers keyed in a desperate message for help.

CHAPTER 00000101 / FIVE

◆━◈━◆

At the top left-hand corner of Phate's screen was a small dialogue box containing:

Trapdoor – Hunt Mode

Target: JamieTT@hol.com

Online: Yes

Operating system: MS–DOS/Windows

Antivirus software: Disabled

On the screen itself Phate was looking at exactly what Jamie Turner was seeing on his own machine, several miles away, in St. Francis Academy.

This particular character in his game had intrigued Phate from the first time he'd invaded the boy's machine, a month ago.

Phate had spent a lot of time browsing through Jamie's files and he'd learned as much about him as he'd learned about the late Lara Gibson.

For instance:

Jamie Turner hated sports and history and excelled at math and science. He read voraciously. The youngster was a MUDhead – he spent hours in the Multiuser Domain chat rooms on the Internet, excelling at role-playing games and active in creating and maintaining the fantasy societies so popular in the MUD realm. Jamie was also a brilliant codeslinger – a self-taught programmer. He'd designed his own Web site, which had gotten a runner-up prize from Web Site Revue Online. He'd come up with an idea for a new computer game that Phate found intriguing and that clearly had commercial potential.

The boy's biggest fear was losing his eyesight; he ordered special shatterproof glasses from an online optometrist.

The only member of his family he spent much time e-mailing and communicating with was his older brother Mark. Their parents were rich and busy and tended to respond to every fifth or sixth e-mail their son sent.

Jamie Turner, Phate had concluded, was brilliant and imaginative and vulnerable.

And the boy was also just the sort of hacker who'd one day surpass him.

Phate – like many of the great computer wizards – had a mystical side to him. He was like those physicists who accept God wholeheartedly or hard-headed politicians who're devoutly committed to Masonic mysticism. There was, Phate believed, an indescribably spiritual side to machines and only those with limited vision denied that.

So it wasn't at all out of character for Phate to be super-stitious. And one of the things that he'd come to believe, as he'd used Trapdoor to stroll through Jamie Turner's computer over the past few weeks, was that the boy had the skill to ultimately replace Phate as the greatest codeslinger of all time.

This was why he had to stop little Jamie T. Turner from continuing his adventures in the Machine World. And Phate planned to stop him in a particularly effective way.

He now scrolled through more files. These, which had been e-mailed to him by Shawn, gave detailed information about the boy's school – St. Francis Academy.

The boarding school was renowned academically but, more important, it represented a true tactical challenge to Phate. If there was no difficulty – and risk to him – in killing the characters in the game then there was no point in playing. And St. Francis offered some serious obstacles. The security was very extensive because the school had been the scene of a break-in several years ago in which one student had been killed and a teacher severely wounded. The principal, Willem Boethe, had vowed to never let that happen again. To reassure parents, he had renovated the entire school and turned it into a fortress. Halls were locked down at night, the grounds double-gated, windows and doors alarmed. You needed passcodes to get in and out of the tall razor-wired wall surrounding the compound.

Getting inside the school was, in short, just the right kind of challenge for Phate. It was a step up from Lara Gibson – moving to a higher, more difficult level in his game. He could—

Phate squinted at the screen. Oh, no, not again. Jamie's computer – and therefore his too – had crashed. It'd happened just ten minutes ago too. This was the *one* bug in Trapdoor. Sometimes his machine and the invaded computer would simply stop working. Then they'd both have to reboot – restart – their computers and go back online.

It resulted in a delay of no more than a minute or so but to Phate it was a terrible flaw. Software had to be perfect, it had to be *elegant*. He and Shawn had been trying to fix this bug for months but had had no luck so far.

A moment later he and his young friend were back online and Phate was browsing through the boy's machine once more.

A small window appeared on Phate's monitor and the Trapdoor program asked:

Target subject has received an instant message from MarkTheMan. Do you want to monitor?

That would be Jamie Turner's brother, Mark. Phate keyed *Y* and saw the brothers' dialogue on his screen.

MarkTheMan: Can you instant message?

JamieTT: Gotta go play sucker I mean SOCCER.

MarkTheMan: LOL. Still on for tonight?

JamieTT: You bet. Santana RULES!!!!!

MarkTheMan: Can't wait. I'll see you across the street by the north gate at 6:30. You ready to rock n roll?

Phate thought, You bet we are.

Wyatt Gillette paused in the doorway and felt as if he'd been transported back in time.

He gazed around him at the California State Police Computer Crimes Unit, which was housed in an old one-story building several miles from the state police's San Jose headquarters. "It's a dinosaur pen."

"Of our very own," Andy Anderson said. He then explained to Bishop and Shelton, neither of whom seemed to want the information, that in the early computing days huge computers like the mainframes made by IBM and Control Data Corporation were housed in special rooms like this, called dinosaur pens.

The pens featured raised floors, beneath which ran massive cables called "boas," after the snakes, which they resembled (and which had been known to uncurl violently at times and injure technicians). Dozens of air conditioner ducts also criss-crossed the room – the cooling systems were necessary to keep the massive computers from over-heating and catching fire.

The Computer Crimes Unit was located off West San Carlos, in a low-rent commercial district of San Jose, near the town of Santa Clara. To reach it you drove past a number of car dealerships – EZ TERMS FOR YOU! SE HABLA ESPAÑOL – and over a series of railroad tracks. The rambling one-story building, in need of painting and repair, was in clear contrast to, say, Apple Computer headquarters a mile away, a pristine, futuristic building decorated with a forty-foot portrait of cofounder Steve Wozniak. CCU's only artwork was a broken, rusty Pepsi machine, squatting next to the front door.

Inside the huge building were dozens of dark corridors and empty offices. The police were using only a small portion of the space – the central work area, in which a dozen modular cubicles had been assembled. There were eight Sun Microsystems workstations, several IBMs and Apples, a dozen laptops. Cables ran everywhere, some duct-taped to the floor, some hanging overhead like jungle vines.

"You can rent these old data-processing facilities for a song," Anderson explained to Gillette. He laughed. "The CCU finally gets recognized as a legit part of the state police and they give us digs that're twenty years out of date."

"Look, a scram switch." Gillette nodded at a red switch on the wall. A dusty sign said EMERGENCY USE ONLY. "I've never seen one."

"What's that?" Bob Shelton asked.

Anderson explained: The old mainframes would get so hot that if the cooling system went down the computers could overheat and catch fire in seconds. With all the resins and plastic and rubber the gases from a burning computer would kill you before the flames would. So all dinosaur pens came equipped with a scram switch – the name borrowed from the emergency shutdown switch in nuclear reactors. If there was a fire you hit the scram button, which shut off the computer, summoned the fire department and dumped halon gas on the machine to extinguish the flames.

Andy Anderson introduced Gillette, Bishop and Shelton to the CCU team. First, Linda Sanchez, a short, stocky, middle-aged Latina in a lumpy tan suit. She was the unit's SSL officer – seizure, search and logging, she explained. She was the one who secured a perpetrator's computer, checked it for booby traps, copied the files and logged hardware and software into evidence. She also was a digital evidence recovery specialist, an expert at "excavating" a hard drive – searching it for hidden or erased data (accordingly, such officers were also know as computer archaeologists). "I'm the team bloodhound," she explained to Gillette.

"Any word, Linda?"

"Not yet, boss. That daughter of mine, she's the laziest girl on earth."

Anderson said to Gillette, "Linda's about to be a grandmother."

"A week overdue. Driving the family crazy."

"And this is my second in command, Sergeant Stephen Miller."

Miller was older than Anderson, close to fifty. He had bushy, graying hair. Sloping shoulders, bearish, pear-shaped. He seemed cautious. Because of his age Gillette guessed he was from the second generation of computer programmers – men and women who were innovators in the computer world in the early seventies.

The third person was Tony Mott, a cheerful thirty-year-old with long, straight blond hair and Oakley sunglasses dangling from a green fluorescent cord around his neck. His cubicle was filled with pictures of him and a pretty Asian girl, snowboarding and mountain biking. A crash helmet sat on his desk, snowboarding boots in the corner. He'd represent the latest generation of hackers: athletic risk-takers, equally at home hacking together script at a keyboard and skateboarding half-pipes at extreme-sport competitions. Gillette noticed too that of all the cops at CCU Mott wore the biggest pistol on his hip – a shiny silver automatic.

The Computer Crimes Unit also had a receptionist but the woman was out sick. CCU was low in the state police hierarchy (it was referred to as the "Geek Squad" by fellow cops) and headquarters wouldn't spring for a temporary replacement. The members of the unit had to take phone messages, sift through mail and file documents by themselves and none of them, understandably, was very happy about this.

Then Gillette's eyes slipped to one of several erasable white-boards, against the wall, apparently used for listing clues. A photo was taped to one. He couldn't make out what it depicted and walked closer. Then he gasped and stopped in shock. The photo was of a young woman in an orange-and-red skirt, naked from the waist up, bloody and pale, lying in a patch of grass, dead. Gillette was shocked. He'd played plenty of computer games – Mortal Kombat and Doom and Tomb Raider – but, as gruesome as those games were, they were nothing compared to this still, horrible violence against a real victim.

Andy Anderson glanced at the wall clock, which wasn't digital, as befit a computer center, but an old, dusty analog model – with big and little hands. The time was 10:00 A.M. The cop said, "We've got to get moving on this. . . . Now, we're taking a two-prong approach to the case. Detectives Bishop and Shelton are going to be running a standard homicide investigation. CCU'll handle the computer evidence – with Wyatt's help here." He glanced at a fax on his desk and added, "We're also expecting a consultant from Seattle, an expert on the Internet and online systems. Patricia Nolan. She should be here any minute."

"Police?" Shelton asked.

"No, civilian," Anderson said.

Miller added, "We use corporate security people all the time. The technology changes so fast we can't keep up with all the latest developments. Perps're always one step ahead of us. So we try to use private consultants whenever we can."

Tony Mott said, "They're usually standing in line to help. It's real chic now to put catching a hacker on your résumé."

Anderson asked Linda Sanchez, "Now, where's the Gibson woman's computer?"

"In the analysis lab, boss." The woman nodded down one of the dark corridors that spidered out from the central room. "A couple of techs from crime scene are fingerprinting it – just in case the perp broke into her house and left some nice, juicy latents. Should be ready in ten minutes."

Mott handed Frank Bishop an envelope. "This came for you ten minutes ago. It's the preliminary crime scene report."

Bishop brushed at his stiff hair with the backs of his fingers. Gillette could see the tooth marks from the comb very clearly in the heavily sprayed strands. The cop glanced through the file but said nothing. He handed the thin stack of papers to Shelton, tucked his shirt in once more then leaned against the wall.

The chunky cop opened the file, read for a few moments then looked up. "Witnesses report the perpetrator was a white male, medium build and medium height, white slacks, a light blue shirt, tie with a cartoon character of some kind on it. Late twenties, early thirties. Looked like every techie in there, the bartender said." The cop walked to the white-board and began to write down these clues. He continued. "ID card around his neck said Xerox Palo Alto Research Center but we're sure that was fake. There were no hard leads to anybody there. He had a mustache and goatee. Blond hair. Also there were several frayed blue denim fibers on the victim that didn't match her clothes or anything in her closet at home. Might've come from the perp. The murder weapon was probably a military Ka-bar knife with a serrated top."

Tony Mott asked, "How'd you know that?"

"The wounds're consistent with that type of weapon." Shelton turned back to the file. "The victim was killed else-where and dumped by the highway."

Mott interrupted. "How could they tell *that?*"

Shelton frowned slightly, apparently not wishing to digress. "Quantity of her blood found at the scene." The young cop's lengthy blond hair danced as he nodded and seemed to record this information for future reference.

Shelton resumed. "Nobody near the body drop site saw anything." A sour glance at the others. "Like they *ever* do. . . . Now, we're trying to trace the doer's car – he and Lara left the bar together and were seen walking toward the back parking lot but nobody got a look at his wheels. Crime scene was lucky; the bartender remembered that the perp wrapped his beer bottle in a napkin and one of the techs found it in the trash. But we printed both the bottle and the napkin and came up with zip. The lab lifted some kind of adhesive off the lip of the bottle but we can't tell what it is. It's nontoxic. That's all they know. It doesn't match anything in the lab database."

Frank Bishop finally spoke. "A costume store."

"Costume?" Anderson asked.

The cop said, "Maybe he needed some help to look like this Will Randolph guy he was impersonating. Might be glue for a fake mustache or beard."

Gillette agreed. "A good social engineer always dresses for the con. I have friends who've sewed together complete Pac Bell linemen uniforms."

"That's good," Tony Mott said to Bishop, adding more data to his continuing education file.

Anderson nodded his approval of this suggestion. Shelton called homicide headquarters in San Jose and arranged to have some troopers check the adhesive against samples of theatrical glue.

Frank Bishop took off his wrinkled suit jacket and hung it carefully on the back of a chair. He stared at the photo and the white-board, arms crossed. His shirt was already billowing out again. He wore boots with pointed toes. When Gillette was a college student he and some friends at Berkeley had rented a skin flick for a party – a stag film from the fifties or sixties. One of the actors had looked and dressed just like Bishop.

Lifting the crime scene file away from Shelton, Bishop flipped through it. Then he looked up. "The bartender said that the victim had a martini and the killer had a light beer. The killer paid. If we can get a hold of the check we might lift a fingerprint."

"How're you going to do that?" It was bulky Stephen Miller who asked this. "The bartender probably pitched them out last night – with a thousand others."

Bishop nodded at Gillette. "We'll have some troopers do what *he* mentioned – Dumpster diving." To Shelton he said, "Have them look through the bar's trash bins for a receipt for a martini and a light beer, time-stamped about seven-thirty P.M."

"That'll take forever," Miller said. But Bishop ignored him and nodded to Shelton, who made the call to follow up on his suggestion.

Gillette then realized that nobody had been standing close to him. He eyed everyone else's clean clothes, shampooed hair, grime-free fingernails. He asked Anderson, "If we've got a few minutes before that computer's ready . . . I don't suppose you have a shower 'round here?"

Anderson tugged at the lobe that bore the stigmata of a past-life earring and broke into a laugh. "I was wondering how to bring that up." He said to Mott, "Take him down to the employee locker room. But stay close."

The young cop nodded and led Gillette down the hallway. He chattered away nonstop – his first topic the advantages of the Linux operating system, a variation on the classic

Unix, which many people were starting to use in place of Windows. He spoke enthusiastically and was well informed.

He then told Gillette about the recent formation of the CCU. They'd only been in existence for less than a year. The Geek Squad, Mott explained, could easily have used another half-dozen full-time cops but they weren't in the budget. There were more cases than they could possibly handle – from hacking to cyberstalking to child pornography to copyright infringement of software – and the workload seemed to get heavier with every passing month.

"Why'd you get into it?" Gillette asked him. "CCU?"

"Hoping for a little excitement. I mean, I love machines and guess I have a mind for 'em but sifting through code to find a copyright violation's not quite what I'd hoped. I thought it'd be a little more rig and rage, you know."

"How 'bout Linda Sanchez?" Gillette asked. "She a geek?"

"Not really. She's smart but machines aren't in her blood. She was a gang girl down in Lettuce Land, you know, Salinas. Then she went into social work and decided to go to the academy. Her partner was shot up pretty bad in Monterey a few years ago. Linda has kids – the daughter who's expecting and a girl in high school – and her husband's never home. He's an INS agent. So she figured it was time to move to a little quieter side of the business."

"Just the opposite of you."

Mott laughed. "I guess so."

As Gillette toweled off after the shower Mott placed an extra set of his own workout clothes on the bench for the hacker. T-shirt, black sweatpants and a warm-up windbreaker. Mott was shorter than Gillette but they had basically the same build.

"Thanks," Gillette said, donning the clothes. He felt exhilarated, having washed away one particular type of filth from his thin frame: the residue of prison.

On the way back to the main room they passed a small kitchenette. There was a coffeepot, a refrigerator and a table on which sat a plate of bagels. Gillette stopped, looked hungrily at the food. Then he eyed a row of cabinets.

He asked Mott, "I don't suppose you have any Pop-Tarts in there."

"Pop-Tarts? Naw. But have a bagel."

Gillette walked over to the table and poured a cup of coffee. He picked up a raisin bagel.

"Not one of those," Mott said. He took it out of Gillette's hand and dropped it on the floor. It bounced like a ball.

Gillette frowned.

"Linda brought these in. It's a joke." When Gillette stared at him in confusion the cop added, "Don't you get it?"

"Get what?"

"What's today's date?"

"I don't have a clue." The days of the month aren't how you mark time in prison.

"April Fools' Day," Mott said. "Those bagels're plastic. Linda and I put 'em out this morning and we've been waiting for Andy to bite – so to speak – but we haven't got him yet. I think he's on a diet." He opened the cabinet and took out a bag of fresh ones. "Here."

Gillette ate one quickly. Mott said, "Go ahead. Have another."

Another followed, washed down with gulps from the large cup of coffee. They were the best thing he'd had in ages.

Mott got a carrot juice from the fridge and they returned to the main area of CCU.

Gillette looked around the dinosaur pen, at the hundreds of disconnected boas lying in the corners and at the air-conditioning vents, his mind churning. A thought occurred to him. "April Fools' Day . . . so the murder was March thirty-first?"

"Right," Anderson confirmed. "Is that significant?"

Gillette said uncertainly, "It's probably a coincidence."

"Go ahead."

"Well, it's just that March thirty-first is sort of a red-letter day in computer history."

Bishop asked, "Why?"

A woman's gravelly voice spoke from the doorway. "Isn't that the date the first Univac was delivered?"

CHAPTER 00000110 / SIX

———◆·▶◀·◆———

They turned to see a hippy brunette in her mid-thirties, wearing an unfortunate gray sweater suit and thick black shoes.

Anderson asked, "Patricia?"

She nodded and walked into the room, shook his hand.

"This's Patricia Nolan, the consultant I was telling you about. She's with the security department of Horizon On-Line."

Horizon was the biggest commercial Internet service provider in the world, larger even than America Online. Since there were tens of millions of registered subscribers and since every one of them could have up to eight different usernames for friends or family members it was likely that, at any given time, a large percentage of the world was checking stock quotes, lying to people in chat rooms, reading Hollywood gossip, buying things, finding out the weather, reading and sending e-mails and downloading soft-core porn via Horizon On-Line.

Nolan kept her eyes on Gillette's face for a moment. She glanced at the palm tree tattoo. Then at his fingers, keying compulsively in the air.

Anderson explained, "Horizon called us when they heard the victim was a customer and volunteered to send some-body to help out."

The detective introduced her to the team and now Gillette examined *her*. The trendy designer eyeglasses, probably bought on impulse, didn't do much to make her masculine, plain face any less plain. But the striking green eyes behind them were piercing and very quick – Gillette could see that she too was amused to find herself in an antiquated dinosaur pen. Nolan's complexion was loose and doughy and obscured with thick makeup that would have been stylish – if excessive – in the 1970s. Her brunette hair was very thick and unruly and tended to fall into her face.

After hands were shaken and introductions made she returned immediately to Gillette. She twined a mass of hair around her fingers and, not caring who heard, said bluntly, "I saw the way you looked at me when you heard I worked for Horizon."

Like all big commercial Internet service providers – AOL, CompuServe, Prodigy and the others – Horizon On-Line was held in contempt by true hackers. Computer wizards used telnet programs to jump directly from their computers to others' and they roamed the Blue Nowhere with customized Web browsers built for interstellar travel. They wouldn't think of using simple-minded, low-horsepower Internet providers like Horizon, which was geared for family entertainment.

Subscribers to Horizon On-Line were known as HOLamers or HOLosers. Or, echoing Gillette's current address, just plain HOs.

Nolan continued, speaking to Gillette. "Just so we get everything on the table, I went to MIT undergrad and Princeton for my masters and doctorate – both in computer science."

"AI?" Gillette asked. "In New Jersey?"

Princeton's artificial intelligence lab was one of the top in the country. Nolan nodded. "That's right. And I've done my share of hacking too."

Gillette was amused that she was justifying herself to *him*, the one felon in the crowd, and not to the police. He could hear an edgy tone in her voice and the delivery sounded rehearsed. He supposed this was because she was a woman; the Equal Employment Opportunity Commission doesn't have jurisdiction to stop the relentless prejudice against women trying to make their way in the Blue Nowhere. Not only are they hounded out of chat rooms and off bulletin boards but they're often blatantly insulted and even threatened. Teenage girls who want to hack need to be smarter and ten times tougher than their male counterparts.

"What were you saying about Univac?" Tony Mott asked.

Nolan filled in, "March 31, 1951. The first Univac was delivered to the Census Bureau for regular operations."

"What was it?" Bob Shelton asked.

"It stands for Universal Automatic Computer."

Gillette said, "Acronyms're real popular in the Machine World."

Nolan said, "Univac is one of the first modern mainframe computers, as we know them. It took up a room as big as this one. Of course nowadays you can buy laptops that're faster and do a hundred times more."

Anderson mused, "The date? Think it's a coincidence?"

Nolan shrugged. "I don't know."

"Maybe our perp's got a theme of some kind," Mott suggested. "I mean, a milestone computer date and a motiveless killing right in the heart of Silicon Valley."

"Let's follow up on it," Anderson said. "Find out if there're any recent unsolved killings that fit this M.O. in other high-tech areas. Try Seattle, Portland – they have the Silicon Forest there. Chicago's got the Silicon Prairie. Route 128 outside of Boston."

"Austin, Texas," Miller suggested.

"Good. And the Dulles Toll Road corridor outside of D.C. Start there and let's see what we can find. Send the request to VICAP."

Tony Mott keyed in some information and a few minutes later he got a response. He read from the screen and said, "Got something in Portland. February fifteenth and seventeenth of this year. Two unsolved killings, same M.O. in both of them, and it was similar to here – both victims stabbed to death, died of chest wounds. Perp was believed to be a white male, late twenties. Didn't seem to know the victims and robbery and rape weren't motives. The vics were a wealthy corporate executive – male – and a professional woman athlete."

"February fifteenth?" Gillette asked.

Patricia Nolan glanced at him. "ENIAC?"

"Right," the hacker said then explained: "ENIAC was similar to Univac but earlier. It came online in the forties. The dedication date was February fifteenth."

"What's *that* acronym?"

Gillette said, "The Electronic Numerical Integrator and Calculator." Like all hackers he was an aficionado of computer history.

"Shit," Shelton muttered, "we've got a pattern doer. Great."

Another message arrived from VICAP. Gillette glanced at the screen and learned that these letters stood for the Department of Justice's Violent Criminal Apprehension Program.

It seemed that cops used acronyms as much as hackers.

"Man, here's one more," Mott said, reading the screen.

"More?" Stephen Miller asked, dismayed. He absently organized some of the mess of disks and papers that covered his desk six inches deep.

"About eighteen months ago a diplomat and a colonel at the Pentagon – both of them with bodyguards – were killed in Herndon, Virginia. That's the Dulles Toll Road high-tech corridor. . . . I'm ordering the complete files."

"What were the dates of the Virginia killings?" Anderson asked.

"August twelfth and thirteenth."

He wrote this on the white-board and looked at Gillette with a raised eyebrow. "Any clue?"

"IBM's first PC," the hacker replied. "The release date was August twelfth." Nolan nodded.

"So he's got a theme," Shelton said.

Frank Bishop added, "And that means he's going to keep going."

The computer terminal where Mott sat gave a soft beep. The young cop leaned forward, his large automatic pistol clanking loudly against his chair. He frowned. "We've got a problem here."

On the screen were the words:

Unable to Download Files

A longer message was beneath it.

Anderson read the text, shook his head. "The case files at VICAP on the Portland and Virginia killings're missing. The note from the sysadmin says they were damaged in a data-storage mishap."

"Mishap," Nolan muttered, sharing a look with Gillette.

Linda Sanchez, eyes wide, said, "You don't think . . . I mean, he *couldn't've* cracked VICAP. Nobody's ever done that."

Anderson said to the younger cop, "Try the state databases: Oregon and Virginia State Police case archives."

In a moment he looked up. "No record of any files on those cases. They vanished."

Mott and Miller eyed each other uncertainly. "This's getting scary," Mott said.

Anderson mused, "But what's his motive?"

"He's a goddamn hacker," Shelton muttered. "*That's* his motive."

"He's not a hacker," Gillette said.

"Then what is he?"

Gillette didn't feel like educating the difficult cop. He glanced at Anderson, who explained, "The word 'hacker' is a compliment. It means an innovative programmer. As in 'hacking together' software. A real hacker breaks into somebody's machine only to see if he can do it and to find out what's inside – it's a curiosity thing. The hacker ethic is it's okay to look but don't touch. People who break into systems as vandals or thieves are called 'crackers.' As in safecrackers."

"I wouldn't even call him that," Gillette said. "Crackers maybe steal and vandalize but they don't hurt people. I'd call him a 'kracker' with a *k*. For killer."

"Cracker with a *c*, kracker with a *k*," Shelton muttered. "What the hell difference does it make?"

"A big difference," Gillette said. "Spell 'phreak' with a *ph* and you're talking about somebody who steals phone services. 'Phishing' – with a *ph* – is searching the Net for someone's identity. Misspell 'wares' with a *z* on the end, not an *s*, and you're not talking about housewares but about stolen software. When it comes to hacking it's all in the spelling."

Shelton shrugged and remained unimpressed by the distinction.

The identification techs from the California State Police Forensics Division returned to the main part of the CCU office, wheeling battered suitcases behind them. One consulted a sheet of paper. "We lifted eighteen partial latents, twelve partial visibles." He nodded at a laptop computer case slung over his shoulder. "We scanned them and it looks like they're all the victim's or her boyfriend's. And there was no evidence of glove smears on the keys."

"So," Anderson said, "he got inside her system from a remote location. Soft access – like we thought." He thanked the techs and they left.

Then Linda Sanchez – all business at the moment, no longer the grandmother-to-be – said to Gillette, "I've secured and logged everything in her machine." She handed him a floppy disk. "Here's a boot disk."

This was a disk that contained enough of an operating system to "boot up," or start, a suspect's computer. Police used boot disks, rather than the hard drive itself, to start the computer in case the owner – or the killer, in this case – had installed some software on the hard drive that would destroy it.

"I've been through her machine three times now and I haven't found any booby traps but that doesn't mean they aren't there. You probably know all this too but keep the victim's machine and any disks away from plastic bags or boxes or folders – they can create static and zap data. Same thing with speakers. They have magnets in them. And don't put any disks on metal shelves – they might be magnetized. You'll find nonmagnetic tools in the lab. I guess you know what to do from here."

"Yep."

She said, "Good luck. The lab's down that corridor there."

The boot disk in hand, Gillette started toward the hallway. Bob Shelton followed.

The hacker turned. "I don't really want anybody looking over my shoulder."

Especially you, he added to himself.

"It's okay," Anderson said to the homicide cop. "The only

exit back there's alarmed and he's got his jewelry on."
Nodding at the shiny metal transmission anklet. "He's not
going anywhere."

Shelton wasn't pleased but he acquiesced. Gillette
noticed, though, that he didn't return to the main room. He
leaned against the hallway wall near the lab and crossed
his arms, looking like a bouncer with a bad attitude.

*If you even get an itchy look that I don't like you're going
to get hurt bad. . . .*

Inside the analysis room Gillette walked up to Lara
Gibson's computer. It was an unremarkable, off-the-shelf
IBM clone.

He did nothing with her machine just yet, though. Instead
he sat down at a workstation and wrote a kludge – a down-
and-dirty program to solve a particular problem. In five
minutes he was finished writing the source code. He named
the program Detective then compiled and copied it to the
boot disk Sanchez had given him. He inserted the disk into
the floppy drive of Lara Gibson's machine. He turned on
the power switch and the drives hummed and snapped with
comforting familiarity.

Wyatt Gillette's thick, muscular fingers slid eagerly onto
the cool plastic of the keys. He positioned his fingertips,
callused from years of keyboarding, on the tiny orientation
bumps on the F and J keys. The boot disk bypassed the
machine's Windows operating system and went straight to
the leaner MS-DOS – the famous Microsoft Disk Operating
System, which is the basis for the more user-friendly
Windows. The C: prompt appeared on the black screen.

His heart raced as he stared at the hypnotically pulsing
cursor.

Then, not looking at the keyboard, he pressed a key, the
one for *d* – the first letter in the command line, detective.exe,
which would start his program.

In the Blue Nowhere time is very different from what we
know it to be in the Real World and, in the first thousandth
of a second after Wyatt Gillette pushed that key, this
happened:

The voltage flowing through the circuit beneath the *d* key
changed ever so slightly.

The keyboard processor noticed the change in current and transmitted an interrupt signal to the computer itself, which momentarily sent the dozens of tasks it was currently performing to a storage area known as the stack and then created a special priority route for codes coming from the keyboard.

The code for the letter *d* was directed by the keyboard processor along this express route into the computer's basic input-output system – the BIOS – which checked to see if Wyatt Gillette had pressed the SHIFT, CONTROL or ALTERNATE keys at the same time he'd hit the *d* key.

Assured that he hadn't, the BIOS translated the letter's keyboard code for the lowercase *d* into another one, its ASCII code, which was then sent into the computer's graphics adapter.

The adapter in turn converted the code to a digital signal, which it forwarded to the electron guns located in the back of the monitor.

The guns fired a burst of energy into the chemical coating on the screen. And, miraculously, the white letter *d* burned into existence on the black monitor.

All this in a fraction of a second.

And in what remained of that second Gillette typed the rest of the letters of his command, *e-t-e-c-t-i-v-e . e-x-e,* and then hit the ENTER key with his right little finger.

More type and graphics appeared, and soon, like a surgeon on the trail of an elusive tumor, Wyatt Gillette began probing carefully through Lara Gibson's computer – the only aspect of the woman that had survived the vicious attack, that was still warm, that retained at least a few memories of who she was and what she'd done in her brief life.

CHAPTER 00000111 / SEVEN

——◆◆◆◆◆——

He walks in a hacker's slump, Andy Anderson thought, watching Wyatt Gillette return from the analysis lab.

Machine people had the worst posture of any profession in the world.

It was nearly 11:00 A.M. The hacker had spent only thirty minutes looking over Lara Gibson's machine.

Bob Shelton, who now dogged Gillette back to the main office, to the hacker's obvious irritation, asked, "So what'd you find?" The question was delivered in a chilly tone and Anderson wondered again why Shelton was riding the young man so hard – especially considering that the hacker was helping them out on a case the detective had volunteered for.

Gillette ignored the pock-faced cop and sat down in a swivel chair, flipped open his notebook. When he spoke it was to Anderson. "There's something odd going on. The killer *was* in her computer. He seized root and—"

"Dumb it down," Shelton muttered. "Seized what?"

Gillette explained, "When somebody has root that means they have complete control over a computer network and all the machines on it."

Anderson added, "When you're root you can rewrite programs, delete files, add authorized users, remove them, go online as somebody else."

Gillette continued, "But I can't figure out how he did it. The only thing unusual I found were some scrambled files – I thought they were some kind of encrypted virus but they turned out to be just gibberish. There's not a trace of any kind of software on her machine that would let him get inside."

Glancing at Bishop, he explained, "See, I could load a virus in your computer that'd let me seize root on your machine and get inside it from wherever I am, whenever I want to, without needing a passcode. They're called 'back door' viruses – as in sneaking in through the back door.

"But in order for them to work I have to somehow actually *install* the software on your computer and activate it. I could send it to you as an attachment to an e-mail, say, and you could activate it by opening the attachment without knowing what it was. Or I could break into your house and install it on your computer then activate it myself. But there's no evidence that happened. No, he seized root some other way."

The hacker was an animated speaker, Anderson noticed. His eyes were glowing with that absorbed animation he'd seen in so many young geeks – even the ones who were sitting in court, more or less convicting *themselves* as they excitedly described their exploits to the judge and jury.

"Then how do you know he seized root?" Linda Sanchez asked.

"I hacked together this kludge." He handed Anderson a floppy disk.

"What's it do?" Patricia Nolan asked, her professional curiosity piqued, as was Anderson's.

"It's called Detective. It looks for things that *aren't* inside a computer." He explained for the benefit of the non-CCU cops. "When your computer runs, the operating system – like Windows – stores parts of the programs it needs all over your hard drive. There're patterns to where and when it stores those files." Indicating the disk, he said, "That showed me that a lot of those bits of programs'd been moved to places on the hard drive that make sense only if somebody was going through her computer from a remote location."

Shelton shook his head in confusion.

But Frank Bishop said, "You mean, it's like you know a burglar was inside your house because he moved furniture and didn't put the pieces back. Even though he was gone when you got home."

Gillette nodded. "Exactly."

Andy Anderson – as much a wizard as Gillette in some areas – hefted the thin disk in his hand. He couldn't help feeling impressed. When he was considering asking Gillette to help them, the cop had looked through some of Gillette's script, which the prosecutor had submitted as evidence in the case against him. After examining the brilliant lines of source code Anderson had two thoughts. The first was that if anyone could figure out how the perp had gotten into Lara Gibson's computer it was Wyatt Gillette.

The second was pure, painful envy of the young man's skills. Throughout the world there were tens of thousands of code crunchers – people who happily churn out tight, efficient software for mundane tasks – and there were just as many script bunnies, the term for kids who write wildly creative but clumsy and largely useless programs just for the fun of it. But only a few programmers have both the vision to conceive of script that's "elegant," the highest form of praise for software, and the skill to write it. Wyatt Gillette was just such a codeslinger.

Once again Anderson noticed Frank Bishop looking around the room absently, his mind elsewhere. He wondered if he should call headquarters and see about getting a new detective on board. Let Bishop go chase his MARINKILL bank robbers – if that's what was so goddamn important to him – and we'll replace him with somebody who at least could pay attention.

The CCU cop said to Gillette, "So the bottom line is he got into her system thanks to some new, unknown program or virus."

"Basically, that's it."

"Could you find out anything else about him?" Mott asked.

"Only what you already know – that he's been trained on Unix."

Unix is a computer operating system, just like MS-DOS or Windows, though it controls larger, more powerful machines than personal computers.

"Wait," Anderson interrupted. "What do you mean, what we already know?"

"That mistake he made."

"What mistake?"

Gillette frowned. "When the killer was inside her system he keyed some commands to get into her files. But they were Unix commands – he must've entered them by mistake before he remembered her machine was running Windows. You *must've* seen them in there."

Anderson looked questioningly at Stephen Miller, who'd apparently been the one analyzing the victim's computer in the first place. Miller said uneasily, "I noticed a couple lines of Unix, yeah. But I just assumed she'd typed them."

"She's a civilian," Gillette said, using the hacker term for a casual computer user. "I doubt she'd even heard of Unix, let alone known the commands." In Windows and Apple operating systems people control their machines by simply clicking on pictures or typing common English words for commands; Unix requires users to learn hundreds of complicated codes.

"I didn't think, sorry," the bearish cop said defensively. He seemed put out at this criticism over what he must have thought was a small point.

So Stephen Miller had made yet another mistake, Anderson reflected. This had been an ongoing problem ever since Miller had joined CCU recently. In the 1970s Miller had headed a promising company that made computers and developed software. But his products were always one step behind IBM's, Digital Equipment's and Microsoft's and he eventually went bankrupt. Miller complained that he'd often anticipated the NBT (the "Next Big Thing" – the Silicon Valley phrase for an innovation that would revolutionize the industry) but the "big boys" were continually sabotaging him.

After his company went under he'd gotten divorced and left the Machine World for a few years, then surfaced as a freelance programmer. Miller drifted into computer security and finally applied to the state police. He wouldn't've been Anderson's first choice for a computer cop but, then again, CCU had very few qualified applicants to choose from (why earn $60,000 a year working a job where there's a chance you might get shot when you can make ten times that at one of Silicon Valley's corporate legends?).

Besides, Miller – who'd never remarried and didn't seem to have much of a personal life – put in the longest hours in the department and could be found in the dinosaur pen long after everyone else had left. He also took work "home," that is, to some of the local university computer departments, where friends would let him run CCU projects on state-of-the-art supercomputers for free.

"What's that mean for us?" Shelton asked. "That he knows this Unix stuff."

Anderson said, "It's *bad* for us. That's what it means. Hackers who use Windows or Apple systems are usually small-time. Serious hackers work in Unix or Digital Equipment's operating system, VMS."

Gillette concurred. He added, "Unix is also the operating system of the Internet. Anybody who's going to crack into the big servers and routers on the Net has to know Unix."

Bishop's phone rang and he took the call. Then he looked around and sat down at a nearby workstation to jot notes. He sat upright; no hacker's slouch here, Anderson observed. When he disconnected the call Bishop said, "Got some leads. One of our troopers heard from some CIs."

It was a moment before Anderson recalled what the letters stood for. Confidential informants. Snitches.

Bishop said in his soft, unemotional voice, "Somebody named Peter Fowler, white male about twenty-five, from Bakersfield's been seen selling guns in this area. Been hawking Ka-bars too." A nod at the white-board. "Like the murder weapon. He was seen an hour ago near the Stanford campus in Palo Alto. Some park near Page Mill, a quarter mile north of 280."

"Hacker's Knoll, boss," Linda Sanchez said. "In Milliken Park."

Anderson nodded. He knew the place well and wasn't surprised when Gillette said that he did too. It's a deserted grassy area near the campus where computer science majors, hackers and chip-jocks hang out. They trade warez and swap stories, smoke weed.

"I know some people there," Anderson said. "I'll go check it out when we're through here."

Bishop consulted his notes again and said, "The report from the lab shows that the adhesive on the bottle is the type of glue used in theatrical makeup. A couple of our people checked the phone book for stores. There's only one store in the immediate area – Ollie's Theatrical Supply on El Camino Real in Mountain View. They sell a lot of the stuff, the clerk said. But they don't keep records of the sales."

"Now," Bishop continued, "we might have a lead on the perp's car. A security guard in an office building across the street from Vesta's, the restaurant where he picked up the Gibson woman, noticed a late-model, light-colored sedan parked in the company lot around the time the victim was in the bar. He thought somebody was inside the sedan. If there was, the driver may've gotten a good view of the perp's vehicle. We should canvass all the employees in the company."

Anderson said to Bishop, "You want to check that out while I'm at Hacker's Knoll?"

"Yessir, that's what I had in mind." Another look at his notes. Then he nodded his crisp hair toward Gillette. "Some crime scene techs *did* find a receipt for a light beer and martini in the trash bins behind the restaurant. They've lifted a couple of prints. They're sending 'em to the bureau for AFIS."

Tony Mott noticed Gillette's frown of curiosity. "Automated Fingerprint Identification System," he explained to the hacker. "It'll search the federal system and then do a state-by-state search. Takes time to do the whole country but if he's been collared for anything in the past eight or nine years we'll probably get a match."

Although he had a real talent for computers Mott was fascinated with what he called "real police work" and was constantly hounding Anderson for a transfer to Homicide or Major Crimes so he could go chase "real perps." He was undoubtedly the only cybercop in the country who wore as his sidearm a car-stopping .45 automatic.

Bishop said, "They'll concentrate on the West Coast first. California, Washington, Oregon and—"

"No," Gillette said. "Go east to west. Do New Jersey, New York, Massachusetts and North Carolina first. Then Illinois and Wisconsin. Then Texas. Do California last."

"Why?" Bishop asked.

"Those Unix commands he typed? They were the East Coast version."

Patricia Nolan explained that there were several versions of the Unix operating system. Using the East Coast commands suggested that the killer had Atlantic seaboard roots. Bishop nodded and called this information into headquarters. He then glanced at his notebook and said, "There's one other thing we should add to the profile."

"What's that?" Anderson asked.

"The ID division said that it looks like the perp was in an accident of some kind. He's missing the tips of most of his fingers. He's got enough of the pads to leave prints but the tips end in scar tissue. The ID tech was thinking maybe he'd been injured in a fire."

Gillette shook his head. "Callus."

The cops looked at him. Gillette held up his own hands. The fingertips were flat and ended in yellow calluses. "It's called a 'hacker manicure,'" he explained. "You pound keys twelve hours a day, this's what happens."

Shelton wrote this on the white-board.

Gillette said, "What I want to do now is go online and check out some of the renegade hacking newsgroups and chat rooms. Whatever the killer's doing is the sort of thing that's going to cause a big stir in the underground and—"

"No, you're not going online," Anderson told him.

"What?"

"Nope," the cop repeated adamantly.

"I *have* to."

"No. Those're the rules. You stay offline."

"Wait a minute," Shelton said. "He *was* online. I saw him."

Anderson's head swiveled toward the cop. "He was?"

"Yeah, in that room in the back – the lab. I looked in on him when he was checking out the victim's computer." He glanced at Anderson. "I assumed you okayed it."

"No, I didn't." Andersen asked Gillette, "Did you log on?"

"No," Gillette said firmly. "He must've seen me writing my kludge and thought I was online."

"Looked like it to me," Shelton said.

"You're wrong."

Shelton smiled sourly and appeared unconvinced.

Anderson could have checked out the log-in files of the CCU computer to find out for certain. But then decided that whether or not he'd gone online didn't really matter. Gillette's job here was finished. He picked up the phone and called HQ. "We've got a prisoner here to be transferred back to the San Jose Correctional Facility."

Gillette turned toward him, dismay in his eyes. "No," he said. "You *can't* send me back."

"I'll make sure you get that laptop we promised you."

"No, you don't understand. I can't stop now. We've got to find out what this guy did to get into her machine."

Shelton grumbled, "You said you couldn't find anything."

"*That's* exactly the problem. If I *had* found something we could understand it. But I can't. That's what's so scary about what he did. I need to keep going."

Anderson said, "If we find the killer's machine – or another victim's – and if we need you to analyze it we'll bring you back."

"But the chat rooms, the newsgroups, the hacker sites . . . there could be a hundred leads there. People *have* to be talking about software like this."

Anderson saw the addict's desperation in Gillette's face, just as the warden had predicted.

The cybercop pulled on his raincoat and said firmly, "We'll take it from here, Wyatt. And thanks again."

CHAPTER 00001000 / EIGHT

❖━━◆━━❖

He wasn't going to make it, Jamie Turner realized with dismay.

The time was nearly noon and he was sitting by himself in the cold, dim computer room, still in his damp soccer outfit (playing in the mist doesn't build character at all, Booty; it just makes you fucking wet). But he didn't want to waste the time on a shower and change of clothes. When he'd been out on the playing field all he'd been able to think about was whether the college computer he'd hacked into had cracked the outer-gate passcode.

And now, peering at the monitor through his thick, misted glasses, he saw that the Cray probably wasn't going to spit out the decrypted password in time. It would take, he estimated, another two days to crack the code.

He thought about his brother, about the Santana concert, about the backstage passes – all just out of reach – and he felt like crying. He began to type some commands to see if he could log on to another of the school's computers – a faster one, in the physics department. But there was a long queue of users waiting to get into that one. Jamie sat back and, out of frustration, not hunger, wolfed down a package of M&Ms.

He felt a painful chill and he looked quickly around the dark, musty room. He shivered in fear.

That damn ghost again . . .

Maybe he should just forget the whole thing. He was sick of being scared, sick of being cold. He should get the hell out of here, go hang with Dave or Totter or some of the guys from French club. His hands went to the keyboard to stop Crack-er and run the cloaking program that would destroy the evidence of his hack.

Then something happened.

On the screen in front of him the root directory of the college's computer suddenly appeared. Way bizarre! Then, all by itself, the computer dialed out to another one, outside of the school. The machines electronically shook hands and a moment later Jamie Turner's Cracker and Booty's password file were transferred to the second computer.

How the hell had that happened?

Jamie Turner was very savvy in the ways of computers but he'd never seen this. The only explanation was that the first computer – the college's – had some kind of arrangement with other computer departments so that tasks that took a long time were automatically transferred to speedier machines.

But what was totally weird was that the machine Jamie's software had been transferred to was the Defense Research Center's massive parallel array of supercomputers in Colorado Springs, one of the fastest computer systems in the world. It was also one of the most secure and was virtually impossible to crack (Jamie knew; he'd tried it). It contained highly classified information and no civilian had even been allowed to use it in the past. Jamie supposed they'd started renting out the system to defray the massive cost of maintaining a parallel array. Ecstatic, he peered at the screen and saw that the DRC's machines were cracking Booty's passcode at a blistering rate.

Well, if there was a ghost in his machine, he decided, maybe it was a good ghost after all. Maybe it was even a Santana fan, he laughed to himself.

Jamie now turned to his next task, the second hack he needed to complete before the Great Escape. In less than sixty seconds he'd transformed himself into a middle-aged overworked service tech employed by West Coast Security Systems, Inc., who'd unfortunately misplaced the schematic diagram for an WCS Model 8872 alarmed fire door he was trying to repair and needed some help from the technical supervisor.

The man was all too happy to oblige.

Phate, sitting at his dining room office, was watching Jamie Turner's program hard at work in the Defense Research Center's supercomputers, where he'd just sent it, along with the password file.

Unknown to the sysadmins at the DRC the huge computers were presently under his root control and were burning about $25,000 of computer time for the sole purpose of letting a sophomore in high school open a single locked gate.

Phate had examined the progress of the first supercomputer Jamie had used at a nearby college and had seen at once that it wasn't going to spit out the passcode in time for the boy to escape from the school for his six-thirty rendezvous with his brother.

Which meant that he'd stay safely tucked away at St. Francis and Phate would lose this round of the game. And that wasn't acceptable.

But, as he'd known, the DRC's parallel array would easily crack the code before the deadline.

If Jamie Turner had actually gotten to the concert that night – which wasn't going to happen now – he'd have had Phate to thank.

Phate then hacked into the San Jose City Planning and Zoning Board computer files and found a construction proposal, submitted by the principal of St. Francis Academy, who'd wanted to put up a gated wall and needed P&Z approval. Phate downloaded the documents and printed out diagrams of the school itself and the grounds.

As he was examining the diagrams his machine beeped and a box flashed onto the screen, alerting him that he'd received an e-mail from Shawn.

He felt the ping of excitement he always did when Shawn sent a message. This reaction struck him as significant, an important insight into Phate's – no, make that Jon Holloway's – personal development. He'd grown up in a household where love was as rare as money was plentiful and he knew that he'd developed into a cold, distant person.

He'd felt this way toward everyone – his family, fellow workers, classmates and the few people he'd tried to have relationships with. And yet the depth of what Phate felt for Shawn proved that he wasn't emotionally dead, that he had within him a vast well of love.

Eager to read the message he logged off the planning and zoning network and called up the e-mail.

But as he read the stark words the smile slipped from his face, his breath grew rapid, his pulse increased. "Oh, Christ," he muttered.

The gist of the e-mail was that the police were much further along on his trail than he'd anticipated. They even knew about the killings in Portland and Virginia.

Then he glanced at the second paragraph and got no further than the reference to Milliken Park.

No, no. . . .

He now had a real problem.

Phate rose from his desk and hurried downstairs to the basement of his house. He glanced at another smear of dried blood on the floor – from the Lara Gibson character – and then opened a footlocker. From it he took his dark, stained knife. He walked to the closet, opened it and flicked the light on.

Ten minutes later he was in his Jaguar, speeding onto the freeway.

In the beginning God created the Advanced Research Projects Agency network, which was called ARPAnet, and the ARPAnet flourished and begat the Milnet, and the ARPAnet and the Milnet begat the Internet, and the Internet and its issue, Usenet newsgroups and the World Wide Web, became a trinity that changed the life of His people forever and ever.

Andy Anderson – who'd described the Net thus when he taught classes on computer history – thought of this slightly too-witty description now as he drove through Palo Alto and saw Stanford University ahead of him. For it was at the nearby Stanford Research Institute that the Department of Defense had established the Internet's predecessor in 1969 to link the SRI with UCLA, the University of

California at Santa Barbara and the University of Utah.

The reverence he felt for the site, however, faded quickly as he drove on through misty rain and saw the deserted hill of Hacker's Knoll ahead of him, in John Milliken Park. Normally the place would be crowded with young people swapping software and tales of their cyber exploits. Today, though, the cold April drizzle had emptied the place.

He parked, pulled on the rumpled gray rain hat his six-year-old daughter had given him as a birthday present and climbed out of the car, striding through the grass, as streamers of rain flew from his shoes. He was discouraged by the lack of possible witnesses who might have a lead to Peter Fowler, the gunrunner. Still, there was a covered bridge in the middle of the park; sometimes kids hung out there when it was rainy or cold.

But as Anderson approached he saw that the bridge too was deserted.

He paused and looked around. The only people here clearly weren't hackers: an elderly woman walking a dog, and a businessman making a cell phone call under the awning of one of the nearby university buildings.

Anderson recalled a coffee shop in downtown Palo Alto, near the Hotel California. It was a place where geeks gathered to sip strong coffee and swap tales of their outrageous hacks. He decided to try the restaurant and see if anyone had heard about Peter Fowler or somebody selling knives in the area. If not, he'd try the computer science building and ask some of the professors and grad students if they'd seen anybody who—

Then the detective saw motion nearby.

Fifty feet away was a young man, walking furtively through the bushes toward the bridge. He was looking around uneasily, clearly paranoid.

Anderson ducked behind a thick stand of juniper, his heart pounding like a pile driver – because this was, he knew, Lara Gibson's killer. He was in his twenties and was wearing the blue jean jacket that must've shed the denim fibers found on the woman's body. He had blond hair and was clean shaven; the beard and mustache he'd worn in the bar *had* been fake, glued on with the theatrical adhesive.

Social engineering . . .

Then the man's jacket fell away for a moment and Anderson could see, protruding from the waistband of the man's jeans, the knobby hilt of a Ka-bar knife. The killer quickly pulled the jacket closed and continued to the covered bridge, where he stepped into the shadows and peered out.

Anderson remained out of sight. He made a call to the state police's field operations central dispatch. A moment later he heard the dispatcher answer and ask for his badge number.

"Four three eight nine two," Anderson whispered in reply. "Request immediate backup. I've got a visual on a suspect in a homicide. I'm in John Milliken Park, Palo Alto, southeast corner."

"Copy, four three eight," the man replied. "Is suspect armed?"

"I see a knife. I don't know about any firearms."

"Is he in a vehicle?"

"Negative," Anderson said. "He's on foot at the moment."

The dispatcher asked him to hold on. Anderson stared at the killer, squinting hard, as if that would keep him frozen in place. He whispered to central, "What's the ETA of that backup?"

"One moment, four three eight. . . . Okay, be advised, they'll be there in twelve minutes."

"Can't you get somebody here faster than that?"

"Negative, four three eight. Can you stay with him?"

"I'll try."

But just then the man began walking again. He left the bridge and started down the sidewalk.

"He's on the move, central. He's heading west through the middle of the park toward some university buildings, I'll stay with him and keep you posted on his location."

"Copy that, four three eight. CAU is on its way."

CAU? he wondered. What the hell was that again? Oh, right: closest available unit.

Hugging the trees and brush, Anderson moved closer to the bridge, keeping out of the killer's sight. What had he come back here for? To find another victim? To cover up some traces of the earlier crime? To buy more weapons from Peter Fowler?

He glanced at his watch. Less than a minute had passed. Should he call back and tell the unit to roll up silently? He didn't know. There were probably procedures for handling this sort of situation – procedures that cops like Frank Bishop and Bob Shelton would surely know well. Anderson was used to a very different kind of police work. *His* stake-outs were conducted sitting in vans, staring at the screen of a Toshiba laptop connected to a Cellscope radio directional-finding system.

Then he remembered: his weapon . . .

He looked down at the chunky butt of the Glock. He pulled it off his hip and pointed it downward, finger outside the trigger, as he vaguely remembered he ought to do.

Ten minutes until the damn CAU rolled up.

Then, through the mist, he heard a faint electronic trill.

The killer had gotten a phone call. He pulled a cell phone off his belt and held it to his ear. He glanced at his watch, spoke a few words. Then he put the phone away and turned back the way he'd come.

Hell, he's going back to his car, the detective thought. I'm going lose him. . . .

Ten minutes till the backup gets here. Jesus. . . .

Andy Anderson decided he had no choice. He was going to do something he'd never done: make an arrest alone.

CHAPTER 00001001 / NINE

———◆———

Anderson moved next to a low bush.

The killer was walking quickly along the path, hands in his pockets.

That was good, Anderson decided – the hands encumbered, which would make it more difficult to get to the knife.

But wait, he wondered: What if he was hiding a pistol in his pocket?

Okay, keep that in mind.

And remember too that he might have Mace or pepper spray or tear gas.

And remember that he might simply turn and sprint away. The cop wondered what he'd do then. What were the fleeing felon rules? Could he shoot the killer in the back?

He'd busted dozens of criminals but he'd always been backed up by cops like Frank Bishop, for whom guns and high-risk arrests were as routine as compiling a program in C++ was for Anderson.

The detective now moved closer to the killer, thankful the rain was obscuring the sound of his footsteps. They were paralleling each other now on opposite sides of a row of tall boxwood. Anderson kept low and squinted through the rain. He got a good look at the killer's face. An intense curiosity coursed through him: What made this young man commit the terrible crimes he was responsible for? This curiosity was similar to what he felt when examining software code or puzzling over the crimes CCU investigated –

but it was stronger now because, though he understood the principles of computer science and the crimes that that science made possible, a criminal like this was a pure enigma to Andy Anderson.

Except for the knife, except for the gun he might or might not be clutching in his hidden hand, the man seemed benign, almost friendly.

The detective wiped his hand on his shirt to dry some of the rain and gripped the pistol firmly once more. He continued on. This's a hell of a lot different from taking down hackers at a public terminal in the mall or serving warrants in houses where the biggest dangers were the plates of putrid food sitting stacked next to a teenager's machine.

Closer, closer . . .

Twenty feet farther on, their paths would converge. Soon Anderson would have no more cover and he'd have to make his move.

For an instant his courage broke and he stopped. He thought of his wife and daughter. And how alien he felt here, how completely out of his depth he was. He thought: Just follow the killer back to his car, get the license plate and follow as best you can.

But then Anderson thought of the deaths this man had caused and the deaths that he'd cause again if not stopped. This might be their only chance to stop him.

He started forward again along the path that would intersect with the killer's.

Ten feet.

Eight . . .

A deep breath.

Watch the hand in the pocket, he reminded himself.

A bird flew close – a gull – and the killer turned to look at it, startled. He laughed.

And that was when Anderson burst from the bushes, shoving the pistol toward the killer, shouting, "Freeze! Police! Hand out of your pocket!"

The man spun around to face the detective, muttering, "Shit." He hesitated for a moment.

Anderson brought the gun even with the killer's chest. "Now! Move slow!"

The hand appeared. Anderson stared at the fingers. What was he holding?

He almost laughed. It was a rabbit's foot. A lucky key chain.

"Drop it."

He did and then lifted his hands in the resigned, familiar way of someone who's been through an arrest before.

"Lie down on the ground and keep your arms spread."

"Jesus," the man spat out. "Jesus. How the fuck did you find me?"

"Do it," Anderson shouted in a quaking voice.

The killer lay down on the ground, half on the grass and half on the sidewalk. Anderson was kneeling over him, shoving his gun into the man's neck as he put the cuffs on, an awkward feat that took several tries. He then frisked the killer and relieved him of the Ka-bar knife and cell phone and wallet. He *had* been carrying a small pistol, it turned out, but that had been in the pocket of his jacket. The weapons, wallet, phone and rabbit's foot went into a pile on the grass nearby. Anderson stepped back, his hands shaking from the adrenaline.

"Where the fuck d'you come from?" the man muttered.

Anderson didn't respond but just stared at his prisoner as the shock of what he'd done was replaced with euphoria. What a story he'd have to tell! His wife would love it. He wanted to tell his little daughter but that would have to wait a few years. Oh, and Stan, his neighbors, who—

Then Anderson realized that he'd forgotten the Miranda warning. He didn't want to blow an arrest like this by making a technical mistake. He found the card in his wallet and read the words stiffly.

The killer muttered that he understood his rights.

"Officer, you okay?" a man's voice called. "You need any help?"

Anderson glanced behind him. It was the businessman he'd seen under the awning. His dark suit, expensive-looking, was dampened by the rain. "I've got a cell phone. You need to use it?"

"No, no, that's okay, everything's under control." Anderson turned back to his prisoner. He holstered his weapon and pulled out his own cell phone to report in. He hit redial but for some reason the call wouldn't go through. He glanced at the screen and the phone reported, NO SIGNAL.

That was odd. Why—

And in an instant – an instant of pure horror – he realized that no street cop in the world would've let an unidentified civilian get behind him during an arrest. As he groped for his pistol and started to turn, the businessman grabbed his shoulder and the detective felt an explosion of pain in his back.

Anderson cried out and dropped to his knees. The man stabbed him again with his own Ka-bar knife.

"No, please, no. . . ."

The man lifted away Anderson's gun and kicked him forward onto the wet sidewalk.

He then walked over to the young man Anderson had just handcuffed. He rolled him over on his side and looked down.

"Man, I'm fucking glad you're here," the cuffed man said. "This guy comes out of nowhere and I thought I was fucked. Get me out of these things, will you? I—"

"Shhhh," the businessman said and turned back to the CCU cop, who was struggling to reach the terrible pain in his back, trying to touch it. If he could only touch it then the searing agony would go away.

The attacker crouched down next to him.

"*You're* the one," Anderson whispered to the businessman. "You killed Lara Gibson." His eyes flicked to the man he'd handcuffed. "And *he's* Fowler."

The man nodded. "That's right." Then he said, "And *you're* Andy Anderson." The awe in his voice was genuine. "I didn't think it'd be *you* coming after me. I mean, I knew you worked for the Computer Crimes Unit and'd be investigating the Gibson case. But not *here*, not in the field. Amazing . . . Andy Anderson. You're a *total* wizard."

"Please . . . I've got a family! Please."

Then the killer did something odd.

Holding the knife in one hand, he touched the cop's abdomen with the other. Then he slid his fingers up slowly to the detective's chest, counting ribs, beneath which his heart was beating so very quickly.

"Please," Anderson pleaded.

The killer paused and lowered his head to Anderson's ear. "You never know somebody the way you know them at a moment like this," he whispered, then resumed his eerie reconnaissance of the cop's chest.

II
DEMONS

———◆·▸◂·◆———

[He] was a new generation of hacker, not
the third generation inspired by innocent
wonder . . . but a disenfranchised fourth
generation driven by anger.

— Jonathan Littman,
The Watchman

CHAPTER 0001010 / TEN

———◆———

At 1:00 P.M. a tall man in a gray suit walked into the Computer Crimes Unit.

He was accompanied by a stocky woman wearing a forest-green pantsuit. Two uniformed state troopers were beside them. Their shoulders were damp from the rain and their faces were grim. They walked to Stephen Miller's cubicle.

The tall man said, "Steve."

Miller stood, brushed his hand through his thinning hair. He said, "Captain Bernstein."

"I've got something to tell you," the captain said in that tone that Wyatt Gillette recognized immediately as the precursor to tragic news. His look included Linda Sanchez and Tony Mott. They joined him. "I wanted to come in person. We found just Andy Anderson's body in Milliken Park. It looks like the perp – the one in the Gibson woman's killing – got him."

"Oh," Sanchez choked, her hand going to her mouth. She began to cry. "Not Andy . . . No!"

Mott's face grew dark. He muttered something Gillette couldn't hear.

Patricia Nolan had spent the past half hour sitting with Gillette, speculating about what software the killer might've used to invade Lara Gibson's computer. As they'd talked she'd opened her purse, taken out a small bottle and, incongruously, started applying nail polish. Now, the tiny brush drooped in her hand. "Oh, my God."

Stephen Miller closed his eyes momentarily. "What happened?" he asked in a shaky voice.

The door pushed open and Frank Bishop and Bob Shelton hurried into the room. "We heard," Shelton said. "We got back here as fast as we could. It's true?"

The tableau of shocked faces before them though left little doubt.

Sanchez asked through the tears, "Have you talked to his wife? Oh, God, and he's got that little girl, Connie. She's only five or six."

"The commander and a counselor are on their way over to the house right now."

"What the hell happened?" Miller repeated.

Captain Bernstein said, "We have a pretty good idea – there was a witness, a woman walking her dog in the park. Seems like Andy'd just collared somebody named Peter Fowler."

"Right," Shelton said. "He was the dealer we think supplied the perp with some of his weapons."

Captain Bernstein continued, "Only it looks like he must've thought that *Fowler* was the killer. He was blond and wearing a denim jacket. Those denim fibers crime scene found on Lara Gibson must've been stuck to the knife the killer bought from Fowler. Anyway, while Andy was busy cuffing Fowler, a white male came up behind him. He was late twenties, dark hair, navy blue suit and carrying a brief-case. He stabbed Andy in the back. The woman went to call for help and that was all she saw. The killer stabbed Fowler to death too."

"Why didn't he call for backup?" Mott asked.

Bernstein frowned. "Well, now, that was odd – we checked his cell phone and the last number he'd dialed was to dispatch. It was a completed three-minute call. But there was no record of central receiving it and none of the dispatchers talked to him. Nobody can figure out how that happened."

"Easy," the hacker said. "The killer cracked the switch."

"You're Gillette." the captain said. He didn't need a nod to verify his identity; the tracking anklet was very evident. "What's that mean, 'cracked the switch'?"

"He hacked into the cell phone company's computer and had all of Andy's outgoing calls sent to his own phone. Probably pretended he was the dispatcher and told him a squad car was on the way. Then he shut down Andy's phone service so he couldn't call anyone else for help."

The captain nodded slowly. "He did all that? Jesus, what the hell're we up against?"

"The best social engineer I've ever heard of," Gillette said.

"Goddamit!" Shelton shouted at him. "Why don't you just can the fucking computer buzzwords?"

Frank Bishop touched his arm to calm his partner and said to the captain, "This'd be my fault, sir."

"Your fault?" Captain Bernstein asked the thin detective. "What do you mean?"

Bishop's slow eyes moved from Gillette to the floor. "Andy was a white-collar cop. He wasn't qualified for a takedown."

"He was still a trained detective," the captain said.

"Training's a lot different than what goes down on the street." Bishop looked up. "In my opinion, sir."

The woman who'd accompanied Bernstein stirred. The captain glanced at her and then announced, "This is Detective Susan Wilkins from Homicide in Oakland. She'll be taking over the case. She's got a task force of troopers – crime scene and tactical – up and running at headquarters in San Jose."

Turning to Bishop, the captain said, "Frank, I've okayed that request of yours – for the MARINKILL case. There's a report that the perps were spotted an hour ago outside a convenience store ten miles south of Walnut Creek. It looks like they're headed this way." He glanced at Miller. "Steve, you'll take over what Andy was doing – the computer side of the case. Working with Susan."

"Of course, Captain. You bet."

The captain turned to Patricia Nolan. "You're the one the commander called us about, right? The security consultant from that computer outfit? Horizon On-Line?"

She nodded.

"They asked if you'd stay on board too."

"They?"

"The powers-that-be in Sacramento."

"Oh. Sure, I'd be happy to."

Gillette didn't merit a direct address. The captain said to Miller, "The troopers here'll take the prisoner back to San Jose."

"Look," Gillette protested, "don't send me back."

"What?"

"You need me. I have to—"

The captain dismissed him with a wave and turned to Susan Wilkins, gesturing at the white-board and talking to her about the case.

"Captain," Gillette called, "you *can't* send me back."

"We need his help," Nolan said emphatically.

But the captain glanced at the two large troopers who'd accompanied him here. They cuffed Gillette, positioned themselves on either side – as if he himself were the murderer – and started out of the office.

"No," Gillette protested. "You don't know how dangerous this man is!"

Another look from the captain was all it took. The troopers escorted him quickly toward the exit. Gillette started to ask Bishop to intervene but the detective was elsewhere mentally, apparently already on his MARINKILL assignment. He stared vacantly at the floor.

"All right," Gillette heard Detective Susan Wilkins say to Miller, Sanchez and Mott. "I'm sorry for what's happened to your boss but I've been through this before and I'm sure you've been through it before and the best way to show that you cared for him is to apprehend this perpetrator and that's what we're going to do. Now, I think we're all on the same page in terms of our approach. I'm up to speed on the file and the crime scene report and I've got a proactive plan in mind. The preliminary report is that Detective Anderson – as well as this Fowler individual – were stabbed. Cause of death was trauma to the heart. They—"

"Wait!" Gillette shouted just as he was about to be led out the door.

Wilkins paused. Bernstein gestured to the cops to get him

out. But Gillette said quickly, "What about Lara Gibson? Was *she* stabbed in the chest too?"

"What's your point?" Bernstein asked.

"Was she?" Gillette asked emphatically. "And the victims in the other killings – in Portland and in Virginia?"

No one said anything for a moment. Finally Bob Shelton glanced at the report on the Lara Gibson killing. "Cause of death was a stab wound to—"

"The heart, right?" Gillette asked.

Shelton glanced at his partner then to Bernstein. He nodded. Tony Mott reminded, "We don't know about Virginia and Oregon – he erased the files."

"It'll be the same," Gillette said. "I guarantee it."

Shelton asked, "How'd you know that?"

"Because I know his motive now."

"Which is?" Bernstein asked.

"Access."

"What does that mean?" Shelton muttered belligerently.

Patricia Nolan said, "That's what all hackers're after. Access to information, to secrets, to data."

"When you hack," Gillette said, "access is God."

"What's that got to do with the stabbings?"

"The killer's a MUDhead."

"Sure," Tony Mott said. "I know MUDs." Miller did too, it seemed. He was nodding.

Gillette said, "Another acronym. It stands for multiuser domain or dimension. It's a bunch of specialized chat rooms – places on the Internet where people log on for role-playing games. Adventure games, knights' quests, science fiction, war. The people who play MUDs're, you know, pretty decent – businessmen, geeks, a lot of students, professors. But three or four years ago there was a big controversy about this game called Access."

"I heard about that," Miller said. "A lot of Internet providers refused to carry it."

Gillette nodded. "The way it worked was that there was a virtual city. It was populated with characters who carried on a normal life – going to work, dating, raising a family, whatever. But on the anniversary of a famous death – like John Kennedy's assassination or the day Lennon was shot or Good Friday – a random number generator picked one of the players to be a killer. He had one week to work his way into people's lives and kill as many of them as he could.

"The killer could pick anyone to be his victim but the more challenging the murder the more points he got. A politician with a bodyguard was worth ten points. An armed cop was worth fifteen. The one limitation on the killer was that he had to get close enough to the victims to stab them in the heart with a knife – that was the ultimate form of access."

"Jesus, that's our perp in a nutshell," Tony Mott said. "The knife, stab wounds to the chest, the anniversary dates, going after people who're hard to kill. He won the game in Portland and Virginia. And here he is, playing it in Silicon Valley." The young cop added cynically, "He's at the expert level."

"Level?" Bishop asked.

"In computer games," Gillette explained, "you move up in the degree of challenge from the beginning level to the hardest – the expert – level."

"So, this whole thing is a fucking game to him?" Shelton said. "That's a little hard to believe."

"No," Patricia Nolan said. "I'm afraid it's pretty *easy* to believe. The FBI's Behavioral Science Unit in Quantico considers criminal hackers compulsive, progressive offenders. Just like lust-driven serial killers. Like Wyatt said, access is God. They have to find increasingly intense crimes to satisfy themselves. This guy's spent so much time in the Machine World he probably doesn't see any difference between a digital character and a human being." With a glance at the white-board Nolan continued, "I'd even say that, to him, the machines themselves're more important than people. A human death is nothing; a crashed hard drive, well, that's a tragedy."

Bernstein nodded. "That's helpful. We'll consider it." He nodded at Gillette. "But you've still got to go back to the prison."

"No!" the hacker cried.

"Look, we're already in deep water getting a federal

prisoner released under a John Doe order. Andy was willing to take that risk. I'm not. That's all there is to it."

He pointed at the troopers and they led the hacker out of the dinosaur pen. It seemed to Gillette that they gripped him harder this time – as if they could sense his desperation and desire to flee. Nolan sighed and shook her head, gave a mournful smile of farewell to Gillette as he was led out.

Detective Susan Wilkins started up her monologue again but her voice soon faded as Gillette stepped outside. The rain was coming down steadily. One of the troopers said, "Sorry about that," though whether it was for his failed attempt to stay at CCU or the absence of an umbrella Gillette didn't know.

The trooper eased him down into the backseat of the squad car and slammed the door.

Gillette closed his eyes, rested his head against the glass. Heard the hollow sound of the rain pelting the top of the car.

He felt utter dismay at this defeat.

Lord, how close he'd come. . . .

He thought of the months in prison. He thought of all the planning he'd done. Wasted. It was all—

The car door opened.

Frank Bishop was crouching down. Water ran down his face, glistening on his sideburns and staining his shirt, but his sprayed hair, at least, was impervious to the drops. "Got a question for you, sir."

Sir?

Gillette asked, "What's that?"

"That MUD stuff. That's not hogwash?"

"Nope. The killer's playing his own version of that game – a real-life version."

"Is anybody still playing it now? On the Internet, I mean."

"I doubt it. Real MUDheads were so offended by it that they sabotaged the games and spammed the players until they stopped."

The detective glanced back at the rusting soda machine in front of the CCU building. He then asked, "That fellow in there, Stephen Miller – he's a lightweight, isn't he?"

Gillette thought for a moment and said, "He's from the elder days."

"The what?"

The phrase meant the sixties and seventies – that revolutionary era in the history of computing that ended more or less with the release of Digital Equipment Corporation's PDP-10, the computer that changed the face of the Machine World forever. But Gillette didn't explain this. He said simply, "He *was* good, I'd guess, but he's past his prime now. And in Silicon Valley that means, yeah, he's a lightweight."

"I see." Bishop straightened up, looking out at the traffic that sped along the nearby freeway. He then said to the troopers, "Bring this man back inside, please."

They looked at each other and, when Bishop nodded emphatically, hustled Gillette out of the squad car.

As they walked back into the CCU office Gillette heard Susan Wilkins's voice still droning on, " . . . liaise with security at Mobile America and Pac Bell if need be and I've established lines of communication with the tactical teams. Now, in my estimation it's probably sixty-forty more efficient to be located closer to main resources so we'll be moving the Computer Crimes Unit to headquarters in San Jose. I understand you're missing some administrative support in terms of your receptionist and at HQ we'll be able to mitigate that . . ."

Gillette tuned out the words and wondered what Bishop was up to.

The cop walked up to Bob Shelton, with whom he whispered for a moment. The conversation ended with Bishop's asking, "You with me on this?"

The stocky cop surveyed Gillette with a disdainful gaze and then muttered something grudgingly affirmative.

As Wilkins continued to speak, Captain Bernstein frowned and walked up to Bishop, who said to him, "I'd like to run this case, sir, and I want Gillette here to work it with us."

"You wanted the MARINKILL case."

"I did, sir. But I changed my mind."

"I know what you said before, Frank. But Andy's death

– that wasn't your fault. He should've known his limits. Nobody forced him to go after that guy alone."

"I don't care if it was my fault or not. That's not what this is about. It's about collaring a dangerous perp before someone else gets killed."

Captain Bernstein caught his meaning and glanced at Wilkins. "Susan's run major homicides before. She's good."

"I know she is, sir. We've worked together. But she's textbook. She's never worked in the trenches, the way I have. I ought to be running the case. But the other problem is that we're way out of our league here. We need somebody sharp on this one." The stiff hair nodded toward Gillette. "And I think he's as good as the perp."

"Probably he is," Bernstein muttered. "But that's not my worry."

"I'll ride point on this one, sir. Something goes bad, it can all come down on me. Nobody else has to take any heat."

Patricia Nolan joined them and said, "Captain, stopping this guy's going to take more than fingerprints and canvassing witnesses."

Shelton sighed. "Welcome to the new fucking millennium."

Bernstein reluctantly nodded to Bishop. "Okay, you got the case. You'll have full tactical and crime scene backup. And pick some people from Homicide in San Jose to help you."

"Huerto Ramirez and Tim Morgan," Bishop said without hesitating. "I'd like them here ASAP if you could arrange that, sir. I want to brief everybody."

The captain called HQ to summon the detectives here. He hung up. "They're on their way."

Bernstein then broke the news to Susan Wilkins and, more perplexed than upset at the loss of the new assignment, she left. The captain asked Bishop, "You want to move the operation back to headquarters?"

Bishop said, "No, we'll stay here, sir." He nodded toward a row of computer screens. "This's where we'll do most of the work, I've got a feeling."

"Well, good luck, Frank."

Bishop said to the troopers who'd come to take Gillette back to San Ho, "You can take the cuffs off."

One of the men did this then he pointed at the hacker's leg. "How 'bout the anklet?"

"No," Bishop said, offering a very uncharacteristic smile. "I think we'll keep that on."

A short while later two men joined the team in CCU: a broad, swarthy Latino who was extremely muscular, Gold's Gym muscular, and a tall, sandy-haired detective in one of those stylish four-button men's suits, dark shirt and dark tie. Bishop introduced Huerto Ramirez and Tim Morgan, the detectives from headquarters Bishop had requested.

"Now, I'd like to say a word," Bishop said, tucking his unruly shirt into his slacks and stepping in front of the team. He looked over everybody, holding their gazes for a moment. "This fellow we're after – he's somebody who's perfectly willing to kill anybody in his way and that includes law enforcers and innocents. He's an expert at social engineering." A glance toward the newcomers, Ramirez and Morgan. "Which is basically disguise and diversion. So it's important that you continually remind yourself what we know about him."

Bishop continued his low, unhesitant monologue. "I think we have enough confirmation to place him in his late twenties. He's medium build, maybe blond but probably darkhaired, clean shaven but sometimes disguised with fake facial hair. He prefers a Ka-bar as a murder weapon and wants to get close enough to his victims to inflict a fatal chest wound. He can break into the phone company and interrupt service or transfer calls. He can hack into law enforcement computers" – Gillette now received a glance – "excuse me, *crack* into computers and destroy police records. He likes challenges, he thinks of killing as a game. He's spent a lot of time on the East Coast and he's somewhere in the Silicon Valley area but we have no exact locale. We think he's bought some items for his disguises at a theatrical supply store on Camino Real in Mountain View. He's a progressive, lust-driven sociopath who's lost touch with reality and is treating what he's doing like it's some big computer game."

Gillette was astonished. The detective's back was to the white-board as he recited all of this information. The hacker realized that he'd misjudged the man. All the time that the detective had seemed to stare absently out the window or at the floor he'd been absorbing the evidence.

Bishop lowered his head but kept his eyes on them all. "I'm not going to lose anybody else on this team. So watch your backs and don't trust another living soul – even people you think you know. Go on this assumption: Nothing is what it seems to be."

Gillette found himself nodding along with the others.

"Now – about his victims . . . We know that he's going after people who're hard to get close to. People with body-guards and security systems. The harder to get to the better. We'll have to keep that in mind when we're trying to anti-cipate him. We're going to keep to the general plan for the investigation. Huerto and Tim, I want you two to run the Anderson crime scene in Palo Alto. Canvass everybody you can find in and around Milliken Park. Bob and I didn't get a chance to find that witness who might've seen the killer's vehicle outside the restaurant where Ms. Gibson was killed. That's what he and I'll do. And, Wyatt, you're going to head up the computer side of the investigation."

Gillette shook his head, not sure he'd understood Bishop correctly. "I'm sorry?"

"You," Bishop responded, "are going to head up the computer side of the investigation." No further explanation. Stephen Miller said nothing though his eyes stared coldly at the hacker as he continued to pointlessly rearrange the sloppy piles of disks and paperwork on his desk.

Bishop asked, "Should we be worried about him listening to our phones? I mean, that's how he killed Andy."

Patricia Nolan replied, "It's a risk, I suppose, but the killer'd have to monitor hundreds of frequencies for the numbers of our cell phones."

"I agree," Gillette said. "And even if he cracked the switch he'd have to sit with a headset all day long, listening to our conversations. Doesn't sound like he's got the time to do that. In the park he was close to Andy. That's how he got his specific frequency."

Besides, as it turned out there wasn't much to do about the risk. Miller explained that, while the CCU did have a scrambler, it would only work when the caller on the other end of the line had a scrambler as well. As for secure cell phones Miller explained, "They're five thousand bucks each." And said nothing more. Meaning, apparently, that such toys weren't in the CCU budget and never would be.

Bishop then sent Ramirez and the *GQ* cop, Tim Morgan, to Palo Alto. After they'd left, Bishop asked Gillette, "You were telling Andy that you thought you could find out more about how this killer got into Ms. Gibson's computer?"

"That's right. Whatever this guy is doing has to've caused some buzz in the hacker underground. What I'll do is go online and—"

Bishop nodded to a workstation. "Just do what you have to do and give us a report in a half hour."

"Just like that?" Gillette asked.

"Make it less if you can. Twenty minutes."

"Uhm." Stephen Miller stirred.

"What is it?" the detective asked him.

Gillette was expecting the cybercop to make a comment about his demotion. But that wasn't what he had in mind. "The thing is," Miller protested, "Andy said he wasn't ever supposed to go online. And then there's that court order that said he couldn't. It was part of his sentencing."

"That's all true," Bishop said, eyes scanning the whiteboard. "But Andy's dead and the court isn't running this case. I am." He glanced over at Gillette with a look of polite impatience. "So I'd appreciate it if you'd get going."

CHAPTER 00001011 / ELEVEN

W
yatt Gillette settled himself in the cheap office chair.
He was in a dim workstation cubicle in the back of
the CCU, quiet, away from the others on the team.

Staring at the blinking cursor on the screen, he rolled the
chair closer and wiped his hands on his pants. Then his
callused fingertips rose and began pounding furiously on the
black keyboard. His eyes never left the screen. Gillette knew
the location of every character and symbol on the keyboard
and touch-typed a 110 words a minute with perfect accu-
racy. When he was starting to hack years ago he found that
eight fingers were too slow so he'd taught himself a new
keyboarding technique in which he used his thumbs on
certain keys too, not just reserving them for the space bar.

Weak otherwise, his forearms and fingers were pure
muscle; in prison, where most inmates spend hours lifting
iron in the yard, Gillette had done only fingertip push-ups
to stay in shape for his passion. Now, the plastic keyboard
danced under his hammering as he prepared to go online.

Most of today's Internet is a combination shopping mall,
USA Today, multiplex cinema and amusement park.
Browsers and search engines are populated with cartoon
characters and decorated with pretty pictures (plenty of
those damn ads too). The point-and-click technology of the
mouse can be mastered by a three-year-old. Simpleminded
Help menus await at every new window. This is the Internet
as packaged for the public through the glossy façade of the
commercialized World Wide Web.

But the *real* Internet – the Internet of the true hacker, lurking *behind* the Web – is a wild, raw place, where hackers use complicated commands, telnet utilities and communications software stripped bare as a dragster to sail throughout the world at, literally, the speed of light.

This is what Wyatt Gillette was about to do.

There was a preliminary matter to take care of, though. A mythological wizard wouldn't go off on a quest without his magic wands and book of spells and potions; computer wizards have to do the same.

One of the first skills hackers learn is the art of hiding software. Since you have to assume that an enemy hacker, if not the police or FBI, will at some point seize or destroy your machine, you never leave the only copy of your tools on your hard drive and backup disks in your home.

You hide them in a distant computer, one that has no link to you.

Most hackers store their stash in university computers because their security is notoriously lacking. But Gillette had spent years working on his software tools, writing code from scratch in many cases, as well as modifying existing programs to suit his needs. It'd be a tragedy for him to lose all that work – and pure hell for many of the world's computer users since Gillette's programs would help even a mediocre hacker crack into nearly any corporate or government site.

So he cached his tools in a slightly more secure location than the data-processing department of Dartmouth or the University of Tulsa. With a glance behind him now to make sure that no one was "shoulder surfing" – standing behind him and reading the screen – he typed a command and linked the CCU's computer with another one several states away. After a moment these words scrolled onto the screen:

Welcome to the United States Air Force Los Alamos Nuclear Weapons Research Facility #Username?

In response to this request he typed *Jarmstrong*. Gillette's father's name was John Armstrong Gillette. It was generally a bad idea for a hacker to pick a screen name or username that had any connection with his real life but he'd allowed himself this one concession to his human side.

The computer then asked:

#Password?

He typed *4%xTtfllk5$$60%4Q,* which was, unlike the username, pure, stone-cold hacker. This series of characters had been excruciating to memorize (part of his *mental* daily calisthenics in prison was recalling two dozen passwords as long as this one) but it would be impossible for someone to guess and, because it was seventeen characters long, would take a supercomputer weeks to crack. An IBM-clone personal computer would have to work continuously for hundreds of years before it spit out a password this complicated.

The cursor blinked for a moment then the screen shifted and he read:

Welcome, Capt. J. Armstrong

In three minutes he'd downloaded a number of files from the fictional Captain Armstrong's account. His weaponry included the famous SATAN program (the Security Administer Tool for Analyzing Networks, used by both sysadmins *and* hackers to check the "hackability" of computer networks), several breaking and entering programs that would let him grab root access on various types of machines and networks, a custom-made Web browser and newsreader, a cloaking program to hide his presence while he was in someone else's computer and which would delete traces of his activities when he logged off, sniffer programs that would "sniff out" – find – usernames, passwords and other helpful information on the Net or in someone's computer, a communications program to send that data back to him, encryption programs and lists of hacker Web sites and anonymizer sites (commercial services that would in effect "launder" e-mails and messages so that the recipient couldn't trace Gillette).

The last of the tools he downloaded was a program he'd hacked together a few years ago, HyperTrace, which could track down other users on the Net.

With these tools downloaded onto a high-capacity disk Gillette logged out of the Los Alamos site. He paused for a moment, flexed his fingers and then sat forward. Pounding on the keys with the subtlety of a sumo wrestler once more, Gillette entered the Net. He began the search in the Multiuser Domains because of the killer's apparent motivation – playing a Real World version of the infamous Access game. No one Gillette queried on the subject, however, had played Access or knew anyone who had – or so they claimed. Still, Gillette came away with a few leads.

From the MUDs he moved to the World Wide Web, which everyone talks *about* but few could define. The WWW is simply an international network of computers, accessed through special computer protocols that let users see graphics and hear sounds and leap through a Web site, and to other sites, by simply clicking on certain places on their screen – hyperlinks. Prior to the Web most of the information on the Net was in text form and navigating from one site to another was extremely cumbersome. The Web is still in its adolescence, having been born a little over a decade ago at CERN, the Swiss physics institute.

Gillette searched through the underground hacking sites on the Web – the eerie, Tenderloin districts of the Net. Gaining entry to some of these sites required an answer to an esoteric question on hacking, finding and clicking on a microscopic dot on the screen or supplying a passcode. None of these barriers, though, barred Wyatt Gillette for more than a minute or two.

From site to site to site, losing himself further and further in the Blue Nowhere, prowling through computers that might have been in Moscow or Cape Town or Mexico City. Or right next door in Cupertino or Santa Clara.

Gillette sped through this world so quickly that he was reluctant to take his fingers off the keys for fear of losing his stride. So rather than jotting notes with pen and paper, as most hackers did, he copied material he thought was useful and pasted it into a word-processing window he kept open on the screen.

From the Web he searched the Usenet – the collection of 80,000 newsgroups, in which people interested in a particular subject can post messages, pictures, programs, movies and sound clips. Gillette scoured the classic hacking newsgroups like alt.2600, alt.hack, alt.virus and alt.binaries.hacking.utilities, cutting and pasting whatever seemed relevant. He found references to dozens of newsgroups that hadn't existed when he'd gone to jail. He jumped to those groups, scrolled through them and found mention of still others.

More scrolling, more reading, more cutting and pasting. A snap under his fingers and on the screen he saw:

mmmmmmmmmmmmmmmmmmmmmmmmmmmmmmmmmmmmmm

One of his powerful keystrokes had jammed the keyboard, which had often happened when he'd been hacking. Gillette unplugged it, tossed it on the floor behind him, hooked up another keyboard and started typing again.

He then logged onto the Internet Relay Chat rooms. The IRC was an unregulated no-holds-barred series of networks where you could find real-time discussions among people who had similar interests. You typed your comment, hit the ENTER key and your words appeared on the screens of everyone who was logged into the room at that time. He logged into the room #hack (the rooms were designated by a number sign followed by a descriptive word). It was in this same room where he'd spent thousands of hours, sharing information, arguing and joking with fellow hackers around the world.

After the IRC Gillette began searching through the BBS, bulletin boards, which are like Web sites but can be accessed for only the cost of a local phone call – no Internet service provider is required. Many were legitimate but many others – with names like DeathHack and Silent Spring – were the darkest parts of the online world. Completely unregulated and unmonitored, these were the places to go for recipes for bombs and poisonous gases and debilitating computer viruses that would wipe the hard drives of half the population of the world.

Following the leads – losing himself in Web sites, news-groups, chat rooms and archives. Hunting . . .

This is what lawyers do when they paw through hoary old shelves searching for that one case that will save their client from execution, what sportsmen do easing through the grass toward where they *thought* they heard the snarl of a bear, what lovers do seeking the core of each other's lust. . . .

Except that hunting in the Blue Nowhere isn't like searching library stacks or a field of tall grass or on your mate's smooth flesh; it's like prowling through the entire ever-expanding universe, which contains not only the known world and its unshared mysteries but worlds past and worlds yet to come.

Endless.

Snap . . .

He had broken another key – the all-important E. Gillette flung this keyboard into the corner of the cubicle, where it joined its dead friend.

He plugged in a new one and kept going.

At 2:30 P.M. Gillette emerged from the cubicle. His back was racked with pure fiery pain from sitting frozen in one place. Yet he could still feel the exhilarating rush from that brief time he'd spent online and the reluctance at leaving the machine, which tugged him back fiercely.

In the main part of the CCU he found Bishop talking with Shelton; the others were on telephones or standing around the white-board, looking over the evidence. Bishop noticed Gillette first and fell silent.

"I've found something," the hacker said, holding up a stack of printouts.

"Tell us."

"Dumb it down," Shelton reminded. "What's the bottom line?"

"The bottom line," Gillette responded, "is that there's somebody named Phate. And we've got a real problem."

CHAPTER 00001100 / TWELVE

———◆◆◆———

"**F**ate?" Frank Bishop asked.

Gillette said. "That's his username – his screen name. Only he spells it p-h-a-t-e. Like p-h phishing, remember? The way hackers do."

It's all in the spelling . . .

"What's his real name?" Patricia Nolan asked.

"I don't know. Nobody seems to know much about him – he's a loner – but the people who've heard of him're scared as hell."

"A wizard?" Stephen Miller asked.

"Definitely a wizard."

Bishop asked, "Why do you think he's the killer?"

Gillette flipped through the printouts. "Here's what I found. Phate and a friend of his, somebody named Shawn, wrote some software called Trapdoor. Now, 'trapdoor' in the computer world means a hole built into a security system that lets the software designers get back inside to fix problems without needing a passcode. Phate and Shawn use the same name for their script but this's a little different. It's a program that somehow lets them get inside *anybody's* computer."

"Trapdoor," Bishop mused. "Like a gallows, too."

"Like a gallows," Gillette echoed.

Nolan asked, "How does it work?"

Gillette was about to explain it to her in the language of the initiated then glanced at Bishop and Shelton.

Dumb it down.

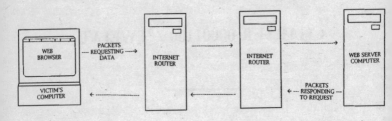

The hacker walked to one of the blank white-boards and drew a chart. He said, "The way information travels on the Net isn't like on a telephone. Everything sent online – an e-mail, music you listen to, a picture you download, the graphics on a Web site – is broken down into small fragments of data called 'packets.' When your browser requests something from a Web site it sends packets out into the Internet. At the receiving end the Web server computer reassembles your request and then sends its response – also broken into packets – back to your machine."

"Why're they broken up?" Shelton asked.

Nolan answered, "So that a lot of different messages can be sent over the same wires at the same time. Also, if some of the packets get lost or corrupted your computer gets a notice about it and resends just the problem packets. You don't have to resend the whole message."

Gillette pointed to his diagram and continued, "The packets are forwarded through the Internet by these routers – huge computers around the country that guide the packets to their final destination. Routers have real tight security but Phate's managed to crack into some of them and put a packet-sniffer inside."

"Which," Bishop said, "looks for certain packets, I assume."

"Exactly," Gillette continued. "It identifies them by somebody's screen name or the address of the machines the packets're coming from or going to. When the sniffer finds the packets it's been waiting for it diverts them to Phate's computer. Once they're there Phate adds something to the packets." Gillette asked Miller, "You ever heard of stenanography?"

The cop shook his head. Tony Mott and Linda Sanchez weren't familiar with the term either but Patricia Nolan said, "That's hiding secret data in, say, pictures or sound files you're sending online. Spy stuff."

"Right," Gillette confirmed. "Encrypted data is woven right into the file itself – so that even if somebody intercepts your e-mail and reads it or looks at the picture you've sent all they'll see is an innocent-looking file and not the secret data. Well, that's what Phate's Trapdoor software does. Only it doesn't hide messages in the files – it hides an application."

"A *working* program?" Nolan said.

"Yep. Then he sends it on its way to the victim."

Nolan shook her head. Her pale, doughy face revealed both shock and admiration. Her voice was hushed with awe as she said, "No one's ever done that before."

"What's this software that he sends?" Bishop asked.

"It's a demon," Gillette answered, drawing a second diagram to show how Trapdoor worked.

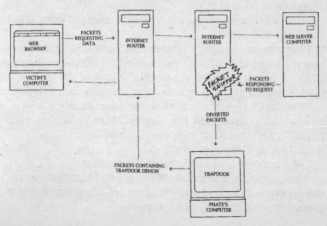

"Demon?" Shelton asked.

"There's a whole category of software called 'bots,'" Gillette explained. "Short for 'robots.' And that's just what they are – software robots. Once they're activated they run completely on their own, without any human input. They can travel from one machine to another, they can reproduce, they can hide, they can communicate with other computers or people, they can kill themselves."

Gillette continued, "Demons are a type of bot. They sit inside your computer and do things like run the clock and automatically back up files. Scut work. But the Trapdoor demon does something a lot scarier. Once it's inside your computer it modifies the operating system and, when you go online, it links your computer to Phate's."

"And he seizes root," Bishop said.

"Exactly."

"Oh, this is bad," Linda Sanchez muttered. "Man. . . ."

Nolan twined more of her unkempt hair around a finger. Beneath the fragile designer glasses her green eyes were troubled – as if she'd just seen a terrible accident. "So if you surf the Web, read a news story, read an e-mail, pay a bill, listen to music, download pictures, look up a stock quotation – if you're online at *all* – Phate can get inside your computer."

"Yep. Anything you get via the Internet might have the Trapdoor demon in it."

"But what about firewalls?" Miller asked. "Why don't they stop it?"

Firewalls are computer sentries that keep files or data you haven't requested out of your machine. Gillette explained, "That's what's brilliant about this: Because the demon's hidden in data that you've *asked* for, firewalls won't stop it."

"Brilliant," Bob Shelton muttered sarcastically.

Tony Mott drummed his fingers absently on his bike helmet. "He's breaking rule number one."

"Which is?" Bishop asked.

Gillette recited, "Leave the civilians alone."

Mott, nodding, continued, "Hackers feel that the government, corporations and other hackers are fair game. But you should never target the general public."

Sanchez asked, "Is there any way to tell if he's inside your machine?"

"Only little things – your keyboard seems a little sluggish, the graphics look a little fuzzy, a game doesn't respond quite as quickly as usual, your hard drive engages for a second or two when it shouldn't. Nothing so obvious that most people'd notice."

Shelton asked, "How come you didn't find this demon thing in Lara Gibson's computer?"

"I did – only what I found was its corpse: digital gibberish. Phate built some kind of self-destruct into it. If the demon senses you're looking for it, it rewrites itself into garbage."

"How did you find all this out?" Bishop asked.

Gillette shrugged. "Pieced it together from these." He handed Bishop the printouts.

Bishop looked at the top sheet of paper.

```
To: Group

From: Triple-X

I heard that Titan233 was asking for a copy
of Trapdoor. Don't do it, man. Forget you
heard about it. I know about Phate and
Shawn. They're DANGEROUS. I'm not kidding.
```

"Who's he?" Shelton asked. "Triple-X? Be good to have a talk with him in person."

"I don't have any clue what his real name is or where he lives," Gillette said. "Maybe he was in some cybergang with Phate and Shawn."

Bishop flipped through the rest of the printouts, all of which gave some detail or rumor about Trapdoor. Triple-X's name was on several of them.

Nolan tapped one. "Can we trace the information in the header back to Triple-X's machine?"

Gillette explained to Bishop and Shelton, "Headers in newsgroup postings and e-mails show the route the message took from the sender's computer to the recipient's.

Theoretically you can look at a header and trace a message back to find the location of the sender's machine. But I checked these already." Nodding at the sheet. "They're fake. Most serious hackers falsify the headers so nobody can find them."

"So it's a dead end?" Shelton muttered.

"I just read everything quickly. We should look at them again carefully," Gillette said, nodding at the printouts. "Then I'm going to hack together a bot of my own. It'll search for any mention of the words 'Phate,' 'Shawn,' 'Trapdoor' or 'Triple-X.'"

"A fishing expedition," Bishop mused. "P-h phishing."

It's all in the spelling. . . .

Tony Mott said, "Let's call CERT. See if they've heard anything about this."

Although the organization itself denied it, every geek in the world knew that these initials stood for the Computer Emergency Response Team. Located on the Carnegie Mellon campus in Pittsburgh, CERT was a clearinghouse for information about viruses and other computer threats. It also warned systems administrators of impending hacker attacks.

After the organization was described to him Bishop nodded. "Let's give them a call."

Nolan added, "But don't say anything about Wyatt. CERT's connected with the Department of Defense."

Mott made the call and spoke to someone he knew at the organization. After a brief conversation he hung up. "They've never heard about Trapdoor or anything similar. They want us to keep them posted."

Linda Sanchez was staring at the picture of Andy Anderson's daughter on his desk. In a troubled whisper she said, "So nobody who goes online is safe."

Gillette looked into the soon-to-be grandmother's round brown eyes. "Phate can find out every secret you've got. He can impersonate you or read your medical records. He can empty your bank accounts, make illegal political contributions in your name, give you a phony lover and send your wife or husband copies of fake love letters. He could get you fired."

"Or," Patricia Nolan added softly, "he could kill you."

"Mr. Holloway, are you with us? . . . Mr. Holloway!"

"Huh?"

"'Huh?' 'Huh?' Is that the response of a respectful student? I've asked you twice to answer the question and you're staring out the window. If you don't do the assignments we're going to have a prob—"

"What was the question again?"

"Let me finish, young man. If you don't do the assignments then we're going to have some problems. Do you know how many deserving students're on the waiting list to get into this school? Of course you don't and you don't care either. Did you read the assignment?"

"Not exactly."

"'Not exactly.' I see. Well, the question is: Define the octal number system and give me the decimal equivalent of the octal numbers 05726 and 12438. But why do you want to know the question if you haven't read the assignment? You can hardly answer—"

"The octal system is a number system with eight digits, like the decimal system has ten and the binary system has two."

"So, you remember something from the Discovery Channel, Mr. Holloway."

"No, I—"

"If you know so much why don't you come up to the board and try to convert those numbers for us. Up to the board, up you go!"

"I don't need to write it out. The octal number 05726 converts to decimal 3030. You made a mistake with the second number – 12438 isn't an octal number. There's no digit 8 in the octal system. Only zero through seven."

"I didn't make a mistake. It was a trick question. To see if the class was on its toes."

"If you say so."

Okay, *"Mr. Holloway, time for a visit to the principal."*

Sitting in the dining room office of his house in Los Altos, listening to a CD of James Earl Jones in *Othello*, Phate was roaming through the files of the young character,

Jamie Turner, and planning that evening's visit to St. Francis Academy.

But thinking of the student had brought back memories of his own academic history – like that difficult recollection of freshman high school math. Phate's early schooling fell into a very predictable pattern. For the first semester he'd get straight A's. But in the spring his grades would plunge to D's or F's. This was because he could stave off the boredom of school for the first three or four months but after that even going to class was too tedious for him and he'd invariably miss most of the second-semester.

Then his parents would ship him off to a new school. And the same thing would happen again.

Mr. Holloway, are you with us?

Well, that had been Phate's problem all along. No, basically he hadn't been with anyone ever; he was light-years ahead of them.

His teachers and counselors would try. They'd put him into gifted-and-talented classes and then *advanced* G&T programs but even those didn't hold his interest. And when he grew bored he became sadistic and vicious. His teachers – like poor Mr. Cummings, the freshman math teacher of the octal number incident – stopped calling on him, for fear that he'd mock them and their own limitations.

After some years of this his parents – both scientists themselves – pretty much gave up. Busy with their own lives (Dad, an electrical engineer; Mom, a chemist for a cosmetics company), they were happy to hand off their boy to a series of tutors after school – in effect, buying themselves a couple of extra hours at their respective jobs. They took to bribing Phate's brother, Richard, two years older, into keeping him occupied – which usually amounted to dropping the boy off on the Atlantic City boardwalk video arcades or at nearby shopping malls with a hundred dollars in quarters at ten A.M. and picking him up twelve hours later.

As for his fellow students . . . they, of course, disliked him on first meeting. He was the "Brain," he was "Jon the Head," he was "Mr. Wizard." They avoided him during the early days of class and, as the semester wore on, teased and insulted him unmercifully. (At least no one bothered to beat him up because, as one football player said, "A fucking *girl* could pound the crap out of him. I'm not gonna bother.")

And so to keep the pressure inside his whirling brain from blowing him to pieces he spent more and more time in the one place that challenged him: the Machine World. Since mom and dad were happy to spend money to keep him out of their hair he always had the best personal computers that were available.

A typical high school day would find him tolerating classes then racing home at three P.M. and disappearing into his room, where he would launch himself into bulletin boards or crack the phone company's switches or slip into the computers of the National Science Foundation, the Centers for Disease Control, the Pentagon, Los Alamos, Harvard and CERN. His parents weighed the $800 monthly phone bills against the alternative – missed work and an endless series of meetings with teachers and counselors – and happily opted to write a check to New Jersey Bell.

Still, though, it was obvious that the boy was on a downward spiral – his increasing reclusiveness and vicious outbursts whenever he wasn't online.

But before he bottomed out and, as he'd thought back then, "did a Socrates" with some clever poison whose recipe he'd downloaded from the Net, something happened.

The sixteen-year-old stumbled onto a bulletin board where people were playing a MUD game. This particular one was a medieval game – knights on a quest for a magic sword or ring, that sort of thing. He watched for a while and then shyly keyed, "Can I play?"

One of the seasoned players welcomed him warmly and then asked, "Who do you want to be?"

Young Jon decided to be a knight and went off happily with his band of brothers, killing orcs and dragons and enemy troops for the next eight hours. That night, as he lay in bed, after signing off, he couldn't stop thinking about that remarkable day. It occurred to him that he didn't *have* to be Jon the Head, he didn't *have* to be the scorned Mr. Wizard. All day long he'd been a knight in the mythical land of Cyrania and he'd been happy. Maybe in the Real World he could be someone else too.

Who do you want to be?

The next day he signed up for an extracurricular activity at school, something he'd never done before. What he picked was drama club. He soon learned that he had a natural ability to act. The rest of his time at that particular school didn't improve – there was too much bad blood between Jon and his teachers and fellow students – but he didn't care; he had a plan. At the end of the semester he asked his parents if he could transfer to yet a different school for the next, his junior, year. Since he said he'd take care of all the paperwork himself and the transfer wouldn't disrupt their lives they agreed.

The next fall among the eager students registering for classes at Thomas Jefferson High School for the Gifted was a particularly eager youngster named Jon Patrick Holloway.

The teachers and counselors reviewed the documentation e-mailed to them from his prior schools – the transcripts, which showed his consistent B+ performance in all grades since kindergarten, counselors' glowing reports describing a well-adjusted and -socialized child, his outstanding placement test scores and a number of recommendation letters from his former teachers. The in-person interview with the polite young man – cutting quite a figure in tan slacks, powder blue shirt and navy blazer – went very well and he was heartily welcomed into the school.

The boy always did his assignments and rarely missed a class. He was consistently in the upper-B and lower-A range – pretty much like the other students at Tom Jefferson. He worked out diligently and took up several sports. He'd sit on the grassy hill outside the school, where the in-crowd gathered, and sneak cigarettes and make jokes about the geeks and losers. He dated, went to dances, worked on homecoming floats.

Just like everybody else.

He sat in Susan Coyne's kitchen, and fumbled under her blouse and tasted her braces. He and Billy Pickford took his dad's vintage Corvette out onto the highway, where they got the car up to a hundred, and then sped home, where they dismantled and reset the odometer.

He was happy some, moody some, boisterous some.

Just like everybody else.

At the age of seventeen Jon Holloway social engineered himself into one of the most normal and popular kids in school.

He was so popular, in fact, that the funeral of his parents and brother was one of the most widely attended in the history of the small New Jersey town where they were living. (It was a miracle, friends of the family remarked, that young Jon just happened to be taking his computer to a repair shop early Saturday morning when the tragic gas explosion took the lives of his family.)

Jon Holloway had looked at life and decided that God and his parents had fucked him up so much that the only way he could survive was to see it as a MUD game.

And he was now playing again.

Who do you want to be?

In the basement of his pleasant suburban house in Los Altos Phate washed the blood off his Ka-bar knife and began sharpening it, enjoying the hiss of the blade against the sharpening steel he'd bought at Williams-Sonoma.

This was the same knife he'd used to tease to stillness the heart of an important character in the game – Andy Anderson.

Hiss, hiss, hiss . . .

Access . . .

As he swiped the knife against the steel Phate's perfect memory recalled a passage from the article, "Life in the Blue Nowhere," which he'd copied into one of his hacking notebooks several years ago:

> *The line between the real world and the machine world is becoming more and more blurred every day. But it's not that we're turning into automatons or becoming slaves to machines. No, humans and machines are simply growing toward each other. We're bending machines to our purposes and nature. In the Blue Nowhere, machines are taking on our personalities and culture – our language, myths, metaphors, philosophy and spirit.*

And those personalities and cultures are in turn being changed more and more by the Machine World itself.

Think about the loner who used to return home from work and spend the night eating junk food and watching TV all night. Now, he turns on his computer and enters the Blue Nowhere, a place where he interacts – he has tactile stimulation on the keyboard, verbal exchanges, he's challenged. He can't be passive anymore. He has to provide input to get some response. He's entered a higher level of existence and the reason is that machines have come to him. *They speak* his *language.*

For good or bad, machines now reflect human voices, spirits, hearts and goals.

For good or bad, they reflect human conscience, or the lack of conscience, too.

Phate finished honing the blade and wiped it clean. He replaced it in his footlocker and returned upstairs to find that his taxpayer dollars had been well spent; the Defense Research Center's supercomputers had just finished running Jamie Turner's program and had spit out the passcode to St. Francis Academy's gates. He was going to get to play his game tonight.

For good or bad . . .

After twenty minutes of poring over the printouts from Gillette's search the team could find no other leads. The hacker sat down at a workstation to write code for the bot that would continue to search the Net for him.

Then he paused and looked up. "There's one thing we have to do. Sooner or later Phate's going to realize that you've got a hacker looking for him and he might try to come after *us*." He turned to Stephen Miller. "What external networks do you have access to from here?"

"Two – the Internet, through our own domain: cspccu.gov. That's the one you've been using to get online. Then we're also hooked to ISLEnet."

Sanchez explained the acronym. "That's the Integrated Statewide Law Enforcement Network."

"Is it quarantined?"

A quarantined network was made up of machines connected only to one another and only by hardwire cables – so that no one could hack in via a phone line or the Internet.

"No," Miller said. "You can log on from anywhere – but you need passcodes and have to get through a couple of firewalls."

"What outside networks could I get to from ISLEnet?"

Sanchez shrugged. "Any state or federal police system around the country – the FBI, Secret Service, ATF, NYPD . . . even Scotland Yard and Interpol. The works."

Mott added, "Since we're a clearing house for all computer crimes in the state, CCU has root authority on ISLEnet. So we have access to more machines and networks than anybody else."

Gillette said, "Then we'll have to cut our links to it."

"Hey, hey, hey, backspace, backspace," Miller said, using the hacker term for Hold on a minute. "Cut the link to ISLEnet? We can't do that."

"We have to."

"Why?" Bishop asked.

"Because if Phate gets inside them with a Trapdoor demon he could jump right to ISLEnet. If he does *that* he'll have access to every law enforcement network it's connected to. It'd be a disaster."

"But we use ISLEnet a dozen times a day," Shelton protested. "The automatic fingerprint identification databases, warrants, suspect records, case files, research. . . ."

"Wyatt's right," Patricia Nolan said. "Remember that this guy's already cracked VICAP and two state police databases. We can't risk him getting into any other systems."

Gillette said, "If you need to use ISLEnet you'll have to go to some other location – headquarters, or wherever."

"That's ridiculous," Stephen Miller said. "We can't drive five miles to log on to a database. It'll add hours to the investigation."

"We're already swimming upstream here," Shelton said. "This perp is way ahead of us. He doesn't need any more advantages." He glanced at Bishop imploringly.

The lean detective glanced down at his sloppy shirttail and tucked it in. After a moment he said, "Go ahead. Do what he says. Cut the connection."

Sanchez sighed.

Gillette quickly keyed in the commands severing the outside links, as Stephen Miller and Tony Mott looked on unhappily. When he finished the job he looked up at the team.

"One more thing. . . . From now on nobody goes online but me."

"Why?" Shelton asked.

"Because I can sense if the Trapdoor demon's in our system."

"How?" the rough-faced cop asked sourly. *"Psychic Friends' Hotline?"*

Gillette answered evenly, "The feel of the keyboard, the delays in the system's responses, the sounds of the hard drive – what I mentioned before."

Shelton shook his head. He asked Bishop, "You're not going to agree to *that*, are you? First, we weren't supposed to let him get near the Net at all but he ended up roaming all over the fucking world online. Now, he's telling us that *he's* the only one who can do that and we can't. That's backwards, Frank. Something's going on here."

"What's going on," Gillette argued, "is that I know what I'm doing. When you're a hacker you get the *feel* for machines."

"Agreed," Bishop said.

Shelton lifted his arms helplessly. Stephen Miller didn't look any happier. Tony Mott caressed the grip of his big gun and seemed to be thinking less about machines and more about how much he wanted a clear shot at the killer.

Bishop's phone rang and he took the call. He listened for a moment and, while he didn't exactly smile, the cop's face grew animated. He picked up a pen and paper and started taking notes. After five minutes of jotting he hung up and glanced at the team.

"We don't have to call him Phate anymore. We've got his name."

CHAPTER 00001101 / THIRTEEN

⬧⬥⬧⬥⬧

"**J**on Patrick Holloway."

"It's *Holloway?*" Patricia Nolan's voice rose in surprise.

"You know him?" Bishop asked.

"Oh, you bet. Most of us in computer security do. But nobody's heard from him in years. I thought he'd gone legit or was dead."

Bishop said to Gillette, "It was thanks to you we found him – that suggestion about the East Coast version of Unix. The Massachusetts State Police had positive matches on the prints." Bishop read his notes. "I've got a little history. He's twenty-seven. Born in New Jersey. Parents and only sibling – a brother – are dead. He went to Rutgers and Princeton, good grades, brilliant computer programmer. Popular on campus, involved in a lot of activities. After he graduated he came out here and got a job at Sun Microsystems doing artificial intelligence and supercomputing research. Left there and went to NEC. Then he went to work for Apple, over in Cupertino. A year later he was back on the East Coast, doing advanced phone-switch design at Western Electric in New Jersey. Then he got a job with Harvard's Computer Science Lab. Looks like he was pretty much your perfect employee – team player, United Way campaign captain, things like that."

"Typical upper-middle-class Silicon Valley codeslinger/ chip-jockey," Mott summarized.

Bishop nodded. "Except there was one problem. All the

while he looked like he was Mr. Upstanding Citizen he'd been hacking at night and running cybergangs. The most famous was the Knights of Access. He founded that with another hacker, somebody named Valleyman. No record of *his* real name."

"The KOA?" Miller said, troubled. "They were bad news. They took on Masters of Evil – that gang from Austin. And the Deceptors in New York. He cracked both gangs' servers and sent their files to the FBI's Manhattan office. Got half of them arrested."

"The Knights were probably the gang that shut down nine-one-one in Oakland for two days." Looking through his notes, Bishop said, "A few people died because of that – medical emergencies that never got reported. But the D.A. could never prove they did it."

"Pricks," Shelton spat out.

Bishop continued, "Holloway didn't go by Phate then. His username was CertainDeath." He asked Gillette, "Do you know him?"

"Not personally. But I've heard of him. Every hacker has. He was at the top of the list of wizards a few years ago."

Bishop returned to his notes.

"Somebody snitched on him when he was working for Harvard and the Massachusetts State Police paid him a visit. His whole life turned out to be fake. He'd been ripping off software and supercomputer parts from Harvard and selling them. The police checked with Western Electric, Sun, NEC – all his other employers – and it seemed he'd been doing the same thing there. He jumped bail in Massachusetts and nobody's seen or heard from him for three or four years."

Mott said, "Let's get the files from the Mass. state police. There's bound to be some good forensics in there that we can use."

"They're gone," Bishop replied.

"He destroyed those files too?" Linda Sanchez asked grimly.

"What else?" Bishop asked sarcastically then glanced at Gillette. "Can you change that bot of yours – the search program? And add the names Holloway and Valleyman?"

"Piece of cake." Gillette began keying in code once more.

Bishop called Huerto Ramirez and spoke to him for a few moments. When they hung up he said to the team, "Huerto said there're no leads from the Andy Anderson crime scene. He's going to run the name Jon Patrick Holloway through VICAP and state networks."

"Be faster to just use ISLEnet here," Stephen Miller muttered.

Bishop ignored the dig and continued, "Then he's going to get a copy of Holloway's booking picture from Massachusetts. He and Tim Morgan are going to leave some pictures around Mountain View, near the theatrical supply store, in case Phate goes shopping. Then they'll call all the employers Phate used to work for and get any internal reports on the crimes."

"Assuming they haven't been deleted too," Sanchez muttered pessimistically.

Bishop looked up at the clock. It was nearly 4:00. He shook his head. "We've gotta move. If his goal is killing as many people as he can in a week he might already have somebody else targeted." He picked up a marker and began transcribing his handwritten notes on the white-board.

Patricia Nolan nodded at the board, where the word "Trapdoor" was prominently written in black marker. She said, "That's the crime of the new century. Violation."

"Violation?"

"In the twentieth century people stole your money. Now, what gets stolen is your privacy, your secrets, your fantasies."

Access is God. . . .

"But on one level," Gillette reflected, "you've got to admit that Trapdoor's brilliant. It's a totally robust program."

A voice behind him asked angrily, "'Robust'? What does that mean?" Gillette wasn't surprised find that the questioner was Bob Shelton.

"I mean it's simple and powerful software."

"Jesus," Shelton said. "It sounds like you wish you'd invented the fucking thing."

Gillette said evenly, "It's an astonishing program. I don't understand how it works and I'd like to. That's all. I'm curious about it."

"Curious? You happen to forget a little matter like he's killing people with it."

"I—"

"You asshole. . . . It's a game to you too, isn't it? Just like him." He stalked out of CCU, calling to Bishop, "Let's get the hell out of here and find that witness. *That's* how we're going to nail this prick. Not with this computer shit." He stormed off.

No one moved for a moment. The team looked awkwardly at the white-board or computer terminals or the floor.

Bishop nodded for Gillette to follow him into the pantry, where the detective poured some coffee into a Styrofoam cup.

"Jennie, that's my wife, keeps me rationed," Bishop said, glancing at the dark brew. "Love the stuff but I've got gut problems. Pre-ulcer, the doctor says. Is that a crazy way to put it, or what? Sounds like I'm in training."

"I've got reflux," Gillette said. He touched his upper chest. "Lot of hackers do. From all the coffee and soda."

"Look, about Bob Shelton . . . He had a thing happen a few years ago." The detective sipped the coffee, glanced down at his blossoming shirt. He tucked it in again. "I read those letters in your court file – the e-mails your father sent to the judge as part of the sentencing hearing. It sounds like you two have a good relationship."

"Real good, yeah," Gillette said, nodding. "Especially after my mom passed away."

"Well, then I think you'll understand this. Bob had a son." *Had?*

"He loved the kid a lot – like your dad loves you, sounds like. Only the kid was killed in a car accident a few years ago. He was sixteen. Bob hasn't been the same since then. I know it's a lot to ask but try to cut him some slack."

"I'm sorry about that." Gillette thought suddenly about his own ex-wife. How he'd spent hours and hours in prison wishing he were still married, wishing that he and Ellie had had a son or daughter, wondering how the hell he'd screwed up so badly and ruined his chances for a family. "I'll try."

"Appreciate that."

They walked back to the main room. Gillette returned to

his workstation. Bishop nodded toward the parking lot. "Bob and I'll be checking out that witness at Vesta's Grill."

"Detective," Tony Mott said, standing up. "How 'bout if I come along with you?"

"Why?" Bishop asked, frowning.

"Thought I could help – you've got the computer side covered here, with Wyatt and Patricia and Stephen. I could help canvassing witnesses maybe."

"You ever *do* any canvassing?"

"Sure." After a few seconds he grinned. "Well, not post-crime on the street exactly. But I've interviewed plenty of people online."

"Well, maybe later, Tony. I think Bob and I'll just go alone on this one." He left the office.

The young cop returned to his workstation, clearly disappointed. Gillette wondered if he was upset that he'd been left to report to a civilian or if he really wanted to get a chance to use that very large pistol of his, the butt of which kept nicking the office furniture.

In five minutes Gillette had finished hacking together his bot.

"It's ready," he announced. He went online and typed the commands to send his creation out into the Blue Nowhere.

Patricia Nolan leaned forward, staring at the screen. "Good luck," she whispered. "Godspeed." Like a ship captain's wife bidding her husband farewell as his vessel pulled out of port on a treacherous voyage to uncharted waters.

Another beep on his machine.

Phate looked up from the architectural diagram he'd downloaded – St. Francis Academy and the grounds surrounding it – and saw another message from Shawn. He opened the mail and read it. More bad news. The police had learned his real name. He was momentarily concerned but then decided this wasn't critical; Jon Patrick Holloway was hidden beneath so many layers of fake personas and addresses that there were no links to him as Phate. Still, the police could get their hands on a picture of him (some parts of our past can't be erased with a delete command)

and they'd undoubtedly distribute it throughout Silicon Valley. But at least he was now forewarned. He'd use more disguises.

Anyway, what was the point of playing a MUD game if it wasn't challenging?

He glanced at the clock on his computer: 4:15. Time to get to St. Francis Academy for tonight's game. He had over two hours but he'd have to stake out the school to see if the patrol routes of the security guards had changed. Besides, he knew little Jamie Turner might be feeling antsy and want to slip out of the school before the appointed hour for a stroll around the block while he waited for his brother.

Phate walked down to the basement of his house and took what he needed from his footlocker – his knife, a pistol, some duct tape. Then he went into the downstairs bathroom and pulled a plastic bottle from under the sink. It contained some liquids he'd mixed together earlier. He could still detect the pungent aroma of the chemicals it contained.

When his tools were ready he returned to the dining room of his house and checked the computer once more in case there were more warnings from Shawn. But he had no messages. He logged off and left the room, shutting out the overhead light in the dining room.

As he did so the screen saver on his computer came on and glowed brightly in the dim room. The words scrolled up the screen slowly. They read:

ACCESS IS GOD.

CHAPTER 00001110 / FOURTEEN

———◆◆◆———

"Here, brought you this."

Gillette turned. Patricia Nolan was offering him a cup of coffee. "Milk and sugar, right?"

He nodded. "Thanks."

"I noticed that's how you like it," she said.

He was about to tell her how prisoners in San Ho would trade cigarettes for packages of real coffee and brew it in hot water from the tap. But as interesting as this trivia might be, he decided he wasn't eager to remind everyone – himself included – that he was a convict.

She sat down beside him, tugged at the ungainly knit dress. Pulled the nail polish out of her Louis Vuitton purse again and opened it. Nolan noticed him looking at the bottle.

"Conditioner," she explained. "All the keying is hell on my nails." She glanced into his eyes once then looked down, examining her fingertips carefully. She said, "I could cut them short but that's not part of my plan." There was a certain emphasis on the word "plan." As if she'd decided to share something personal with him – facts that he, however, wasn't sure he wanted to know.

She said, "I woke up one morning earlier this year – New Year's Day, as a matter of fact – after I'd spent the holiday on a plane by myself. And I realized that I'm a thirty-four-year-old single geek girl who lives with a cat and twenty thousand dollars' worth of semiconductor products in her bedroom. I decided I was changing my ways. I'm no fashion model but I thought I'd fix some of the things that could be fixed. Nails, hair, weight. I hate exercise but I'm at the health club every morning at five. The step-aerobics queen at Seattle Health and Racquet."

"Well, you've got really nice nails," Gillette said.

"Thanks. Really good thigh muscles too," she said with averted eyes. (He decided that her plan should probably include a little work on flirtation; she could use some practice.)

She asked, "You married?"

"Divorced."

Nolan said, "I came close once. . . ." She let it go at that but glanced at him to gauge his reaction.

Gillette gave her no response but he thought, Don't waste your time on me, lady. I'm a no-win proposition. Yet at the same time he saw that her interest in him was palpable and Wyatt Gillette knew that it didn't matter that he was a skinny, obsessive geek with a year left on a prison term. He'd seen her adoring gaze as he'd hacked together his bot and he knew that her attraction to him was rooted in his mind and his passion for his craft. Which'll ultimately beat a handsome face and a Chippendale body any day.

But the topic of romance and single life put in his mind thoughts of his ex-wife, Elana, and that depressed him. He fell silent and nodded as Nolan told him about life at Horizon On-Line, which really was, she kept asserting, more stimulating than he might think (though nothing she said bore out that proposition), about life in Seattle with friends and her tabby cat, about the bizarre dates she'd had with geeks and chip-jocks.

He absorbed all the data politely, if vacantly, for ten minutes. Then his machine beeped loudly and Gillette glanced at the screen.

```
Search results:

Search Request: Phate

Location: alt.pictures.true.crime

Status: newsgroup reference
```

"My bot caught a fish," he called. "There's a reference to Phate in a newsgroup."

Newsgroups – those collections of special-interest messages on every topic under the sun – are contained on a subdivision of the Internet known as Usenet, which stands for Unix user network. Started in 1979 to send messages between the University of North Carolina and Duke University, the Usenet was purely scientific at first and contained strict prohibitions against topics like hacking, sex and drugs. In the eighties, though, a number of users thought these limitations smacked of censorship. The "Great Rebellion" ensued, which led to the creation of the Alternate category of newsgroups. From then on the Usenet was like a frontier town. You can now find messages on every subject on earth, from hard-core porn to literary criticism to Catholic theology to pro-Nazi politics to irreverent swipes at popular culture (such as alt.barney.the.dinosaur.must.die).

Gillette's bot had learned that someone had posted a message that included Phate's name in one of these alternate newsgroups, alt.pictures.true.crime, and had alerted its master.

Gillette loaded up his newsgroup reader and went online. He found the group and then examined the screen. Somebody with the screen name Vlast453 had posted a message that mentioned Phate's name. He'd included a picture attachment.

Mott, Miller and Nolan crowded around the screen.

Gillette clicked on the message. He glanced at the header:

From: "Vlast" <vlast@euronet.net>

Newsgroups: alt.pictures.true.crime.

Subject: A old one from Phate. Anyboddy have others.

Date: 1 April 23:54:08 + 0100

Lines: 1323

Message-ID: <8hj345d6f7$1@newsg3.svr.pdd.co.uk>

References: <20000606164328.26619.00002274-@ng-fm1.hcf.com>

NNTP-Posting-Host: modem-76.flonase.dialup.pol.co.uk

```
X-Trace: newsg3.svr.pdd.co.uk 960332345
11751 62.136.95.76

X-Newsreader: Microsoft Outlook Express
5.00.2014.211

X-MimeOLE: Produced By Microsoft MimeOLE
V5.00.2014.211

Path: news.Alliance-news.com!traffic.Alliance-
news.com!Budapest.usenetserver.com!News-
out.usenetserver.com!diablo.theWorld.net!news
.theWorld.net!newspost.theWorld.net!
```

Then he read the message that Vlast had sent.

```
To The Group:

I am receved this from our friend Phate it
was sixths months ago, I am not hearing
from him after then. Can anyboddy post
more like this.
                          — Vlast
```

Tony Mott observed, "Look at the grammar and spelling. He's from overseas."

The language people used on the Net told a great deal about them. English was the most common choice but serious hackers mastered a number of languages – especially German, Dutch and French – so they could share information with as many fellow hackers as possible.

Gillette downloaded the picture that accompanied Vlast's message. It was an old crime scene photograph and showed a young woman's naked body – stabbed a dozen times.

Linda Sanchez, undoubtedly mindful of her own daughter and her fetal grandchild, looked at the picture once and then quickly away. "Disgusting," she muttered.

It was, Gillette agreed. But he forced himself to think past the image. "Let's try to trace this guy," he suggested. "If we can get to him maybe he can give us some leads to Phate."

There are two ways to trace someone on the Internet. If

you have the real header of an e-mail or newsgroup posting you can examine the path notation, which will reveal where the message entered the Internet and the route it followed to get to the computer from which Gillette had downloaded it. If presented with a court order, the sysadmin of that initial network might give the police the name and address of the user who sent the message.

Usually, though, hackers use fake headers so that they can't be traced. Vlast's header, Gillette noted immediately, was bogus – real Internet routes contain only lowercase words and this one contained uppercase and lowercase. He told the CCU team this then added, however, that he'd try to find Vlast with the second type of trace: through the man's Internet address – Vlast453@euronet.net. Gillette loaded up HyperTrace. He typed in Vlast's address and the program went to work. A map of the world appeared and a dotted line moved outward from San Jose – the location of CCU's computer – across the Pacific. Every time it hit a new Internet router and changed direction the machine gave an electronic tone called a "ping" – named after a submarine's sonar beep, which is just what it sounded like.

Nolan said, "This is your program?"

"Right."

"It's brilliant."

"Yeah, it was a fun hack," Gillette said, noting that his prowess had earned him a bit more adoration from the woman.

The line representing the route from CCU to Vlast's computer headed west and finally stopped in central Europe, ending in a box that contained a question mark.

Gillette looked at the graph and tapped the screen. "Okay, Vlast isn't online at the moment or he's cloaking his machine's location – that's the question mark where the trail ends. The closest we can get is his service provider: Euronet.bulg.net. He's logging on through Euronet's Bulgarian server. I should've guessed that."

Nolan and Miller nodded their agreement. Bulgaria probably has more hackers per capita than any other country. After the fall of the Berlin Wall and the demise of Central European Communism the Bulgarian government tried to turn the country into the Silicon Valley of the former Soviet Bloc and imported thousand of codeslingers and chip-jocks. To their dismay, however, IBM, Apple, Microsoft and other U.S. companies swept through the world markets. Foreign tech companies failed in droves and the young geeks were left with nothing to do except hang out in coffee shops and hack. Bulgaria produces more computer viruses annually than any other country in the world.

Nolan asked Miller, "Do the Bulgarian authorities co-operate?"

"Never. The government doesn't even answer our requests for information." Stephen Miller then suggested, "Why don't we e-mail him directly, Vlast?"

"No," Gillette said. "He might warn Phate. I think this's a dead end."

But just then the computer beeped as Gillette's bot signaled yet another catch.

```
Search results:

Search Request: "Triple-X"

Location: IRC, #hack

Status: Currently online
```

Triple-X was the hacker Gillette had tracked down earlier, the one who seemed to know a great deal about Phate and Trapdoor.

"He's in the hacking chat room on the Internet Relay Chat," Gillette said. "I don't know if he'll give up anything about Phate to a stranger but let's try to trace him." He asked Miller, "I'll need an anonymizer before I log on. I'd have to modify mine to run on your system."

An anonymizer, or cloak, is a software program that blocks any attempts to trace you when you're online by making it appear that you're someone else and are in a different location from where you really are.

"Sure, I just hacked one together the other day."

Miller loaded the program into the workstation in front of Gillette. "If Triple-X tries to trace you all he'll see is that you're logging on through a public-access terminal in

Austin. That's a big high-tech area and a lot of Texas U students do some serious hacking."

"Good." Gillette returned to the keyboard, examined Miller's program briefly and then keyed his new fake username, Renegade334, into the anonymizer. He looked at the team. "Okay, let's go swimming with some sharks," he said. And hit the ENTER key.

"That's where it was," said the security guard. "Parked right there, a light-colored sedan. Was there for about an hour, just around the time that girl was kidnapped. I'm pretty sure somebody was in the front seat."

The guard pointed to a row of empty parking spaces in the lot behind the three-story building occupied by Internet Marketing Solutions Unlimited, Inc. The spaces overlooked the back parking lot of Vesta's Grill in Cupertino where Jon Holloway, aka Phate, had social engineered Lara Gibson to her death. Anyone in the mystery sedan would have had a perfect view of Phate's car, even if they hadn't witnessed the actual abduction itself.

But Frank Bishop, Bob Shelton and the woman who ran Internet Marketing's human resources department had just interviewed all of the thirty-two people who worked in the building and hadn't been able to identify the sedan.

The two cops were now interviewing the guard who'd noticed it to see if they could learn anything else that would help them find the car.

Bob Shelton asked, "And it *had* to belong to somebody who worked for the company?"

"Had to," the tall guard confirmed. "You need an employee pass to get through the gate into this lot."

"Visitors?" Bishop asked.

"No, they park in front."

Bishop and Shelton shared a troubled glance. Nobody's leads were panning out. After leaving the Computer Crimes Unit they'd stopped by state police headquarters in San Jose and picked up a copy of Jon Holloway's booking picture from the Massachusetts State Police. It showed a thin young man with dark brown hair and virtually no distinguishing features – a dead ringer for 10,000 other young men in Silicon Valley. Huerto Ramirez and Tim Morgan had also drawn a blank when they'd canvassed Ollie's Theatrical Supply in Mountain View; the only clerk on hand didn't recognize Phate's picture.

The team at CCU had found a lead – Wyatt Gillette's bot had turned up a reference to Phate, Linda Sanchez had told Bishop in a phone call – but that too was a dead end.

Bulgaria, Bishop thought cynically. What kind of case *is* this?

The detective now said to the security guard, "Let me ask you a question, sir. Why'd you notice the car?"

"I'm sorry?"

"It's a parking lot. It'd be normal for a car to be parked here. Why'd you pay any attention to the sedan?"

"Well, the thing is, it's *not* normal for cars to be parked back here. It was the only one I've seen here for a while." He looked around and, making sure the three men were alone, added, "See, the company ain't doing so well. We're down to forty people on the payroll. Was nearly two hundred last year. The whole staff can park in the front lot if they want. In fact, the president encourages it – so the company don't look like it's on its last legs." He lowered his voice. "You ask me, this dot-com Internet crap ain't the golden egg everybody makes it out to be. I myself am looking for work at Costco. Retail . . . now, *that's* a job with a future."

Okay, Frank Bishop told himself, gazing at Vesta's Grill. Think about it: a car parked here by itself when it doesn't have to be parked here. Do something with that.

He had a wisp of a thought but it eluded him.

They thanked the guard and returned to their car, walking along a gravel path that wound through a park surrounding the office building.

"Waste of time," Shelton said. But he was stating a simple truth – most investigating is a waste of time – and didn't seem particularly discouraged.

Think, Bishop repeated silently.

Do something with that.

It was quitting time and some employees were walking along the path to the front lot. Bishop saw a businessman in his thirties walking silently beside a young woman in a business suit. Suddenly the man turned aside and took the woman by the hand. They laughed and vanished into a stand of lilac bushes. In the shadows they threw their arms around each other and kissed passionately.

This liaison brought his own family to mind and Bishop wondered how much he'd see of his wife and son over the next week. He knew it wouldn't be much.

Then, as happened sometimes, two thoughts merged in his mind and a third was born.

Do something . . .

He stopped suddenly.

. . . with that.

"Let's go," Bishop called and started running back the way they'd come. Far thinner than Shelton but not in much better shape he puffed hard as they returned to the office building, his shirt enthusiastically untucking itself once again.

"What the hell's the hurry?" his partner gasped.

But the detective didn't answer. He ran through the lobby of Internet Marketing, back to the human resources department. He ignored the secretary, who rose in alarm at his blustery entry, and opened the door of the human resources director's office, where the woman sat speaking with a young man.

"Detective," the surprised woman said. "What is it?"

Bishop struggled to catch his breath. "I need to ask you some questions about your employees." He glanced at the young man. "Better in private."

"Would you excuse us, please?" She nodded at the man across from her and he fled the office.

Shelton swung the door closed.

"What sort of questions? Personnel?"

"No, *personal.*"

CHAPTER 00001111 / FIFTEEN

———◆◈◆———

Here is the land of fulfillment, here is the land of plenty. The land of King Midas, where the golden touch, though, isn't the sly trickery of Wall Street or the muscle of Midwest industry but pure imagination.

Here is the land where some secretaries and janitors are stock-option millionaires and others ride the number 22 bus all night long on its route between San Jose and Menlo Park just so they can catch some sleep – they, like one third of the homeless in this area, have full-time jobs but can't afford to pay a million dollars for a tiny bungalow or $3,000 a month for an apartment.

Here is Silicon Valley, the land that changed the world.

Santa Clara County, a green valley measuring twenty-five by ten miles, was dubbed "The Valley of the Heart's Delight" long ago though the joy referred to when that phrase was coined was culinary rather than technological. Apricots, prunes, walnuts and cherries grew abundantly in the fertile land nestled fifty miles south of San Francisco. The valley might have remained linked forever with produce, like other parts of California – Castroville with its artichokes, Gilroy with garlic – except for an impulsive decision in 1909 by a man named David Starr Jordan, the president of Stanford University, which was located smack in the middle of Santa Clara Valley. Jordan decided to put some venture capital money on a little-known invention by a man named Lee De Forest.

The inventor's gadget – the audion tube – wasn't like

the phonograph player or the internal-combustion engine. It was the type of innovation that the general public couldn't quite understand and, in fact, didn't care about one bit at the time it was announced. But Jordan and other engineers at Stanford believed that the device might have a few practical applications and before long it became clear how stunningly correct they were – the audion was the first electronic vacuum tube, and its descendants ultimately made possible radio, television, radar, medical monitors, navigation systems and computers themselves.

Once the tiny audion's potential was unearthed nothing would ever be the same in this green, placid valley.

Stanford University became a breeding ground for electronics engineers, many of whom stayed in the area after graduation – David Packard and William Hewlett, for instance. Russell Varian and Philo Farnsworth too, whose research gave us the first television, radar and microwave technologies. The early computers like ENIAC and Univac were East Coast inventions but their limitations – massive size and scalding heat from vacuum tubes – sent innovators scurrying to California, where companies were making advances with tiny devices known as semiconductor chips, far smaller, cooler and more efficient than tubes. Once chips were developed, in the late 1950s, the Machine World raced forward like a spaceship, from IBM to Xerox's PARC to Stanford Research Institute to Intel to Apple to the thousands of dot-com companies scattered throughout this lush landscape today.

The Promised Land, Silicon Valley . . .

Through which Jon Patrick Holloway, Phate, now drove southeast on the rain-swept 280 freeway, toward St. Francis Academy and his appointment with Jamie Turner.

In the Jaguar's CD player was a recording of yet another play, *Hamlet* – Laurence Olivier's performance. Reciting the words in unison with the actor, Phate turned off the freeway at a San Jose exit and five minutes later he was cruising past the brooding Spanish colonial St. Francis Academy. It was 5:15 and he had more than an hour to stake out the structure.

He parked on a dusty commercial street, near the north

gate, through which Jamie was planning on making his escape. Unfurling a planning and zoning commission diagram of the building and a recorder of deeds map of the grounds, Phate pored over the documents for ten minutes. Then he got out of the car and circled the school slowly, studying the entrances and exits. He returned to the Jaguar.

Turning the volume up on his CD, he reclined the seat, and watched people stroll and bicycle along the wet sidewalk. He squinted at them with fascination. They were no more – or less – real to him than the tormented Danish prince in Shakespeare's play and Phate was not sure for a moment whether he was in the Machine World or the Real. He heard a voice, maybe his own, maybe not, reciting a slightly different version of a passage from the play. "What a piece of work is a machine. How noble in reason. How infinite in faculty. In form, in moving, how express and admirable. In operation how like an angel. In access how like a god. . . ."

He checked his knife and the squeeze bottle containing the pungent liquid concoction, all carefully arranged in the pockets of his gray coveralls, on whose back he'd carefully embroidered the words "AAA Cleaning and Maintenance Company."

He looked at his watch, then closed his eyes again, leaning back in the sumptuous leather of his car. Thinking: only forty minutes till Jamie Turner sneaks into the school yard to meet his brother.

Only forty minutes until Phate would find out if he'd win or lose this round of the game.

He rubbed his thumb carefully against the razor-sharp blade of the knife.

In operation how like an angel.

In access how like a god.

In his persona as Renegade334, Wyatt Gillette had been lurking – observing but saying nothing – in the #hack chat room.

Before you social engineer someone you have to learn as much about them as you can to make the scam credible.

He'd call out observations and Patricia Nolan would jot down whatever Gillette had deduced about Triple-X. The woman sat close to him. He smelled a very pleasant perfume and he wondered if this particular scent had been part of her makeover plan.

So far Gillette had learned this about Triple-X:

He was currently in the Pacific time zone (he'd made a reference to cocktail happy hour in a bar nearby; it was nearly 5:50 P.M. on the West Coast).

He was probably in Northern California (he'd complained about the rain – and according to CCU's high-tech meteorology source, the Weather Channel, most of the rain on the West Coast was currently concentrated in and around the San Francisco Bay area).

He was American, older and probably college educated (his grammar and punctuation were very good for a hacker – too good for a high school cyberpunk – and his use of slang was correct, indicating he wasn't your typical Eurotrash-hacker, who often tried to impress others with their use of idioms and invariably got them wrong).

He was probably in a shopping mall, dialing into the Internet Relay Chat from a commercial Internet access location, a cybercafé probably (he'd referred to a couple of girls he'd just seen go into Victoria's Secret; the happy-hour comment too suggested this).

He was a serious, and potentially dangerous, hacker (ditto the shopping center public access – most people doing risky hacks tended to avoid going online out of their houses on their own machines and used public dial-up terminals instead).

He had a huge ego and he considered himself a wizard and an older brother to the youngsters in the group (tirelessly explaining esoteric aspects of hacking to novices in the chat room but having no patience for know-it-alls).

With this profile in mind, Gillette was now almost ready to trace Triple-X.

It's easy to find someone in the Blue Nowhere if they don't mind being found. But if they're determined to remain hidden then tracing is an arduous and usually unsuccessful task.

To track a connection back to an individual's computer

while he's online you need an Internet tracing tool – like Gillette's HyperTrace – but you might also need a phone company trace.

If Triple-X's computer was hooked up to his Internet service provider via a fiberoptic or other high-speed cable connection, rather than a telephone line, then HyperTrace could lead them to the exact longitude and latitude of the shopping mall where the hacker's computer sat.

If, however, Triple-X's machine was connected to the Net over a standard phone line via a modem – a dial-up connection, like most personal computers at home – Gillette's HyperTrace could trace the call back only to Triple-X's Internet service provider and would stop there. Then the phone company's security people would have to trace the call from the service provider to Triple-X's computer itself.

Tony Mott then snapped his fingers, looked up from his phone with a grin and said, "Okay, Pac Bell's set to trace."

"Here we go," said Gillette. He typed a message and hit ENTER. On the screens of everyone logged on to the #hack chat room appeared this message:

Renegade334: Hey Triple how you doing.

Gillette was now "imping" – pretending to be someone else. In this case he'd decided to be a seventeen-year-old hacker with marginal education but plenty of balls and adolescent attitude – just the sort you'd expect to find in this room.

Triple-X: Good, Renegade. Saw you lurking.

In chat rooms you can see who's logged on even if they're not participating in the conversation. Triple-X was reminding Gillette that he was vigilant, the corollary of which was: Don't fuck with me.

Renegade334: Im at a public terminal and people keep walking bye, its pissing me off.

Triple-X: Where you hanging?

* * *

Gillette glanced at the Weather Channel.

> **Renegade334: Austin, man the heat sucks.**
> **You ever been hear.**
>
> **Triple-X: Only Dallas.**
>
> **Renegade334: Dallas sucks, Austin rules!!!!**

"Everybody ready?" Gillette called. "I'm going to try to get him alone."

Affirmative responses from around him. He felt Patricia Nolan's leg brush his. Stephen Miller sat next to her. Gillette keyed a phrase and hit ENTER.

> **Renegade334: Triple – How bout ICQ?**

ICQ (as in "I seek you") was like instant messaging – it would link their machines together so that no one else would be able to see the conversation. A request to ICQ suggested that Renegade might have something illegal or furtive to share with Triple-X – a temptation that few hackers could resist.

> **Triple-X: Why?**
> **Renegade334: can't go into it hear.**

A moment later a small window opened on Gillette's screen.

> **Triple-X: So what's happening, dude?**

"Run it," Gillette called to Stephen Miller, who started HyperTrace. Another window popped up on the monitor, depicting a map of Northern California. Blue lines appeared on the map as the program traced the route from CCU back to Triple-X.

"It's tracing," Miller called. "Signal goes from here to Oakland to Reno to Seattle. . . ."

> **Renegade334: thanks man for the ICQ. Thing**

is I got a problem and Im scared. This
dudes on my case and the word is your a
total wizard and I heard you might know
somthing.

You can never massage a hacker's ego too much, Wyatt
Gillette knew.

Triple-X: What dude?

Renegade334: His names Phate.

There was no response.

"Come on, come on," Gillette urged in a whisper. Don't
vanish. I'm a scared kid. You're a wizard. Help me. . . .

Triple-X: What aobut him? I mean, about.

Gillette glanced at the window on his computer screen that
showed HyperTrace's progress in locating the routing
computers. Triple-X's signal was jumping all over the
western United States. Finally it ended at the last hub, Bay
Area On-Line Services, located in Walnut Creek, which was
just north of Oakland.

"Got his service provider," Stephen Miller called. "It's a
dial-in service."

"Damn," Patricia Nolan muttered. This meant that a
phone company trace was necessary to pinpoint the final
link from the server in Walnut Creek to the computer café
where Triple-X was sitting.

"We can do it," Linda Sanchez called enthusiastically, a
cheerleader. "Just keep him on the line, Wyatt."

Tony Mott called Bay Area On-Line and told the head
of the security department what was going on. The security chief in turn called his own technicians, who would
coordinate with Pacific Bell and trace the connection from
Bay Area back to Triple-X's location. Mott listened for a
moment then called, "Pac Bell's scanning. It's a busy area.
Might take ten, fifteen minutes."

"Too long, too long!" Gillette said. "Tell 'em to speed it up."

But from his days as a phone phreak, breaking into Pac Bell himself, Gillette knew that phone company employees might have to physically run through the switches – which are huge rooms filled with electrical relays – visually finding the connections, in order to trace a call back to its source.

```
Renegade334: I heard about this totally
robust hack of Phates I mean totally and I
saw him online and I asked him about it
only he just dissed me. then Weird stuff
started happening after that and I heard
about this script he wrote called trapdoor
and now Im totally paranoyd.
```

A pause, then:

```
Triple-X: So what're you asking?
```

"He's scared," Gillette said. "I can feel it."

```
Renegade334: this trapdoor thing, does it
really get him in your machine and go
through all your shit, I mean like EVERY-
THING, and you don't even know it.
```

```
Triple-X: I don't think it really exists. Like
an urban legend.
```

```
Renegade334: I don't know man I think its
real, I saw my fucking files OPENING and no
way was I doing it.
```

"We've got incoming," Miller said. "*He's* pinging *us.*"

Triple-X was, as Gillette had predicted, running his own version of HyperTrace to check out Renegade334. The anonymizing program that Stephen Miller had hacked together, however, would make Triple-X's machine think Renegade was in Austin. The hacker must have gotten this report and believed it because he didn't log off.

*   *   *

Triple-X: Why do you care about him? You're
at a public terminal. He can't get into your
files there.

Renegade334: I'm just hear today cause my
fucking parents' took away my Dell for a
week cause a my grades. At home I was
online and the keyboard was fucked up and
then files started opening all by themself. I
freaked. I mean, totally.

Another long pause. Then finally the hacker responded.

Triple-X: You oughta be freaked. I know
Phate.

Renegade334: Yeah how?

Triple-X: Just started talking to him in a
chat room. Helped me debug some script.
Traded some warez.

"This guy is gold," Tony Mott whispered.

Nolan said, "Maybe he knows Phate's address. Ask him."

"No," Gillette said. "We can't scare him off."

There was no message for a moment then:

Triple-X: BRB

Chat room regulars have developed a shorthand of initials
that represent phrases – to save keyboarding time and
energy. BRB meant Be right back.

"Is he headed for the hills?" Sanchez asked.

"The connection's still open," Gillette said. "Maybe he
just went to take a leak or something. Keep Pac Bell on the
trace."

He sat back in the chair, which creaked loudly. Moments
passed. The screen remained unchanged.

BRB.

Gillette glanced at Patricia Nolan. She opened her purse, as bulky as her dress, took out her fingernail conditioner again and absently began to apply it.

The cursor continued to blink. The screen remained blank.

The ghosts were back and this time there were plenty of them.

Jamie Turner could hear them as he moved along the corridors of St. Francis Academy.

Well, the sound was probably only Booty or one of the teachers, making certain that windows and doors were secure. Or students, trying to find a place to sneak a cigarette or play their Game Boys.

But he couldn't get ghosts out of his mind: the spirits of Indians tortured to death and the student murdered a couple of years ago by that crazy guy who broke in – the one who, Jamie now realized, also added to the ghost population by getting shot dead by the cops in the old lunchroom.

Jamie Turner was certainly a product of the Machine World – a hacker and scientist – and he *knew* ghosts and mythical creatures and spirits didn't exist. So why did he feel so damn scared?

Then this weird idea occurred to him. He wondered if maybe, thanks to computers, life had returned to an earlier, more spiritual – and more witchy – time. Computers made the world seem like a place out of one of those books from the 1800s by Washington Irving or Nathaniel Hawthorne. *Sleepy Hollow* and *The House of Seven Gables*. Back then people believed in ghosts and spirits and weird stuff going on that you couldn't exactly see. Now, there was the Net and code and bots and electrons and things you couldn't see – just *like* ghosts. They could float around you, they could appear out of nowhere, they could *do* things.

These thoughts scared the hell out of him but he forced them away and continued down the dark corridors of St. Francis Academy, smelling the musty stucco, hearing the muted conversations and music from the students' rooms recede as he left the residence area and slipped past the gym.

Ghosts. . . .

No, forget it! he told himself.

Think about Santana, think about hanging out with your brother, think about what a great night you're going to have.

Think about backstage passes.

Then, finally, he came to the fire door, the one that led out into the garden.

He looked around. No sign of Booty, no sign of the other teachers who occasionally wandered through the halls like guards in some prisoner-of-war movie.

Dropping to his knees, Jamie Turner looked over the alarm bar on the door the way a wrestler sizes up his opponent.

WARNING: ALARM SOUNDS IF DOOR IS OPENED.

If he didn't disable the alarm, if it went off when he tried to open the door, bright lights would come on throughout the school and the police and the fire department would be here in minutes. He'd have to sprint back to his room and his entire evening would be fucked. He now unfolded a small sheet of paper, which contained the wiring schematic of the alarm that the door manufacturer's service chief had kindly sent him.

Playing a small flashlight over the sheet he studied the diagram once more. Then he caressed the metal of the alarm bar, observing how the triggering device worked, where the screws were, how the power supply was hidden. In his quick mind he matched what he saw in front of him with the schematic.

He took a deep breath.

He thought of his brother.

Pulling on his thick glasses to protect his precious eyes, Jamie Turner reached into his pocket, pulled out the plastic case containing his tools and selected a Phillips head screwdriver. He had plenty of time, he told himself. No need to hurry.

Ready to rock n roll. . . .

CHAPTER 00010000 / SIXTEEN

F rank Bishop parked the unmarked navy blue Ford in front of the modest colonial house on a pristine plot of land – only an eighth of an acre, he estimated, yet being in the heart of Silicon Valley it'd be worth an easy million dollars.

Bishop noted that a new, light-colored Lexus sedan sat in the driveway.

They walked to the door, knocked. A harried forty-something woman in jeans and a faded floral blouse opened the door. The smell of cooking onions and meat escaped. It was 6:00 P.M. – the Bishop family's normal suppertime – and the detective was struck by a blast of hunger. He realized he hadn't eaten since that morning.

"Yes?" the woman asked.

"Mrs. Cargill?"

"That's right. Can I help you?" Cautious now.

"Is your husband home?" Bishop asked, displaying his shield.

"Uhm. I—"

"What is it, Kath?" A stocky man in chinos and a button-down pink dress shirt came to the door. He was holding a cocktail. When he noticed the badges the men displayed he put the liquor out of sight on an entryway table.

Bishop said, "Could we talk to you for a minute, please, sir?"

"What's this about?"

"What's going on, Jim?"

He glanced at her with irritation. "I don't know. If I knew I wouldn't've asked now, would I?"

Grim-faced, she stepped back.

Bishop said, "It'll just take a minute." He and Shelton walked halfway down the front path and paused.

Cargill followed the detectives. When they were out of earshot of the house Bishop said, "You work for Internet Marketing Solutions in Cupertino, right?"

"I'm a regional sales director. What's this—"

"We have reason to believe that you may have seen a vehicle we're trying to track down as part of a homicide investigation. Yesterday at about seven P.M., this car was parked in the lot behind Vesta's Grill, across the street from your company. And we think you might've gotten a look at it."

He shook his head. "Our human resources director asked me about that. But I told her I didn't see anything. Didn't she tell you that?"

"She did, sir," Bishop said evenly. "But I have reason to believe you weren't telling her the truth."

"Hey, hold on a minute—"

"You were parked in the lot behind the company around that time in your Lexus, engaging in sexual activity with Sally Jacobs, from the company's payroll department."

The priceless look of shock, morphing into horror, told Bishop that he was right on the money but Cargill said what he had to. "That's bullshit. Whoever told you that's lying. I've been married for seventeen years. Besides, Sally Jacobs . . . if you saw her you'd know how idiotic that suggestion is. She's the ugliest girl on the sixteenth floor."

Bishop was aware of the fleeting time. He recalled Wyatt Gillette's description of the Access game – to murder as many people as possible in a week. Phate could already be close to another victim. The detective said shortly, "Sir, I don't care about your personal life. All I care about is that yesterday you saw a car parked in the lot behind Vesta's. It belonged to a suspected killer and I need to know what kind of car it was."

"I *wasn't* there," Cargill said adamantly, looking toward

the house. His wife's face was peering at them from behind a lace curtain.

Bishop said calmly, "Yes, sir, you were. And I know you got a look at the killer's car."

"No, I didn't," the man growled.

"You did. Let me explain why I know."

The man gave a cynical laugh.

The detective said, "A late-model, light-colored sedan – like your Lexus – was parked in the back lot of Internet Marketing yesterday around the time the victim was abducted from Vesta's. Now, I know that the president of your company encourages employees to park in front of the building so that clients don't notice that you're down to less than half the staff. So, the only logical reason to park in the back portion of the lot is to do something illicit and not be seen from the building or the street. That would include use of some controlled substances and/or sexual relations."

Cargill stopped smiling.

Bishop continued, "Since it's an access-controlled lot, whoever was parked there was a company employee, not a visitor. I asked the personnel director which employee who owns a light-colored sedan either has a drug problem or was having an affair. She said you were seeing Sally Jacobs. Which, by the way, everybody in the company knows."

Lowering his voice so far that Bishop had to lean forward to hear, Cargill muttered, "Fucking office rumors – that's all they are."

Twenty-two years as a detective, Bishop was a walking lie detector. He continued, "Now, if a man is parked with his mistress—"

"She's not my mistress!"

"—in a parking lot he's going to check out every car nearby to make sure it's not his wife's or a neighbor's. So, therefore, sir, you saw the suspect's car. What kind was it?"

"I didn't see anything," the businessman snapped.

It was Bob Shelton's turn. "We don't have time for any more bullshit, Cargill." He said to Bishop, "Let's go get Sally and bring her over here. Maybe the two of them together can remember a little more."

The detectives had already talked to Sally Jacobs – who

was far from being the ugliest girl on the sixteenth, or any other, floor of the company – and she'd confirmed her affair with Cargill. But being single and, for some reason, in love with this jerk she was far less paranoid than he and hadn't bothered to check out nearby cars. She'd thought there'd been one but she couldn't remember what type. Bishop had believed her.

"Bring her here?" Cargill asked slowly. "Sally?"

Bishop gestured to Shelton and they turned. He called over his shoulder, "We'll be back."

"No, don't," Cargill begged.

They stopped.

Disgust flooded into Cargill's face. The most guilty always look the most victimized, street-cop Bishop had learned. "It was a Jaguar convertible. Late model. Silver or gray. Black top."

"License number?"

"California plate. I didn't see the number."

"You ever see the car in the area before?"

"No."

"Did you see anybody in or around the car?"

"No, I didn't."

Bishop decided he was telling the truth.

Then a conspiratorial smile blossomed in Cargill's face. "Say, Officer, man-to-man, you know how it is. . . . We can keep this between you and me, right?" He glanced back at house, indicating his wife.

The polite façade remained on Bishop's face as he said, "That's not a problem, sir."

"Thanks," the businessman said with massive relief.

"Except for the final statement," the detective added. "That *will* have a reference to your affair with Ms. Jacobs."

"Statement?" Cargill asked uneasily.

"That our evidence department'll mail to you."

"Mail? To the house?" he asked breathlessly.

"It's a state law," Shelton said. "We have to give every witness a copy of their final statement."

"You can't do that."

Unsmiling by nature, unsmiling because of circumstance

now, Bishop said, "Actually we have to, sir. As my partner said. It's a state law."

"I'll drive down to your office and pick it up."

"Has to be mailed – comes from Sacramento. You'll be getting it within the next few months."

"*Few months?* Can't you tell me when exactly?"

"We don't know ourselves, sir. Could be next week, could be July or August. You have a nice night. And thanks for your cooperation, sir."

They hurried back to their navy-blue Crown Victoria, leaving the mortified businessman undoubtedly thinking up wild schemes for intercepting the mail for the next two or three months so his wife didn't see the report.

"Evidence department?" Shelton asked with a cocked eyebrow.

"Sounded good to me." Bishop shrugged. Both men laughed.

Bishop then called central dispatch and requested an EVL – an emergency vehicle locator on Phate's car. This request pulled all Department of Motor Vehicles records on late-model silver or gray Jaguar convertibles. Bishop knew that if Phate used this car in the crime it would either be stolen or registered under a fake name and address, which meant that the DMV report probably wouldn't help. But an EVL would also alert every state, county and local law enforcer in the Northern California area to immediately report any sightings of a car fitting that description.

He nodded for Shelton, the more aggressive – and faster – driver of the two, to get behind the wheel.

"Back to CCU," he said.

Shelton mused, "So he's driving a Jag. Man, this guy's no ordinary hacker."

But, Bishop reflected, we already knew that.

A message finally popped up on Wyatt Gillette's machine at CCU.

```
Triple-X: Sorry, dude. This guy had to ask
me some shit about breaking screen saver
passcodes. Some luser.
```

For the next few minutes Gillette, in his persona as the alienated Texas teenager, told Triple-X about how he defeated Windows screen saver passcodes and let the hacker give him advice on better ways to do it. Gillette was digitally genuflecting before the guru when the door to the CCU opened and he glanced up to see Frank Bishop and Bob Shelton returning.

Nolan said excitedly, "We're close to finding Triple-X. He's in a cybercafé in a mall somewhere around here. He said he knows Phate."

Gillette called to Bishop, "But he's not saying anything concrete about him. He knows things but he's scared."

"Pac Bell and Bay Area On-Line say they'll have his location in five minutes," Tony Mott said, listening into his headset. "They're narrowing down the exchange. Looks like he's in Atherton, Menlo Park or Redwood City."

Bishop said, "Well, how many malls can there be? Get some tactical troops into the area."

Bob Shelton made a call and then announced, "They're rolling. Be in the area in five minutes."

"Come on, come on," Mott said to the monitor, fondling the square butt of his silver gun.

Bishop, reading the screen, said, "Steer him back to Phate. See if you can get him to give you *something* concrete."

```
Renegade334: man this phate dude, isnt
their some thing I can do I mean to stop
him. I'd like to fuck him up.

Triple-X: Listen, dude. You don't fuck up
Phate. He fucks YOU up.

Renegade334: You think?

Triple-X: Phate is walking death, dude. Same
with his friend Shawn. Don't go close to
them. If Phate got you with Trapdoor, burn
your drive and install a new one. Change
your screen name.
```

Renegade334: Could he get to me do you
think, even in texas? wheres he hang?

"Good," said Bishop.

But Triple-X didn't answer right away. After a moment this message appeared on the screen:

Triple-X: I don't think he'd get to Austin.
But I ought tell you something, dude . . .

Renegade334: Whats that?

Triple-X: Your ass ain't the least bit safe in
Northern California, which is where you're
sitting right at the moment, you fucking
poser!!!!

"Shit, he made us!" Gillette snapped.

Renegade334: Hey man I'm in Texas.

Triple-X: "Hey, man" no, you're not. Check
out the response times on your anonymizer.
ESAD!

Triple-X logged off.

"Goddamn," Nolan said.

"He's gone," Gillette told Bishop and slammed his palm onto the workstation desktop in anger.

The detective glanced at the last message on the screen. He nodded toward it. "What's he mean by response times?"

Gillette didn't answer right away. He typed some commands and examined the anonymizer that Miller had hacked together.

"Hell," he muttered when he saw what had happened. He explained: Triple-X had been tracing CCU's computer by sending out the same sort of tiny electronic pings that Gillette was sending to find *him*. The anonymizer *did* tell Triple-X that Renegade was in Austin, but, when he'd typed BRB, the hacker must've run a further test, which showed that the length of time it took the pings to get to and from Renegade's computer was far too short for the electrons to make the round-trip all the way to Texas and back.

This was a serious mistake – it would have been simple to build a short delay into the anonymizer to add few milliseconds and make it appear that Renegade was a thousand miles farther away. Gillette couldn't understand why Miller hadn't thought of it.

"Fuck!" the cybercop said, shaking his head when he realized his mistake. "That's my fault. I'm sorry. . . . I just didn't think."

No, you sure as hell hadn't, Gillette thought.

They'd been so close.

In a soft, discouraged voice, Bishop said, "Recall SWAT."

Shelton pulled out his cell phone and made the call.

Bishop asked, "That other thing Triple-X typed. 'ESAD.' What does that mean?"

"Just a friendly acronym," Gillette said sourly. "It means Eat shit and die."

"Bit of a nasty temper," Bishop observed.

Then a phone rang – it was his cell – and the detective answered. "Yes?" Then tersely he asked, "Where?" He jotted notes and then said, "Get every available unit in the area over there now. Call the San Jose metro police too. *Move* on it and I mean big."

He hung up then looked at the team. "We got a break. There was a response to our emergency vehicle locator. A traffic cop in San Jose saw a parked gray late-model Jag about a half hour ago. It was in an old area of town where you don't see expensive cars very often." He walked to the map and made an *X* at the intersection where the car had been seen.

Shelton said, "I know the area a little. There're a lot of apartments near there. Some bodegas, a few package stores. Pretty low-rent district."

Then Bishop tapped a small square on the map. It was labeled "St. Francis Academy."

"Remember that case a few years ago?" the detetctive asked Shelton.

"Right."

"Some psycho got into the school and killed a student or teacher. The principal put in all kinds of security, real high-tech stuff. It was in all the papers." He nodded at the white-board. "Phate likes challenges, remember?"

"Jesus," Shelton muttered in fury. "He's going after kids now."

Bishop grabbed the phone and called in an assault-in-progress code to central dispatch.

No one dared to mention out loud what everybody was thinking: that the EVL report had placed the car there a half hour ago. Which meant Phate had already had plenty of time to play his macabre game.

It was just like life, Jamie Turner reflected.

With no fanfare, no buzzing, no satisfying ka-chunks like in the movies, without even a faint click, the light on the alarmed door went out.

In the Real World you don't get sound effects. You do what you set out to do and there's nothing to commemorate it except a light silently going dark.

He stood up and listened carefully. From far off down the halls of St. Francis Academy he heard music, some shouting, laughter, tinny arguing on a talk-radio show – which he was leaving all behind, on his way to spend a totally perfect evening with his brother.

Easing the door open.

Silence. No alarms, no shouts from Booty.

The smell of cold air, fragrant with grass, filled his nose. It reminded him of those long, lonely hours after dinner at his parents' house in Mill Valley during the summer – his brother Mark in Sacramento where he'd taken a job to get away from home. Those endless nights. . . . His mother giving Jamie desserts and snacks to keep him out of their hair, his father saying, "Go outside and play," while they and their friends told pointless stories that got more and more fuzzy as everybody guzzled local wines.

Go outside and play. . . .

Like he was in fucking kindergarten!

Well, Jamie hadn't gone outside at all. He'd gone *inside* and hacked like there was no tomorrow.

That's what the cool spring air reminded him of. But at the moment he was immune to these memories. He was thrilled that he'd been successful and that he was going to spend the night with his brother.

He taped the door latch down so that he could get back inside when he returned to the school later that night. Jamie paused and turned back, listening. No footsteps, no Booty, no ghosts. He took a step outside.

His first step to freedom. Yes! He'd made it! He—

It was then that the ghost got him.

Suddenly a man's arm gripped him painfully around the chest and a powerful hand covered his mouth.

God god god. . . .

Jamie tried to leap back into the school but his attacker, wearing some kind of maintenance man uniform, was strong and wrestled him to the ground. Then the man pulled the thick safety glasses off the boy's nose.

"What've we got here?" he whispered, tossing them on the ground and caressing the boy's eyelids.

"No, no!" Jamie cried, trying to raise his arms to protect his eyes. "What're you doing?"

The man took something from the coveralls he wore. It looked like a spray bottle. He held it close to Jamie's face. What was – ?

A stream of milky liquid shot from the nozzle into his eyes.

The terrible burn started a moment later and the boy began to cry and shake in utter panic. His worst fear was coming true. Blindness!

Jamie Turner shook his head furiously to fling off the pain and horror but the stinging only got worse. He was screaming,"No, no, no," the words muffled under the strong grip of the hand around his mouth.

The man leaned close and began to whisper in the boy's ear but Jamie had no idea what he said; the pain – and the horror it represented – consumed him like fire in dry bush.

CHAPTER 00010001 / SEVENTEEN

Frank Bishop and Wyatt Gillette walked through the old archway of the entrance to St. Francis Academy, their shoes sounding in gritty scrapes on the cobblestones.

Bishop nodded a greeting to Huerto Ramirez, whose massive bulk filled half the archway, and asked, "It's true?"

"Yep, Frank. Sorry. He got away."

Ramirez and Tim Morgan, who was presently canvassing witnesses along the streets around the school, had been among the first at the scene.

Ramirez turned and led Bishop, Gillette and, behind them, Bob Shelton and Patricia Nolan into the school proper. Linda Sanchez, pulling a large wheelie suitcase, joined them.

Outside were two ambulances and a dozen police cars, their lights flashing silently. A large crowd of the curious stood on the sidewalk across the street.

"What happened?" Shelton asked him.

"As near as we can tell, the Jaguar was outside that gate over there." Ramirez pointed into a yard separated from the street by a high wall. "We were all on silent roll-up but it looks like he heard we were coming and sprinted out of the school and got away. We set up roadblocks eight and sixteen blocks away but he got through them. Used alleys and side-streets probably."

As they walked through the dim corridors Nolan fell into step beside Gillette. She seemed to want to say something but changed her mind and remained silent.

Gillette noticed no students as they walked down the

hallways; maybe the teachers were keeping them in their rooms until parents and counselors arrived.

"Crime scene finding anything?" Bishop asked Ramirez.

"Nothing that, you know, jumps up and gives us the perp's address."

They turned a corner and at the end of it saw an open door, outside of which were dozens of police officers and several medical technicians. Ramirez glanced at Bishop and then whispered something to him. Bishop nodded and said to Gillette, "It's pretty unpleasant in there. It was like Andy Anderson and Lara Gibson. The killer used his knife again – in the heart. But it looks like it took him a while to die. It's pretty messy. Why don't you wait outside? When we need you to look at the computer I'll let you know."

"I can handle it," the hacker replied.

"You sure?"

"Yep."

Bishop asked Ramirez, "How old?"

"The kid? Fifteen."

Bishop lifted an eyebrow at Patricia Nolan, asking her if she too could tolerate the carnage. She answered, "It's okay."

They walked inside the classroom.

Despite his measured response to Bishop's question Gillette stopped in shock. There was blood everywhere. An astonishing amount – on the floor, walls, chairs, picture frames, white-board, the lectern. The color was different depending on what substance the blood covered, ranging from bright pink to nearly black.

The body lay under a dark-green rubberized blanket on the floor in the middle of the room. Gillette glanced at Nolan, expecting her to be repulsed too. But after a glance at the crimson spatters and streaks and puddles around the room, her eyes simply scanned the classroom, maybe looking for the computer they were going to analyze.

"What's the boy's name?" Bishop asked.

A woman officer from the San Jose Police Department said, "Jamie Turner."

Linda Sanchez walked into the room and inhaled deeply

when she saw the blood and the body. She seemed to be deciding if she was going to faint or not. She stepped outside again.

Frank Bishop walked into the classroom next door to the murder site, where a teenage boy sat clutching himself and rocking back and forth in a chair. Gillette joined the detective.

"Jamie?" Bishop asked. "Jamie Turner?"

The boy didn't respond. Gillette noticed that his eyes were bright red and the skin around them seemed inflamed. Bishop glanced at another man in the room. He was thin and in his mid-twenties. He stood beside Jamie and had his arm on the boy's shoulder. The man said to the detective, "This is Jamie, that's right. I'm his brother. Mark Turner."

"Booty's dead," Jamie whispered miserably and pressed a damp cloth on his eyes.

"Booty?"

Another man – in his forties, wearing chinos and an Izod shirt – identified himself as the assistant principal at the school and said, "It was the boy's nickname for him." He nodded toward the room where the body bag rested. "For the principal."

Bishop crouched down. "How you feeling, young man?"

"He killed him. He had this knife. He stabbed him and Mr. Boethe just kept screaming and screaming and running around, trying to get away. I . . ." He lost his voice to a cascade of sobbing. His brother gripped his shoulders tighter.

"He all right?" Bishop asked one of the medical techs, a woman whose jacket was adorned with a stethoscope and hemostat clamps. She said, "He'll be fine. Looks like the perp squirted him in the eyes with water that had a little ammonia and Tabasco mixed in. Just enough to sting, not enough to do any damage."

"Why?" Bishop asked.

She shrugged. "You got me."

Bishop pulled up a chair and sat down. "I'm sorry this happened, Jamie. I know you're upset. But it's real important you tell us what you know."

After a few minutes the boy calmed and explained that he'd broken out of the school to go to a concert with his brother. But as soon as he'd gotten the door open this man in a uniform like a janitor's grabbed him and squirted some stuff in his eyes. He'd told Jamie it was acid and that if the boy led him to where Mr. Boethe was he'd give him an antidote. But if he didn't the acid'd eat his eyes away.

The boy's hands shook and he started to cry.

"It's his big fear," Mark said angrily, "going blind. The bastard found that out somehow."

Bishop nodded and said to Gillette, "The principal was his target. It's a big school – Phate needed Jamie to find the victim fast."

"And it hurt so much! It really, really did. . . . I told him I wasn't going to help him. I didn't *want* to, I *tried* not to but I couldn't help it. I . . ." He fell silent.

Gillette felt there was something more that Jamie wanted to say but couldn't bring himself to.

Bishop touched the boy's shoulder. "You did exactly the right thing. You did just what I would've done, son. Don't you worry about it. Tell me, Jamie, did you e-mail anybody about what you were going to do tonight? It's important that we know."

The boy swallowed and looked down.

"Nothing's going to happen to you, Jamie. Don't worry. We just want to find this guy."

"My brother, I guess. And then . . ."

"Go ahead."

"What it was, I kind of went online to find some passcodes and stuff. Passcodes to the front gate. He must've hacked my machine and seen them and that's how he got into the courtyard."

"How about you being afraid of going blind?" Bishop asked. "Could he have read about that online?"

Jamie nodded again.

Gillette said, "So Phate made Jamie himself a trapdoor – to get inside."

"You've been real brave, young man," Bishop said kindly.

But the boy was beyond consoling.

The medical examiner's technicians took the principal's

body away and the cops conferred in the corridor, Gillette and Nolan with them. Shelton reported what he'd learned from the forensic techs. "Crime scene doesn't have dick. A few dozen obvious fingerprints – they'll run those but, hell, we already know it's Holloway. He was wearing shoes without distinctive tread marks. There're a million fibers in the room. Enough to keep the bureau's lab busy for a year. Oh, they found this. It's the Turner kid's."

He handed a sheet of paper to Bishop, who read it and passed it on to Gillette. It appeared to be the boy's notes about cracking the passcode and deactivating the door alarm.

Huerto Ramirez told them, "Nobody was exactly sure where the Jaguar was parked. In any case, the rain's washed away any tread marks. We got a ton of trash by the roadside but whether our perp dropped any of it or not, who knows?"

Nolan said, "He's a cracker. That means he's an organized offender. He's not going to be pitching out junk mailers with his address on them while he's staking out a victim."

Ramirez continued, "Tim's still pounding the pavement with some troopers from HQ but nobody's seen anything at all."

Bishop glanced at Nolan, Sanchez and Gillette. "Okay, secure the boy's machine and check it out."

Linda Sanchez asked, "Where is it?"

The assistant principal said he'd lead them to the school's computer department. Gillette returned to the room where Jamie was sitting and asked him which machine he'd used.

"Number three," the boy sullenly replied and continued pressing the cloth into his eyes.

The team started down the dim corridor. As they walked, Linda Sanchez made a call on her cell phone. She learned – Gillette deduced from the conversation – that her daughter still hadn't started labor. She hung up, saying, *"Dios."*

In the basement computer room, a chill and depressing place, Gillette, Nolan and Sanchez walked up to the machine marked NO. 3. Gillette told Sanchez not to run any of her excavation programs just yet. He sat down and said, "As far as we know the Trapdoor demon hasn't self-destructed. I'm going to try to find out where it's resident in the system."

Nolan looked around the damp, gothic room. "Feels like we're in *The Exorcist*. . . . Spooky atmosphere and demonic possession."

Gillette gave a faint smile. He powered up the computer and examined the main menu. He then loaded various applications – a word processor, a spreadsheet, a fax program, a virus checker, some disk-copying utilities, some games, some Web browsers, a password-cracking program that Jamie had apparently written (some very robust code writing for a teenager, Gillette noticed).

As he typed he'd stare at the screen, watching how soon the character he typed would appear in the glowing letters on the monitor. He'd listen to the grind of the hard drive to see if it was making any sounds that were out of sync with the task it was supposed to be performing at that moment.

Patricia Nolan sat close to him, also gazing at the screen.

"I can feel the demon," Gillette whispered. "But it's odd – it seems to move around. It jumps from program to program. As soon as I open one it slips into the software – maybe to see if I'm looking for it. When it decides that I'm not, it leaves. . . . But it has to be resident somewhere."

"Where?" Bishop asked.

"Let's see if we can find out." Gillette opened and closed a dozen programs, then a dozen more, all the while typing furiously. "Okay, okay. . . . This is the most sluggish directory." He looked over a list of files then gave a cold laugh. "You know where Trapdoor hangs out?"

"Where?"

"The Solitaire program."

"What?"

"The card game."

Sanchez said, "But that comes with almost every computer sold in America."

Nolan said, "That's probably why Phate wrote the code that way."

Bishop shook his head. "So anybody with a Solitaire program on his computer could have Trapdoor in it?"

Nolan asked, "What happens if you disabled Solitaire or erased it?"

They debated this for a moment. Gillette was very curious about how Trapdoor worked and wanted to extract the demon and examine it. If they deleted the game program the demon might kill itself – but knowing that this would kill it would give them a weapon; anyone who suspected the demon was inside could simply remove the game.

They decided to copy the contents of the hard drive from the computer Jamie had used and then Gillette would delete Solitaire and they'd see what happened.

Once Sanchez was finished copying the contents Gillette erased the Solitaire program. But he noticed a faint delay in the delete operation. He tested various programs again then laughed bitterly. "It's still there. It jumped to another program and's alive and well. How the *hell* does it do that?" The Trapdoor demon had sensed its home was about to be destroyed and had delayed the delete program just long enough to escape from the Solitaire software to another program.

Gillette stood up and shook his head. "There's nothing more I can do here. Let's take the machine back to CCU and—"

There was a blur of motion as the door to the computer room swung open fast, shattering glass. A raging cry filled the room and a figure charged up to the computer. Nolan dropped to her knees, giving a faint scream of surprise.

Bishop too was knocked aside. Linda Sanchez fumbled for her gun.

Gillette dove for cover just as the chair swung past his head and crashed into the monitor he'd been sitting at.

"Jamie!" the assistant principal cried sharply. "No!"

But the boy drew back the heavy chair and slammed it into the monitor again, which imploded with a loud pop and scattered glass shards around them. Smoke rose from the carcass of the unit.

The administrator grabbed the chair and ripped it from Jamie's hand, pulling the boy aside and shoving him to the floor. "What the hell are you doing, mister?"

The boy scrambled to his feet, sobbing, and made another grab for the computer. But Bishop and the administrator restrained him. "I'm going to smash it! It killed him! It killed Mr. Boethe!"

The assistant principal shouted, "You cut that out this minute, young man! I'm not going to have that kind of behavior in my students."

"Get your fucking hands off me!" the boy raged. "It killed him and I'm going to kill it!" The boy shook with anger.

"Mr. Turner, you will calm down this instant! I'm not going to tell you again."

Mark, Jamie's brother, ran into the computer room. He put his arm around the boy, who collapsed against him, sobbing.

"The students have to behave," the shaken administrator said, looking at the cool faces of the CCU team. "That's the way we do things around here."

Bishop glanced at Sanchez, who was surveying the damage. She said, "Central processor's okay. The monitor's all he nailed."

Wyatt Gillette pulled a couple of chairs into the corner and motioned Jamie over to him. The boy looked at his brother, who nodded, and he joined the hacker.

"I think that fucks up the warranty," Gillette said, laughing and nodding at the monitor.

The boy flashed a weak smile but it vanished almost immediately.

After a moment the boy said, "It's my fault Booty died." The boy looked at him. "I hacked the passcode to the gate, I downloaded the schematic for the alarms. . . . Oh, I wish I was fucking dead!" He wiped his face on his sleeve.

There was more on the boy's mind, Gillette could see once again. "Go on, tell me," he encouraged softly.

The boy looked down and finally said, "That man? He said that if I hadn't been hacking, Mr. Boethe'd still be alive. It was *me* who killed him. And I should never touch another computer again because I might kill somebody else."

Gillette was shaking his head. "No, no, no, Jamie. The

man who did this is a sick fuck. He got it into his head that he was going to kill your principal and nothing was going to stop him. If he hadn't used you he would've used somebody else. He said those things to you 'cause he's afraid of you."

"Afraid of me?"

"He's been watching you, watching you write script and hack. He's scared of what you might do to *him* someday."

Jamie said nothing.

Gillette nodded at the smoking monitor. "You can't break all the machines in the world."

"But I can fuck up that one!" he raged.

"It's just a tool," Gillette said softly. "Some people use screwdrivers to break into houses. You can't get rid of all the screwdrivers."

Jamie sagged against a stack of books, crying. Gillette put his arm around the boy's shoulders. "I'm never going on a fucking computer again. I hate them!"

"Well, that's going to be a problem."

The boy wiped his face again. "Problem?"

Gillette said, "See, we need you to help us."

"Help you?"

The hacker nodded at the machine. "You wrote that script? Crack-er?"

The boy nodded.

"You're good, Jamie. You're really good. There are *sys-admins* who couldn't run the hacks you did. We're going to take that machine with us so we can analyze it at headquarters. But I'm going to leave the other ones here and I was hoping you'd go through them and see if there's anything you can find that might help us catch this asshole."

"You want me to do that?"

"You know what a white-hat hacker is?"

"Yeah. A good hacker who helps find bad hackers."

"Will you be our white hat? We don't have enough people at the state police. Maybe you'll find something we can't."

The boy now seemed embarrassed he'd been crying. He angrily wiped his face. "I don't know. I don't think I want to."

"We sure could use your help."

The assistant principal said, "Okay, Jamie, it's time to get back to your room."

His brother said, "No way. He's not staying here tonight. We're going to that concert and then he can spend the night with me."

The assistant principal said firmly, "No. He needs written permission from your parents and we couldn't get in touch with them. We have rules here and, after all this" – he waved his hands vaguely toward the crime scene – "we're not deviating from them."

Mark Turner leaned forward and whispered harshly, "Jesus Christ, loosen up, will you? The kid's had the worst night of his life and you're—"

The administrator responded, "You have no say about how I deal with my students."

Then Frank Bishop said, "But *I* do. And Jamie's not doing either – staying here *or* going to any concerts. He's coming to police headquarters and making a statement. Then we'll take him to his parents."

"I don't want to go there," the boy said miserably. "Not my parents."

"I'm afraid I don't have any choice, Jamie," said the detective.

The boy sighed and looked like he was going to start crying again.

Bishop glanced at the assistant principal and said, "I'll take care of it from here. You're going to have your hands full with the other boys tonight."

The man glanced distastefully at the detective – and at the broken door – and left the computer room.

After he was gone Frank Bishop smiled and said to the boy, "Okay, young man, you and your brother get on out of here now. You might miss the opening act but if you move fast you'll probably make the main show."

"But my parents? You said—"

"Forget what I said. I'll call your mom and dad and tell them you're spending the night with your brother." He looked at Mark. "Just make sure he's back here in time for classes tomorrow."

The boy couldn't smile – not after everything that had

happened – but he offered a faint, "Thanks." He walked toward the door.

Mark Turner shook the detective's hand.

"Jamie," Gillette called.

The boy turned.

"Think about what I asked – about helping us."

Jamie looked at the smoking monitor for a moment. He turned and left without responding.

Bishop asked Gillette, "You think he can find something?"

"I don't have any idea. That's not why I asked him to help. I figured that after something like this he needs to get back on the horse." Gillette nodded at Jamie's notes. "He's brilliant. It'd be a real crime if he got gun-shy and gave up machines."

The detective laughed faintly. "The more I know you, the more you don't seem like the typical hacker."

"Who knows? Maybe I'm not."

Gillette helped Linda Sanchez go through the ritual of disconnecting the computer that had been a co-conspirator in the death of poor Willem Boethe. She wrapped it in a blanket and strapped it onto a wheelie cart carefully, as if she were afraid that jostling or rough treatment would dislodge any fragile clues to the whereabouts of their adversary.

At the Computer Crimes Unit the investigation stalled.

The bot's alarm that would alert them to the presence of Phate or Shawn on the Net hadn't gone off, nor had TripleX gone back online.

Tony Mott, who still seemed unhappy missing a chance to play "real cop," was grudgingly poring over sheets of legal paper on which he and Miller had taken numerous notes while the rest of the team had been at St. Francis Academy. He announced, "There was nothing helpful in VICAP or the state databases under the name 'Holloway.' A lot of the files were missing and the ones still there don't tell us shit."

Mott continued, "We talked to some of the places that Holloway'd worked: Western Electric, Apple, and Nippon Electronics – that's NEC. A few of the people who remember him say that he was a brilliant codeslinger . . . and a brilliant social engineer."

"TMS," Linda Sanchez recited, "IDK."

Gillette and Nolan laughed.

Mott translated yet another acronym from the Blue Nowhere for Bishop and Shelton. "Tell me something I don't know." He continued, "But – surprise, surprise – all the files were gone from their personnel and audit departments."

"I can see how he hacks in and erases computer files," Linda Sanchez said, "but how's he get rid of the dead-tree stuff?"

"The what?" Shelton asked.

"Paper files," Gillette explained. "But that's easy: he hacks into the file-room computer and issues a memo to the staff to shred them."

Mott added that several of the security officers at Phate's former employers believed he'd made his living – and might still be making it now – by brokering stolen supercomputer parts, for which there was huge demand, especially in Europe and third-world nations.

Their hopes blossomed for a moment when Ramirez called in to say that he'd finally heard from the owner of Ollie's Theatrical Supply. The man had looked at the booking picture of young Jon Holloway and confirmed that he'd come into the store several times in the past month. The owner couldn't recall exactly what he'd bought but he remembered the purchases were large and had been paid for with cash. The owner had no idea where Holloway lived but he did remember a brief exchange. He'd asked Holloway if he was an actor and, if so, wasn't it hard to get jobs?

The owner had added, "I remember that he said, 'Nope, it's not hard at all. I act every single day.'"

A half hour later, Frank Bishop stretched and looked around the dinosaur pen.

The energy was low in the room. Linda Sanchez was on the phone with her daughter, who still wasn't in labor. Stephen Miller sat sullenly by himself, looking over notes, perhaps still troubled by the mistake he'd made with the anonymizer, which had let Triple-X get away. Gillette was in the analysis lab, checking out the contents of Jamie Turner's computer. Patricia Nolan was in a nearby cubicle, making phone calls. Bishop wasn't sure where Bob Shelton was.

Bishop's phone rang and he took the call. It was from the highway patrol.

A motorcycle officer had found Phate's Jaguar in Oakland.

There wasn't any direct evidence linking the car to the hacker but it had to be his; the only reason to douse a $60,000 vehicle with copious amounts of gasoline and set it aflame was to destroy evidence.

Which the fire did with great efficiency, according to the crime scene unit; there were no clues that might help the team.

Bishop turned back to the preliminary crime scene report from St. Francis Academy. Huerto Ramirez had compiled it in record time but there wasn't much that was helpful here either. The murder weapon had again been a Ka-bar knife. The duct tape used to bind Jamie Turner was untraceable, as were the Tabasco and ammonia that had stung his eyes. They'd found plenty of Holloway's fingerprints – but those were useless now since they already knew his identity.

Bishop walked to the white-board and gestured to Mott for the marker, who pitched it to him. The detective wrote these details on the board but when he started to write "Fingerprints," he paused.

Phate's fingerprints . . .

The burning Jaguar . . .

These facts troubled him for some reason. Why? he wondered, brushing his sideburns with his knuckles.

Do something with that . . .

He snapped his fingers.

"What?" Linda Sanchez asked. Mott, Miller and Nolan looked at him.

"Phate didn't wear gloves this time."

At Vesta's, when he'd kidnapped Lara Gibson, Phate had

carefully wrapped a napkin around his beer bottle to obscure his prints. At St. Francis he hadn't bothered. "That means he *knows* we have his real identity." Then the detective added, "And the car too. The only reason to destroy it is if he knew that we'd found out he was driving a Jaguar. How'd he do that?"

The press hadn't mentioned his name or the fact that the killer was driving a Jaguar.

"We have ourselves a spy, you think?" Linda Sanchez said.

Bishop's eyes fell again on the white-board and he noticed the reference to Shawn, Phate's mysterious partner. He tapped the name and asked, "What's the whole point of this game of his? It's to find some hidden way of getting access to your victim's life."

Nolan said, "You're thinking Shawn's a trapdoor? An insider?"

Tony Mott shrugged. "Maybe he's a dispatcher at headquarters? Or a trooper?"

"Or somebody from California State Data Management?" Stephen Miller suggested.

"Or maybe," a man's voice growled, "*Gillette* is Shawn."

Bishop turned and saw Bob Shelton standing in front of a cubicle toward the back of the room.

"What're you talking about?" Patricia Nolan asked.

"Come here," he said, gesturing them toward the cubicle.

Inside, on the desk, a computer monitor glowed with text. Shelton sat down and scrolled through it as the others on the team crammed into the cubicle.

Linda Sanchez looked over the screen. With some concern she said, "You're on ISLEnet. Gillette said we weren't supposed to log on from here."

"Of *course* he said that," Shelton spat out bitterly. "Know why? Because he was afraid we'd find this—" He scrolled a little further down and gestured toward the screen. "It's an old Department of Justice report I found in the Contra Costa County archives. Phate might've erased the copy in Washington but he missed this one." Shelton tapped the screen. "Gillette was Valleyman. He and Holloway ran that gang – Knights of Access – together. They *founded* it."

"Shit," Miller muttered.

"No," Bishop whispered. "Can't be."

Mott spat out, "*He* fucking social engineered us too!"

Bishop closed his eyes, seared by the betrayal.

Shelton muttered, "Gillette and Holloway've known each other for years. 'Shawn' could be one of Gillette's screen names. Remember that the warden said he'd been caught going online. He was probably contacting Phate. Maybe this whole thing was a plan to get Gillette out of prison. What a fucking son of bitch."

Nolan pointed out, "But Gillette programmed his bot to search for Valleyman too."

"Wrong." Shelton pushed a printout toward Bishop. "Here's how he modified his program."

The printout read:

```
Search: IRC, Undernet, Dalnet, WAIS,
gopher, Usenet, BBSs, WWW, FTP,
ARCHIVES

Search for: (Phate OR Holloway OR "Jon
Patrick Holloway" OR "Jon Holloway") BUT
NOT Valleyman OR Gillette
```

Bishop shook his head. "I don't understand it."

"The way he wrote the request," Nolan said, "his bot would retrieve anything that had a reference to Phate, Holloway or Trapdoor in it unless it also referred to Gillette or Valleyman. Those it would ignore."

Shelton continued, "He's the one who's been warning Phate. That's why he got away from St. Francis in time. And Gillette told him that we knew what kind of car he was driving, so he burned it."

Miller added, "And he was so desperate to stay and help us, remember?"

"Sure he was," Shelton said, nodding. "Otherwise, he'd lose his chance to—"

The detectives looked at each other.

Bishop whispered, "—escape."

They sprinted down the corridor that led to the analysis lab. Bishop noticed that Shelton had drawn his weapon.

The door to the lab was locked. Bishop pounded but there was no response. "Key!" he called to Miller.

But Shelton growled, "Fuck the key—" and kicked the door in, raising his gun.

The room was empty.

Bishop continued to the end of the corridor and pushed into a storeroom in the back of the building.

He saw the fire door, which led outside into the parking lot. It was wide open. The fire alarm in the door-opener bar had been dismantled – just as Jamie Turner had done to escape from St. Francis Academy.

Bishop closed his eyes and leaned against the damp wall. He felt the betrayal deep within his heart, as sharp as Phate's terrible knife.

"The more I know you, the more you don't seem like the typical hacker."

"Who knows? Maybe I'm not."

Then the detective turned and hurried back into the main area of the CCU. He picked up the phone and called the Department of Corrections Detention Coordination Office at the Santa Clara County Building. The detective identified himself and said, "We've got a fugitive on the run wearing an anklet. We need an emergency trace. I'll give you the number of his unit." He consulted his notebook. "It's—"

"Could you call back later, Lieutenant?" came the weary response.

"Call back? Excuse me, sir, you don't understand. We just had an escape. Within the last thirty minutes. We need to trace him."

"Well, we're not *doing* any tracing. The whole system's down. Crashed like the Hindenburg. Our tech people can't figure out why."

Bishop felt the chill run through his body. "Tell them you've been hacked," he said. "*That's* why."

The voice on the other end of the line gave a condescending

laugh. "You've been watching too many movies, Detective. Nobody can get into *our* computers. Call back in three or four hours. Our people're saying we should be up and running by then."

III
SOCIAL ENGINEERING

[A]nonymity is one thing that the next
wave of computing will abolish.

— *Newsweek*

CHAPTER 00010010 / EIGHTEEN

———◆◆◆———

*H*e *takes things apart.*
    Wyatt Gillette was jogging through the chill evening rain down a sidewalk in Santa Clara, his chest aching, breathless. It was 9:30 P.M. and he'd put nearly two miles between him and CCU headquarters since he'd escaped.

He knew his way around this neighborhood – he wasn't far from one of the houses where he'd lived as a boy – and he was thinking of the time his mother had told a friend, who'd asked if ten-year-old Wyatt preferred baseball to soccer, "Oh, he doesn't like sports. He takes things apart. That seems to be all he likes to do."

A police car approached and Gillette eased to a quick walk, keeping his head under the umbrella he'd found in the computer analysis lab at CCU.

The car disappeared without slowing. The hacker sped up once again. The anklet tracking system would be down for several hours but he couldn't afford to dawdle.

He takes things apart. . . .

Nature had cursed Wyatt Edward Gillette with a raging curiosity that seemed to grow exponentially with every new year. But that perverse gift had at least been mitigated somewhat by the blessing of hands and a mind skillful enough to, more often than not, satisfy his obsession.

He lived to understand how things worked and there was only one way to do that: take them apart.

Not a single thing in the Gillette house had been safe from the boy and his tool kit.

His mother would return home from her job to find young Wyatt sitting in front of her food processor, happily examining its component parts.

"Do you know how much that cost?" she'd ask angrily.

Didn't know, didn't care.

But ten minutes later it would be reassembled and working fine, neither better nor worse for its dismemberment.

And the Cuisinart's surgery had occurred when the boy was only five years old.

Soon, though, he'd taken apart and put back together all the things mechanical in the house. He understood pulleys and wheels and gears and motors and they began to bore him so it was on to electronics. For a year he preyed upon stereos and record players and tape decks.

Taking 'em apart, putting 'em back together . . .

It didn't take long before the boy had dispensed with the mysteries of vacuum tubes and circuit boards, and his curiosity began to prowl like a tiger with a reawakened hunger.

But then he discovered computers.

He thought of his father, a tall man with the perfect posture and trim hair that had been his legacy from the air force. The man had taken him to a Radio Shack when his son was eight and told him he could pick out something for himself. "You can get anything you want."

"Anything?" asked the boy, eyeing the hundreds of items on the shelves.

Anything you want . . .

He'd picked a computer.

It was a perfect choice for a boy who takes things apart – because the little Trash-80 computer was a portal to the Blue Nowhere, which is infinitely deep and infinitely complex, made up of layer upon layer of parts small as molecules and big as the exploding universe. It's the place where curiosity can roam free forever.

Schools, however, tend to prefer their students' minds to be compliant first and curious second, if at all, and as he moved up through his grades young Wyatt Gillette began to founder.

Before he bottomed out, though, a wise counselor plucked him out of the stew of high school, sized him up and sent him off to Santa Clara Magnet School Number Three.

The school was billed as a "haven for gifted but troubled students residing in Silicon Valley" – a description that could, of course, be translated only one way: hacker heaven. A typical day for a typical student at Magnet Three involved cutting P.E. and English classes, tolerating history and acing math and physics, all the while concentrating on the only schoolwork that really mattered: talking with your buddies nonstop about the Machine World.

Now, walking down a rainy sidewalk, not far from this very school in fact, he had many memories of his early days in the Blue Nowhere.

Gillette clearly remembered sitting in the Magnet Three school yard, practicing his whistle for hour upon hour. If you could whistle into a fortress phone at just the right tone you could fool the phone switches into thinking you yourself were another switch and would be rewarded with the golden ring of *access*. (Everybody knew about Captain Crunch – the username of a legendary young hacker who had discovered that the whistle given away with the cereal of the same name generated a tone of 2600 megahertz, the exact frequency that let you break into the phone company's long-distance lines and make free calls.)

He remembered all the hours he'd spent in the Magnet Three cafeteria, which smelled like wet dough, or in study hall or the green corridors, talking about CPUs, graphics cards, bulletin boards, viruses, virtual disks, passwords, expandable RAM, and the bible – that is, William Gibson's novel, *Neuromancer,* which popularized the term "cyberpunk."

He remembered the first time he cracked into a government computer and the first time he got busted and sentenced to detention for hacking – at seventeen, still a juvenile. (Though he still had to do time; the judge was stern with boys who seized root of Ford Motor Company's mainframe when they should've been out playing baseball – and the old jurist was more stern yet with boys who lectured *him,* adamantly pointing out that the world'd be in pretty shitty shape today if Thomas Alva Edison had been more concerned with sports than inventing.)

But the most prominent memory at the moment was of an event that occurred a few years after he graduated from Berkeley: his first online meeting with a young hacker named CertainDeath, the user name of Jon Patrick Holloway, in the #hack chat room.

Gillette was working as a programmer during the day. But like many code crunchers he was bored with that life and counted the hours until he could get home to his machine to explore the Blue Nowhere and meet kindred souls, which Holloway certainly was; their first online conversation lasted four and a half hours.

Initially they traded phone phreaking information. They then put theory into practice and pulled off what they declared to be some "totally moby" hacks, cracking into the Pac Bell, AT&T and British Telecom switching systems. As far as they knew they were the only hackers in America who'd ever placed free calls from a pay phone in Golden Gate Park to one in Red Square in Moscow.

From these modest beginnings they began prowling through corporate and government machines. Their reputation spread and pretty soon other hackers began to seek them out, running Unix "finger" searches on the Net to find them by name and them sitting at the young men's virtual feet to learn what the gurus had to teach. After a year or so of hanging out online with various regulars he and Holloway realized that they'd become a cybergang – a rather legendary one, as a matter of fact. CertainDeath, the leader and bona fide wizard. Valleyman, the second in command, the thoughtful philosopher of the group and nearly as good a codeslinger as CertainDeath. Sauron and Klepto, not as smart but half crazy and willing to do anything online. Others, too: Mosk, Replicant, Grok, NeuRO, BYTEr. . . .

They needed a name and Gillette had delivered: "Knights of Access" had occurred to him after playing a medieval MUD game for sixteen hours straight.

Their notoriety spread around the world – largely because they wrote programs that could get computers to do amazing things. Far too many hackers and cyberpunks weren't programmers at all – they were referred to contemptuously as "point-and-clickers." But the leaders of the Knights were skilled software writers, so good that they didn't even bother to compile many of their programs – turning the raw source code into working software – because they knew clearly how the software would perform. (Elana – Gillette's ex-wife, whom he'd met around this time – was a piano teacher and she said Gillette and Holloway reminded her of Beethoven, who could imagine his music so perfectly in his head that once he'd written it the performance was anticlimactic.)

Recalling this, he now thought of his ex-wife. Not far from here was the beige apartment where he and Elana had lived for several years. He could picture the time they spent together so clearly; a thousand images leapt from deep memory. But unlike the Unix operating system or a math coprocessor chip, the relationship between him and Elana was something he *couldn't* understand. He didn't know how to take it apart and look at the components.

And therefore it was something he couldn't fix.

This woman still consumed him, he longed for her, he wanted a child with her . . . but in the matter of love Wyatt Gillette knew he was no wizard.

He now put these reflections aside and stepped under the awning of a shabby Goodwill store near the Sunnyvale town line. Once he was out of the rain he looked around him then, seeing he was alone, reached into his pocket and extracted a small electronic circuit board, which he'd had with him all day. When he'd gone back to his cell at San Ho that morning to collect the magazines and clippings for his excursion to the CCU office he'd taped the board to his right thigh, near his groin.

This board, which he'd been working on for the past six months, was what he'd intended to smuggle out of prison from the beginning – not the phone phreaking red box, which he'd slipped into his pocket so that the guards would find that and, he hoped, let him leave prison without going through the metal detector again.

In the computer analysis lab back at CCU forty minutes ago he'd pulled the board off his skin and successfully tested it. Now in the pale, fluorescent light from the Goodwill shop he examined the circuit again and found that it had survived his jog from CCU just fine.

He slipped it back into his pocket and stepped inside the store, nodding a greeting to the night clerk, who said, "We close at ten."

Gillette knew this – he'd checked their hours out earlier. "I won't be long," he assured the man then proceeded to pick out a change of clothing, which, in the best tradition of social engineering, were the sort of things he wouldn't normally wear.

He paid with money he'd lifted from a jacket in CCU and started toward the door. He paused and turned back to the clerk. "Excuse me. There's a bus stop around here, isn't there?"

The old man pointed to the west of the store. "Fifty feet up the street. It's a transfer point. You can get a bus there that'll take you anywhere you want to go."

"Anywhere?" Wyatt Gillette asked cheerfully. "Who could ask for more than that?" And he stepped back into the rainy night, opening his borrowed umbrella.

The Computer Crimes Unit was mute from the betrayal.

Frank Bishop felt the hot pressure of silence around him. Bob Shelton was coordinating with the local police Tony Mott and Linda Sanchez were also on the phones, checking leads. They spoke in quiet tones, reverent almost, suggesting the intensity of their desire to recapture their betrayer.

The more I know you, the more you don't seem like the typical hacker . . .

After Bishop, it was Patricia Nolan who seemed the most upset and took the young man's escape personally. Bishop had sensed a connection between them – well, *she* at least was attracted to the hacker. The detective wondered if this crush might've fit a certain pattern: the smart but ungainly woman would fall hard and fast for a brilliant renegade, who'd charm her for a while but then would slip out of her life. For the fiftieth time that day Bishop pictured his wife Jennie and thought how glad he was to be contentedly married.

The reports came back but there were no leads. No one in the buildings near CCU had seen Gillette escape. No cars were missing from the parking lot but the office was right next to a major county bus route and he could easily have escaped that way. No county or municipal police cars reported seeing anyone fitting his description on foot.

With the absence of hard evidence as to where Gillette had gone Bishop decided to look at the hacker's history – try to track down his father or brother. Friends too and former coworkers. Bishop looked over Andy Anderson's desk for copies of Gillette's court and prison files but he couldn't find them. When Bishop put in an emergency request for copies of the files from central records he learned that they were gone.

"Someone issued a memo to shred them, right?" Bishop asked the night clerk.

"As a matter of fact, sir, that's right. How'd you know?"

"Wild guess." The detective hung up.

Then an idea occurred to him. He recalled that the hacker had done juvenile time.

So Bishop called a friend at the night magistrate's office. The man did some checking and learned that, yes, they did have a file on Wyatt Gillette's arrest and sentencing when he'd been seventeen. They'd send a copy over as soon as possible.

"He forgot to have those shredded," Bishop said to Nolan. "At least we've got one break."

Suddenly Tony Mott glanced at a computer terminal and leapt to his feet, shouting, "Look!"

He ran to the terminal and started banging on the keyboard.

"What?" Bishop asked.

"A housekeeping program just started to wipe the empty space on the hard drive," Mott said breathlessly as he keyed. He hit ENTER then looked up. "There, it's stopped."

Bishop noted the alarm in his face but had no clue what was going on.

It was Linda Sanchez who explained. "Almost all the data on a computer – even things you've deleted or that vanish when you shut the computer off – stay in the empty space

of your hard drive. You can't see them as files but they're
easy to recover. That's how we catch a lot of bad guys who
think they deleted incriminating evidence. The only way to
completely destroy that information is to run a program that
'wipes' the empty space. It's like a digital shredder. Before
he escaped Wyatt must've programmed it to start running."

"Which means," Tony Mott said, "that he doesn't want
us to see what he was just doing online."

Linda Sanchez said, "I've got a program that'll find whatever he was looking at."

She flipped through a box containing floppy disks and
loaded one into the machine. Her stubby fingers danced
over the keyboard and in a moment cryptic symbols filled
the screen. They made no sense whatsoever to Frank Bishop.
He noticed though that this must have been a victory for
their side because Sanchez smiled faintly and motioned her
colleagues over to the terminal.

"This's interesting," Mott said.

Stephen Miller nodded and began taking notes.

"What?" Bishop asked.

But Miller was too busy writing to reply.

CHAPTER 00010011 / NINETEEN

P hate sat in the dining room of his house in Los Altos, listening to *Death of a Salesman* on his Diskman.

Hunching over his laptop, though, he was distracted. He was badly shaken up by the close call at St. Francis Academy. He remembered standing with his arm around trembling Jamie Turner – both of them watching poor "Booty" thrash about in his death throes – and telling the kid to stay away from computers forever. But his compelling monologue had been interrupted by Shawn's emergency page, which alerted him that the police were on their way to the school.

Phate had sprinted out of St. Francis and gotten away just in time, as the police cruisers approached from three different directions.

How on earth had they figured that out?

Well, he was shaken, true, but – an expert at MUD games, a supreme strategist – Phate knew that there was only one thing to do when the enemy has a near success.

Attack again.

He needed a new victim. He scrolled through his computer's directory and opened a folder labeled Univac Week, which contained information on Lara Gibson, St. Francis Academy and other potential victims in Silicon Valley. He started reading through some of the articles from local newspaper Web sites; there were stories about people like paranoid rap stars who traveled with armed entourages, politicians who supported unpopular causes and abortion doctors who lived in virtual fortresses.

But whom to pick? he wondered. Who'd be more challenging than Boethe and Lara Gibson?

Then his eye caught a newspaper article that Shawn had sent to him about a month ago. It concerned a family who lived in an affluent part of Palo Alto.

High Security in a High-Tech World

Donald W. is a man who's been to the edge. And he didn't like it.

Donald, 47, who agreed to be interviewed only if we didn't use his last name, is chief executive officer of one of Silicon Valley's most successful venture capital firms. While another man might brag about this accomplishment, Donald tries desperately to keep his success, and all the other facts about his life, completely hidden.

There's a very good reason for this: six years ago, while in Argentina to close a deal with investors, he was kidnapped at gunpoint and held for two weeks. His company paid an undisclosed amount of ransom for his release.

Donald was subsequently found unharmed by Buenos Aires police, but he says he hasn't been the same since.

"You look death right in the face and you think, I've taken so much for granted. We think we live in a civilized world, but that's not the case at all."

Donald is among a growing number of wealthy executives in Silicon Valley who are starting to take security seriously.

He and his wife even picked a private school for their only child, Samantha, 8, on the basis of its high-security facilities.

Perfect, Phate thought and went online.

The anonymity of these characters was, of course, merely a slight inconvenience and in ten minutes he'd hacked into the newspaper's editorial computer system and was browsing through the notes of the reporter who'd written the article. He soon had all the details he needed on Donald Wingate,

32983 Hesperia Way, Palo Alto, married to Joyce, forty-two, neé Shearer, who were the parents of a third grader at Junípero Serra School, 2346 Rio Del Vista, also in Palo Alto. He learned too about Wingate's brother, Irving, and Irv's wife, Kathy, and about the two bodyguards in Wingate's employ.

There were some MUDhead game players who'd consider it bad strategy to hit the same type of target – a private school, in this case – twice in a row. Phate, on the contrary, thought it made perfect sense and that the cops would be caught completely off guard.

He scrolled through the files again slowly.

Who do you want to be?

Patricia Nolan said, "You're not going to hurt him, are you? It's not like he's dangerous. You *know* that."

Frank Bishop snapped that they weren't going to shoot Gillette in the back but, beyond that, there were no guarantees. His response wasn't very civil but his goal at the moment was to find the fugitive, not to comfort consultants who had a crush on him.

The main CCU phone line rang.

Tony Mott took the call, listened, nodding his head broadly, eyes slightly wider than they normally were. Bishop frowned, wondering who was on the other end of the line. In a respectful voice Mott said, "Please hold a minute." The young cop then handed the receiver to the detective as if it were a bomb.

"It's for you," the cop whispered uncertainly. "Sorry."

Sorry? Bishop lifted an eyebrow.

"It's Washington, Frank. The Pentagon."

The Pentagon. It was after 1:00 A.M. East Coast time. This is trouble . . .

He took the receiver. "Hello?"

"Detective Bishop?"

"Yessir."

"This's David Chambers. I run the Department of Defense's Criminal Investigation Division."

Bishop shifted the phone, as if the news he was about to hear would hurt less in his left ear.

"I've heard from various sources that a John Doe release

order was issued in the Northern District of California. And that that order might concern an individual we have some interest in." Chambers added quickly, "Don't mention that person's name over the phone line."

"That's right," Bishop responded.

"Where is he now?"

Brazil, Cleveland, Paris, hacking into the New York Stock Exchange to bring the world economy to a halt.

"In my custody," Bishop said.

"You're a California *state* trooper, is that right?"

"I am, yessir."

"How the hell d'you get a federal prisoner released? And more important, how the hell d'you get him out on a John Doe? Even the warden at San Jose doesn't know anything . . . or claims he doesn't."

"The U.S. attorney and I're friends. We closed the Gonzalez killings a couple of years ago and we've been working together ever since."

"This is a murder case you're running?"

"Yessir. A hacker's been breaking into people's computers and using the information inside to get close to his victims."

Bishop looked at Bob Shelton's concerned face and drew his finger across his own throat. Shelton rolled his eyes.

Sorry. . . .

"You know why we're after this individual, don't you?" Chambers asked.

"Something about him writing some software that cracks *your* software." Trying to be as vague as he could. He guessed that in Washington two conversations often went on simultaneously: the one you meant and the one you said out loud.

"Which, if he did, is illegal to start with and if a copy of what this person wrote gets out of the country it's treason."

"I understand that." Bishop filled the ensuing silence with: "And you want him back in prison, is that it?"

"That's right."

"We've got three days on the order," Bishop said firmly.

A laugh from the other end of the phone. "I make one phone call and that order becomes toilet paper."

"I imagine you could do that. Yessir."

There was a pause.

Then Chambers asked, "The name's Frank?"

"Yessir."

"Okay, Frank. Cop to cop: Has this individual been helpful with the case?"

Aside from one slight glitch . . .

Bishop responded, "Very. See, the perpetrator's a computer expert. We're no match for him without somebody like this person we've been talking about."

Another pause. Chambers said, "I'll say this – I personally don't think he's the devil incarnate like he's made out to be 'round here. There wasn't any good evidence that he cracked our system. But there're plenty of people in Washington who think he did and it's becoming a witch-hunt in the department here. If he did anything illegal he'll go to jail. But I'm on the side that he's innocent until proven otherwise."

"Yessir," Bishop said, then added delicately, "Of course, you could also look at it that if some kid could crack the code maybe you might want to write a better one."

The detective thought: Okay, now, that remark may just get me fired.

But Chambers laughed. He said, "I'm not sure Standard 12 is all it's touted to be. But there're a lot of people involved in encryption here who don't want to hear that. They don't like to get shown up and they really hate it if they get shown up in the media. Now, there's an assistant undersecretary, Peter Kenyon, who'd shit bricks if he thought there was a chance our unnamed individual was out of prison and might end up on the news. See, Kenyon was the one in charge of the task force that commissioned Standard 12."

"I was wondering."

"Kenyon doesn't know the boy's out but he's heard rumors and if he does find out it could be bad for me and for a lot of people." He let Bishop mull these intra-agency politics over for a moment. Chambers then said, "I was a cop before I got into this bureaucracy stuff."

"Where, sir?"

"I was an M.P. in the navy. Spent most of my time in San Diego."

"Broke up some fights, did you?" Bishop asked.

"Only if the army was winning. Listen, Frank, if that boy is helping you catch this perp, okay, go ahead. You can keep him until the release order expires."

"Thank you, sir."

"But I don't need to tell you that *you're* the one who'll get hung out to dry if he hacks into somebody's Web site. Or if he disappears."

"I understand, sir."

"Keep me informed, Frank."

The phone went dead.

Bishop hung up, shook his head.

Sorry. . . .

"What was that all about?" Shelton asked.

But the detective's explanation was interrupted when they head a triumphant shout from Miller. "Got something here!" he called excitedly.

Linda Sanchez was nodding her weary head. "We've managed to recover a list of Web sites Gillette logged on to just before he escaped."

She handed Bishop some printouts. They contained a lot of gibberish, computer symbols and fragments of data and text that made no sense to him. But among the fragments were references to a number of airlines and information about flights that evening from San Francisco International to other countries.

Miller handed him another sheet of paper. "He also down-loaded this – the schedule of buses from Santa Clara to the airport." The pear-shaped detective smiled with pleasure – presumably at having recovered from his earlier bumbling.

"But how would he pay for the airfare?" Shelton wondered out loud.

"Money? Are you kidding?" Tony Mott asked with a sour laugh. "He's probably at an ATM right now, emptying *your* bank account."

Bishop had a thought. He went to the phone in the analysis lab and picked it up, hit REDIAL.

The detective spoke with someone on the other end of the line for a moment. Then he hung up.

Bishop reported his conversation to the team. "The last number Gillette dialed was a Goodwill store a couple of miles from here in Santa Clara. They're closed but the clerk's still there. He said somebody fitting Gillette's description came in about twenty minutes ago. He bought a black trench coat, a pair of white jeans, an Oakland A's cap and a gym bag. He remembered him because he kept looking around and seemed really nervous. Gillette also asked the clerk where the nearest bus stop was. There's one near the store and the airport bus *does* stop there."

Mott said, "It takes the bus about forty-five minutes to get up to the airport." He checked his pistol and started to rise.

"No, Mott," Bishop said. "We've been through this before."

"Come on," the young man urged. "I'm in better shape than ninety percent of the rest of the force. I bicycle a hundred miles a week and I run two marathons a year."

Bishop said, "We're not paying you to run Gillette to ground. You stay here. Or better yet go home and get some rest. You too, Linda. Whatever happens with Gillette we're still going to be working overtime to find the killer."

Mott shook his head, not at all happy about the detective's order. But he agreed.

Bob Shelton said, "We can be at the airport in twenty minutes. I'll call in his description to the Port Authority police. They'll cover all the bus stops. But I tell you – *I'm* personally going to be at the international terminal. I can't wait to see the look in that man's eyes when I say hello." The stocky detective cracked the first smile Bishop had seen in days.

CHAPTER 00010100 / TWENTY

❖

Wyatt Gillette stepped off the bus and watched it pull away from the curb. He looked up into the night sky. Specters of clouds moved quickly overhead and sprinkled droplets of cold rain on the ground. The moisture brought out the smells of Silicon Valley: auto exhaust and the medicinal scent of eucalyptus trees.

The bus – which wasn't bound for the airport at all but was making local stops in Santa Clara County – had deposited him on a dark, empty street in the pleasant suburb of Sunnyvale. He was a good ten miles from the San Francisco airport, where Bishop, Shelton and a slew of police officers would be frantically searching for an Oakland A's fan in white jeans and a black raincoat.

As soon as he'd left the Goodwill store he'd pitched put those clothes and had stolen what he now wore – a tan jacket and blue jeans – from the collection box in front of the shop. The canvas gym bag was the only purchase still with him.

Opening his umbrella and starting up a dimly lit street, Gillette inhaled deeply to calm his nerves. He wasn't worried about recapture – he'd covered his tracks at CCU just fine, logging on to airline Web sites, looking up international flight information then running EmptyShred – to catch the attention of the team and to draw them to the fake clues he'd planted about leaving the country.

No, Gillette was nervous as hell because of where he was now headed.

It was after ten-thirty and many of the houses in this hardworking town were dark, their owners already asleep; days begin early in Silicon Valley.

He walked north, away from El Camino Real, and soon the sound of traffic on that busy commercial street faded.

Ten minutes later he saw the house and slowed down.

No, he reminded himself. Keep going. . . . Don't act suspicious. He started walking again, eyes on the sidewalk, avoiding the glances of the few people on the street: A woman in a silly plastic rain hat, walking her dog. Two men hunched over a car's open hood. One held an umbrella and flashlight while the other struggled with a wrench.

Still, as he drew closer to the house – an old classic California bungalow – Gillette found his steps slowing until, twenty feet away, he stopped altogether. The circuit board in the gym bag, which weighed only a few ounces, seemed suddenly to be heavy as lead.

Go ahead, he told himself. You have to do it. Go on.

A deep breath. He closed his eyes, lowered the umbrella and looked upward. He let the rain fall on his face.

Wondering if what he was about to do was brilliant or completely foolish. What was he risking?

Everything, he thought.

Then he decided that it didn't matter. He had no choice.

Gillette started forward, toward the house.

No more than three seconds later they nailed him.

The dog walker turned suddenly and sprinted toward him, the dog – a German shepherd – growling fiercely. A gun was in the woman's hand and she was shouting, "Freeze, Gillette! Freeze!"

The two men supposedly working on the car also drew weapons and raced toward him, shining flashlights in his eyes.

Dazed, Gillette dropped the umbrella and the gym bag. He lifted his hands and backed up slowly. He felt someone grip his shoulder and he turned. Frank Bishop had come up behind him. Bob Shelton was there too, holding a large black pistol pointed at his chest.

"How did you—?" Gillette began.

But Shelton lashed out with his fist and struck Gillette

squarely in the jaw. His head popped back and, stunned, he fell hard to the sidewalk.

Frank Bishop handed him a Kleenex, nodded toward his jaw.

"You missed some there. No, to the right."

Gillette wiped the blood away.

Shelton's punch hadn't been that hard but his knuckles had cut skin and the rain flowed into it, making the wound sting fiercely.

Other than offering the tissue, Bishop gave no reaction to the blow delivered by his partner. He crouched, opened the canvas bag. He took out the circuit board. He turned it over and over in his hands.

"What is it, a bomb?" he asked with a lethargy that suggested he didn't think it was explosive.

"Just something I made," Gillette muttered, pressing his palm to his nose. "I'd rather you didn't get it wet."

Bishop stood, put it in his pocket. Shelton, his scarred face wet and red, kept staring at him. Gillette tensed slightly, wondering if the cop was going to lose control and hit him again.

"How?" Gillette asked again.

Bishop said, "We *were* on the way to the airport but then I started thinking. If you'd really gone online and looked up something about where you were going, you'd've just destroyed the hard drive and done it as soon as you left. Not timed that program to run later. Which all it did was draw our attention to the clues you'd left about the airport. Like you'd planned, right?"

Gillette nodded.

The detective then added, "And why on earth would you pretend to go to Europe? You'd get stopped at customs."

"I didn't have a lot of time to plan," Gillette muttered.

The detective looked up the street. "You know how we found out you were coming here, don't you?"

Of course he knew. Bishop had called the phone company and learned what number had been dialed from the phone in the lab *before* he'd called Goodwill. Then Bishop had gotten the address of that location – the house in front of them – and they'd staked out the approaches.

If Bishop's handling of the escape had been software, the hacker within Gillette would have called it one moby kludge.

He said, "I should've cracked the switch at Pac Bell and changed the local-call records. I would've done that if I'd had time."

Shock at the arrest was diminishing, replaced by despair – as he looked at the outline of his electronic creation in Bishop's raincoat pocket. How close he'd come to the goal that had obsessed him for months. He looked at the house he'd been headed for. The lights glowed warmly, beckoning.

Shelton said, "You're Shawn, aren't you?"

"No, I'm not. I don't know who Shawn is."

"But you were Valleyman, right?"

"Yes. And I was in the Knights of Access."

"You know Holloway?"

"I *did* know him, yes."

"Jesus Christ," the bulky detective continued, "of *course* you're Shawn. All you assholes have a dozen different IDs. You're him and you're on your way to meet Phate right now." He grabbed the hacker by the collar of his cheap Goodwill jacket.

This time Bishop intervened and touched Shelton's shoulder. The big cop released the hacker but continued in his low, threatening voice, nodding at the house up the street. "Phate's going by the identity of Donald Papandolos. He's the one you called – and you called him a couple of times today from CCU. To tip him off about us. We saw the fucking phone records."

Gillette was shaking his head. "No. I—"

Shelton continued, "We've got tactical troopers surrounding the place. And you're going to help us get him out."

"I have no idea where Phate is. But I'll guarantee you he's not in there."

"Who is, then?" Bishop asked.

"My wife. That's her father's house."

CHAPTER 00010101 / TWENTY-ONE

"Elana's the one I called," Gillette explained. He turned to Shelton. "And you were right. I *did* go online when I first got to CCU. I lied about it. I hacked into DMV to see if she was still living at her father's. Then I called her tonight to see if she was home."

"You're divorced, I thought," Bishop said.

"I *am* divorced." He hesitated. "I still think of her as my wife."

"Elana," Bishop said. "Last name Gillette?"

"No. She went back to her maiden name. Papandolos."

Bishop said to Shelton, "Run the name."

The cop made the call and a moment later nodded. "It's her. This's her address. House owned by Donald and Irene Papandolos. No warrants."

Bishop pulled on a headset mike. He said into his mouthpiece, "Alonso? It's Bishop. We're pretty sure there're only innocents inside the house. Check it out and tell me what you see. . . ." A pause of a few minutes. Then he listened into the microphone. He looked up at Gillette. "There's a woman in her sixties, gray hair."

"Elana's mother. Irene."

"A man in his twenties."

"Curly black hair?"

Bishop repeated the question, listened to the response then nodded.

"That's her brother, Christian."

"And a blonde in her mid-thirties. She's reading to two little boys."

"Elana has dark hair. That's probably Camilla, her sister. She used to be a redhead but she'd change her hair color every few months. The kids're hers. She's got four of them."

Bishop said into the microphone, "Okay, it's sounding legit. Tell everybody to stand down. I'm releasing the scene." The detective asked Gillette, "What's this all about? You were going to check the computer from St. Francis and instead you escaped."

"I *did* check the machine. There was nothing that'd help us find him. As soon as I booted up, the demon sensed something – probably that we'd disconnected the modem – and killed itself. If I'd found anything helpful I would've left you a note."

"Left us a note?" Shelton snapped. "You make it sound like you're running to the goddamn 7-Eleven for cigarettes. You fucking escaped from custody."

"I didn't escape." He pointed at the anklet. "Check out the tracking system. It's set to go back on in an hour. I was going to call you from her house and have somebody come get me and take me back to CCU. I just needed some time to see Ellie."

Bishop eyed the hacker closely then asked, "Does *she* want to see *you?*"

Gillette hesitated. "Probably not. She doesn't know I'm coming."

"But you called her, you said," Shelton pointed out.

"And I hung up as soon as she answered. I just wanted to make sure she was home tonight."

"Why's she living at her parents'?"

"Because of me. She doesn't have any money. She spent it all on my defense and on the fine. . . ." He nodded toward Bishop's pocket. "That's why I've been working on that – what I smuggled out."

"It was hidden under that phone box thing in your pocket, right?"

Gillette nodded.

"I should've had them sweep you with the wand twice. I got careless. What's this thing got to do with your wife?"

"I was going to give it to Ellie. She can patent it and license it to a hardware company. Make some money. It's a new kind of wireless modem you can use with your laptop. You can go online when you're traveling and not have to use your cell phone. It uses global positioning to tell a cellular switch where you are and then automatically links you to the best signal for data transmission. It—"

Bishop waved off the tech-speak. "You made it? With things you found in prison?"

"Found or bought."

"Or *stole*," Shelton said.

"Found or bought," Gillette repeated.

Bishop asked, "Why didn't you tell us you were Valleyman? And that you and Phate were in Knights of Access?"

"Because you'd send me right back to prison. And then I wouldn't've been able to help you track him down." He paused. "And I wouldn't've had a chance to see Ellie. . . . Look, if there was anything I knew about Phate that would've helped catch him I would've told you. Sure, we were in Knights of Access together but that was years ago. In cybergangs you never see the people you're running with – I didn't even know what he looked like, whether he was gay or straight, married or single. All I knew was his real name and that he was in Massachusetts. But you found that out by yourselves at the same time I did. And I never heard about Shawn until today."

Shelton said angrily, "So you were one of those assholes with him – sending out viruses and bomb recipes and shutting down nine-one-one?"

"No," Gillette said adamantly. He went on to explain that for the first year or so Knights of Access *was* one of the world's premiere cybergangs but they never did anything harmful to civilians. They fought hacking battles with other gangs and cracked your typical corporate and government sites. "The worst we did was we wrote our own freeware that did the same things that expensive commercial software did and gave copies away. So a half-dozen big companies lost a few thousand bucks in profit. That's it."

But, he continued, he began to realize there was another person inside of CertainDeath – Holloway's screen name back then. He was becoming dangerous and vindictive and started looking for more and more of a particular type of access – the access that let you hurt people. "He kept getting confused about who was real and who was a character in the computer games he was playing."

Gillette spent long hours instant messaging with Holloway, trying try to talk him out of his more vicious hacks and his plans for "getting even" with people he saw as his enemies.

Finally he cracked Holloway's machine and found, to his shock, that he'd been writing deadly viruses – programs like the one that took down Oakland's 911 system or that would block transmissions from air-traffic controllers to pilots. He downloaded the viruses and wrote inoculations against them then posted those on the Net. Gillette found stolen Harvard University software in Holloway's machine. He sent a copy to the school and to the Massachusetts State Police, along with CertainDeath's e-mail address. Holloway was arrested.

Gillette retired Valleyman as a username and – fully aware of Holloway's vindictive nature – came up with a number of other online identities when he began hacking again.

Shelton said, "Let's get the scumbag back to San Ho. We've wasted enough time."

"No, don't. Please!"

Bishop studied him with some amusement. "You want to keep working with us?"

"I *have* to. You've seen how good Phate is. You need somebody as good as me to stop him."

"Man," Shelton said, laughing. "You've got some balls."

"I know you're good, Wyatt," Bishop said. "But you also just escaped from my custody and that could've cost me my job. It's going to be pretty tough to trust you now, isn't it? We'll make do with somebody else."

"You can't 'make do' when it comes to somebody like Phate. Stephen Miller can't handle it. He's in over his head. Patricia Nolan is just security – as good as they are, security people're always one step behind the hackers. You need somebody who's been in the trenches."

"Trenches," Bishop said softly. The comment seemed to amuse him. He fell silent and finally said, "I believe I'm going to give you one more chance."

Shelton's eyes fluttered with dark resentment. "Bad mistake."

Bishop gave a faint nod, as if acknowledging that it might very well be. Then he said to Shelton, "Tell everybody to get some dinner and a few hours sleep. I'm taking Wyatt back to San Ho for the night."

Shelton shook his head, dismayed at his partner's plans, but went off to do what he'd been asked.

Gillette rubbed his jaw and said, "Give me ten minutes with her."

"Who?"

"My wife."

"You're serious, aren't you?"

"Ten minutes is all I'm asking."

"Not an hour ago I got a call from David Chambers at the Department of Defense, who's about an inch away from rescinding that release order."

"They found out?"

"They sure did. So I'll tell you, son, this fresh air you're breathing and those free hands of yours – those're all just gravy. By rights you should be sleeping on a prison mattress right now." The detective took the hacker's wrist. But before the metal of the cuff closed around it, Gillette asked, "You married, Bishop?"

"Yes, I am."

"Do you love your wife?"

The cop said nothing for a moment. He looked up at the rainy sky then put the cuffs away. "Ten minutes."

He saw her first in silhouette, lit from behind.

But there was no doubt it was Ellie. Her sensuous figure, the mass of long, black hair that became wilder and more tangled as it reached her lower back. Her round face.

The only evidence of the tension she'd surely be feeling was the way she gripped the doorjamb on the other side of the screen. Her pianist's fingers were red from the fierce pressure.

"Wyatt," she whispered. "Did they . . .?"

"Release me?" He shook his head.

A glint in the shadow of her eyes as she looked over his

shoulder and saw vigilant Frank Bishop on the sidewalk.

Gillette continued, "I'm just out for a few days. Sort of a temporary parole. I'm helping them find somebody – Jon Holloway."

She muttered, "Your gang friend."

He asked, "Have you heard from him?"

"Me? No. Why would I? I don't see any of your *friends* anymore." Looking over her shoulder at her sister's children, she stepped farther outside and pulled the door shut, as if she wanted to separate him – and the past – firmly from her present life.

"What are you doing here? How did you know I was . . . Wait. Those phone calls, the hang ups. They came up 'call blocked' on caller ID. That was you."

He nodded. "I wanted to make sure you were home."

"Why?" she asked bitterly.

He hated her tone. He remembered it from the trial. He remembered that single word too. *Why?* She'd asked that often in the days before he went to prison.

Why didn't you give up your goddamn machines? You wouldn't be going to jail, you wouldn't be losing me, if you had. Why?

"I wanted to talk to you," he said to her now.

"We have *nothing* to talk about, Wyatt. We had years to talk – but you had other things to do with your time."

"Please," he said, sensing that she was about to bolt back inside. Gillette heard the desperation in his voice but he was past pride.

"The plants've grown." Gillette nodded toward a thick boxwood. Elana glanced at it and for a moment her façade softened. One balmy November night years ago they'd made love beside that very shrub while her parents were inside, watching election night results.

More memories of their life together flooded into Gillette's thoughts – a health food restaurant in Palo Alto they ate at every Friday, midnight runs for Pop-Tarts and pizza, bicycling through the Stanford campus. For a moment Wyatt Gillette was hopelessly entangled in those memories.

Then Elana's face hardened once more. She gave another glance inside the house through the lace-covered window.

The children, now in their pajamas, trotted out of sight. She turned back and looked at the tattoo of the palm tree and seabird on his arm. Years ago, he'd told her he wanted to get it removed and she'd seemed to like the idea but he never had. Now he felt he'd disappointed her.

"How's Camilla and the kids?"

"Fine."

"Your parents?"

Exasperated, Elana asked, "What do you want, Wyatt?"

"I brought you this."

He handed her the circuit board and explained what it was.

"Why're you giving it to me?"

"It's worth a lot of money." He gave her a technical specification sheet for the device that he'd written out on the bus ride from the Goodwill store. "Find yourself a Sand Hill Road lawyer and sell it to one of the big companies. Compaq, Apple, Sun. They'll want to license it and that's okay but make sure they pay you a big advance up front. Nonreturnable. Not just royalties. The lawyer'll know all about it."

"I don't want it."

"It's not a present. I'm just repaying you. You lost the house and your savings because of me. You should make enough to recover that."

She looked down at the board but didn't take it from his out-stretched hand. "I should go."

"Wait," he said. There was more he'd wanted to say, so much more. He'd rehearsed his speech in prison for days, trying to figure out the best way to present his arguments.

Her strong fingers – tipped in faint purple polish – now kneaded the wet porch banister. She looked out over the rainy yard.

He stared at her, studying her hands, her hair, her chin, her feet.

Don't say it, he told himself. Do. Not. Say. It.

But say it he did. "I love you."

"No," she responded sternly and help up a hand as if to deflect the words.

"I want to try again."

"It's too late for that, Wyatt."

"I was wrong. What I did won't ever happen again."

"Too late," she repeated.

"I got carried away. I wasn't there for you. But I will be. I promise. You wanted children. Well, we can have children."

"You have your machines. Why do you need children?"

"I've changed."

"You've been in jail. You haven't had a chance to prove to anybody – yourself included – that you *can* change."

"I want to have a family with you."

She walked to the door, opened the screen. "I wanted that too. And look what happened."

He blurted, "Don't move to New York."

Elana froze. She turned. "New York?"

"You're moving to New York. With your friend Ed."

"How do you know about Ed?"

Out of control now, he asked, "Are you going to marry him?"

"How do you know about him?" she repeated. "How do you know about New York?"

"Don't do it, Elana. Stay here. Give me a—"

"How?" she snapped.

Gillette looked down at the porch, at the spattering of rain on the gray deck paint. "I cracked your online account and read your e-mail."

"You *what?*" She let the screen door swing shut. Luxurious Greek temper flooded into her beautiful face.

There was no going back now. Gillette blurted, "Do you love Ed? Are you going to marry him?"

"Christ, I don't believe you! From prison? You hacked into my e-mail from prison?"

"Do you love him?"

"Ed's none of your goddamn business. You had every chance in the world to have a family with me and you chose not to. You have absolutely no right to say a word about my personal life!"

"Please—"

"No! Well, Ed and I *are* going to New York. And we leave in three days. And there's not a single goddamn thing in the world you can do to stop me. Goodbye, Wyatt. Don't bother me again."

"I love—"

"You don't love anyone," she interrupted. "You social engineer them."

She walked inside, closing the door quietly.

He walked down the steps to Bishop.

Gillette asked, "What's the phone number at CCU?"

Bishop gave it to him and the hacker wrote the number on the specification sheet and jotted, "Please call me." He wrapped the sheet around the circuit board and left it in the mailbox.

Bishop led him back down the gritty, wet sidewalk. He gave no reaction to what he'd just witnessed on the porch.

As the two of them approached the Crown Victoria, one with perfect posture, the other with a permanent slouch, a man appeared out of the shadows across the street from Elana's house.

He was in his late thirties, thin, with trim hair and a mustache. Gillette's first impression was that he was gay. He was wearing a raincoat but had no umbrella. Gillette noticed that the detective's hand was hovering near his pistol as the man approached.

The stranger slowed and cautiously held up a wallet, revealing a badge and an ID card. "I'm Charlie Pittman. Santa Clara County Sheriff's Department."

Bishop read the card carefully and seemed satisfied with Pittman's credentials.

"You're state police?" Pittman asked.

"Frank Bishop."

Pittman glanced at Gillette. "And you're . . .?"

Before Gillette could speak, Bishop asked, "What can we do for you, Charlie?"

"I'm investigating the Peter Fowler case."

Gillette recalled: He was the gun dealer killed by Phate, along with Andy Anderson, on Hacker's Knoll earlier that day.

Pittman explained, "We heard there was a related operation here tonight."

Bishop shook his head. "False alarm. Nothing that'll help

you out. Good night, sir." He started to walk past, gesturing Gillette to come with him, but Pittman said, "We're swimming upstream on this one, Frank. Anything you can tell us'd be a big help. The Stanford people're all shook up 'cause somebody was selling guns on campus. *We're* the ones they're beating up on."

"We're not pursuing the weapon side of the investigation. We're after the perp who killed Fowler but if you want any information you'll have to go through troop headquarters in San Jose. You know the drill."

"Is that where you're working out of?"

Bishop must've known police politics as well as he knew life on the mean streets of Oakland. He was suitably evasive as he said, "They're the ones you ought to talk to. Captain Bernstein can help you out."

Pittman's deep eyes scanned Gillette up and down. Then he glanced into the murky sky. "I'm sure sick of this weather. Been raining way too long." He looked back to Bishop. "You know, Frank, we get the scut work, we county folks. We're always getting lost in the shuffle and end up having to do the same work somebody else's already done. Get kind of tired of it sometimes."

"Bernstein's a straight shooter. He'll help you out if he can."

Pittman looked over Gillette once more, probably wondering what a skinny young man in a muddy jacket – clearly not a cop – was doing here.

"Good luck to you," Bishop said.

"Thanks, Detective." Pittman walked back into the night.

When they were inside the squad car Gillette said, "I really don't want to go back to San Ho."

"Well, I'm going back to CCU to look over the evidence and grab a few winks. And I didn't see any lockup there."

Gillette said, "I'm not going to escape again."

Bishop didn't respond.

"I don't really want to go back to jail." The detective remained silent and the hacker added, "Handcuff me to a chair if you don't trust me."

Bishop said, "Put your seat belt on."

CHAPTER 00010110 / TWENTY-TWO

———•✦•———

The Junípero Serra School looked idyllic in the early-morning fog.

The exclusive private school, located on eight landscaped acres, was sandwiched between Xerox's Palo Alto Research Center and one of the many Hewlett-Packard facilities near Stanford University. It enjoyed a wonderful reputation and was known for launching virtually all of its students to advanced schools of their (well, their parents') choice. The grounds were beautiful and the staff was paid extremely well.

At the moment, however, the woman who'd been the receptionist of the school for the past few years wasn't basking in the benefits of her working environment; her eyes were filled with tears and she struggled to control the tremors in her voice. "My God, my God," she whispered. "Joyce just dropped her off a half-hour ago. I saw her. She was fine. I mean, just a half *hour*."

Standing in front of her was a young man, with reddish hair and mustache, wearing an expensive business suit. His eyes were red, as if he'd been crying too, and he clasped his hands in a way that suggested that he was very upset. "She and Don were driving to Napa for the day. To the vineyard. They were meeting some of Don's investors for lunch."

"What happened?" she asked breathlessly.

"One of those buses with migrant workers . . . it veered right into them."

"Oh, God," she muttered again. Another woman walked past and the receptionist said, "Amy, come here."

The woman, wearing a bright red suit and carrying a sheet of paper headed with the words "Lesson Plan," walked to the desk. The receptionist whispered, "Joyce and Don Wingate were in an accident."

"No!"

"It sounds bad." The receptionist nodded. "This's Don's brother, Irv."

They nodded and stricken Amy said, "How are they?"

The brother swallowed and cleared his emotion-thickend throat. "They'll live. At least that's what the doctors're saying now. But they're both unconscious still. My brother broke his back." He forced back tears.

The receptionist wiped away her own. "Joyce's so active in the PTA. Everybody loves her. What can we do?"

"I don't know yet," Irv said, shaking his head. "I'm not thinking real clearly."

"No, no, of course not."

Amy said, "But everybody at the school'll be here for you, whatever you need." Amy summoned a stocky woman in her fifties. "Oh, Mrs. Nagler!"

The gray-suited woman approached and glanced at Irv, who nodded at her. "Mrs. Nagler," he said. "You're the director here, right?"

"That's right."

"I'm Irv Wingate, Samantha's uncle. I met you at the spring recital last year."

She nodded and shook his hand.

Wingate recapped the story of the accident.

"Oh, my God, no," Mrs. Nagler whispered. "I'm so sorry."

Irv said, "Kathy – that's my wife – she's up there now. I'm here to pick up Sammie."

"Of course."

But Mrs. Nagler, sympathetic though she was, nonetheless ran a tight ship and wasn't going to deviate from the rules. She leaned over the computer keyboard and typed with blunt, polish-free nails on the keys. She read the screen and then said, "You're on the authorized list of relatives to release Samantha to." She hit another key and a picture popped up – the driver's license photo of Irving Wingate. She looked up at him. It was a perfect match. Then she said, "But I'm afraid there're two other things we have to verify. First, could I see your driver's license, please?"

"Sure." He displayed the card. It matched both his appearance and the photo on the computer.

"Just one more thing. I'm sorry. Your brother was very security minded, you know."

"Oh, sure," Irv said. "The password." He whispered to her, "It's S-H-E-P." Mrs. Nagler nodded in confirmation. Irv gazed out the window at the liquid sunlight falling on a boxwood hedge. "That was Donald's first Airedale, Shep. We got it when he was twelve. He was a great dog. He still raises them, you know."

Mrs. Nagler said sadly, "I know. We sometimes e-mail each other pictures of our dogs. I've got two weimaraners." Her voice faded and she put this sorrowful thought away. She made a call, spoke to the girl's teacher and asked that she be brought to the main reception area.

Irv said, "Don't say anything to Sammie, please. I'll break the news to her on the way up."

"Of course."

"We'll stop for breakfast on the way. Egg McMuffins're her favorite."

Amy of the crimson suit choked at this bit of trivia. "That's what she had on the class trip to Yosemite. . . ." She covered her eyes and cried silently for a moment.

An Asian woman – presumably the girl's teacher – led a skinny redheaded girl into the office. Mrs. Nagler smiled and said, "Your uncle Irving's here."

"Irv," he corrected. "She calls me Uncle Irv. Hi, Sammie."

"Wow, you grew your mustache back like totally fast."

Wingate laughed. "Your aunt Kathy said I looked more distinguished." He crouched down. "Listen, your mommy and daddy decided you could take the day off school. We're going to go spend the day with them in Napa."

"They went up to the vineyard?"

"That's right."

A frown crossed the girl's freckled face. "Dad said they couldn't go till next week. Because of the painters."

"They changed their mind. And you get to go up there with me."

"Cool!"

The teacher said, "You go get your book bag now. Okay?"

The girl ran off and Mrs. Nagler told the teacher what'd happened. "Oh, no," the woman whispered as she shouldered her portion of the tragedy. A few minutes later Samantha reappeared, her heavy book bag hooked over her shoulder. She and Uncle Irv started out the door. The receptionist said to Mrs. Nagler, "Thank God she'll be in good hands."

And Irv Wingate must've heard her say this because he turned and nodded. Still, the receptionist did a brief double take; the smile he offered seemed just a little off, like an eerie gloat. But the woman decided she was wrong and put the look down to the terrible stress the poor man had to be under.

"Rise and shine," the snappy voice said.

Gillette opened his eyes and looked up at Frank Bishop, who was shaved and showered and absently tucking in his ornery shirttail.

"It's eight-thirty," Bishop said. "They let you sleep late at prison?"

"I was up till four," the hacker grumbled. "I couldn't get comfortable. But that's not really a surprise, is it?" He nodded at the large iron chair that Bishop had handcuffed him to.

"It was your idea, the cuffs and the chair."

"I didn't think you'd take it literally."

"What's to take literally?" Bishop asked. "Either you handcuff somebody to a chair or you don't."

The detective unhooked Gillette and the hacker rose stiffly, rubbing his wrist. He went into the kitchen and got coffee and a day-old bagel.

"By any chance, you ever get any Pop-Tarts around here?" Gillette called, returning to the main room of CCU.

"I don't know," Bishop responded. "This isn't my office, remember? Anyway, I'm not much for sweets. People should have bacon and eggs for breakfast. You know, hearty food." He sipped his coffee. "I was watching you – when you were asleep."

Gillette didn't know what to do with that. He lifted an eyebrow.

"You were typing in your sleep."

"They call it *keying* nowadays, not *typing.*"

"Did you know you did that?"

The hacker nodded. "Ellie used to tell me I did. I sometimes dream in code."

"You do what?"

"I see script in my dreams – you know, lines of software source code. In Basic or C++ or Java." He looked around. "Where is everybody?"

"Linda and Tony're on their way. Miller too. Linda's still not a grandmother. Patricia Nolan called from her hotel." He held Gillette's eyes for a moment. "She asked if you were okay."

"She did?"

The detective nodded with a smile. "Gave me hell for cuffing you to the chair. She said you could've spent the night on the couch in her hotel room. Make of that what you will."

"Shelton?"

Bishop said, "He's at home with his wife. I called him but there was no answer. Sometimes he just has to disappear and spend time with her – you know, because that trouble I told you about before. His son dying."

A beep sounded from a nearby workstation. Gillette rose and went to look at the screen. His tireless bot had worked through the night, traveling the globe and it now had another prize to show for its efforts. He read the message and told Bishop, "Triple-X's online again. He's back in the hacker chat room."

Gillette sat down at the computer.

"We going to social engineer him again?" Bishop asked.

"No. I've got another idea."

"What?"

"I'm going to try the truth."

Tony Mott sped his expensive Fisher bicycle east, along

Stevens Creek Boulevard, outpacing many of the cars and trucks, and turned fast into the Computer Crimes Unit parking lot.

He always rode the 6.3 miles from his home in Santa Clara to the CCU building at a good pace – the lean, muscular cop bicycled as fast as he did all his other sports, whether he was skiing the chutes at A-basin in Colorado, heli-skiing in Europe, white-water rafting or rapelling down the sheer rock faces of the mountains he loved to climb.

But today he'd biked particularly fast, thinking that sooner or later he'd wear down Frank Bishop – the way he hadn't been able to wear down Andy Anderson – and strap on body armor and do some real police work. He'd worked hard at the academy and, though he was a good cybercop, his assignment at CCU wasn't any more exciting than working on a graduate thesis. It was as if he were being discriminated against just because of his 3.97 grade point average at MIT.

Hooking the old, battered Kryptonite lock through the frame of his cycle, he glanced up to see a slim, mustachioed man in a raincoat striding up to him.

"Hi," the man offered, smiling.

"Hi, there."

"I'm Charlie Pittman, Santa Clara County Sheriff's Department."

Mott shook the offered hand. He knew many of the county detectives and didn't recognize this man but he gave a fast glance at the ID badge dangling from his neck and saw that the picture matched.

"You must be Tony Mott."

"Right."

The county cop admired the Fisher. "I heard that you cycle like a son of a bitch."

"Only when I'm going downhill," Mott said, smiling modestly, even though the truth was that, yes, he *did* cycle like a son of a bitch, whether it was downhill, uphill or on the flats.

Pittman laughed too. "I don't get half the exercise I should. Especially when we're after some perp like this computer guy."

Funny – Mott hadn't heard anything about somebody from the county working the case. "You going inside?" Mott pulled off his helmet.

"I was just in there. Frank was briefing me. This is one crazy case."

"I hear that," Mott agreed, stuffing the shooting gloves that doubled as biking gloves in the waistband of his spandex shorts.

"That guy that Frank's been using – that consultant? The young guy?"

"You mean Wyatt Gillette?"

"Yeah, that's his name. He really knows his stuff, doesn't he?"

"The man is a wizard," Mott said.

"How long's he going to be helping you out?"

"Till we catch this asshole, I guess."

Pittman looked at his watch. "I better run. I'll check in later."

Tony Mott nodded as Pittman walked away, pulling out his cell phone and placing a call. The county cop walked all the way through the CCU parking lot and into the one next door. Mott noticed this and thought momentarily that it was odd he'd parked that far away when there were plenty of spaces right in front of CCU. But then he started toward the office, thinking of nothing except the case and how, one way or another, he was going to finagle a spot on the dynamic entry team when they kicked in the door to collar Jon Patrick Holloway.

"Ani, Ani, Animorphs," the little girl said.

"What?" Phate asked absently. They were driving in an Acura Legend, which had been recently stolen but was duly registered to one of his identities, en route to the basement of his house in Los Altos, where duct tape, the Ka-bar knife and a digital camera awaited little Samantha Wingate's arrival.

"Ani, Ani, Animorphs. Hey, Uncle Irv, you like Animorphs?"

No, not one fucking little bit, thought Phate. But Uncle Irv said, "You bet I do."

"Why was Mrs. Gitting upset?" Sammie Wingate asked.

"Who?"

"The lady at the front desk."

"I don't know."

"Like, are Mom and Dad in Napa already?"

"That's right."

Phate didn't have a clue where they were. But wherever it was he knew they'd be enjoying the last moments of peace before the storm of horror descended. It was only a matter of minutes before somebody from the Junípero Serra School started calling the Wingates' friends and family and would learn that there'd been no accident.

Phate wondered who'd feel the greatest level of panic: the parents of the missing child or the principal and teachers who'd released her to a killer?

"Ani, Ani, Ani, Ani, Animorphs. Who's your favorite?"

"Favorite what?" Phate asked.

"What do you think?" little Samantha asked – a bit disrespectfully, thought both Phate and Uncle Irv.

The girl said, "Favorite *Animorph.* I think Rachel's my favorite. She turns into a lion. I made up this story about her. And it was totally cool. What happened was—"

Phate listened to the inane story as the girl continued to drone on and on. The little brat kept up the prattle without the least encouragement from old Uncle Irv, whose only comfort at the moment was the razor-sharp knife at home and the anticipation of Donald Wingate's reaction when the businessman received the plastic bag containing a rather gruesome present later that day. In accordance with the point system in the Access game, Phate himself would be the deliveryman who dropped off the package and got the signature of D. Wingate on the receipt. This would earn him 25 points, the highest for any particular murder.

He reflected on his social engineering at the school. Now *that* had been a good hack. Challenging yet clean (even though uncooperative Uncle Irv apparently had shaved off his mustache after his last driver's license photo).

The girl bounced obnoxiously on her seat. "You think we can ride that pony Dad got me? Man, that is so neat.

Billy Tomkins was talking all about this stupid dog he got, like, who *doesn't* have a dog? I mean, everybody has a dog. But *I've* got a pony."

Phate glanced at the girl. Her perfectly done hair. The expensive watch whose leather band she'd defaced with indecipherable pictures drawn in ink. The shoes polished by someone else. The cheesy breath.

He decided that Sammie wasn't like Jamie Turner, whom he'd been reluctant to kill because he reminded him so much of himself. No, *this* kid was like all the other little shits who'd made young Jon Patrick Holloway's life at school pure hell.

Taking some pictures of little Samantha before the trip to the basement and little Samantha after – now, *that* would give him a great deal of satisfaction.

"You want to ride on Charizard, Uncle Irv?"

"Who?" Phate asked.

"Duh, my *pony.* The one Dad got me for my birthday. You were, like, there."

"Right. I forgot."

"Dad and me go riding sometimes. Charizard's pretty cool. He knows his way back to the barn all by himself. Or, I know, you could take Dad's horse and we could go around the lake together. *If* you can keep up."

Phate wondered if he could wait long enough to get the girl into the basement.

Suddenly a loud beeping filled the car and, as the girl continued to prattle on about morphing dogs or lions or whatever, Phate pulled the pager off his belt and scrolled through the display.

His reaction was an audible gasp.

The gist of Shawn's message was that Wyatt Gillette was at CCU headquarters.

Phate felt the shock as if he'd touched a live wire. He had to pull off the road.

Jesus in Heaven. . . . Gillette – Valleyman – was helping the cops! *That's* why they'd learned so much about him and were so close on his trail. Instantly hundreds of memories from the Knights of Access days came back to him. The incredible hacks. The hours and hours of mad conversations, typing as fast as they could out of fear that an idea might escape. The paranoia. The risks. The exhilaration of going places online where nobody else could go.

And just yesterday he'd been thinking about that article Gillette had written. He remembered the last line: *Once you've spent time in the Blue Nowhere, you can never completely return to the Real World.*

Valleyman – whose childlike curiosity and dogged nature didn't let him rest until he'd understood everything there was to know about something new to him.

Valleyman – whose brilliance in writing code approached and sometimes surpassed Phate's own.

Valleyman – whose betrayal had destroyed Holloway's life and shattered the Great Social Engineering. And who was alive now only because Phate hadn't yet focused on killing him.

"Uncle Irv, um, how come we're stopped here? I mean, is there something wrong with the car?"

He glanced at the girl. Then looked around the deserted road.

"Well, Sammie, you know what – I think there may be. How 'bout you take a look?"

"Um, me?"

"Yeah."

"I'm not sure what to do."

"Just see if the tire's flat," kindly Uncle Irv said. "Could you do that?"

"I guess. Like, which tire?"

"Right rear."

The girl looked left.

Phate pointed the other way.

"Um, okay, that one. What should I look for?"

"Well, what would the Animorphs look for?"

"I don't know. Maybe if there was a nail in it or something."

"That's good. Why don't you look and see if there's a nail."

"Okay."

Phate unhooked the girl's seat belt.

Then he reached across Sammie for the door handle.

"I can do it myself," she said defiantly. "You don't have to."

"Okay." Phate sat back and watched the girl fumble with the latch then push the door open.

Sammie got out and walked to the back of the car. "It looks okay to me," she called.

"Good," Phate called. And gunned the engine, racing forward. The door slammed shut and the tires sprayed Sammie with dust and gravel. She started to scream, "Wait, Uncle Irv . . ."

Phate skidded onto the highway.

The sobbing girl ran after the car but she was soon obscured by a huge cloud of dust from the spinning wheels. Phate, for his part, had stopped thinking about little Samantha Wingate the moment the door slammed.

CHAPTER 00010111 / TWENTY-THREE

—•◆◆◆•—

> Renegade334: Triple-X, it's me again. I want
> to talk to you. NBS.

"The acronym means No bullshit," Patricia Nolan explained to Frank Bishop as they gazed at the computer screen in front of Wyatt Gillette.

Nolan had arrived from her hotel a few minutes before, as Gillette was hurrying to a nearby workstation. She'd hovered near him as if she was about to hug him good morning. But she seemed to sense his complete concentration and chose not to. She pulled up a chair and sat close to the monitor. Tony Mott too sat nearby. Bob Shelton had called and told Bishop that his wife was sick and that he'd be in late.

Gillette typed another message and hit RETURN.

> Renegade334: Are you there? I want to talk.

"Come on," Gillette encouraged in a whisper. "Come on. . . . Talk to me."

Finally an ICU window opened and Triple-X responded.

> Triple-X: You're keying a lot fucking better
> now. Grammar and spelling too. BTW, I'm
> launching from an anonymous platform in
> Europe. You can't trace me.

> Renegade334: We're not trying to. I'm sorry

```
about before. About trying to trick you.
We're desperate. We need your help. I'm
asking for your help.

Triple-X: Who the fuck are you?

Renegade334: You ever hear of Knights of
Access?

Triple-X: EVERYBODY'S heard of KOA. You're
saying you were in it?

Renegade334: I'm Valleyman.

Triple-X: You're Valleyman? NFW.
```

"No fucking way," Tony Mott translated this one for Bishop.

The door to CCU opened and Stephen Miller and Linda Sanchez arrived. Bishop briefed them about what was going on.

```
Renegade334: I am. Really

Triple-X: If you are then tell me what you
cracked six years ago — the big one, you
know what I mean.
```

"He's testing me," Gillette said. "He probably heard about a KOA hack from Phate and wants to see if I know it." He typed:

```
Renegade334: Fort Meade.
```

Fort Meade, Maryland, was home of the National Security Agency and had more supercomputers than anywhere in the world. It also had the tightest security of any government installation.

"Jesus Christ," Mott whispered. "You cracked Meade?"

Gillette shrugged. "Just the Internet connection. Not the black boxes."

"But still, Jesus. . . ."

Triple-X: So how did you get through their
firewalls?

Renegade334: We heard NSA was installing a
new system. We got in through the sendmail
flaw in Unix. We had three minutes after
they installed the machine before they
loaded the patch to fix it. That's when we
got in.

The famous sendmail flaw was a bug in an early version
of Unix, later fixed, that let someone send a certain type of
e-mail to the root user – the systems administrator – that
would sometimes let the sender seize control of the
computer.

Triple-X: Man, you're a wizard. Everybody's
heard about you. I thought you were in jail.

Renegade334: I am. I'm in custody. But
don't worry – they're not after you.

Mott whispered, "Please. . . . Don't run for the hills."

Triple-X: What do you want?

Renegade334: We're trying to find Phate –
Jon Holloway.

Triple-X: Why do you want him?

Gillette looked at Bishop, who nodded his okay to tell all.

Renegade334: He's killing people.

Another pause. Gillette typed invisible messages in the air
for thirty seconds before Triple-X replied.

Triple-X: I heard rumors. He's using that
program of his, Trapdoor to go after people,
right?

Renegade334: That's right.

Triple-X: I KNEW he'd use it to hurt people.
That man is one sick MF.

No translation necessary for *those* initials, Gillette
concluded.

Triple-X: What do you want from me?

Renegade334: Help finding him.

Triple-X: IDTS.

Bishop tried, "I don't think so."
Linda Sanchez laughed. "That's it, boss. You're learning
the lingo." Gillette noticed that Bishop had finally earned
the title, "boss," which Sanchez had apparently reserved for
Andy Anderson.

Renegade334: We need help.

Triple-X: You have no clue how dangerous
that fucker is. He's psycho. He'll come after
me.

Renegade334: You can change your username
and system address.

Triple-X: LTW.

Nolan said to Bishop, "Like, that'd work. Sarcastic."

Triple-X: He'd find me in ten minutes.

Renegade334: Then stay offline till we get him.

Triple-X: And when you were hacking was there a single day you weren't online?

Now Gillette paused. Finally he typed:

Renegade334: No.

Triple-X: And you want me to risk my life and stay off the Net because you can't find this asshole?

Renegade334: He's KILLING civilians.

Triple-X: He could be watching us now. Trapdoor could be in your machine right now. Or mine. He could be watching everything we're writing.

Renegade334: No, he's not. I could feel him if he was. And you could feel him too. You've got the touch, right?

Triple-X: True.

Renegade334: We know he likes snuff pics and crime scene photos. Do you have anything he's sent you?

Triple-X: No, I wiped everything. I didn't want any connection with him.

Renegade334: Do you know Shawn?

Triple-X: He hangs with Phate is all I know. Word is Phate couldn't hack Trapdoor together by himself and Shawn helped him.

Renegade334: He a wizard too?

```
Triple-X: That's what I hear. And that HE'S
fucking scary too.

Renegade334: Where is Shawn?

Triple-X: Got the idea he's in the Bay area.
But that's all I know.

Renegade334: You sure it's a man?

Triple-X: No, but how many skirt hackers
you know?

Renegade334: Will you help us? We need
Phate's real e-mail address, Internet
address, web sites he visits, FTP sites he
uploads to — anything like that.
```

Gillette said to Bishop, "He won't want to contact us online or here at CCU. Give me your cell phone number."

Bishop did and Gillette relayed it to Triple-X. The man didn't acknowledge receiving the number and typed only:

```
Triple-X: I'm logging off. We've been talking
too long. I'll think about it.

Renegade334: We need your help.
Please. . . .

Triple-X: That's weird.

Renegade334: What?

Triple-X: I don't think I ever saw a hacker
write please before.
```

The connection terminated.

After Phate had learned that Wyatt Gillette was helping the cops look for him and had left the little Animorph crying by the side of the road he'd ditched his car – the whiny brat could identify it – and bought a used clunker with cash. He then sped through the chill overcast to the warehouse he rented near San Jose.

When he played his Real World game of Access he'd travel to a different city and set up house for a while but this warehouse was more or less his permanent residence. It was where he kept everything that was important to him.

If, in a thousand years, archaeologists dug through layers of sand and loam and found this webby, dust-filled place they might believe that they'd discovered a temple from the early computer age, as significant a find as explorer Howard Carter's unearthing the tomb of pharaoh Tutankhamen in Egypt.

Here in this cold, empty space – an abandoned dinosaur pen – were all of Phate's treasures. A complete EAI TR-20 analog computer from the sixties, a 1956 Heath electronic analog kit computer, Altair 8800 and 680b computers, a twenty-five-year-old IBM 510 portable, a Commodore KIM-1, the famous TRS-80, a Kaypro portable, a COSMAC VIP, a number of Apples and Macs, tubes from the original Univac, brass gears and a number disk from a prototype of Charles Babbage's never-completed Difference Engine from the 1800s and notes about it jotted down by Ada Byron – Lord Byron's daughter and Babbage's companion – who wrote instructions for his machines and is therefore considered the world's first computer programmer. Dozens of other items of hardware too.

On shelves were all the Rainbow Books – the technical manuals that cover every aspect of computer networking and security, their jackets standing out in the gloom with their distinctive oranges, reds, yellows, aquas, lavenders and teal greens.

Perhaps Phate's favorite souvenir was a framed poster of correspondence bearing the letterhead of the Traf-O-Data company, Bill Gates's original name for Microsoft.

But the warehouse was not simply a museum. It served a purpose too. Here were rows and rows of boxes of disks, a dozen working computers and perhaps two million dollars' worth of specialized computer components, most of them for supercomputer construction and repair. Buying and selling these products through shell companies was how Phate made his substantial income.

This also was his staging area – where he planned his games and where he changed his description and personality. Most of his costumes and disguises were here. In the corner was an ID 4000 – a security identification pass maker – complete with magnetic strip burner. Other machines let him make *active* identification cards, which broadcast passwords for access to particularly secure facilities. With these machines – and a brief hack into the Department of Motor Vehicles, various schools and departments of vital records – he could become anyone he wanted to be and create the documentation to prove it. He could even write himself a passport.

Who do you want to be?

He now surveyed his equipment. From a shelf above his desk he took a cell phone and several powerful Toshiba laptops, into one of which he loaded a jpeg – a compressed photo image. He also found a large disk-storage box, which would serve his needs nicely.

The shock and dismay of finding that Valleyman was among his adversaries was gone and had turned to electric excitement. Phate was now thrilled that the game he was playing had taken a dramatic twist, one that was familiar to anybody who'd ever played Access or other MUD games: This was the moment when the plot turns 180 degrees and the hunters became the prey.

Cruising through the Blue Nowhere like a dolphin, in coves close to shore, in open sea, breaking the surface or nosing through dim vegetation on the impenetrable bottom, Wyatt Gillette's tireless bot sent an urgent message back to its master.

In CCU headquarters the computer beeped.

"What do we have?" Patricia Nolan asked.

Gillette nodded at the screen.

```
Search results:
Search request: "Phate"
Location: Newsgroup: alt.pictures.true.crime
Status: Posted message
```

* * *

Gillette's face bristled with excitement. He called to Bishop, "Phate's posted something himself." He called up the message.

```
Message-ID:
<1000423454210815.NP16015@k2rdka>
X-Newsposter: newspost-1.2
Newsgroups: alt.pictures.true.crime
From: <phate@icsnet.com>
To: Group
Subject: A recent character
Encoding: .jpg
Lines: 1276
NNTP-Posting-Date: 2 April
Date: 2 Apr 11:12 a.m.
Path:news.newspost.com!southwest.com!newsc
om.mesh.ad.jp!counterculturesystems.com!lari
vegauche.fr.net!frankfrt.de.net!swip.net!newss
erve.deluxe.interpost.net!internet.gateway.net!
roma.internet.it!globalsystems.uk!

Remember: All the world's a MUD, and the
people in it merely characters.
```

No one could figure out what Phate's paraphrase of Shakespeare might mean.

Until Gillette downloaded the picture that was attached to the message.

It slowly appeared on the screen.

"Oh, my God," Linda Sanchez muttered, her eyes fixed on the terrible image.

"Son of a bitch," Tony Mott whispered. Stephen Miller said nothing at first then he looked away.

On the screen was a picture of Lara Gibson. She was half naked and lying on a tile floor – in a basement somewhere, it appeared. There were slashes on her body and she was covered with blood. Her dim eyes were gazing hopelessly at the camera. Gillette, sickened by the picture, supposed that it had been taken when she'd had only a few minutes left to live. He – like Stephen Miller – had to turn away.

Bishop asked, "That address? Phate@icsnet.com? Any chance it's real?"

Gillette ran his HyperTrace and checked the address.

"Fake," he said, not surprising anyone with this news.

Miller suggested, "The picture – we know Phate's in the area here somewhere. How about if you send troopers to canvass the one-hour photo-processing places? They might recognize it."

Before Gillette could respond Patricia Nolan said impatiently, "He's not going to risk taking film to a photo lab. He'll use a digital camera."

Even nontechno Frank Bishop had figured this out.

"So, this isn't any help to us," the detective said.

"Well, it might be," Gillette said. He leaned forward and tapped the screen, indicating the line that was labeled Path. He reminded Bishop about the pathway in e-mail headers, which identified the networks that Phate's message had made its way through to get to the computer server they'd downloaded it from.

"They're just like street directions. The hacker in Bulgaria? Vlast? *His* path listings were all faked. But this one might be real or at least have some networks that Phate really used to upload the Gibson woman's picture."

Gillette began checking every network listed in the Path heading with HyperTrace. The program revealed that one was legitimate.

"*That's* the network Phate's computer was actually connected to: newsserve.deluxe.interpost.net."

Gillette ordered HyperTrace to dig up more information about the company. In a moment, this popped up on the screen:

```
Domain Name: Interpost.net
Registered to: Interpost Europe SA
23443 Grand Palais
Bruges, Belgium
Services: Internet Service Provider, Web
hosting, anonymous browsing and remailing.
```

"It's a chainer," Gillette said, shaking his head. "I'm not surprised."

Nolan explained to Bishop why this was discouraging: "It's a service that hides your identity when you send e-mails or post messages."

Gillette continued, "Phate sent the picture to Interpost and their computers stripped out his real return address, added the fake ones in place of his and then sent it on its way."

"We can't trace it?" Bishop asked.

"No," Nolan said. "It's a dead end. That's why Phate didn't bother to write a fake header, the way Vlast did."

"Well," the cop pointed out, "*Interpost* knows where Phate's computer is. Let's get their phone number, call them up and find out."

The hacker shook his head. "Chainers stay in business because they guarantee that *nobody* can find out who the sender is, even the police."

"So we're dead in the water," Bishop said.

But Wyatt Gillette said, "Not necessarily. I think we ought to do some more fishing." And he loaded one of his own search engines into the CCU machine.

CHAPTER 00011000 / TWENTY-FOUR

———◆◆◆———

As the computer at the state police's CCU was sending out a request for information about Interpost, Phate sat in the Bay View Motel, a decrepit inn along a sandy stretch of commercial sprawl in Freemont, California, just north of San Jose. Staring at the laptop's monitor, he was following the progress of Gillette's search.

Gillette would of course know that a foreign chainer like Interpost wouldn't give any U.S. cop as much as the courtesy of a reply to a request for a client's identity. So, as Phate had anticipated, Gillette had used a search engine to look for general information about Interpost, in hopes of retrieving something that might let the cops beg or bribe some cooperation from the Belgium Internet service.

Within seconds Gillette's search engine had found dozens of sites in which Interpost was mentioned and was shooting their names and addresses back to the CCU computer. But the packets of data that made up this information took a detour – they were diverted to Phate's laptop. Trapdoor then modified the packets to insert its hardworking demon and sent them on their way to CCU.

Phate now got this message:

Trapdoor
Link complete
Do you wish to enter subject's computer? Y/N

Phate keyed Y, hit ENTER and a moment later was wandering around inside CCU's system.

He typed more commands and began looking through files, reflecting that the cops at CCU had thought that, like some slobbering serial killer, Phate had posted the picture of the dying Gibson woman just to threaten them or to get off on some weird sado-sexual exhibitionist thing. But no, he'd posted the picture as bait – to find the Internet address of the CCU machine. Once he'd uploaded the picture he'd instructed a bot to tell him the address of everybody who'd downloaded it. One of those had been a California state government computer in the western San Jose area – which had to be the CCU office.

Phate now raced through the police computer, copying information, then he went straight to a folder labeled Personnel Records – Computer Crimes Unit.

The contents were – not surprisingly – encrypted. Phate pulled down a screen window on Trapdoor and clicked on Decrypt. The program went to work to crack the code.

As the hard drive moaned, Phate stood and fetched a Mountain Dew from a cooler sitting on the motel room floor. He stirred in a No-Doz and, sipping the sweet drink, walked to the window, where shafts of brilliant sunlight had momentarily broken through the storm clouds. The flood of jarring light agitated him and he pulled the shade down quickly, then turned back to the muted colors of the computer screen, which were far more pleasing to him than God's palette could ever be.

"We've got him," Gillette announced to the team. "Phate's inside our machine. Let's start the trace."

"All right!" Tony Mott said, offering an deafening whistle of victory.

Gillette began HyperTrace and, with faint pings, one by one the route between CCU's computer and Phate's appeared on the screen as a tiny yellow line.

"Our boy's good, whatta you say, boss?" Linda Sanchez offered, nodding an admiring head toward Gillette.

"Looks like he got it right," Bishop said.

Ten minutes before, Gillette had had a thought: that Phate's message was a feint. He decided that the killer had been setting them up like a master MUD player and that he'd posted the picture of Lara not to taunt or threaten them but so he could find out CCU's Internet address and get inside their computer.

Gillette had explained this to the team and then added, "And we're going to let him."

"So *we* can trace *him*," Bishop said.

"You got it," Gillette confirmed.

Waving a hand at the CCU machines, Stephen Miller protested, "But we can't let him in our system."

Gillette said shortly, "I'll transfer out all the real data to backup tapes and load some encrypted files. While he's trying to decrypt them we'll track him down."

Bishop agreed and Gillette had transferred all the sensitive data, like the real personnel files, to tape and replaced them with scrambled files. Then Gillette sent out a search request about Interpost and, when the results came back, the Trapdoor demon came with them.

"It's like he's a rapist," Linda Sanchez said, seeing the folders in their system opening and closing as Phate examined them.

Violation is the crime of the new century. . . .

"Come on, come on," Gillette encouraged his HyperTrace program, which was issuing faint sonar pings each time another link in the chain of connection was identified.

"What if *he's* using an anonymizer?" Bishop asked.

"I doubt that he is. If I were him I'd be doing a hit and run, probably logging on from a pay phone or hotel room. And I'd be using a hot machine."

Nolan explained, "That's a computer you use once and abandon. It doesn't have anything on it that could be traced back to you."

Gillette sat forward, staring intently at the screen as the HyperTrace lines slowly made their way from CCU toward Phate. Finally they stopped at a location northeast of them. "I've got his service provider!" he shouted, reading the information on the screen. "He's dialing into ContraCosta

On-Line in Oakland." He turned to Stephen Miller. "Get Pac Bell on it now!"

The phone company would complete the trace from ContraCosta On-Line to Phate's machine itself. Miller spoke urgently to the Pac Bell security staff.

"Just a few more minutes," Nolan said, her voice edgy. "Stay on the line, stay on the line . . . Please."

Then Stephen Miller, on the phone, stiffened and his face broke into a smile. He said, "Pac Bell's got him! He's in the Bay View Motel – in Fremont."

Bishop pulled out his cell phone. He called central dispatch and had them alert the tactical team. "Silent roll up," he ordered. "I want troopers there in five minutes. He's probably sitting in front of the window, watching the parking lot, with his car running. Let the SWAT folks know that." Then he contacted Huerto Ramirez and Tim Morgan and directed them to the motel too.

Tony Mott saw this as one more chance to play real cop. This time, though, Bishop surprised him. "Okay, Officer, you're coming along on this one. Only you stay to the rear."

"Yessir," the young cop said gravely and pulled an extra box of bullets from his desk.

Bishop nodded at Mott's belt. "I think the two clips you've got with you'll be enough."

"Sure. Okay." Though when Bishop turned away Mott slipped a furtive handful of bullets into his windbreaker pocket.

Bishop said to Gillette, "You come with me. We'll stop by Bob Shelton's place, pick him up. It's on the way. Then let's go catch ourselves a killer."

Detective Robert Shelton lived in a modest neighborhood of San Jose not far from the 280 freeway.

The yards of the houses were filled with the plastic toys of youngsters, the driveways with inexpensive cars – Toyotas and Fords and Chevys.

Frank Bishop pulled up to the house. He didn't get out immediately but appeared to be debating. Finally he said, "Just want to let you know, about Bob's wife. . . . Their son dying in that car crash? She never really got over it.

She drinks a bit too much. Bob says she's sick. But that's not what it is."

"Got it."

They walked to the house. Bishop pushed the doorbell button. There was no ring inside but they could hear muted voices. Angry voices.

Then a scream.

Bishop glanced at Gillette, hesitated a moment then tried the door. It was unlocked. He pushed inside, his hand on his pistol. Gillette entered after him.

The house was a mess. Dirty dishes, magazines, clothes littered the living room. There was a sour smell to the place – unwashed clothing and liquor. An uneaten meal for two – sad-looking American cheese sandwiches – was on the table. It was 12:30, lunchtime, but Gillette couldn't tell if the food was meant for today or leftover from yesterday or even before. They couldn't see anyone but heard a crash and footsteps from a back room.

Both Bishop and Gillette were startled by a shout – a woman's slurred voice: "I'm fucking fine! You think you can control me. I don't know why the hell you think that. . . . *You're* the reason I'm not fine."

"I'm not—" Bob Shelton's voice said. But his words were lost in another crash as something fell – or maybe was flung by his wife. "Oh, Jesus," he shouted. "Now look what you've done."

The hacker and the detective stood helplessly in the living room, not sure what to do now that they'd intruded on this difficult domestic situation.

"I'm cleaning it up," Shelton's wife muttered.

"No, I'll get—"

"Just leave me alone! You don't understand anything. You're never here. How could you understand?"

Gillette happened to glance into the open doorway of a room nearby. He squinted. The room was dark and from it came an unpleasant musty odor. What caught his attention, though, wasn't the smell but what sat near the doorway. A square metal box.

"Look at that."

"What is it?" Bishop asked.

Gillette examined it. He gave a surprised laugh. "It's an old Winchester hard drive. A big one. Nobody uses them anymore but a few years ago they were state of the art. Most people used them for running bulletin boards and early Web sites. I thought Bob didn't know much about computers."

Bishop shrugged.

The question as to why Bob Shelton had a server drive never got answered, though, because just then the detective stepped into the hallway and blinked in shock at the presence of Bishop and Gillette.

"We rang the bell," Bishop said.

Shelton remained frozen, as if trying to decide how much the two intruders had heard.

"Emma okay?" Bishop asked.

"She's fine," he responded cautiously.

"She didn't sound—" Bishop began.

"Just has the flu," he said quickly. He looked coldly at Gillette. "What's *he* doing here?"

"We came by to pick you up, Bob. We have a lead to Phate in Fremont. We've got to move."

"Lead?"

Bishop explained about the tactical operation at the Bay View Motel.

"Okay," the cop said, with a glance toward where his wife now seemed to be crying softly. "I'll be out in a minute. Can you wait in the car?" He then glanced at Gillette. "I don't want him in my house. Okay?"

"Sure, Bob."

Shelton waited until Bishop and Gillette were at the front door before turning back into the bedroom. He hesitated, as if working up his courage, then walked through the doorway into the dim room beyond.

CHAPTER 00011001 / TWENTY-FIVE

———◆◆◆◆———

It all comes down to this. . . .
   One of his mentors on the state police had shared these
words with rookie Frank Bishop years ago, on their way to
kick in the door of a walk-up apartment near the Oakland
docks. Inside were five or six kilos of something the tenants
weren't willing to part with, along with some automatic
weapons they were all too willing to use.
   "It all comes down to this," the older cop had said.
"Forget about the backup and medevac choppers and
newscasters and public affairs and the brass in Sacramento
and radios and computers. What it comes down to is you
versus a perp. You kick in a door, you chase somebody
down a blind alley, you walk up to the driver's side of a
car where the guy behind the wheel's staring straight
ahead, maybe a fine citizen, maybe holding his wallet and
license, maybe holding his dick, maybe holding a
Browning .380, hammer back to single action and safety
off. See what I'm saying?"
   Oh, Bishop saw perfectly: Going through that door was
what being a cop was all about.
   Speeding now toward the Bay View Motel in Fremont,
where Phate was currently raiding the CCU's computer,
Frank Bishop was thinking of what that cop had told him
so many years ago.
   He was thinking too of what he'd noticed in the San Ho
warden's file on Wyatt Gillette – the article the hacker had
written, calling the computer world the Blue Nowhere.

Which was, Frank Bishop decided, a phrase that could apply
to the cop world too.

Blue for the uniform.

Nowhere because that place on the other side of the door
you're about to kick in, or down that alleyway, or in that
front seat of the stopped car is different from anywhere else
on God's good earth.

It all comes down to this . . .

Shelton, still moody from the incident at his home, was
driving. Bishop sat in the back. Gillette was in the front
passenger seat (Shelton wouldn't hear of an unshackled prisoner sitting *behind* two officers).

"Phate's still online, trying to crack the CCU files,"
Gillette said. The hacker was studying the screen on a
laptop, online via a cell phone.

They arrived at the Bay View Motel. Bob Shelton braked
hard and skidded into the parking lot where a uniformed
cop directed him.

There were a dozen state police and highway patrol cars
in the lot and a number of uniformed, plainclothes and
armor-suited tactical officers clustered around them. This
lot was next door to the Bay View but was out of sight of
the windows.

In another Crown Victoria were Linda Sanchez, along
with Tony Mott, who was decked out in his Oakley
sunglasses – despite the overcast and mist – and rubberized
shooting gloves. Bishop wondered how he could keep Mott
from hurting himself and anyone else during the operation.

Stylish Tim Morgan, today in a double-breasted forest-
green suit, whose cut was ruined by a bulletproof vest,
noticed Bishop and Shelton and ran up to the car. Bent
down to the window.

Catching his breath, he said, "Guy fitting Holloway's
description checked in two hours ago under the name Fred
Lawson. Paid cash. He filled out the car information on the
motel registration card but there's no match in the lot. The
tag number was fake. He's in room one-eighteen. The
blinds're down but he's still on the phone."

Bishop glanced at Gillette. "He still online?"

Gillette looked at his laptop screen. "Yep."

Bishop, Shelton and Gillette climbed from the car. Sanchez and Mott joined them.

"Al," Bishop called to a well-built black trooper. Alonso Johnson was head of the state police's tactical team in San Jose. Bishop liked him because he was as calm and methodical as an inexperienced officer like, say, Tony Mott, was dangerously gung ho. "What's the scenario?" Bishop asked.

The tactical cop opened a diagram of the motel. "We've got troopers here, here, here." He tapped various places around the grounds and in the first-floor corridor. "We don't have much leeway. It'll be a typical motel room takedown. We'll secure the rooms on either side and above his. We've got the passkey and a chain cutter. We'll just go in through the front door and take him. If he tries to get out the patio door there'll be the second team outside. Snipers're ready – just in case he's got a weapon."

Bishop glanced up and saw Tony Mott strapping on body armor. He picked up a short black automatic shotgun and studied it lovingly. With his wraparound sunglasses and biker shorts he looked like a character in a bad science-fiction film. Bishop motioned the young man over. He asked Mott, "What're you doing with that?" Gesturing at the gun.

"I just thought I ought to have some better firepower."

"You ever fire a scattergun before, Officer?"

"Anybody can—"

"Have you ever fired a shotgun?" Bishop repeated patiently.

"Sure."

"Since firearms training at the academy?"

"Not exactly. But—"

Bishop said, "Put it back."

"And, Officer?" Alonso Johnson muttered. "Lose the sunglasses." He rolled his eyes toward Bishop.

Mott stalked off and handed the gun to a tactical officer.

Linda Sanchez, on her cell phone – undoubtedly with her extremely pregnant daughter – hung back well to the rear. She, for one, didn't need reminding that tactical operations weren't her expertise.

Then Johnson cocked his head as he received a

transmission. He nodded slightly and then looked up. "We're ready."

Bishop said, "Go ahead," as casually as if he were politely letting someone precede him into an elevator.

The SWAT commander nodded and spoke into the tiny microphone. Then he motioned a half dozen other tactical officers after him and they ran through a line of bushes toward the motel. Tony Mott followed, keeping to the rear as he'd been ordered.

Bishop walked back to the car and tuned the radio to the tactical operations frequency.

It all comes down to this. . . .

From the radio headset he heard Johnson suddenly call, "Go, go, go!"

Bishop tensed, leaning forward. Was Phate waiting for them with a gun? Bishop wondered. Would he be completely surprised? What would happen?

But the answer was: nothing.

A staticky transmission cut through the air on his radio. Alonso Johnson said, "Frank, the room's empty. He's not here."

"Not there?" Bishop asked doubtfully. Wondering if there was a mix-up about which room Phate was in.

Johnson came back on the radio a moment later. "He's gone."

Bishop turned to Wyatt Gillette, who glanced at the computer in the Crown Victoria. Phate was still online and Trapdoor was still trying to crack the personnel file folder. Gillette pointed to the screen and shrugged.

The detective radioed to Johnson, "We can see him transmitting from the motel. He *has* to be there."

"Negative, Frank," was Johnson's response. "Room's empty, except for a computer here – hooked up to the phone line. A couple of empty cans of Mountain Dew. A half-dozen boxes of computer disks. That's it. No suitcase, no clothes."

Bishop said, "Okay, Al, we're coming in to take a look."

Inside the hot, close motel room a half-dozen troopers opened drawers and checked out closets. Tony Mott stood in the corner, searching as diligently as the rest. The soldier's Kevlar headgear looked a lot less natural on him than his biker's helmet, Gillette concluded.

Bishop motioned Gillette toward the computer, which sat on the cheap desk. On the screen he saw the decryption program. He typed a few commands then frowned. "Hell, it's fake. The software's decrypting the same paragraph over and over again."

"So," Bishop considered, "he tricked us into thinking he was here. . . . But why?"

They debated this for a few minutes but no one could come to any solid conclusion – until Wyatt Gillette happened to open the lid of a large plastic disk-storage box and glance inside. He saw an olive-drab metal box, stenciled with these words:

> U.S. ARMY ANTIPERSONNEL CHARGE.
> HIGH EXPLOSIVE.
> THIS SIDE TOWARD ENEMY.

It was attached to a small black box, on which a single red eye began to blink rapidly.

CHAPTER 00011010 / TWENTY-SIX

❦

P hate *did* happen to be in a motel at the moment. That
motel *was* in Fremont, California. And he *was* in front
of a laptop computer.

However, the motel was a Ramada Inn two miles away
from the Bay View, where Gillette – the Judas traitor
Valleyman – and the cops were undoubtedly fleeing the
room at the moment, escaping from the antipersonnel bomb
they were certain would detonate at any minute.

It wouldn't; the box was filled with sand and the only
thing the device was capable of doing was scaring the shit
out of anyone who was standing close enough to it to see
the made-for-TV blinking light on the supposed detonator.

Phate, of course, would never kill his adversaries in such
an inelegant way. That would've been far too gauche a tactic
for Phate, whose goal was, like a player of the MUD game
Access, to get close enough to his victims to feel their
quaking hearts as he slipped a blade into them. Besides,
killing a dozen cops would have brought in the feds in a
big way and he'd have been forced to give up on the game
here in Silicon Valley. No, he was content to keep Gillette
and the cops from the CCU busy for an hour or so at the
Bay View while the bomb squad got the mean-looking
device out of the room – and giving Phate a chance to do
what he'd planned all along: Use the Computer Crime Unit's
machine to crack into ISLEnet. He needed to log on through
CCU because ISLEnet would then recognize him as a root
user and give him unlimited access to the network.

Phate had played plenty of MUD games with Valleyman and knew that Gillette anticipated Phate would break into CCU's machine and would try to trace him when he did.

So, after Trapdoor had broken into CCU's computer Phate had driven from the Bay View Motel to *this* place, where his second laptop was warmed up and waiting for him, online via a virtually untraceable cell phone connection through a South Carolina Internet provider, linked to an anonymizing Net launch pad in Prague.

Phate now looked at some of the files he'd copied when he'd first cracked into CCU's system. These files had been erased but not wiped – that is, permanently obliterated – and he now restored them easily with Restore8, a powerful undelete program. He found the CCU's computer identification number and then, after a bit more searching, the following data:

```
System: ISLEnet

Login: RobertSShelton

Password: BlueFord

Database: California State Police Criminal
Activity Archives

Search Request: (Wyatt Gillette OR Gillette,
Wyatt OR Knights of Access OR Gillette, W.)
AND (compute* OR hack*).
```

He then changed his own laptop computer's identity number and Internet address to that of CCU's machine then ordered the computer's modem to dial the general ISLEnet access phone number. He heard the whistle and hum of the electronic handshake. This was the moment when the firewall protecting ISLEnet would have rejected any outsider's attempt to get inside but, because Phate's computer appeared to be CCU's, ISLEnet recognized it as a super-access "trusted system" and Phate was instantly welcomed inside. The system then asked:

```
Username?
```

Phate typed: *RobertSShelton*

Passcode?

He typed: *BlueFord*

Then the screen went blank and some very boring graphics appeared, followed by:

```
            California Integrated State
            Law Enforcement Network

                   Main Menu
       Department of Motor Vehicles
       State Police
       Department of Vital Statistics
       Forensic Services
       Local Law Enforcement Agencies
          Los Angeles
          Sacramento
          San Francisco
          San Diego
          Monterey County
          Orange County
          Santa Barbara County
          Other
       Office of the State Attorney General
       Federal Agencies
          FBI
          ATF
          Treasury
          U.S. Marshals
          IRS
          Postal Service
          Other
       Mexican Federal Police, Tijuana
       Legislative Liaison
       Systems Administration
```

Like a lion grabbing a gazelle's neck, Phate went straight into the systems administration file. He cracked the passcode and seized root, which gave him unrestricted access to ISLEnet and to all of the systems ISLEnet was in turn connected to.

He then returned to the main menu and clicked on another entry.

```
State Police
   Highway Patrol Division
   Human Resources
   Accounting
   Computer Crimes
   Violent Felonies
   Juvenile
   Criminal Activity Archive
   Data Processing
   Administrative Services
   Tactical Operations
   Major Crimes
   Legal Department
   Facilities Management
   Felony Warrants Outstanding
```

Phate didn't need to waste any time making up his mind. He already knew exactly where he wanted to go.

The bomb squad had taken the gray box out of the Bay View Motel and dismantled it, only to find that it was filled with sand.

"What the hell was the point of *that?*" Shelton snapped. "Is this part of his fucking games? Messing with our minds?"

Bishop shrugged.

The squad had also examined Phate's computer with nitrogen-sensing probes and declared it explosives-free. Gillette now scrolled through it quickly. The machine contained hundreds of files – he opened some at random.

"They're gibberish."

"Encrypted?" Bishop asked.

"No – look, just snatches of books, Web sites, graphics. It's all filler." Gillette looked up, squinting, staring at the ceiling, his fingers typing in the air. "What's it all mean, the fake bomb, the gibberish files?"

Tony Mott, who'd discarded his armor and helmet, said, "All right. Phate set this whole thing up to get us out of the office, to keep us busy. . . . Why?"

"Oh, Jesus Christ," Gillette snapped. "I know why!"

Frank Bishop did too. He looked quickly at Gillette and said, "He's trying to crack ISLEnet!"

"Right!" Gillette confirmed. He grabbed the phone and called CCU.

"Computer Crimes. Sergeant Miller here."

"It's Wyatt. Listen—"

"Did you find him?"

"No. Listen to me. Call the sysadmin at ISLEnet and have him suspend the entire network. Right now."

A pause. "They won't do that," Miller said. "It's—"

"They have to. Now! Phate's trying to crack it. He's probably inside already. Don't shut it down – make sure it's suspended. That'll give me a chance to assess the damage."

"But the whole state relies on—"

"You have to do it now!"

Bishop grabbed the phone. "That's an order, Miller. Now!"

"Okay, okay, I'll call. They aren't going to like it. But I'll call."

Gillette sighed. "We got out-thought. This whole thing was a setup – posting the picture of Lara Gibson to get our address, going through CCU's computer, sending us here. Man, I thought *we* were one step ahead of *him*."

Linda Sanchez logged all the evidence, attached chain of custody cards and loaded the disks and computer into the folding cardboard boxes she'd brought with her like a Mayflower mover. They packed up their tools and left the room.

As Frank Bishop walked with Wyatt Gillette back to the car, they noticed a slim man with a mustache watching them from the far end of the parking lot.

There was something familiar about him and after a moment Gillette recalled: Charles Pittman, the Santa Clara County detective.

Bishop said, "I can't have him poking around our operations. Half those county boys handle surveillance like it was a frat party." He started toward Pittman but the officer had already climbed into his unmarked car. He started the engine and drove off.

Bishop called the county sheriff's office. He was put through to Pittman's voice mail and left a message asking the cop to call Bishop back as soon as he could.

Bob Shelton took a call, listened and then disconnected. "That was Stephen Miller. The systems administrator's hopping mad but ISLEnet's suspended." The cop barked at Gillette, "You said you were making sure he couldn't get inside ISLEnet."

"I *did* make sure," Gillette said to him. "I took the system offline and then shredded every reference to usernames and passwords. He probably cracked ISLEnet because *you* went back online from CCU to check me out. Phate must've found out the CCU machine's identity number to get through the firewall and then he logged on with your username and passcode."

"Impossible. I erased everything."

"Did you *wipe* the free space on the drives? Did you overwrite the temp and slack files? Did you encrypt the logs and overwrite them?"

Shelton was silent. He broke eye contact with Gillette and looked up at the fast-moving tatters of fog flowing over them toward San Francisco Bay.

Gillette said, "No, you didn't. *That's* how Phate got online. He ran an undelete program and got everything he needed to crack into ISLEnet. So don't give *me* any crap about it."

"Well, if you hadn't lied about being Valleyman and knowing Phate, I wouldn't've gone online," Shelton responded defensively.

Gillette turned angrily and continued on to the Crown Victoria. Bishop fell into step beside him.

"If he got into ISLEnet you know what he'd have access to, don't you?" Gillette asked the detective.

"Everything," Bishop said. "He'd have access to everything."

* * *

Wyatt leapt from the car before Bishop had brought it to a complete stop in the CCU headquarters parking lot. He sprinted inside.

"Damage assessment?" he asked. Both Miller and Patricia Nolan were at workstations but it was Nolan to whom he directed this question.

She replied, "They're still offline but one of the sysadmin's assistants walked a disk of the log files over. I'm just going through it now."

Log files retain information on which users have been connected to a system, for how long, what they do online and if they log on to another system while they're connected.

Gillette took over and began keying furiously. He absently picked up his coffee cup from that morning, took a sip and shuddered at the cold, bitter liquid. He put the cup down and returned to the screen, pounding keys hard as he roamed through the ISLEnet log files.

A moment later he was aware of Patricia Nolan sitting beside him. She put a fresh cup of coffee next to him. He glanced her way. "Thanks."

She offered a smile and he nodded back, holding her eye for a moment. Sitting this close Gillette noticed a tautness to her facial skin and he supposed she'd taken her makeover plan so seriously that she'd had some plastic surgery. He had the passing thought that if she used less of the thick makeup, bought some better clothes and stopped shoving her hair off her face every few minutes she'd be attractive. Not beautiful, or demure, but handsome.

He turned back to the screen and continued to key. His fingers slammed down angrily. He kept thinking about Bob Shelton. How could somebody who knew enough about computers to own a Winchester server drive be so careless?

Finally, he sat back and announced, "It's not as bad as it could be. Phate *was* in ISLEnet but only for about forty seconds before Stephen suspended it."

Bishop asked, "Forty seconds. That's not enough time to get anything useful to him, is it?"

"No way," the hacker said. "He might've looked at the main menus and gotten into a couple of files but to get to anything classified he'd need other passcodes and'd have to run a cracking program for those. That'd take him a half hour at best."

Bishop nodded. "At least we got *one* break."

In the outside world it was nearly 5:00 P.M., rainy again, and a hesitant rush hour was under way. But for a hacker there is no afternoon, there is no morning, no night. There is simply time you spend in the Machine World and time you do not.

Phate was, for the moment, offline.

Though he was, of course, still in front of his computer in his lovely façade of a house off El Monte in Los Altos. He was scrolling through page after page of data, all of which he'd downloaded from ISLEnet.

The Computer Crimes Unit believed Phate had been inside ISLEnet for only forty-two seconds. What they didn't know, however, was that as soon as he'd had gotten inside the system one of Trapdoor's clever demons had taken over the internal clock and rewritten all the connection and download logs. In reality Phate had spent a leisurely fifty-two minutes inside ISLEnet, downloading gigabytes of information.

Some of this intelligence was mundane but – because CCU's machine had root access – some was so classified that only a handful of law enforcers in the state and federal governments were allowed to see it: access numbers and passcodes to top-secret government computers; tactical assault codes; encrypted files about ongoing operations; surveillance procedures; rules of engagement and classified information about the state police, the FBI, the Bureau of Alcohol, Tobacco and Firearms, the Secret Service and most other law enforcement agencies.

Now, as soft rain streaked the windows of his house, Phate was scrolling through one of these classified folders – the state police human resource files. These contained information on every individual employed by the California State Police. There were many, many subfolders but at the moment Phate was interested only in the one he was looking through now. It was labeled Detective Division and it contained some very useful data.

IV
ACCESS

———◆◆◆———

The Internet is about as safe as a convenience store in East L.A. on Saturday night.
                                    – Jonathan Littman,
                                    The Fugitive Game

CHAPTER 00011011 / TWENTY-SEVEN

F or the rest of the evening the Computer Crimes Unit team pored over the reports from the Bay View Motel, continuing to search for any leads to Phate and listening in fearful anticipation to the police-band scanners for reports of more killings.

There'd been a report that a young girl had been kidnapped from a private school that morning by a man impersonating her uncle and then released. It was certainly Phate's M.O. but when Huerto Ramirez and Tim Morgan had checked out the school and interviewed the girl but they came away with no leads. The hysterical student couldn't even remember the color of her abductor's car.

Other officers had canvassed most of the guests at the Bay View Motel and surrounding areas and had found no witnesses who'd seen what kind of car or truck Phate had been driving.

A clerk in a 7-Eleven in Fremont had sold two six-packs of Mountain Dew to someone fitting Phate's description several hours ago. But the killer hadn't said anything that would help in tracing him. No one inside or outside the convenience store got a look at his car either.

The crime scene search of the motel room had revealed nothing useful in tracing Phate to a specific location.

Wyatt Gillette had helped Stephen Miller, Linda Sanchez and Tony Mott perform the forensic analysis on the computer left in the room. The hacker reported that it was indeed a hot machine, loaded with just enough software for the break-in.

There was nothing contained in it that gave any indication where Phate might be. The serial number of the Toshiba indicated that it had been part of a shipment to Computer World in Chicago six months ago. The purchaser had paid cash and had never filled out the warranty registration card or registered online. All of the computer disks Phate had left in the room were blank. Linda Sanchez, queen of the computer archaeologists, tested each one with the Restore8 program and found that none had ever contained any data.

Sanchez continued to be preoccupied with her daughter and called her every few hours to see how she was doing. She clearly wanted to visit the poor girl and so Bishop sent her home. He dismissed the rest of the troops too and Miller and Mott – the blond cop in much better spirits after his SWAT experience – left to get some dinner and sleep.

Patricia Nolan, on the other hand, was in no hurry to return to her hotel. She sat next to Gillette and together they scrolled through ISLEnet files, trying to find out more about the clever Trapdoor demon. There was, however, no sign of it and Gillette suspected that the bot had killed itself.

Once, Gillette leaned back wearily, cracked his knuckles and stretched. Bishop watched him spot a wad of pink phone-message slips. His face brightened and he picked them up eagerly. He was clearly disappointed that none were for him – probably upset that his ex-wife hadn't called, as he'd asked her to do last night.

Well, Frank Bishop knew that feelings about loved ones weren't limited to upstanding citizens. He'd collared dozens of worthless killers who'd broken into tears when they were led away in cuffs – not at the thought of the hard years ahead of them in prison but because they'd be separated from their wives and children.

Bishop noted that once again the hacker's fingers had started typing – no, *keying* – in the air as he stared at the ceiling. Was he writing something to his wife right now? Or maybe he was asking his father – the engineer in the dusty sand fields of the Middle East – for some advice or support, or telling his brother that once he was released he'd like to spend some time with him.

"Nothing," Nolan muttered. "We're not getting anywhere."

For a moment Bishop felt the same discouragement he saw in her face. But then he thought, wait a minute . . . I'm getting distracted here. He realized that he had been pulled deep under the hypnotic, addictive spell of the Blue Nowhere. It had skewed his thoughts. He now walked to the white-board and stared at the notations about the evidence, the printouts and pictures. These were part of the world he was familiar with.

Do something with that . . .

Bishop glanced at the printout of the terrible picture of Lara Gibson.

Do something . . .

The detective walked closer to the picture, studied it carefully.

"Look at this," he said to Shelton. The stocky, sullen cop joined him.

"What about it?"

"What do you see?"

Shelton shrugged. "I don't know. What do *you* see?"

"I see *clues*," Bishop responded. "The other *things* in the picture – what's on the floor, the walls. . . . They can tell us something about where Phate killed her, I'll bet."

Gillette scooted forward and stared at the gruesome photo.

The picture showed the poor girl in the foreground. Bishop pointed out what else the shot revealed: The floor she lay on was greenish tile. There was a square galvanized-metal duct running from a beige air-conditioning or furnace unit. The wall was the backside of unpainted Sheetrock nailed to wooden studs. This was probably the furnace room in a partially unfinished basement. You could also see part of a white-painted door and what seemed to be a trash can next to it, brimming with refuse.

Bishop said, "We'll send the picture to the FBI. Let their techs look it over."

Shelton shook his head. "I don't know, Frank. I think he's too smart to piss where he eats. Way too traceable." He nodded toward the picture. "He took her someplace else to kill her. That's not where he lives."

But Nolan said, "I don't agree. You're right that he's smart but he doesn't see things the way we do."

"What's that mean?"

Gillette seemed to understand exactly. "Phate doesn't think about the Real World. He'd try to cover up any computer evidence but I think he'd tend to overlook physical clues."

Bishop nodded at the picture. "The basement looks pretty new – the furnace too. Or air conditioner, whatever it is. The FBI might be able to figure out if there's a particular builder who makes residential properties with those brands of materials. We could narrow down the building."

Shelton shrugged. "It's a long shot. But what can it hurt?"

Bishop called a friend of his in the bureau. He told him about the picture and what they needed. They conversed for a moment or two and the detective hung up.

"He's going to download an original of the picture himself and send it to the lab," Bishop said. The detective then glanced down at a nearby desk and noticed a large envelope addressed to him. The routing slip indicated it had come from the California State Police Juvenile Division central files department and must have arrived when he was at the Bay View. He opened it and read through the contents. It was the juvenile court file he'd requested on Gillette when the hacker had escaped last night. He dropped it on the desk then glanced up at the dusty wall clock. It was 10:30. "I think we all need some rest," he said.

Shelton hadn't mentioned his wife but Bishop sensed he was eager to return home to her. The brawny detective left with a nod to his partner. "See you in the morning, Frank." He smiled at Nolan. Gillette received neither a word nor a gesture of farewell.

Bishop said to Gillette, "I don't feel like spending the night here again. I'm going home. And you're coming with me."

Patricia Nolan's head swiveled toward the hacker when she heard this. She said casually, "I've got plenty of room at my hotel. My company's paying for a suite. You're welcome to stay there if you want. Got a great minibar."

But the detective chuckled and said, "I'm running toward

unemployment fast enough with this case. Think it'd be better if he came with me. Prisoner in custody, you know."

Nolan took the defeat well – Bishop supposed she was beginning to give up on Gillette as romantic material. She gathered up her purse, a pile of floppy disks and her laptop and left.

As Bishop and Gillette walked out the door the hacker asked, "You mind if we make a stop on the way?"

"A stop?"

"There's something I want to pick up," Gillette said. "Oh, and speaking of which – can I borrow a couple of dollars?"

CHAPTER 00011100 / TWENTY-EIGHT

"Here we are," Bishop said.

They pulled up in front of a ranch house, small but situated in a verdant yard that looked to be about a half acre, a huge lot for this part of Silicon Valley.

Gillette asked what town this was and Bishop told him Mountain View. Then he added, "Of course, I can't exactly *see* any mountains. The only view's my next-door neighbor's Dodge up on blocks and, on a clear day, that big hangar at Moffett field." He pointed north, across the lights of traffic streaming along Highway 101.

They walked along a winding sidewalk, which was badly cracked and buckled. Bishop said, "Watch your step there. I've been meaning to get around to fixing that. You have the San Andreas fault to thank. Which is all of about three miles thataway. Say, wipe your feet if you don't mind."

He unlocked the door and ushered the hacker inside.

Frank Bishop's wife, Jennie, was a petite woman in her late thirties. Her pug face wasn't beautiful but was appealing in a wholesome way. While Bishop – with his sprayed hair, sideburns and short-sleeved white shirts – was a time traveler from the 1950s, his wife was very much an up-to-date housewife. Long hair in a French braid, jeans, a designer work shirt. She was trim and athletic-looking, though to Gillette, now out of prison and surrounded by tanned Californians, she seemed very pale.

She didn't appear the least put out – or even surprised – that her husband had brought a felon home to spend the night and Gillette supposed she'd received a phone call earlier about their houseguest.

"Have you eaten?" she asked.

"No," Bishop said.

But Gillette held up the paper bag containing what they'd stopped for on the way here from CCU. "I'm fine with these."

Jennie unabashedly took the bag from him, looked inside. She laughed. "You're not having Pop-Tarts for dinner. You need real food."

"No, really—" With a smile on his face and sorrow in his heart Gillette watched the pastry disappear into the kitchen.

So near, yet so far . . .

Bishop unlaced his shoes, pulled them off and put on moccasin slippers. The hacker took his shoes off and, in stocking feet, stepped into the living room, looking around.

The place reminded Gillette of his own childhood homes. White wall-to-wall carpet in need of replacing. Furniture from JCPenney or Sears. An expensive TV and a cheap stereo. The chipped dining room table doubled tonight as a desk; this seemed to be bill-paying day. A dozen envelopes were carefully laid out to be mailed. Pacific Bell, Mervyn's, MasterCard, Visa.

Gillette looked over some of the many framed pictures on the mantelpiece. There were four or five dozen of them. More on the walls, tables and bookshelves. The couple's wedding picture revealed a young Frank Bishop identical to today's, sideburns and sprayed hair included (though the white shirt under the tuxedo jacket was held firmly in place by a cummerbund).

Bishop saw Gillette studying them. "Jennie calls us World O' Frames. We've got more pictures than any two families on our block combined." He nodded toward the back of the house. "Plenty more in the bedroom and bathroom too. That one you're looking at – that's my father and mother."

"Was he a cop? Wait, do you mind being called a cop?"

"Do you mind being called a hacker?"

Gillette shrugged. "Nope. It fits."

"Same with 'cop.' But, no, Dad owned a printing company in Oakland. Bishop and Sons. The 'sons' part isn't exactly accurate since two of my sisters run it along with most of my brothers."

"'Two of'?" Gillette said, lifting an eyebrow. "'Most of'?"

Bishop laughed. "I'm the eighth of nine. Five boys and four girls."

"That's quite a family."

"I've got twenty-nine nieces and nephews," the detective said proudly.

Gillette looked at a picture of a lean man in a shirt as baggy as Bishop's, standing in front of a one-story building, on the façade of which was a sign, BISHOP & SONS PRINTING AND TYPESETTING.

"You didn't want to be in the business?"

"I like the idea of a company staying in the family." He picked up the picture and gazed at it himself. "I think family's the most important thing in the world. But, I tell you, I'd've been pretty bad at the printing business. Boring, you know. The thing about being a cop is that it's . . . how do I say it? It's like it's infinite. There's always something new, every day. As soon as you think you've figured out the criminal mind, bang, you find a whole new perspective."

There was motion nearby. They turned.

"Look who we have here," Bishop said.

A boy of about eight was peeking into the living room from the corridor.

"Come on in here, young man."

Wearing pajamas decorated with tiny dinosaurs, the boy walked into the living room, looking up at Gillette.

"Say hi to Mr. Gillette, son. This's Brandon."

"Hello."

"Hi, Brandon," Gillette said. "You're up late."

"I like to say good night to my dad. If he doesn't get home too late mom lets me stay up."

"Mr. Gillette writes software for computers."

"You write script?" the boy asked enthusiastically.

"That's right," Gillette said, laughing at the way the

programmer's shorthand for software tripped easily off his tongue.

The boy said, "We write programs at our computer lab in school. The one we did last week made a ball bounce around the screen."

"That sounds like fun," Gillette offered, noting the boy's round, eager eyes. His features were mostly his mother's.

"Naw," Brandon said, "it was totally boring. We had to use QBasic. I'm gonna learn O-O-P."

Object-oriented programming – the latest trend, exemplified by the sophisticated C++ language.

The boy shrugged. "Then Java and HTML for the Net. But, like, *everybody* oughta know that."

"So you want to go into computers when you grow up."

"Naw, I'm going to play pro baseball. I just want to learn O-O-P 'cause it's where everything's happening now."

Here was a grade-schooler who was already tired of Basic and had his eyes set on the cutting edge of programming.

"Why don't you go show Mr. Gillette your computer."

"You play Tomb Raider?" the boy asked. "Or Earthworm Jim?"

"I don't play games much."

"I'll show you. Come on."

Gillette followed the boy into a room cluttered with books, toys, sports equipment, clothes. The Harry Potter books sat on the bedside table, next to a Game Boy, two 'N Sync CDs and a dozen floppy disks. Well, here's a snapshot of our era, Gillette thought.

In the center of the room was an IBM-clone computer and dozens of software instruction manuals. Brandon sat down and, with lightning-fast keystrokes, booted up the machine and loaded a game. Gillette recalled that when he was the boy's age the state of the art in personal computing was the Trash-80 he'd selected when his father had told him he could pick out a present for himself at Radio Shack. That tiny computer had thrilled him but it was, of course, just a rudimentary toy compared with even this cheap, mail-order machine he was now looking at. At that time – just a few years ago – only a handful of people in the world had owned machines as powerful as the one on which

Brandon Bishop was now directing a beautiful woman in a tight green top through caverns with a gun in her hand.

"You want to play?"

But this brought to mind the terrible game of Access and Phate's digital picture of the murdered girl (her name, Lara, was the same as that of the heroine of this game of Brandon's); he wanted nothing to do with violence, even two-dimensional, at the moment.

"Maybe later."

He watched the boy's fascinated eyes dance around the screen for a few minutes. Then the detective stuck his head in the door. "Lights out, son."

"Dad, look at the level I'm at! Five minutes."

"Nope. It's bedtime."

"Aw, Dad . . ."

Bishop made sure the boy's teeth were brushed and his homework was in his book bag. He kissed his son good night, powered down the computer and shut out the over-head light, leaving a *Star Wars* spaceship night-light as the only source of illumination in the room.

He said to Gillette, "Come on. I'll show you the back forty."

"The what?"

"Follow me."

Bishop led Gillette through the kitchen, where Jennie was making sandwiches, and out the back door.

The hacker stopped abruptly on the back porch, surprised at what he saw in front of him. He gave a laugh.

"Yep, I'm a farmer," Bishop announced.

Rows of fruit trees – probably fifty altogether – filled the backyard.

"We moved in eighteen years ago – just when the Valley was starting to take off. I borrowed enough to buy two lots. This one had some of the original farm on it. These're apricot and cherry."

"What do you do, sell it?"

"Give it away mostly. At Christmas, if you know the Bishops, you're going to get preserves or dried fruit. People we *really* like get brandied cherries."

Gillette examined the sprinklers and smudge pots. "You take it pretty seriously," the hacker observed.

"Keeps me sane. I come home and Jennie and I come out here and tend to the crop. It kind of shuts out all the bad stuff I deal with during the day."

They walked through the rows of trees. The backyard was filled with plastic pipes and hoses, the cop's irrigation system. Gillette nodded at them. "You know, you could make a computer that ran on water."

"You could? Oh, you mean a waterfall'd run a turbine for the electricity."

"No, I mean instead of current going through wires you could use water running through pipes, with valves to shut the flow on or off. That's all computers do, you know. Turn a flow of current on or off."

"Is that right?" Bishop asked. He seemed genuinely interested.

"Computer processors are just little switches that let bits of electricity through or don't let them through. All the pictures you see on a computer, all the music, movies, word processors, spreadsheets, browsers, search engines, the Internet, math calculations, viruses . . . *everything* a computer does can be boiled down to that. It's not magic at all. It's just turning little switches on or off."

The cop nodded then he gave Gillette a knowing look. "Except that you don't believe that, do you?"

"How do you mean?"

"You think computers're *pure* magic."

After a pause Gillette laughed. "Yeah, I do."

They remained standing on the porch for a few minutes, looking out over the glistening branches of the trees. Then Jennie Bishop summoned them to dinner. They walked into the kitchen.

Jennie said, "I'm going to bed. I've got a busy day tomorrow. Nice meeting you, Wyatt." She shook his hand firmly.

"Thanks for letting me stay. I appreciate it."

To her husband she said, "My appointment's at eleven tomorrow."

"You want me to go with you? I will. Bob can take over the case for a few hours."

"No. You've got your hands full. I'll be fine. If Dr.

Williston sees anything funny I'll call you from the hospital. But that's not going to happen."

"I'll have my cell phone with me."

She started to leave but then she turned back with a grave look. "Oh, but there *is* something you have to do tomorrow."

"What's that, honey?" the detective asked, concerned.

"The Hoover." She nodded toward a vacuum cleaner sitting in the corner, the front panel off and a dusty hose hanging from the side. Several other components lay nearby on a newspaper. "Take it in."

"I'll fix it," Bishop said. "There's just some dirt in the motor or something."

She chided, "You've had a month. Now it's time for the experts."

Bishop turned toward Gillette. "You know anything about vacuum cleaners?"

"Nope. Sorry."

The detective glanced at his wife. "I'll get to it tomorrow. Or the next day."

A knowing smile. "The address of the repair place is on that yellow sticky tab there. See it?"

He kissed her. "Night, love." Jennie disappeared into the dim hallway.

Bishop rose and walked to the refrigerator. "I guess I can't get into any more trouble than I'm already in if I offer a prisoner a beer."

Gillette shook his head. "Thanks but I don't drink."

"No?"

"That's one thing about hackers: We never drink anything that'll make us sleepy. Go to a hacking newsgroup sometime – like alt.hack. Half the postings are about taking down Pac Bell switches or cracking into the White House and the other half are about the caffeine content of the latest soft drinks."

Bishop poured himself a Budweiser. He glanced at Gillette's arm, the tattoo of the seagull and the palm tree. "That's mighty ugly, I have to say. That bird especially. Why'd you have it done?"

"I was in college – at Berkeley. I'd been up hacking for about thirty-six hours straight and I went to this party."

"And what? You did it on a dare?"

"No, I fell asleep and woke up with it. Never did find out who did it to me."

"Makes you look like some kind of ex-marine."

The hacker glanced around – to make sure Jennie was gone and then walked to the counter, where she'd left the Pop-Tarts. He opened them up and took four of the pastries, offered one to Bishop.

"Not for me, thanks."

"I'll eat the roast beef *too*," Gillette said, nodding at Jennie's sandwiches. "It's just, I dream about these in prison. They're the best kind of hacker food – full of sugar and you can buy 'em by the case and they don't go bad." He wolfed down two at once. "They probably even have vitamins in them. I don't know. This'd be my staple when I was hacking. Pop-Tarts, pizza, Mountain Dew and Jolt cola." After a moment Gillette asked in a low voice, "Is your wife all right? That appointment she mentioned?"

He saw a faint hesitation in the detective's hand as he lifted the beer and took a sip. "Nothing serious. . . . A few tests." Then, as if to deflect the course of this conversation, he said, "I'm going to check on Brandon."

When he returned a few minutes later Gillette held up the empty box of Pop-Tarts. "Didn't save any for you."

"That's okay." Bishop laughed and sat down again. "How's your son?"

"Asleep. Did you and your wife have children?"

"No. We didn't want to at first. . . . Well, I should say *I* didn't want to. By the time I *did* want to, well, I'd been busted. And then we were divorced."

"So you'd like kids?"

"Oh, yeah." He shrugged, brushed the pastry crumbs into his hand and deposited them on a napkin. "My brother's got two, a boy and a girl. We have a lot of fun together."

"Your brother?" Bishop asked.

"Ricky," Gillette said. "He lives in Montana. He's a park ranger, believe it or not. He and Carole – that's his wife – have this great house. Sort of a log cabin, a big one though." He nodded toward Bishop's backyard. "You'd appreciate their vegetable patch. She's a great gardener."

Bishop's eyes dipped to the tabletop. "I read your file."

"My file?" Gillette asked.

"Your juvenile file. The one you forgot to have shredded."

The hacker slowly rolled up his napkin then unrolled it. "I thought those were sealed."

"From the public they are. Not from the police."

"Why'd you do that?" Gillette asked coolly.

"Because you escaped from CCU. I ordered a copy when we found you'd skedaddled. I thought we might get some information that'd help track you down." The detective's imperturbable voice continued, "The social worker's report was included. About your family life. Or *lack* of family life. . . . So tell me – why'd you lie to everybody?"

Gillette said nothing for a long moment.

Why'd you lie? he thought.

You lie because you *can.*

You lie because when you're in the Blue Nowhere you can make up whatever you want and nobody knows that what you're saying isn't true. You can drop into any chat room and tell the world that you live in a big beautiful house in Sunnyvale or Menlo Park or Walnut Creek and that your father is a lawyer or doctor or pilot and your mother is a designer or runs a flower store and your brother Rick is a state champion track star. And you can go on and on to the world about how you and your father built an Altair computer from a kit, six nights straight after he got home from work, and that's what got you hooked on computers.

What a great guy he is. . . .

You can tell the world that even though your mother died of a tragic and unexpected heart attack you're still real close to your dad. He travels all over the world as a petroleum engineer but he always gets home to visit you and your brother for the holidays. And when he's in town you go over to his house every Sunday for dinner with him and his new wife, who's really nice, and you and he sometimes go into his den and debug script together or play a MUD game.

And guess what?

The world believes you. Because in the Blue Nowhere

the only thing people have to go by are the bytes you key with your numb fingers.

The world never knows it's all a lie.

The world never knows you're the only child of a divorced mother who worked late three or four nights a week and went out with her "friends" – always male – the other nights. And that it wasn't her failed heart that killed her but her liver and her spirit, which both disintegrated at about the same time, when you were eighteen.

The world never knows that your father, a man of vague occupation, fulfilled the only potential he'd ever seemed destined for by leaving your mother and you on the day you entered third grade.

And that your homes were a series of bungalows and trailers in the shabbiest parts of Silicon Valley, that your only treasure was a cheap computer and that the only bill that ever got paid on time was the phone bill – because you paid it yourself out of paper-delivery money so that you'd be able to stay connected to the one thing that kept you from going mad with sorrow and loneliness: the Blue Nowhere.

Okay, Bishop, you caught me. No father, no siblings. An addictive, selfish mother. And me – Wyatt Edward Gillette, alone in my room with my companions: my Trash-80, my Apple, my Kaypro, my PC, my Toshiba, my Sun SPARCstation. . . .

Finally he looked up and did what he'd never done before – not even to his wife – he told this entire story to another human being. Frank Bishop remained motionless, looking intently at Gillette's dark, hollow face. When the hacker had finished, Bishop said, "You social engineered your whole childhood."

"Yep."

"I was eight when he left," Gillette said, hands around his cola can, callused fingertips pressing the cold metal as if he were keying the words. *I W-A-S E-I-G-H-T W-H-E-N* . . . "He was ex-air force, my dad. He'd been stationed at Travis and when he got discharged he stayed in the area. Well, he stayed in the area *occasionally.* Mostly he was out with his service buddies or . . . well, you can figure out where he was when he didn't come home at night. The day he left was the only time we ever had a serious talk. My mother was out somewhere and he came into my room and said he had some shopping to do, why didn't I come along with him. That was pretty weird because we never did *anything* together."

Gillette took a breath, tried to calm himself. His fingers keyed a silent storm against the soda can.

P-E-A-C-E O-F M-I-N-D . . . P-E-A-C-E O-F M-I-N-D . . .

"We were living in Burlingame, near the airport, and my father and I got in the car and drove to this strip mall. He bought some things in a drugstore and then took me to the diner next to the railroad station. The food came but I was too nervous to eat. He didn't even notice. All of a sudden he put his fork down and looked at me and told me how unhappy he was with my mother and how he had to leave. I remembered how he put it. He said his peace of mind was jeopardized and he needed to move on for his personal growth."

P-E-A-C-E O-F . . .

Bishop shook his head. "He was talking to you like you were some buddy of his in a bar. Not a little boy, not his son. That was really bad."

"He said it was a tough decision to leave but it was the right thing to do and asked if I felt happy for him."

"He asked you *that?*"

Gillette nodded. "I don't remember what I said. Then we left the restaurant and we were walking down the street and maybe he noticed I was upset and he saw this store and said, 'Tell you what, son, you go in there and buy anything you want'."

"A consolation prize."

Gillette laughed and nodded. "I guess that's exactly what it was. The store was a Radio Shack. I just walked in and stood there, looking around. I didn't see anything, I was so hurt and confused, trying not to cry. I just picked the first thing I saw. A Trash-80."

"A what?"

"A TRS-80. One of the first personal computers."

A-N-Y-T-H-I-N-G Y-O-U W-A-N-T . . .

"I took it home and started playing with it that night. Then I heard my mother come home and she and my father had a big fight and then he was gone and that was it."

T-H-E B-L-U-E N-O-

Gillette smiled briefly, fingers tapping.

"That article I wrote? 'The Blue Nowhere'?"

"I remember," Bishop said. "It means cyberspace."

"But it also means something else," Gillette said slowly.

N-O-W-H-E-R-E.

"What?"

"My father was air force, like I said. And when I was really young he'd have some of his military buddies over and they'd get drunk and loud and a couple of times they'd sing the air force song, 'The Wild Blue Yonder.' Well, after he left I kept hearing that song in my head, over and over, only I changed 'yonder' to 'nowhere,' the 'Wild Blue Nowhere,' because he was gone. He was nowhere." Gillette swallowed hard. He looked up. "Pretty stupid, huh?"

But Frank Bishop didn't seem to think there was anything stupid about this at all. With his voice filled with the sympathy that made him a natural family man he asked, "You ever hear from him? Or hear what happened to him?"

"Nope. Have no clue." Gillette laughed. "Every once in a while I think I should track him down."

"You'd be good at finding people on the Net."

Gillette nodded. "But I don't think I will."

Fingers moving furiously. The ends were so numb because of the calluses that he couldn't feel the cold of the soda can he was tapping them against.

O-F-F W-E G-O, I-N-T-O T-H-E

"It gets even better – I learned Basic, the programming language, when I was nine or ten, and I'd spend hours writing programs. The first ones made the computer talk to me. I'd key, 'Hello,' and the computer'd respond, 'Hi, Wyatt. How are you?' Then I'd type, 'Good,' and it would ask, 'What did you do in school today?' I tried to think of things for the machine to say that'd be what a real father would ask."

A-N-Y-T-H-I-N-G Y-O-U W-A-N-T . . .

"All those e-mails supposedly from my father to the judge

and those faxes from my brother about coming to live with him in Montana, all the psychologists' reports about what a great family life I had, about my dad being the best? . . . I wrote them all myself."

"I'm sorry," Bishop said.

Gillette shrugged. "Hey, I survived. It doesn't matter."

"It probably does," Bishop said softly.

They sat in silence for a few minutes. Then the detective rose and started to wash the dishes. Gillette joined him and they chatted idly – about Bishop's orchard, about life in San Ho. When they'd finished drying the plates Bishop drained his beer then glanced coyly at the hacker. He said, "Why don't you give her a call."

"Call? Who?"

"Your wife."

"It's late," Gillette protested.

"So wake her up. She won't break. Doesn't sound to me like you've got a lot to lose anyway." Bishop pushed the phone toward the hacker.

"What should I say?" He lifted the receiver uncertainly.

"You'll think of something."

"I don't know . . ."

The cop asked, "You know the number?"

Gillette dialed it from memory – fast, before he balked – thinking: What if her brother answers? What if her mother answers? What if—

"Hello."

His throat seized.

"Hello?" Elana repeated.

"It's me."

A pause while she undoubtedly checked a watch or clock. No comment about the lateness of the hour was forthcoming, however.

Why wasn't she saying anything?

Why wasn't *he?*

"Just felt like calling. Did you find the modem? I left in it the mailbox."

She didn't answer for a moment. Then she said, "I'm in bed."

A searing thought: Was she *alone* in bed? Was Ed next

to her? In her *parents'* house? But he pushed the jealousy aside and asked softly, "Did I wake you up?"

"Is there something you want, Wyatt?"

He looked at Bishop but the cop merely gazed at him with an eyebrow raised in impatience.

"I . . ."

Elana said, "I'm going to sleep now."

"Can I call you tomorrow?"

"I'd rather you didn't call the house. Christian saw you the other night and he wasn't very happy about it."

Her twenty-two-year-old brother, an honors marketing student with a Greek fisherman's temperament, had actually threatened to beat up Gillette at the trial.

"Then you call *me* when you're alone. I'll be at that number I gave you yesterday."

Silence.

"Have you got it?" he asked. "The number?"

"I've got it." Then: "Good night."

"Don't forget to call a lawyer about that—"

The phone clicked silent and Gillette hung up.

"I didn't handle that too well."

"At least she didn't hang up on you right away. That's something." Bishop put the beer bottle in the recycling bin. "I hate working late – I can't have supper without my beer but then I have to wake up a couple times during the night and pee. That's 'cause I'm getting old. Well, we've got a tough day tomorrow. Let's get some shut-eye."

Gillette asked, "You going to handcuff me somewhere?"

"Escaping twice in two days'd be bad form, even for a hacker. I think we'll forgo the bracelet. Guest room's in there. You'll find towels and a fresh toothbrush in the bathroom."

"Thanks."

"We get up at six-fifteen around here." The detective disappeared down the dim hallway.

Gillette listened to the creak of boards, the sound of water in pipes. A door closing.

Then he was alone, surrounded by the particularly thick silence of someone else's house late at night, his fingers spontaneously keying a dozen messages on an invisible machine.

*   *   *

But it wasn't six-fifteen when his host woke him. It was just after five.

"Must be Christmas," the detective said, clicking on the overhead light. He was wearing brown pajamas. "We got a present."

Gillette, like most hackers, felt that sleep should be avoided like the flu but he wasn't at his best upon waking. Eyes still closed, he muttered, "A present?"

"Triple-X called me on my cell phone five minutes ago. He's got Phate's real e-mail address. It's deathknell@mol.com."

"MOL? Never heard of an Internet provider with that name." Gillette rolled from bed, fighting the dizziness.

Bishop continued, "I called everybody on the team. They're on their way to the office now."

"Which means us too?" the hacker muttered sleepily.

"Which means us too."

Twenty minutes later they were showered and dressed. Jennie had coffee ready in the kitchen but they passed on food; they wanted to get to the CCU office as soon as possible. Bishop kissed his wife. He took her hands in his and said, "About that appointment thing of yours. . . . All you have to do is say the word and I'll be at the hospital in fifteen minutes."

She kissed his forehead. "I'm having a few tests done, honey. That's all."

"No, no, no, you listen," he said solemnly. "If you need me I'll be there."

"If I need you," she conceded, "I'll call. I promise."

As they were heading out the door a sudden roaring filled the kitchen. Jennie Bishop rolled the reassembled Hoover back and forth over the rug. She shut it off and gave her husband a hug.

"Works great," Jennie said. "Thanks, honey."

Bishop frowned in confusion. "I—"

Gillette interrupted quickly. "A job like that must've taken half the night."

"And he cleaned up afterward," Jennie Bishop said with a wry smile. "That's the miraculous part."

"Well—" Bishop began.

"We better be going," Gillette interrupted.

Jennie waved them off and started making breakfast for Brandon, glancing affectionately at her resurrected vacuum.

As the two men walked outside Bishop whispered to the hacker, "So? *Did* it take you half the night?"

"To fix the vacuum?" Gillette replied. "Naw, only ten minutes. I could've done it in five but I couldn't find any tools. I had to use a dinner knife and a nutcracker."

The detective said, "I didn't think you knew anything about vacuum cleaners."

"I didn't. But I was curious why it didn't work. So now I know *all* about vacuum cleaners." Gillette climbed into the car then turned to Bishop. "Say, any chance we could stop at that 7-Eleven again? As long as it's on the way."

CHAPTER 00011101 / TWENTY-NINE

———◆◆◆◆◆———

But, despite what Triple-X had told Bishop in his phone call, Phate – in his new incarnation as Deathknell – continued to remain out of reach.

Once Gillette was back at the Computer Crimes Unit he booted up HyperTrace and ran a search on MOL.com. He found that the full name of the Internet service provider was Monterey Internet On-Line. Its headquarters were in Pacific Grove, California, about a hundred miles south of San Jose. But when they contacted Pac Bell security in Salinas about tracing the call from MOL to Phate's computer it turned out that there *was* no Monterey Internet On-Line and the real geographic location of the server was in Singapore.

"Oh, that's smart," a groggy Patricia Nolan muttered, sipping a Starbucks coffee. Her morning voice was low; it sounded like man's. She sat down next to Gillette. She was as disheveled as ever in her floppy sweater dress – green today. Obviously not an early riser, Nolan wasn't even bothering to brush her hair out of her face.

"I don't get it," Shelton said. "What's smart? What's it all mean?"

Gillette said, "Phate created his own Internet provider. And he's the only customer. Well, probably Shawn is too. And the server they're connecting through is in Singapore – there's no way we can trace back to their machines."

"Like a shell corporation in the Cayman Islands," said Frank Bishop, who, even if he'd had little prior knowledge of the Blue Nowhere, was good at coming up with apt Real World metaphors.

"But," Gillette added, seeing the discouraged faces of the team, "the address is still important."

"Why?" Bishop asked.

"Because it means we can send him a love letter."

Linda Sanchez walked through the front door of CCU, toting a Dunkin' Donuts bag, bleary-eyed and moving slow. She looked down and noticed that her tan suit jacket was buttoned incorrectly. She didn't bother to fix it and set the food out on a plate.

"Any new branches on your family tree?" Bishop asked.

She shook her head. "So what happens is this – I get this scary movie, okay? My grandmother told me you can induce labor by telling ghost stories. You heard about that, boss?"

"News to me," Bishop said.

"Anyway, we figure a scary movie'll work just as good. So I rent *Scream* okay? What happens? My girl and her husband fall asleep on the couch but the movie scares *me* so much *I* can't get any sleep. I was up all night."

She disappeared into the coffee room and brought the pot out.

Wyatt Gillette gratefully took the coffee – his second cup that morning – but for breakfast he stuck with Pop-Tarts.

Stephen Miller arrived a few minutes later, with Tony Mott right behind him, sweating from the bike ride to the office.

Gillette explained to the rest of the team about Triple-X's sending them Phate's real e-mail address and his plans to send Phate a message.

"What's it going to say?" Nolan asked.

"'Dear Phate,'" Gillette said. "'Having a nice time, wish you were here, and, by the way, here's a picture of a dead body.'"

"*What?*" Miller asked.

Gillette asked Bishop, "Can you get me a crime scene photo? A picture of a corpse?"

"I suppose," the detective replied.

Gillette nodded toward the white-board. "I'm going to

imp that I'm that hacker in Bulgaria he used to trade pictures with, Vlast. I'll upload a picture for him."

Nolan laughed and nodded. "And he'll get a virus along with it. You'll take over *his* machine."

"I'm going to try to."

"Why do you need to send a picture?" Shelton asked. He seemed uneasy with the idea of sending evidence of gruesome crimes into the Blue Nowhere for all to see.

"My virus isn't as clever as Trapdoor. With mine Phate has to *do* something to activate it so I can get into his system. He'll have to open the attachment containing the picture for the virus to work."

Bishop called headquarters and had a trooper fax a copy of a crime scene photo in a recent murder case to CCU.

Gillette glanced at the picture – of a young woman bludgeoned to death – but looked away quickly. Stephen Miller scanned it into digital form so they could upload it with the e-mail. The cop seemed immune to the terrible crime depicted in the picture and matter-of-factly went through the scanning procedure. He handed Gillette a disk containing the picture.

Bishop asked, "What if Phate sees an e-mail from Vlast and writes him to ask if it's really from him or sends him a reply?"

"I thought about that. I'm going to send Vlast another virus, one that'll block any e-mails from the U.S."

Gillette went online to get his tool kit from his cache at the air force lab in Los Alamos. From it he downloaded and modified what he needed – the viruses and his own anonymizing e-mail program – he wasn't trusting Stephen Miller anymore. He then sent a copy of the MailBlocker virus to Vlast in Bulgaria and, to Phate, Gillette's own version of Backdoor-G. This was a well-known virus that let a remote user take over someone else's computer, usually when they're both on the same computer network – for instance two employees working for the same company. Gillette's version, though, would work with any two computers; they didn't need to be connected through a network.

"I've got an alert on our machine. If Phate opens the picture my virus'll go active and a tone sounds here. I'll get into his computer and we'll see if we can find anything that'll lead us to him or Shawn . . . or to the next victim."

The phone rang and Miller answered. He listened and said to Bishop, "For you. It's Charlie Pittman."

Bishop, pouring milk in his coffee, hit the speaker button on the phone.

"Thanks for calling back, Officer Pittman."

"Not a problem, Detective." The man's voice was distorted by the cheap speaker. "What can I do for you?"

"Well, Charlie, I know you have that Peter Fowler investigation open. But next time we have an operation underway, I'm going to have to ask that you or somebody at the county police comes to me first so we can coordinate."

Silence. Then: "How's that?"

"I'm speaking of the operation at the Bay View Motel yesterday."

"The, uh, what?" The voice in the tinny speaker was perplexed.

"Jesus," Bob Shelton said, turning his troubled eyes toward his partner. "He doesn't *know* about it. The guy you saw wasn't Pittman."

"Officer," Bishop asked urgently, "did you introduce yourself to me two nights ago in Sunnyvale?"

"We got a misunderstanding going on here, sir. I'm in Oregon, fishing. I've been on vacation for a week and I'll be here for another three days. I just called the office to get messages. I heard yours and called you back. That's all I know."

Tony Mott leaned toward the speaker. "You mean you weren't at the state police Computer Crimes Unit headquarters yesterday?"

"Uh, no, sir. Like I said. Oregon. Fishing."

Mott looked at Bishop. "This guy claiming to be Pittman was outside yesterday. Said he'd had a meeting here. I didn't think anything of it."

"No, he wasn't here," Miller said.

Bishop asked Pittman, "Officer, was there some kind of memo about your vacation?"

"Sure. We always send one around."

"On paper? Or was it on e-mail?"

"We use e-mails for everything nowadays," the officer said defensively. "People think the county's not so up-to-date as everybody else but that's not so."

Bishop explained, "Well, somebody's been using your name. With a fake shield and ID."

"Damn. Why?"

"Probably has to do with a homicide investigation we're running."

"What should I do?"

"Call your commander and get a report on the record. But for the moment we'd appreciate it if you'd keep this to yourself otherwise. It'd be helpful if the perp doesn't know we're on to him. Don't send anything by e-mail. Only use the phone."

"Sure. I'll call my HQ right now."

Bishop apologized to Pittman for the dressing-down and hung up. He glanced at the team. "Social engineered again." He said to Mott, "Describe him, the guy you saw."

"Thin, mustache. Wore a dark raincoat."

"Same one we saw in Sunnyvale. What was he doing here?"

"Looked like he was leaving the office but I didn't actually see him come out the door. Maybe he was snooping around."

Gillette said, "It's Shawn. Has to be."

Bishop concurred. He said to Mott, "Let's you and me come up with a picture of what he looks like." He turned to Miller, "You have an Identikit here?"

This was a briefcase containing plastic overlays of different facial attributes that could be combined so witnesses could reconstruct an image of a suspect – essentially it was a police artist in a box.

But Linda Sanchez shook her head. "We don't usually do much with facial IDs."

Bishop said, "I've got one in the car. I'll be right back."

In his dining room office Phate was typing contentedly away when a flag rose on screen, indicating that he had an e-mail – one sent to his private screen name, Deathknell.

He noticed that it'd been sent by Vlast, his Bulgarian friend. An attachment was included. They'd traded snuff pictures regularly at one time but hadn't for a while and he wondered if that's what his friend had sent him.

Phate was curious what the man had sent but he'd have to wait until later to find out. At the moment he was too excited about his latest hunt with Trapdoor. After an hour of serious passcode cracking on borrowed supercomputer time Phate had finally seized root in a computer system not far away from his house in Los Altos.

He now scrolled through the menu.

Stanford-Packard Medical Center
Palo Alto, California

Main Menu

1. Administration
2. Personnel
3. Patient Admissions
4. Patient Records
5. Departments by Specialty
6. CMS
7. Facilities management
8. Tyler-Kresge Rehabilitation Center
9. Emergency Services
10. Critical Care Unit

He spent some time exploring and finally chose number 6. A new menu appeared.

Computerized Medical Services

1. Surgical Scheduling
2. Medicine Dosage and Administration
   Scheduling
3. Oxygen Replenishment
4. Oncological Chemo/Radiation Scheduling
5. Patient Dietary Menus and Scheduling

He typed 2 and hit ENTER.

In the parking lot of the Computer Crimes Unit Frank Bishop, on his way to fetch the Identikit, sensed the threat before he actually looked directly at the man.

Bishop knew the intruder – fifty feet away, half hidden through the early-morning mist and fog – was dangerous the way you know somebody is carrying a weapon just because of the way he steps off the curb. The way you *know* that a threat awaits you behind the door, down the alley, in the front seat of the stopped car.

Bishop hesitated for only a moment. But then he continued on his way as if he suspected nothing. He couldn't see the intruder's face clearly but he knew it had to be Pittman – well, Shawn. He'd been staking out the place yesterday when Tony Mott had seen him and he was staking it out again.

Only today the detective had a sense that Shawn might be doing more than surveillance; maybe he was hunting.

And Frank Bishop, veteran of the trenches, guessed that if this man was here then he'd know what kind of car Bishop drove and that he was going to cut Bishop off on the way to his vehicle, that he'd already checked angles and shooting zones and backgrounds.

So the detective continued on his way toward the car, patting his pockets as if looking for the cigarettes that he'd given up smoking years ago and gazing up at the rain with a perplexed frown on his face, trying to fathom the weather.

Nothing makes perps more skittish and likely to flee – or attack – than unpredictability and sudden motion by cops.

He knew he could sprint back inside CCU for help but if he did that Shawn would vanish and they might never get this chance again. No, Bishop would no more miss this chance to nail the killer's partner than he'd ignore his son's tears.

Keep walking, keep walking.

It all comes down to this. . . .

A bit of dark motion ahead, as Shawn, now hiding beside a large Winnebago camper, peeked out to gauge Bishop's position and then ducked back again. The detective continued strolling over the asphalt, pretending that he hadn't seen.

When he was nearly to the Winnebago, the detective ducked to the right, pulling his well-worn gun from his holster, and sprinted as fast as he could around the corner of the camper. He raised his weapon.

But he stopped fast.

Shawn was gone. In the few seconds that it had taken him to circle behind the vehicle Phate's partner had vanished.

To his right, across the parking lot, a car door slammed. Bishop spun toward the sound, crouching and raising his weapon. But he saw that the noise had come from a delivery van. A heavyset black man was carrying a box from the vehicle to a nearby factory.

Well, where could Shawn have gotten to?

Then he found out – the door to the camper behind him flew open and, before he could turn, Bishop felt a pistol barrel nestle itself against the back of his head.

The detective had a fast glimpse of the slight man's mustachioed face as Shawn leaned forward and his hand shot out like a snake to rip Bishop's weapon away.

Bishop thought of Brandon and then of Jennie.

He sighed.

It all comes down to this. . . .

Frank Bishop closed his eyes.

CHAPTER 00011110 / THIRTY

T he chime on the CCU computer was merely an off-the-
shelf .wav sound but to the team it blared like a siren.

Wyatt Gillette ran to the workstation. "Yes!" he whispered. "Phate's looked at the picture. The virus is in his
machine."

On the screen flashed these words:

Config.sys modified

"That's it. But we don't have much time – all he has to do
is check his system once and he's going to see that we're
inside."

Gillette sat down at the computer. Lifted his hands to the
keyboard, feeling the unparalleled excitement he always did
just before he started a journey into an uncharted part – an
illicit part – of the Blue Nowhere.

He started to key.

"Gillette!" a man's voice shouted as the front door of the
CCU crashed open.

The hacker turned to see someone striding into the
dinosaur pen. Gillette gasped. It was Shawn – the man
who'd pretended to be Charles Pittman.

"Jesus," Shelton called, startled.

Tony Mott moved fast, reaching for his large silver pistol.
But Shawn had his own weapon out of his holster and,
before Mott could even draw, Shawn's was cocked and
aimed at the young cop's head. Mott lifted his hands slowly.

Shawn motioned Sanchez and Miller back and continued on toward Gillette, pointing the gun at him.

The hacker stood and backed away, his arms up.

There was nowhere to run.

But, wait. . . . What was going on?

Frank Bishop, grim-faced, walked through the front door. He was flanked by two large men in suits.

So, he *wasn't* Shawn.

An ID appeared in the man's hand. "I'm Arthur Backle, with the Department of Defense Criminal Investigation Division." He nodded at his two partners. "These're Agents Griffin and Cable."

"You're CID? What's going on here?" Shelton barked.

Gillette said to Bishop, "We're linked to Phate's machine. But we've only got a few minutes. I've got to go in now!"

Bishop started to speak but Backle said to one of his partners, "Cuff him."

The man stepped forward and ratcheted handcuffs on Gillette. "No!"

Mott said, "You told me you were Pittman."

Backle shrugged. "I was working undercover. I had reason to suspect you might not cooperate if I identified myself."

"Fucking right we wouldn't've cooperated," Bob Shelton said.

Backle said to Gillette, "We're here to escort you back to the San Jose Correctional Facility."

"You can't!"

Bishop said, "I talked to the Pentagon, Wyatt. It's legit We got busted." He shook his head.

Mott said, "But the director approved his release."

"Dave Chambers is out," the detective explained. "Peter Kenyon's acting director of CID. He rescinded the release order."

Kenyon, Gillette recalled, was the man who'd overseen the creation of the Standard 12 encryption program. The man who was the most likely to end up embarrassed – if not unemployed – if it was cracked. "What happened to Chambers?"

"Financial impropriety," narrow-faced Backle said

prissily. "Insider trading, off-shore corporations. I don't know and I don't care." Backle then said to Gillette, "We have an order to look through all the files you've had access to and see if there's evidence related to your improper accessing of Department of Defense encryption software."

Tony Mott said desperately to Bishop, "We're online with Phate, Frank. Right now!"

Bishop started at the screen. He said to Backle, "Please! We have a chance to find out where this suspect is. Wyatt's the only one who can help us."

"Let him go online? In your dreams."

Shelton snapped, "You need a warrant if—"

The blue-backed paper appeared in the hands of one of Backle's partners. Bishop read it quickly and nodded sourly. "They can take him back and confiscate all his disks and any computers he's used."

Backle looked around, saw an empty office and told his partners to lock Gillette inside while they searched for the files.

"Don't let them do it, Frank!" Gillette called. "I was just about to seize root of his machine. This is his *real* machine, not a hot one. It could have addresses in it. It could have Shawn's real name. It could have the address of his next victim!"

"Shut up, Gillette," Backle snapped.

"No!" the hacker protested, struggling against the agents, who easily dragged him toward the office. "Get your fucking hands off me! We—"

They pitched him inside and closed the door.

"Can *you* get inside Phate's machine?" Bishop asked Stephen Miller.

The big man looked at the screen of the workstation uneasily. "I don't know. Maybe. It's just . . . If you hit one key wrong Phate'll know we're inside."

Bishop was in agony. This was their first real break and it was being stolen away from them because of pointless infighting and government bureaucracy. This was their only chance to look inside the electronic mind of the killer.

"Where're Gillette's files?" Backle asked. "And his disks?"

No one volunteered the information. The team gazed defiantly at the agent. Backle shrugged and said in a cheerful tone, "We'll confiscate everything. Doesn't matter to us. We'll just take it and you'll see it in six months – if you're lucky."

Bishop nodded at Sanchez.

"That workstation there," she muttered, pointing.

Backle and the other agents started looking over three-and-a-half-inch floppy disks as if they could see through the colorful plastic coverings and identify the data inside with their naked eyes.

As Miller stared at the screen uneasily, Bishop turned to Patricia Nolan and Mott. "Can either of *you* run Wyatt's program?"

Nolan said, "I know how it works in theory. But I've never cracked into somebody's machine with Backdoor-G. All I've done is try to find the virus and inoculate against it."

Mott said, "Same with me. And Wyatt's program is a hybrid he hacked together himself. It's probably got some unique command lines."

Bishop made the decision. He picked the civilian, saying to Patricia Nolan, "Do the best you can."

She sat down at the workstation. Wiped her hands on her bulky skirt and shoved her hair out of her face, staring at the screen, trying to understand the commands on the menu, which were, to Bishop, as incomprehensible as Russian.

The detective's cell phone rang. He answered. "Yes?" He listened for a moment. "Yessir. Who, Agent Backle?"

The agent looked up.

Bishop continued into the phone. "He's here, sir. . . . But . . . No, this isn't a secure line. I'll have him call you on one of the landlines in the office. Yessir. I'll do it right now, sir." The detective scribbled a number and hung up. He lifted an eyebrow at Backle. "That was Sacramento. You're supposed to call the secretary of Defense. At the Pentagon. He wants you to call on a secure line. Here's his private number."

One of his partners glanced at Backle uncertainly. "Secretary Metzger?" he whispered. The reverent tone suggested that calls like this were unprecedented.

Backle slowly took the phone that Bishop pushed toward him. "You can use this one," the detective said.

The agent hesitated then punched the number into the phone. After a moment he came to attention. "This is CID agent Backle, sir. I'm on a secure line. . . . Yessir." Backle nodded broadly. "Yessir. . . . It was on Peter Kenyon's orders. The California State Police kept it from us, sir. They got him out on John Doe. . . . Yessir. Well, if that's what you'd like. But you understand what Gillette's done, sir. He—" More nodding. "Sorry, I didn't mean to be insubordinate. I'll handle it, sir."

He hung up and said to his partners, "Somebody's got friends in fucking high places." He nodded at the whiteboard. "Your suspect? Holloway? One of the men he killed in Virginia was related to some big White House contributor. So Gillette's supposed to stay out of jail until you collar the perp." He hissed a disgusted sigh. "Fucking politics." A glance toward the partners. "You two stand down. Go on back to the office." To Bishop he said, "You can keep him for the time being. But I'm baby-sitting till the case is over with."

"I understand, sir," Bishop said, running to the office where the agents had thrown Gillette and unlocking the door.

Without even asking why he'd been sprung Gillette sprinted to the workstation. Patricia Nolan gratefully yielded the chair to him.

Gillette sat down. He looked up at Bishop, who said, "You're still on the team for the time being."

"That's good," the hacker said formally, scooting closer to the keyboard. But, out of earshot of Backle, Bishop gave a laugh and whispered to Gillette, "How on earth d'you pull that off?"

For it hadn't been the Pentagon calling Bishop; it was Wyatt Gillette himself. He'd rung Bishop's cell phone from one of the phones in the office where he'd been locked up. The real conversation had been a bit different from the apparent:

Bishop had answered, *"Yes?"*

Gillette: *"Frank, it's Wyatt. I'm on a phone in the office.*

Pretend I'm your boss. Tell me that Backle's there."

"Yessir. Who, Agent Backle?"

"Good," the hacker had replied.

"He's here, sir."

*"Now tell him to call the secretary of Defense. But make
sure he calls from the main phone line in the CCU office.
Not his cell phone or anybody else's. Tell him that's a secure
line."*

"But—"

Gillette had reassured, *"It's okay. Just do it. And give
him this number."* He'd then dictated to Bishop a
Washington, D.C., phone number.

*"No, this isn't a secure line. I'll have him call you on
one of the landlines in the office. Yessir. I'll do it right now,
sir."*

Gillette now explained in a whisper, "I cracked the local
Pac Bell switch with the machine in there and had all calls
from CCU to that number I gave you transferred to me."

Bishop shook his head, both troubled and amused.
"Whose number is it?"

"Oh, it really *is* the secretary of Defense's. It was just as
easy to crack his line as anybody else's. But don't worry –
I reset the switch." Gillette impatiently studied the screen.

He began keying.

Gillette's variation of the Backdoor-G program launched
him right into the middle of Phate's computer. The first
thing he saw was a folder named Trapdoor.

Gillette's heart began to pound and he sizzled with a
mixture of agitation and exhilaration as his curiosity took
over his soul like a drug. Here was a chance to learn about
this miraculous software, maybe even glimpse the source
code itself.

But he had a dilemma: Although he could slip into the
Trapdoor folder and look at the program, because he had root
control, he would be very vulnerable to detection – the same
way that Gillette had been able to see Phate when the killer
had invaded the CCU computer. If that happened Phate would
immediately shut down his machine and create a new Internet
service provider and e-mail address. They'd never be able to

find him again, certainly not in time to save the next victim.

No, he understood that – as powerfully as he felt his curiosity – he'd have to forgo a look at Trapdoor and search for clues that might give them an idea of where they might find Phate or Shawn or who that next victim might be.

With painful reluctance Gillette turned away from Trapdoor and began to prowl stealthily through Phate's computer.

Many people think of computer architecture as a perfectly symmetrical and antiseptic building: proportional, logical, organized. Wyatt Gillette, however, knew that the inside of a machine was much more organic than that, like a living creature, a place that changes constantly whenever the user adds a new program, installs new hardware or even does something as simple as turning the power off or on. Each machine contains thousands of places to visit and myriad different paths by which get to each destination. And each machine is unique from every other. Examining someone else's computer was like walking through the local Silicon Valley tourist attraction, the nearby Winchester Mystery House, a rambling 160-room mansion where the widow of the inventor of the Winchester repeating rifle had lived. It was a place filled with hidden passages and secret chambers (and, according to the eccentric mistress of the house, ghosts).

The virtual passageways of Phate's computer lead finally to a folder labeled Correspondence, and Gillette went after it like a shark.

He opened the first of the subfolders, Outgoing.

This contained mostly e-mails to Shawn@MOL.com from Holloway under both of his usernames, Phate and Deathknell.

Gillette murmured, "I was right. Shawn's on the same Internet provider Phate is – Monterey On-Line. There's no way to track him down either."

He flipped open some of the e-mails at random and read them. He observed right away that they used only their screen names, Phate or Deathknell and Shawn. The correspondence was highly technical – software patches and copies of engineering data and specifications down-

loaded from the Net and various databases. It was as if
they were worried that their machines might be seized
and had agreed never to refer to their personal lives or
who they were outside of the Blue Nowhere. There wasn't
a shred of evidence as to who Shawn might be or where
he or Phate lived.

But then Gillette found a somewhat different e-mail. It
had been sent from Phate to Shawn several weeks ago – at
three A.M., which is considered the witching hour by
hackers, the time when only the most hard-core geeks are
online.

"Check this one out," Gillette said to the team.

Patricia Nolan was reading over Gillette's shoulder. He
felt her brush against him as she reached forward and tapped
the screen. "Looks like they're a little more than just
friends."

He read the beginning to the team. "'*Last night I'd
finished working on the patch and lay in the bed. Sleep was
far, far away, and all I could do was think about you, the
comfort you give me . . . I started touching myself. I really
couldn't stop. . . .*'"

Gillette looked up. The entire team – DoD agent Backle
too – was staring at him. "Should I keep going?"

"Is there anything in it that'll help track him down?"
Bishop asked.

The hacker skimmed the rest of the e-mail quickly. "No.
It's pretty X-rated."

"Maybe you could just keep looking," Frank Bishop said.

Gillette backed out of Outgoing and examined the
Incoming correspondence file. Most were messages from
list servers, which were e-mailing services that automatically sent bulletins on topics of interest to subscribers. There
were some old e-mails from Vlast and some from Triple-
X – technical information about software and warez. It
wasn't helpful. All the others were from Shawn but they
were responses to Phate's requests about debugging
Trapdoor or writing patches for other programs. These
e-mails were even more technical and less revealing than
Phate's.

He opened another.

From: Shawn

To: Phate

Re: FWD: Cellular Phone Companies

Shawn had found an article on the Net describing which mobile phone companies were the most efficient and forwarded it to Phate.

Bishop looked at it and said, "Might be something in there about which phones they're using. Can you copy it?"

The hacker hit the print-screen – also called the screen-dump – button, which sent the contents on the monitor to the printer.

"Download it," Miller said. "That'll be a lot faster."

"I don't think we want to do that." The hacker went on to explain that a screen dump does nothing to affect the internal operations of Phate's computer but simply sends the images and text on the CCU's monitor to the printer. Phate would have no way of knowing that Gillette was copying the data. A download, however, would be far easier for Phate to notice. It might also trigger an alarm in Phate's computer.

He continued searching through the killer's machine.

More files scrolled past, opening, closing. A fast scan, then on to another file. Gillette couldn't help but feel exhilarated – and overwhelmed – by the sheer amount, and brilliance, of the technical material on the killer's machine.

"Can you tell anything about Shawn from his e-mails?" Tony Mott asked.

"Not much," Gillette replied. He gave his opinion that Shawn was brilliant, matter-of-fact, cold. Shawn's answers were abrupt and assumed a great deal of knowledge on Phate's part, which suggested to Gillette that Shawn was arrogant and would have no patience for people who couldn't keep up with him. He probably had at least one college degree from a good school; even though he rarely bothered to write in complete sentences his grammar, syntax and punctuation were excellent. Much of the software code sent back and forth between the two was written for the East Coast version of Unix – not the Berkeley version.

"So," Bishop speculated, "Shawn might've known Phate at Harvard."

The detective noted this on the white-board and had Bob Shelton call the school to see if anyone named Shawn had been a student or on the faculty in the past ten years.

Patricia Nolan glanced at her Rolex watch and said, "You've been inside for eight minutes. He could check on the system at any time."

Bishop nodded. "Let's move on. See if we can find out something about the next victim."

Keying softly now, as if Phate could hear him, Gillette returned to the main directory – a tree diagram of folders and subfolders.

```
A:/

C:/
   -Operating System
   -Correspondence
   -Trapdoor
   -Business
   -Games
   -Tools
   -Viruses
   -Pictures

D:/
   -Backup
```

"Games!" Gillette and Bishop shouted simultaneously and the hacker entered this directory.

```
   -Games
      -ENIAC week
      -IBM PC week
      -Univac week
      -Apple week
      -Altair week
      -Next year's projects
```

"The fucker's got it all laid out there, neat and organized," Bob Shelton said.

"And more killings lined up." Gillette touched the screen. "The date the first Apple was released. The old Altair computer. And, Jesus, next year too."

"Check out this week – Univac," Bishop said.

Gillette expanded the directory tree.

```
-Univac week.
  -Completed games
  -Lara Gibson
  -St. Francis Academy
  -Next projects
```

"There!" Tony Mott called. "'Next Projects.'"

Gillette clicked on it.

The folder contained dozens of files – page after page of dense notes, graphics, diagrams, pictures, schematics, newspaper clippings. There was too much to read quickly so Gillette started at the beginning, scrolled through the first file, hitting the screen-dump button every time he jumped to the next page. He moved as quickly as he could but screen dumps are slow; it took about ten seconds to print out each page.

"It's taking too much time," he said.

"I think we should download it," Patricia Nolan said.

"That's a risk," Gillette said. "I told you."

"But remember Phate's ego," Nolan countered. "He thinks there's nobody good enough to get inside his machine so he might not've put a download alarm on it."

"It *is* awfully slow," Stephen Miller said. "We've only got three pages so far."

"It's your call," Gillette said to Bishop.

The detective leaned forward, staring at the screen, while Gillette's hands hung in the empty space in front of him, furiously pounding on a keyboard that didn't exist.

Phate was sitting comfortably at his laptop in the immaculate dining room of his house.

Though he wasn't really here at all.

He was lost in the Machine World, roaming through the computer he'd hacked earlier and planning his attack for later that day.

Suddenly an urgent beeping sounded from his machine's speakers. Simultaneously a red box appeared in the upper-right corner of his screen. Inside the box was a single word:

ACCESS

He gasped in shock. Someone was trying to download files from his machine! This had *never* happened. Stunned, sweat bursting out on his face, Phate didn't even bother to examine the system to discover what was happening. He knew instantly: the picture supposedly sent by Vlast had in fact been e-mailed to him by Wyatt Gillette to implant a back-door virus in his computer.

The fucking Judas Valleyman was prowling through his system right now!

Phate reached for the power switch – the way a driver instinctively goes for the brake when he sees a squirrel in the road.

But then, like some drivers, he smiled coldly and let his machine keep running at full speed.

His hands returned to the keyboard and he held down the SHIFT and CONTROL keys on his computer while simultaneously pressing the E key.

CHAPTER 0001111 / THIRTY-ONE

On the monitor in front of Wyatt Gillette the words
flashed in hot type:

BEGIN BATCH ENCRYPTION

A moment later another message:

ENCRYPTING – DEPARTMENT OF DEFENSE
STANDARD 12

"No!" Gillette cried, as the download of Phate's files
stopped and the contents of the Next Projects file turned to
digital oatmeal.

"What happened?" Bishop asked.

"Phate *did* have a download alarm," Nolan muttered,
angry with herself. "I was wrong."

Gillette scanned the screen hopelessly. "He aborted the
download but he didn't log off. He hit a hot key and's
encrypting everything that's on his machine."

"Can you decode it?" Shelton called.

Agent Backle was watching Gillette carefully.

"Not without Phate's decryption key," the hacker said
firmly. "Even Fort Meade running parallel arrays couldn't
decrypt this much data in a month."

Shelton said, "I wasn't asking if you had the key. I was
asking if you can crack it."

"I can't. I told you that. I don't know how to crack Standard 12."

"Fuck," muttered Shelton, staring at Gillette. "People're going to die if we can't find out what's in his computer."

DoD agent Backle sighed. Gillette noticed his eyes straying to the picture of Lara Gibson on the white-board and he said to Gillette, "Go ahead. If it'll save lives go ahead and do it."

Gillette turned back to the screen. For once his fingers, dangling in front of him, refrained from air-keying as he saw the streams of dense gibberish flow past on the screen. Any one of these blocks of type could have a clue as to who Shawn was, where Phate might be, what the address of the next victim was.

"Do it, for Christ's sake," Shelton muttered.

Backle whispered, "I mean it. I'll turn my back on this one."

Gillette watched the data flow past hypnotically. His hands went to the keys. He felt everyone's eyes on him.

But then Bishop asked in a troubled voice, "Wait. Why didn't he just go offline? Why did he encrypt? That doesn't make sense."

"Oh, Jesus," Gillette said. And he knew the answer to that question immediately. He swiveled around and pointed to a gray box on the wall; a red button rose prominently from the middle of it. "Hit the scram switch! Now!" he cried to Stephen Miller, who was closest to it.

Miller glanced at the switch then back to Gillette. "Why?"

The hacker leapt up, sending his chair flying behind him. He made a dive for the button. But it was too late. Before he could push it there was a grinding sound from the main box of the CCU computer and the monitors of every machine in the room turned solid blue as the system failed – the notorious "blue screen of death."

Bishop and Shelton leapt back as sparks shot from one of the vents on the box. Choking smoke and fumes began to fill the room.

"Christ almighty . . ." Mott stepped clear of the machine. The hacker slapped the scram switch with his palm and the power went off; halon gas shot into the computer housing and extinguished the flames.

"What the hell happened?" Shelton asked.

Gillette muttered angrily, "That's why Phate encrypted his data but stayed online – so he could send *our* system a bomb."

"What'd he do?" Bishop asked.

The hacker shook his head. "I'd say he sent a command that shut down the cooling fan and then ordered the hard drive head to a sector on the disk that doesn't exist. That jammed the drive motor and it overheated."

Bishop surveyed the smoldering box. He said to Miller, "I want to be up and running again in a half hour. Take care of that, will you?"

Miller said doubtfully, "I don't know what kind of hardware central services has in inventory. They're pretty backlogged. Last time it took a couple of days to get a replacement drive, let alone a machine. The thing is—"

"No." Bishop said, furious. "A half hour. Tops."

The pear-shaped man's eyes scanned the floor. He nodded toward some small personal computers. "We could probably do a mini-network with those and reload the backup files. Then—"

"Just do it," Bishop said and lifted the sheets of paper out of the printer – what they'd managed to steal from Phate's computer via the screen dump before he encrypted the data. To the rest of the team he said, "Let's see if we've caught anything."

Gillette's eyes and mouth burned from the fumes of the smoldering computer. He noticed that Bishop, Shelton and Sanchez had paused and were staring at the smoking machine uneasily, undoubtedly thinking the same thing he was: How unnerving it was that something as insubstantial as software code – mere strings of digital ones and zeros – could so easily caress your physical body with a hurtful, even lethal, touch.

Under the gaze of his faux family, watching him from the pictures in the living room, Phate paced throughout the room, nearly breathless with anger.

Valleyman had gotten inside *his* machine. . . .

And, worse, he'd done this with a simple-minded back-door program, the kind that a high school geek could hack together.

He'd immediately changed his machine's identity and his Internet address, of course. There was no way Gillette could break in again. But what troubled Phate now was this: What had the police seen? Nothing in this machine would lead them to his house in Los Altos but it had a lot of information about his present and future attacks. Had Valleyman seen the Next Projects folder? Had he seen what Phate was about to do in a few hours?

All the plans were made for the next assault. . . . Hell, it was already under way.

Should he pick a new victim?

But the thought of giving up on a plan that he'd spent so much effort and time on was hard for him. More galling than the wasted effort, however, was the thought that if he abandoned his plans it would be because of a man who'd betrayed him – the man who'd turned him in to the Massachusetts police, exposed the Great Social Engineering and, in effect, murdered John Patrick Holloway, forcing Phate underground forever.

He sat at the computer screen once more, rested his callused fingers on plastic keys smooth as a woman's polished nails. He closed his eyes and, like any hacker trying to figure out how to debug some flawed script, he let his mind wander where it wished.

Jennie Bishop was wearing one of those terrible, open-up-the-back robes they give you in hospitals.

And what exactly, she thought, is the point of those tiny blue dots on the cloth?

She propped up the pillow and looked absently around the yellow room as she waited for Dr. Williston. It was eleven-fifteen and the doctor was late.

She was thinking about what she had to do after the tests here were completed. Shopping, picking up Brandon after school, shepherding him to the tennis courts. Today the boy would be playing against Linda Garland, who was the cutest, little thing in fourth grade – and a total brat whose only strategy was to rush the net every chance she got, in an attempt, Jennie was convinced, to break her opponents' noses with a killer volley.

Thinking about Frank too, of course. And deciding how vastly relieved she was that her husband wasn't here. He was *such* a contradiction. Chasing bad men through the streets of Oakland. Unfazed as he arrested killers twice his size and chatted happily with prostitutes and drug dealers. She didn't think she'd ever seen him shaken up.

Until last week. When a medical checkup had shown that Jennie's white blood cell count was out of whack for no logical reason. As she told him the news Frank Bishop went sheet white and had fallen silent. He'd nodded a dozen times, his head rising and falling broadly. She'd thought he was going to cry – something she'd never seen – and Jennie wondered how exactly she'd have handled *that*.

"So what does it all mean?" Frank had asked in a shaky voice.

"Might be some kind of weird infection," she told him, looking him right in the eye, "or it might be cancer."

"Okay, okay," he'd repeated in a whisper, as if speaking more loudly or saying anything else would pitch her into imminent peril.

They'd talked about some meaningless details – appointment times, Dr. Williston's credentials – and then she'd booted him outside to tend his orchard while she got supper ready.

Might be some kind of weird infection . . .

Oh, she loved Frank Bishop more than she'd ever loved anyone, more than she ever *could* love anyone. But Jennie was very grateful that her husband wasn't here. She wasn't in any mood to hold somebody else's hand at the moment.

Might be cancer. . . .

Well, she'd know soon enough what it was. She looked at the clock. Where was Dr. Williston? She didn't mind hospitals, didn't mind having unpleasant tests but she hated waiting. Maybe there was something on TV. When did *The Young and the Restless* come on? Or she could listen to the radio, maybe—

A squat nurse wheeling a medical cart pushed into the room. "Morning," the woman said in a thick Latino accent.

"Hello."

"You Jennifer Bishop?"

"That's right."

The nurse hooked Jennie up to a vital functions monitor mounted to the wall above the bed. A soft beep began to sound rhythmically. Then the woman consulted a computer printout and looked over a wide array of medicines.

"You Dr. Williston's patient, right?"

"That's right."

She looked at Jennie's plastic wrist bracelet and nodded. Jennie smiled. "Didn't believe me?"

The nurse said, "Always double-check. My father, he was carpenter, you know. He always say, 'Measure twice, cut once.'"

Jennie struggled to keep from laughing, thinking that this probably wasn't the best expression to share with patients in a hospital.

She watched the nurse draw some clear liquid into the hypodermic and asked, "Dr. Williston ordered an injection?"

"That's right."

"I'm only in for some tests."

Checking the printout again, the woman nodded. "This is what he ordered."

Jennie looked at the sheet of paper but it was impossible to make sense out of the words and numbers on it.

The nurse cleaned her arm with an alcohol wipe and injected the drug. After she withdrew the needle Jennie felt an odd tingle spread through her arm near the site of the injection – a burning coldness.

"The doctor be with you soon."

She left before Jennie could ask her what the injection was. It troubled her a little, the shot. She knew you had to be careful with medicines in her condition but then she told herself there wasn't anything to worry about. The fact that she was pregnant was clearly shown in the records, Jennie knew, and surely no one here would do anything to jeopardize the baby.

CHAPTER 0010000 / THIRTY-TWO

"All I need is the numbers of the cell phone he's using and, oh, about one square mile to call my own. And I can walk right up this fellow's backside."

This reassurance came from Garvy Hobbes, a blond man of indeterminate age, lean except for a seriously round belly that suggested an affection for beer. He was wearing blue jeans and a plaid shirt.

Hobbes was the head of security for the main cellular phone service provider in Northern California, Mobile America.

Shawn's e-mail on cellular phone service, which Gillette had found in Phate's computer, was a survey of companies that provided the best service for people wishing to use their mobile phones to go online. The survey listed Mobile America as number one and the team assumed that Phate would follow Shawn's recommendation. Tony Mott had called Hobbes, with whom the Computer Crimes Unit had often worked in the past.

Hobbes confirmed that many hackers used Mobile America because to go online with a cellular phone you needed a consistently high-quality signal, which Mobile America provided. Hobbes nodded toward Stephen Miller, who was hard at work with Linda Sanchez getting the CCU computers hooked up and online again. "Steve and I were just talking about that last week. He thought we should change our company's name to Hacker's America."

Bishop asked how they could track down Phate now that

they knew he was a customer, though probably an illegal one.

"All you need is the ESN and the MIN of the phone he's using," Hobbes said.

Gillette – who'd done his share of phone phreaking – knew what these initials meant and he explained: Every cell phone had both an ESN (the electronic serial number, which was secret) and an MIN (the mobile identification number – the area code and seven-digit number of the phone itself).

Hobbes went on to explain that if he knew these numbers, and if he was within a mile or so of the phone when it was being used, he could use radio direction finding equipment to track down the caller to within a few feet. Or, as Hobbes repeated, "Right up his backside."

"How do we find out what the numbers of his phone are?" Bishop asked.

"Ah, that's the hard part. Mostly we know the numbers 'cause a customer reports his phone's been stolen. But this fellow doesn't sound like the sort to pickpocket one. However you find out, though, we need those numbers – otherwise we can't do a thing for you."

"How fast can you move if we do get them?"

"Me? Lickety-split. Even faster if I get to ride in one of those cars with the flashing lights on top of it," he joked. He handed them a business card. Hobbes had two office numbers, a fax number, a pager and two cell phone numbers. He grinned. "My girlfriend likes it that I'm highly accessible. I tell her it's 'cause I love her but, fact is, with all the call jacking going on, the company wants me available. Believe you me, stolen cellular service is gonna be *the* big crime of the new century."

"Or one of them," Linda Sanchez muttered, her eyes on the desktop photo of Andy Anderson and his family.

Hobbes left and the team went back to looking over the few documents they'd had a chance to print out from Phate's computer before he encrypted the data.

Miller announced that CCU's improvised network was up and running. Gillette checked it out and supervised the installation of the most current backup tapes – he wanted to make sure there was still no link to ISLEnet from this machine. He'd just finished running the final diagnostic check when the machine started to beep.

Gillette looked at the screen, wondering if his bot had found something else. But, no, the sound was announcing an incoming e-mail. It was from Triple-X.

Reading the message out loud, Gillette said, "'Here's a phile with some good stuff on our phriend.'" He looked up. "File, p-h-i-l-e. Friend, p-h-r-i-e-n-d."

"It's all in the spelling," Bishop mused. Then said, "I thought Triple-X was paranoid – and was only going to use the phone."

"He didn't mention Phate's name and the file itself's encrypted." Gillette noticed the Department of Defense agent stir and he added, "Sorry to disappoint you, Agent Backle – it's not Standard 12. It's a commercial public key encryption program." Then he frowned. "But he never sent us the key to open it. Did anybody get a message from Triple-X?"

No one had taken any calls from the hacker.

"Do you have his number?" Gillette asked Bishop.

The detective said no, that when Triple-X had called earlier with Phate's e-mail address the caller ID on Bishop's phone indicated the hacker was calling from a pay phone.

But Gillette examined the encryption program. He laughed and said, "I'll bet I can crack it without the key." He slipped the disk containing his hacker tools into one of the PCs and loaded a decryption cracker he'd hacked together a few years ago.

Linda Sanchez, Tony Mott and Shelton had been looking over the few pages of material that Gillette had managed to screen dump out of Phate's Next Projects folder before the killer stopped the download and encrypted the data.

Mott taped the sheets up on the white-board and the team stood in a cluster in front of them.

Bishop noted, "There're a lot of references to facilities management – janitorial, parking, security and food services, personnel, payroll. It sounds like the target is a big place."

Mott said, "The last page, look. Medical services."

"A hospital," Bishop said. "He's going after a hospital."

Shelton added, "Makes sense – high security, lots of victims to choose from.

Nolan nodded. "It fits his profile for challenges and game playing. And he could pretend to be anybody – a surgeon or nurse or janitor. Any clue which one he's thinking of?"

But no one could find any reference to a specific hospital on the pages.

Bishop pointed to a block of type on one of the printouts.

CSGEI Claims ID Numbers – Unit 44

"Something about that looks familiar."

Below the words was a long list of what seemed to be social security numbers.

"CSGEI," Shelton said, nodding, also trying to place it. "Yeah, I've heard that before."

Suddenly Linda Sanchez said, "Oh, sure, I know: It's our insurer – the California State Government Employees Insurance Company. Those must be the social security numbers of patients."

Bishop picked up the phone and called CSGEI's office in Sacramento. He told a claims specialist what the team had found and asked what the information designated. He nodded as he listened and then looked up. "They're recent claims for medical services by state employees." Bishop then spoke into the phone again. "What's Unit 44?"

He listened. Then a moment later he frowned. He glanced at the team. "Unit 44's the state police – the San Jose office. That's us. That information's confidential. . . . How did Phate get it?"

"Jesus," Gillette muttered. "Ask if the records for that unit are on ISLEnet."

Bishop did. He nodded. "They sure are."

"Goddamn," Gillette spat out. "When he broke into ISLEnet Phate wasn't online for only forty seconds – shit, he changed the log files just to make us think that. He must've downloaded gigabytes of data. We should—"

"Oh, no," a man's voice gasped, filled with wrenching alarm.

The team turned to see Frank Bishop, mouth open, stricken, pointing at the list of numbers taped to the whiteboard.

"What's wrong, Frank?" Gillette asked.

"He's going to hit Stanford-Packard Medical Center," the detective whispered.

"How do you know?"

"The second line from the bottom, that social security number? It's my wife's. She's in the hospital right now."

A man walked into the doorway of Jennie Bishop's room.

She looked away from the silent TV set – on which she'd been absently watching the melodramatic close-ups on a soap opera and checking out actresses' hairstyles. She was expecting Dr. Williston but the visitor was somebody else – a man in a dark blue uniform. He was young and had a thick black mustache, which didn't quite match his sandy hair. Apparently the facial hair was an attempt to give some maturity to a youthful face. "Mrs. Bishop?" He had a faint southern accent, rare in this part of California.

"That's right."

"My name's Hellman. I'm with the hospital security staff. Your husband called and asked me to stay in your room."

"Why?"

"He didn't tell us. He just said to make sure nobody comes into your room except him or policemen or your doctor."

"Why?"

"He didn't say."

"Is my son all right? Brandon?"

"Haven't heard that he *isn't*."

"Why didn't Frank call me directly?"

Hellman toyed with the can of Mace on his belt. "The phones at the hospital went down about a half hour ago. Repairmen're working on it now. Your husband got through on the radio we use for talking to, you know, our ambulances."

Jennie had her cell phone in her purse but she'd seen a sign on the wall warning that you couldn't use mobiles in hospitals – that the signal sometimes interfered with heart pacemakers and other equipment.

The guard looked around the room and then pulled a chair close to the bed and sat down. She didn't look directly at the young man but she sensed him studying her, scanning her body, as if he were trying to look into the armholes of the dotted gown and see her breasts. She turned to him with a stern glare but he looked away just before she caught him.

Dr. Williston, a round, balding man in his late fifties walked into the room.

"Hello, Jennie, how're you this morning?"

"Okay," she said uncertainly.

Then the doctor noticed the security guard and glanced at him with raised eyebrows.

The man answered, "Detective Bishop asked me to stay with his wife."

Dr. Williston looked the man over and then asked, "You're with hospital security?"

"Yessir."

Jennie said, "Sometimes we run into a little trouble with the cases Frank's working on. He likes to be cautious."

The doctor nodded and then put on his reassuring face. "Okay, Jennie, these tests won't take too long today but I'd like to talk to you about what we're going to be doing – and what we're going to be looking for." He nodded at the bandage on her arm from the injection. "They've already taken blood, I see, and—"

"No. That was from the shot."

"The . . .?"

"You know, the injection."

"How's that?" he asked, frowning.

"About twenty minutes ago. The injection you ordered."

"There was no injection scheduled."

"But . . ." She felt the ice of fear run through her – as cold and stinging as the medicine spreading up her arm from the shot. "The nurse who did it. . . . she had a computer printout. It said you'd ordered an injection!"

"What was the medication? Do you know?"

Breathing fast now, in panic, she whispered, "I don't know! Doctor, the baby . . ."

"Don't worry," he said. "I'll find out. Who was the nurse?"

"I didn't notice her name. She was short, heavy, black hair. Hispanic. She had a cart." Jennie started to cry.

The security guard leaned forward. "Something happened here? Something I can do?"

They both ignored him. The doctor's face scared the absolute hell out of her – he too was panicked. He leaned forward and pulled a flashlight from his pocket. He shone it into her eyes and took her blood pressure. He then looked up at the Hewlett-Packard monitor. "Pulse and pressure are a little high. But let's not worry yet. I'll go find out what happened."

He hurried out of the room.

Let's not worry yet. . . .

The security guard rose and shut the door.

"No," she said. "Leave it open."

"Sorry," he responded calmly. "Your husband's orders."

He sat down again, pulled the chair closer to her. "Pretty quiet in here. How 'bout we turn up that TV."

Jennie didn't respond.

Let's not worry yet. . . .

The guard picked up the remote control and turned the volume up high. He clicked the channel selector to a different soap opera and leaned back.

She sensed him looking at her again but Jennie was hardly thinking about the guard at all. There were only two things in her mind: the horrible memory of the stinging injection. And her baby. She closed her eyes, praying that everything would be all right and cradling her belly, where her two-month-old child lay, perhaps sleeping, perhaps floating motionless as it listened to the fierce, frightened drumming of its mother's troubled heart, a sound that surely filled the tiny creature's entire, dark world.

CHAPTER 00100001 / THIRTY-THREE

⬥————⬥

Feeling stiff, feeling irritated, Department of Defense agent Arthur Backle moved his chair to the side so that he could get a better view of Wyatt Gillette's computer.

The hacker glanced down – at the scraping sound the agent's chair made on the cheap linoleum floor – then back to the screen and continued keying. His fingers flew across the keyboard.

The two men were alone in the Computer Crimes Unit office. When he'd learned that his wife might be the killer's next target Bishop had sped to the hospital. Everyone else had followed, except Gillette, who'd stayed to decode the e-mail they'd received from that guy with the weird name, Triple-X. The hacker had suggested Backle might be more useful at the hospital but the agent had merely offered the inscrutable half smile that he knew infuriated suspects and pulled his chair closer to Gillette's.

Backle couldn't get over the speed with which the hacker's blunt, callused fingertips danced over the keys.

Curiously, the agent was someone who could appreciate talented computer keying. For one thing, his employer, the Department of Defense, was the federal agency that'd been involved in the computer world the longest of any (and was – as DoD public affairs was quick to remind – one of the creators of the Internet). Also, as part of his regular training, the agent had attended various computer crimes courses, hosted by the CIA, the Justice Department and the

Department of Defense. He'd spent hours watching tapes of hackers at work.

Watching Gillette type now brought to mind a recent course in Washington, D.C.

Sitting at cheap fiberboard tables in one of the Pentagon's many conference rooms, the Criminal Investigation Division agents had spent hours under the tutelage of two young men who weren't your typical army continuing ed instructors. One had shoulder-length hair and wore macrame sandals, shorts and a rumpled T-shirt. The other was dressed more conservatively but *did* have extensive body piercings and his crew-cut hair was green. The two had been part of a "tiger team" – the term for a group of former bad-boy hackers who'd turned from the Dark Side (generally after realizing how much money there was to be made by protecting companies and government agencies from their former colleagues).

Skeptical at first about these punks, Backle had nonetheless been won over by their brilliance and their ability to simplify the otherwise incomprehensible subjects of encryption and hacking. The lectures had been the most articulately delivered and understandable of any that he'd attended in his six years with the Criminal Investigation Division of the DoD.

Backle knew he was no expert but, thanks to the class, he was following in general terms what Gillette's cracking program was now doing. It didn't seem to have anything to do with the DoD's Standard 12 encryption system. But Mr. Green Hair had explained how you could camouflage programs. You could, for instance, put a shell around Standard 12 to make it look like some other kind of program – even a game or word processor. And that was why he was now leaning forward, noisily sharing his irritation.

Gillette's shoulders tensed once again and he stopped keying. He looked at the agent. "I *really* need to concentrate here. And you breathing down my neck's a little distracting."

"What's that program you're running again?"

"There's no 'again' about it. I never told you what it was in the first place."

The faint smile again. "Well, tell me, would you? I'm curious."

"An encryption/decryption program I downloaded from the HackerMart Web site and modified myself. It's freeware so I guess I'm not guilty of a copyright violation. Which isn't your jurisdiction anyway. Hey, you want to know the algorithm it uses?"

Backle didn't answer, just stared at the screen, making sure the half-smile was annoyingly lodged on his face.

Gillette said, "Tell you what, Backle, I need to do this. How 'bout if you go get some coffee and a bagel or whatever they have in the canteen up the hall there and let me do my job?" He added cheerfully, "You can look through it when I'm done and then arrest me on some more bullshit charges if you want."

"My, we're a little touchy here, aren't we?" Backle said, scraping the chair legs loudly. "I'm just doing my job."

"And I'm trying to do mine." The hacker turned back to the computer.

Backle shrugged. The hacker's attitude didn't do a thing to diminish his irritation but he did like the idea of a bagel. He stood up, stretched and walked down the corridor, following the smell of coffee.

Frank Bishop skidded the Crown Victoria into the parking lot of the Stanford-Packard Medical Center and leapt from the car, forgetting to shut the engine off or close the door.

Halfway to the front entrance he realized what he'd done and stopped abruptly, turned back. But he heard a woman's voice call, "Go ahead, boss. I got it." It was Linda Sanchez. She, Bob Shelton and Tony Mott were in the unmarked car right behind Bishop's – because he'd been in such a hurry to get to his wife he'd left CCU without waiting for the rest of the team. Patricia Nolan and Stephen Miller were in a third car.

He continued breathlessly on to the front door.

In the main reception area he sped past a dozen waiting patients. At the sign-in desk, three nurses were huddled around the receptionist, staring at a computer screen. No one looked at him right away. Something was wrong. They were all frowning, taking turns at the keyboard.

"Excuse me, this is police business," he said, flashing his shield. "I need to know which room Jennie Bishop is in."

A nurse looked up. "Sorry, Officer. The system's haywire. We don't know what's going on but there's no patient information available."

"I have to find her. Now."

The nurse saw the agonized look on his face and walked over to him. "Is she an in-patient?"

"What?"

"Is she staying overnight?"

"No. She's just having some tests. For an hour or two. She's Dr. Williston's patient."

"Oncology outpatient." The nurse understood. "Okay, that'd be the third floor, west wing. That way." She pointed and started to say something else but Bishop was already sprinting down the hall. A flash of white beside him. He glanced down. His shirt was completely untucked. He shoved it back into his slacks, never breaking stride.

Up the stairs, through the corridor, which seemed to be a mile long, to the west wing.

At the end of the hallway he found a nurse and she directed him to a room. The young blonde had an alarmed expression on her face but whether that was because of something she knew about Jennie or because of *his* concerned expression, Bishop didn't know.

He ran down the hall and burst through the doorway, nearly knocking into a trim young security guard, sitting beside the bed. The man stood up fast, reaching for his pistol.

"Honey!" Jennie cried.

"It's okay," Bishop said to the guard. "I'm her husband."

His wife was crying softly. He ran to her and enfolded her in his arms.

"A nurse gave me a shot," she whispered. "The doctor didn't order it. They don't know what it is. What's going on, Frank?"

He glanced at the security guard, whose name badge read "R. Hellman." The man said, "Happened before I got here, sir. They're looking for that nurse now."

Bishop was thankful the guard was here at all. The

detective had had a terrible time getting through to the hospital security staff to have someone sent to Jennie's room. Phate had crashed the hospital phone switch and the transmissions on the radio had been so staticky he hadn't even been sure what the person on the other end of the radio was saying. But apparently the message had been received all right. Bishop was further pleased that the guard – unlike most of the others he'd seen at the hospital – was wearing a sidearm.

"What is it, Frank?" Jennie repeated.

"That fellow we're after? He found out you were in the hospital. We think he might be here someplace."

Linda Sanchez jogged into the room fast. The guard looked at her police ID, dangling from a chain around her neck and motioned her in. The women knew each other but Jennie was too upset to nod a greeting.

"Frank, what about the baby?" She was sobbing now. "What if he gave me something that hurts the baby?"

"What'd the doctor say?"

"He doesn't know!"

"It's going to be all right, honey. You'll be okay."

Bishop told Linda Sanchez what happened and the stocky woman sat on Jennie's bed. She took the patient's hand, leaned forward and said in a friendly but firm voice, "Look at me, honey. Look at me. . . ." When Jennie did, Sanchez said, "Now, we're in a hospital, right?"

Jennie nodded.

"So if anybody did anything he shouldn't've they can fix you up just fine in no time." The officer's dark, stubby fingers rubbed Jennie's arms vigorously as if the woman had just come inside from a freezing rainstorm. "There're more doctors here per square inch here than anywhere in the Valley. Right? Look at me. Am I right?"

Jennie wiped her eyes and nodded. She seemed to relax a bit.

Bishop did too, glad to partake in this reassurance. But that bit of relief sat right beside another thought: that if his wife or the baby were harmed in any way neither Shawn nor Phate would make it into custody alive.

Tony Mott jogged through the door, not the least winded

from his sprint to the room, unlike Bob Shelton, who staggered into the doorway, leaning against the jamb, gasping for breath. Bishop said, "Phate might've done something with Jennie's medicine. They're checking on it now."

"Jesus," Shelton muttered. For once Bishop was glad that Tony Mott was at the front lines and that he carried that big chrome-plated Colt on his hip. His opinion now was that you couldn't have too many allies, or too much firepower, when you were up against perps like Phate and Shawn.

Sanchez kept her comforting grip on Jennie's hand, whispering nonsense, telling her how good she looked and how terrible the food here would probably be and, man oh man, wasn't that orderly up the hall a hunk. Bishop thought what a lucky woman Sanchez's daughter was to have a mother like this – who would surely be stationed right beside her during labor when the girl finally brought her own lazy baby into the world.

Mott had had the foresight to bring photocopies of Holloway's Massachusetts booking picture. He'd handed these to some guards downstairs, he explained, and they were distributing them to hospital personnel. So far, though, no one had seen the killer.

The young cop added to Bishop, "Patricia Nolan and Miller're in the hospital's computer department, trying to figure out how bad the hack was."

Bishop nodded and then said to Shelton and Mott, "I want you to—"

Suddenly the vital signs monitor on the wall began to buzz with a loud sound. The diagram showing Jennie's heart rate was jumping frantically up and down.

Then a message popped up on the screen in glowing red type.

WARNING: Fibrillation

Jennie gasped and tilted her head up, staring at the monitor. She screamed.

"Jesus!" Bishop cried and grabbed the call button. He began pushing it frantically. Bob Shelton ran into the hallway and started shouting, "We need help here! Here! Now!"

Then the lines on the screen suddenly went flat. The warning tone changed to a piercing squeal and a new message burned onto the monitor.

WARNING: Cardiac Arrest

"Honey," Jennie sobbed. Bishop hugged her hard, feeling utterly helpless. Sweat poured from her face and she shivered but she remained conscious. Linda Sanchez ran to the door and cried, "Get a goddamn doctor in here now!"

A moment later Dr. Williston ran into the room. He glanced at the monitor and then at his patient and reached up, shut off the machine.

"Do something!" Bishop cried.

Williston listened to her chest then took her blood pressure. Then he stepped back and announced, "She's fine."

"Fine?" Mott asked.

Sanchez looked as if she was about to grab the doctor by the jacket and drag him back to his patient. "Check her again!"

"There's nothing wrong with her," he told the policewoman.

"But the monitor . . ." Bishop stammered.

"Malfunction," the doctor explained. "Something happened in the main computer system. Every monitor on this floor's been doing the same thing."

Jennie closed her eyes and pressed her head back in the pillow. Bishop held her tightly.

"And that injection?" the doctor continued. "I tracked it down. Somehow central pharmaceutical got an order for you to receive a vitamin shot. That's all it was."

"A vitamin?"

Bishop, trembling with relief, fought down the tears.

The doctor said, "It won't hurt you or the fetus in any way." He shook his head. "It was strange – the order went out under my name and whoever did it got my passcode to authorize it. I keep that in a private file in my computer. I can't imagine how anybody got it."

"Can't imagine," Tony Mott said with a sardonic glance at Bishop.

A man in his fifties with a military bearing walked into the room. He wore a conservative suit. He introduced himself as Les Allen. He was head of security at the hospital. Hellman, the guard in the room, nodded to Allen, who didn't respond. He asked Bishop, "What's going on here, Detective?"

Bishop told him about what had happened with his wife and the monitors.

Allen said, "So he got into our main computer. . . . I'll bring that up with the security committee today. But at the moment, what should we do? You think this guy's here someplace?"

"Oh, yeah, he's here." Bishop waved at the dark monitor above Jennie's head. "He did this as a diversion, to get us to focus on Jennie and this wing. Which means he's targeting a different patient."

"Or patient*s*," Bob Shelton said.

Mott added, "Or somebody on the staff."

Bishop said, "This suspect likes challenges. What would be the hardest place in the hospital to break into?"

Dr. Williston and Les Allen considered this. "What do you think, Doctor? The operating suites? They all have controlled-access doors."

"That'd be my guess."

"And where are they?"

"In a separate building – you get to them through a tunnel from this wing."

"And most doctors and nurses there would be masked and gowned, right?" Linda Sanchez asked.

"Yes."

So Phate could roam his killing grounds freely. Bishop then asked, "Is there anyone being operated on right now?"

Dr. Williston laughed. "Any*one*? We've got probably twenty procedures going on right now, I'd say." He turned to Jennie. "I'll be back in ten minutes. We'll get those tests over with and get you home." He left the room.

"Let's go hunting," Bishop said to Mott, Sanchez and Shelton. He hugged Jennie again. As he left, the young security guard pulled his chair closer to the bedside. Once they were in the corridor the guard swung the door shut. Bishop heard it latch.

They walked down the hall quickly, Mott keeping his hand near his automatic, looking around, as if he were about to draw and shoot anybody who bore the least resemblance to Phate.

Bishop too felt unnerved, recalling that the killer was a chameleon and, with his disguises, could be walking past them right now and they might never know it.

They were at the elevator when something occurred to Bishop. Alarmed, he looked back toward the closed door of Jennie's room. He didn't go into the details of Phate's social engineering skills but said to Allen, "The thing about our suspect is that we're never quite sure what he'll look like next. I didn't pay much attention to that guard in my wife's room. He's about the perp's age and build. You're sure he works for your department?"

"Who? Dick Hellman back there?" Allen answered, nodding slowly. "Well, what I can tell you for sure is that he's my daughter's husband and I've known him for eight years. As far as the 'work' part of your question goes – if putting in a four-hour day during an eight-hour shift is work then I guess the answer's yes."

In the tiny canteen at the Computer Crimes Unit, Agent Art Backle rummaged futilely through the refrigerator for milk or half-and-half. Since Starbucks had arrived in the Bay area Backle hadn't drunk any other kind of coffee and he knew that the boiled-down burnt-smelling brew here would taste vile without something to take the edge off. With some disgust he poured a large dose of Coffee-mate into the cup. The liquid turned gray.

He took a bagel from the plate and bit down into what turned out to be rubber. Goddamn. . . . He flung the phony bagel across the room, realizing of course that Gillette had sent him back here as a practical fucking joke. He decided that when the hacker went back to prison he'd—

What was that noise?

He started to turn toward the doorway.

But by the time he identified the sound as sprinting footsteps his attacker was already on top of him. He slammed into the slim agent's back, pitching him into the wall and knocking the wind out of his lungs.

The attacker flicked the lights out. The windowless room went completely black. Then the man grabbed Backle by the collar and flung him facedown to the floor. His head slammed into the concrete with a quiet thud.

Gasping for breath, the agent groped for his pistol.

But another hand got there first and lifted it away.

Who do you want to be?

Phate walked slowly down the main corridor of the state police's Computer Crimes Unit offices. He was wearing a worn, stained Pacific Gas and Electric uniform and a hard hat. Hidden just inside the coveralls was his Ka-bar knife and a large automatic pistol – a Glock – with three clips of ammunition. He carried another weapon as well but it was one that might not be recognized as such, not in the hands of a repairman: a large monkey wrench.

Who do you want to be?

Someone the cops here would trust, someone they wouldn't think twice about seeing in their midst. *That's* who.

Phate looked around, surprised that the CCU had picked a dinosaur pen for their headquarters. Had it been a coincidence that they'd set up shop here? Or had it been intentional on the part of the late Andy Anderson?

He paused and oriented himself then continued slowly – and quietly – toward a cubicle on the shadowy edge of the pen's central control area. From inside the cubicle he could hear furious keying.

Surprised too that CCU was this empty, he'd expected at least three or four people here – hence the large pistol and the extra ammunition – but everyone was apparently at the hospital where Mrs. Frank Bishop was probably suffering quite a bit of trauma as a result of the nutrient-rich vitamin B shot he'd ordered for her that morning.

Phate had considered actually killing the woman – he could've done so easily by ordering central medication to administer a large dose of insulin, say – but that wouldn't've been the best tactic for this segment of the game. Alive and screaming in panic, she was valuable in her role as the diversionary character. If she died the police might've concluded that she was his intended target and returned here to headquarters immediately. Now the police were scurrying through the hospital trying to find the real victim.

In fact, this victim *was* elsewhere. Only that person was neither a patient nor a staff member at Stanford-Packard Medical Center. He was right here, at CCU.

And his name was Wyatt Gillette.

Who was now only twenty feet away from Phate in that dingy cubicle in front of him.

Phate listened to the astonishing staccato of Valleyman's fast and powerful keyboarding. His touch was relentless, as if his brilliant ideas would vanish like smoke if he didn't pound them instantly into the central processing unit of his machine.

He slowly moved closer to the cubicle, gripping the heavy wrench.

In the days when the two young men had been running Knights of Access, Gillette had often said that hackers must become adept at the art of improvising.

It was a skill Phate too had developed and so, today, he had improvised.

He'd decided there was too great a risk that Gillette had found out about the attack at the hospital when he'd broken into Phate's machine. So he'd changed the plans slightly. Instead of killing several patients in one of the operating suites, as he'd intended, he'd pay a visit to CCU.

There'd been a chance, of course, that Gillette would go with the police to the hospital, so he'd sent some encrypted gibberish, a message that appeared to come from Triple-X, to make sure he'd remain here and try to decrypt it.

This was, he decided, a perfect round. Not only would it be a real challenge for Phate to get into CCU – worth a solid 25 points in the Access game – but, if he was successful, it would finally give him the chance to destroy the man he'd been after for years.

He looked around again, listened. Not a soul in the huge

room other than Judas Valleyman. And the defenses were much less stringent here than he'd expected. Still, he didn't regret going to so much trouble – the PG&E uniform, the faked work order to check some circuit boxes, the laminated badge he'd painstakingly made on his ID machine, the time-consuming lock picking. When you're playing Access against a true wizard you can't be too careful, especially when that wizard happens to be ensconced in the police department's own dungeon.

He was now only feet away from his adversary, a man whose painful death Phate had idled away so very many hours imagining.

But, unlike the traditional game of Access, where you pierce the beating heart of your victim, Phate had something else in mind for Gillette.

An eye for an eye . . .

A fast blow to the man's head with the wrench to stun him and then, gripping Valleyman's head, he'd go to work with the Ka-bar knife. He'd taken the idea from his young trapdoor at St. Francis Academy, Jamie Turner. As the young man had once written in an e-mail to his brother:

```
JamieTT: Man, can you think of anything
scarier than going blind if you're a hacker?
```

No, Jamie, I sure can't, Phate now answered him silently.

He paused beside the cubicle and crouched, listening to the steady clatter of the keys. Taking a deep breath, he stepped inside fast, drawing back the wrench for good leverage.

CHAPTER 00100010 / THIRTY-FOUR

———◆·◆·◆———

Phate stepped into the center of the empty cubicle, the wrench raised above his head.

"No!" he whispered.

The sounds of keyboarding weren't coming from Wyatt Gillette's fingers at all. The source was the speaker connected to the workstation's computer. The cubicle was empty.

But as he dropped the wrench and started to pull his pistol from the coverall, Gillette stepped out from the cubicle next to this one and pressed the gun he'd just lifted off poor Agent Backle into Phate's neck. He pulled the killer's pistol from his hand.

"Don't move, Jon," Gillette told him and went through his pockets. He lifted out a Zip disk, a portable CD player and headset, a set of car keys and a wallet. Then he found the knife. He placed everything on the desk.

"That was good," Phate said, nodding at the computer. Gillette hit a key and the sound stopped.

"You recorded yourself on a .wav file. So I'd think you were in here."

"That's right."

Phate smiled bitterly and shook his head.

Gillette stepped back and the wizards surveyed each other. This was their first face-to-face meeting. They'd shared hundreds of secrets and plans – and millions of words – but those communications had never been in person; they'd all been in the miraculous incarnation of electrons coursing through copper wire or fiberoptic cables.

Phate, Gillette concluded, seemed trim and healthy looking for a hacker. He had a mild tan but Gillette knew that the color was from a bottle; no hacker in the world would trade machine time for even ten minutes at the beach. The man's face seemed amused but his eyes were hard as chips of stone.

"Nice tailor," Gillette said, nodding at the Pac Bell uniform. He picked up the Zip disk that Phate had brought and lifted an eyebrow.

"My version of Hide and Seek," Phate explained. This was a powerful virus that would sweep through every machine at CCU and encode the data files and operating system. The only problem was that there was no key to decode them.

He asked Gillette, "How'd you know I was coming?"

"I figured you really *were* going to kill somebody at the hospital – until you started to worry that I might've seen some of your notes when I got inside your machine. So you changed your plans. You led everybody else off and came after me."

"That's pretty much it."

"You made sure I'd stay here by sending us that encrypted e-mail – supposedly from Triple-X. That's what tipped me off that you were coming. He wouldn't've sent an e-mail to us; he would've called. With Trapdoor around he was too paranoid you'd find out he was helping us."

"Well, I found out anyway, didn't I?" Phate then added, "He's dead, you know. Triple-X."

"What?"

"I made a stop on the way here." A nod toward the knife. "That's his blood on there. His Real World name was Peter C. Grodsky. Lived alone in Sunnyvale. Worked as a code cruncher for a credit bureau during the day, hacked at night. He died next to his machine. For what that's worth."

"How did you find out?"

"That you two were sharing information about me?" Phate scoffed. "Do you think there's a single fact in the world I can't find if I want to?"

"You son of a bitch." Gillette thrust the gun forward and waited for Phate to cringe or cry out in fear. He did neither. He simply looked back, unsmiling, into Gillette's eyes and continued. "Anyway, Triple-X *had* to die. He was the betraying character."

"The what?"

"In the *game* we're playing. Our MUD game. Triple-X was the turncoat. They all *have* to die – like Judas. Or Boromir in the *Lord of the Rings*. Your character's part is pretty clear too. You know what it is?"

Characters . . . Gillette remembered the message that had accompanied the picture of the dying Lara Gibson. *All the world's a MUD, and the people in it merely characters. . . .*

"Tell me."

"You're the hero with the flaw – the flaw usually gets them into trouble. Oh, you'll do something heroic at the end and save some lives and the audience'll cry for you. But you'll still never make it to the final level of the game."

"So what's my flaw?"

"Don't you know? Your curiosity."

Gillette then asked, "And what character are you?"

"I'm the *antagonist* who's better and stronger than you and I'm not held back by moral compunction. But I have the forces of good lined up against me. That makes it a bitch for me to win. . . . Let's see, who else? Andy Anderson? He was the wise man who dies but whose spirit lives on. Obi-Wan Kenobi. Frank Bishop is the soldier. . . ."

Gillette was thinking: Hell, we could've had a police guard protecting Triple-X. We could've done *something*.

Amused again, Phate looked down at the pistol in Gillette's hand. "They let you have a gun?"

"I borrowed it," Gillette explained. "From a guy who stayed here to baby-sit me."

"And he's, what, knocked out? Bound and gagged?"

"Something like that."

Phate nodded. "And he didn't see you do it so you're going to tell them that it was me."

"Pretty much."

A bitter laugh. "I'd forgotten what a fucking good MUD tactician you were. You were the quiet one in Knights of

Access, you were the poet. But, damn, you played a good game."

Gillette pulled a pair of handcuffs out of his pocket. These too he'd lifted off Backle's belt after he body slammed the agent in the coffee room. He felt far less guilty about the assault than he supposed he ought to. He tossed the cuffs to Phate and stepped back. "Put them on."

The hacker took them but didn't ratchet them around his wrists. He simply stared at Gillette for a long moment. Then: "Let me ask you a question – why'd you go over to the other side?"

"The handcuffs," Gillette muttered, gesturing toward them. "Put them on."

But with imploring eyes, Phate said passionately, "Come on, man. You're a *hacker*. You were born to live in your Blue Nowhere. What're you doing working for them?"

"I'm working for them because I *am* a hacker," Gillette snapped. "You're not. You're just a goddamn loser who happens to use machines to kill people. That's not what hacking's about."

"*Access* is what hacking's about. Getting as deep as you can into someone's system."

"But you don't stop with somebody's C: drive, Jon. You have to keep going, to get inside their body too." He waved angrily at the white-board, where the pictures of Lara Gibson and Willem Boethe were taped. "You're *killing* people. They're not characters, they're not bytes. They're human beings."

"So? I don't see a bit of difference between software code and a human being. They're both created, they serve a purpose, then people die and code's replaced by a later version. Inside a machine or outside, inside a body or out, cells or electrons, there's no difference."

"Of course there's a difference, Jon."

"Is there?" he asked, apparently perplexed by Gillette's comment. "Think about it. How did life start? Lightning striking the primordial soup of carbon, hydrogen, nitrogen, oxygen, phosphate and sulfate. Every living creature is made up of those elements, every living creature functions because of electrical impulses. Well, every one of those elements, in one form or another, you'll find in a machine. Which functions because of electrical impulses."

"Save the bogus philosophy for the kids in the chat rooms, Jon. Machines're wonderful toys; they've changed the world forever. But they're not alive. They don't reason."

"Since when is reasoning a prerequisite for life?" Phate laughed. "Half the people on earth are fools, Wyatt. Trained dogs and dolphins reason better than they do."

"For Christ's sake, what happened to you? Did you get so lost in the Machine World that you can't tell the difference?"

Phate's eyes grew wide with anger. "Lost in the Machine World? I don't *have* any other world! And whose fault is that?"

"What do you mean?"

"Jon Patrick Holloway had a life in the Real World. He lived in Cambridge, he worked at Harvard, he had friends, he'd go out to dinner, he'd go on dates. His was as real as anybody else's fucking life. And, you know what? He *liked* it! He was going to meet somebody, he was going to have a family!" His voice broke. "But what happened? *You* turned him in and destroyed him. And the only place left for him to go was the Machine World."

"No," Gillette said evenly. "The real you was cracking into networks and stealing code and hardware and crashing nine-one-one. Jon Holloway's life was totally fake."

"But it was *something!* It was the closest I ever came to having a life!" Phate swallowed and for a moment Gillette wondered if he was going to cry. But the killer controlled his emotions fast and, smiling, glanced around the dinosaur pen. He noticed the two broken keyboards sitting in the corner. "You've only busted two of them?" He laughed.

Gillette himself couldn't help but smile. "I've only been here a couple of days. Give me time."

"I remember you saying you never developed a light touch."

"I was hacking one time, must've been five years ago, and I broke my little finger. I didn't even know it. I kept keying for another couple of hours – until I saw my hand start to turn black."

"What was your endurance record?" Phate asked him.

Gillette thought back. "Once I keyed for thirty-nine hours straight."

"Mine was thirty-seven," Phate responded. "Would've been longer but I fell asleep. When I woke up I couldn't move my hands for two hours. . . . Man, we did some serious shit, didn't we?"

Gillette said, "Remember that guy – the air force general? We saw him on CNN. He said that their recruiting Web site was tighter than Fort Knox and that no punks would ever hack it."

"And we got inside their VAX in, what, about ten minutes?"

The young hackers had uploaded Kimberly-Clark advertisements onto the site; all the exciting pictures of jet fighters and bombers were replaced by product shots of Kotex boxes.

"That was a good hack," Phate said.

"Oh, and how 'bout when we turned the White House Press Office main line into a pay phone?" Gillette mused.

They fell silent for a moment. Finally Phate said, "Oh, man, you were better than me . . . you just got derailed. You married that Greek girl. What was her name? Ellie Papandolos, right?" He looked Gillette over closely as he mentioned her name. "You got divorced . . . but you're still in love with her, right? I can see it."

Gillette said nothing.

Phate continued, "You're a *hacker,* man. You've got no business being with a woman. When machines're your life you don't need a lover. They'll only hold you back."

Gillette countered, "What about Shawn?"

A darkness crossed Phate's face. "That's different. Shawn understands exactly who I am. There aren't many people who do."

"Who is he?"

"Shawn's none of your business," Phate said ominously, then a moment later he smiled. "Come on, Wyatt, let's work together. I know you want the scoop on Trapdoor. Wouldn't you give *anything* to know how it works?"

"I *do* know how it works. It's a packet-sniffer to divert messages. Then you use stenanography to embed a demon in the packets. The demon self-activates as soon as it's inside the target machine and resets the communications protocols. It hides in the Solitaire program and self-destructs when somebody comes looking for it."

Phate laughed. "But that's like saying, 'Oh, that man flaps his arms and flies.' *How* did I do it? *That's* what you don't know. That's what *nobody* knows. . . . Don't you wonder what the source code looks like? Wouldn't you *love* to see that code, Mr. Curious? It'd be like getting a look at God, Wyatt. You know you want to."

For an instant Gillette's mind scrolled through line after line of software programming – what he himself would write to duplicate Trapdoor. But when he got to a certain point, the screen in his mind's eye went blank. He could see no further and he felt the terrible lust of curiosity consuming him. Oh, yes, he *did* want to see the source code. So very badly.

But he said, "Just put the cuffs on."

Phate glanced at the clock on the wall. "Remember what I used to say about revenge when we were hacking?"

"'Hacker revenge is patient revenge.' What about it?"

"I just want to leave you with that thought. Oh, one other thing. . . . You ever read Mark Twain?"

Gillette frowned and didn't answer.

Phate continued, "*A Connecticut Yankee in King Arthur's Court.* No? Well, it's about this man in the 1800s who's transported back in time to medieval England. There's this totally moby scene where the hero or somebody is in some kind of hot water and the knights're going to kill them, or whatever."

"Jon, put the cuffs on." Gillette extended the gun.

"Only what happens . . . this is pretty good. What happens is he has an almanac with him and he looks up the date in whatever year it is and he sees that there was a total eclipse of the sun then. So he tells the knights if they don't back off he'll turn day to night. And of course they don't believe him but then the eclipse happens and everybody freaks and the hero's saved."

"So?"

"I was worried *I* might get into some kind of hot water here."

"What's your point?"

Phate said nothing. But the point became evident a few seconds later when the clock hit exactly twelve-thirty and the virus Phate must have loaded in the electric company's computer shut off the power to the CCU office.

The room was plunged into blackness.

Gillette leapt back, raising Backle's gun and squinting into the dark for a target. Phate's powerful fist slammed into his neck and stunned him. Then he shouldered Gillette hard into the cubicle wall, knocking him to the floor.

He heard a jangling as Phate grabbed his keys and other things on the desk. Gillette reached up, trying for the man's wallet. But Phate already had that and all Gillette could save was the CD player. He felt another stunning pain as the monkey wrench slammed into his shin. Gillette staggered to his knees, lifted Backle's gun toward where he thought Phate was and pulled the trigger.

But nothing happened. Apparently the safety was on. As he started to fiddle with it a foot slammed into his jaw. The gun fell from his hand and he went down onto the floor once again.

V
THE EXPERT LEVEL

There are only two ways to get rid of hackers and phreakers. One is to get rid of computers and telephones. . . . The other way is to give us what we want, which is free access to ALL information. Until one of those two things happen, we are not going anywhere.

– A hacker known as Revelation,
quoted in *The Ultimate Beginner's Guide
to Hacking and Phreaking*

CHAPTER 00100011 / THIRTY-FIVE

————◆————

"Are you all right?" Patricia Nolan asked, looking at the blood on Gillette's face, neck and pants.

"I'm fine," he said.

But she didn't believe him and played nurse anyway, disappearing into the canteen and returning with damp paper towels and liquid soap. She bathed his eyebrow and cheek where he'd been cut in the fight with Phate. He smelled fresh nail conditioner on her strong hands and wondered when, in light of Phate's assault on the hospital and here, she'd found time for cosmetics.

She made him tug his pants cuff up and she cleaned the small gash on his leg, holding his calf firmly. She finished and offered him an intimate smile.

Forget it, Patty, he thought once more. . . . I'm a felon, I'm out of work, I'm in love with another woman. Really, don't bother.

"That doesn't hurt?" she asked, touching the damp cloth to the cut.

It seared like a dozen bee stings. "Just itches a little," he said, hoping to discourage the relentless mothering.

Tony Mott ran back inside CCU, holstering his massive weapon. "No sign of him."

Shelton and Bishop walked inside a moment later. All three men had returned to CCU from the medical center and had spent the last half hour scouring the area, looking for any signs of Phate or witnesses who'd seen him arrive at or flee the CCU. But the homicide partners' faces revealed that they'd had no more luck than Mott.

Bishop sat wearily in an office chair. "So what happened?" he asked the hacker.

Gillette briefed them about Phate's attack on CCU.

"He say anything that's helpful?"

"No. Not a thing. I almost got his wallet but just ended up with that." He nodded at the CD player. A tech from the Crime Scene Identification Unit had printed it and found that the only prints were Phate's and Gillette's.

Then the hacker delivered the news that Triple-X was dead.

"Oh, no," Frank Bishop said, looking heartsick that a civilian who'd taken a risk to help them had been killed. Bob Shelton sighed angrily.

Mott walked to the evidence board and wrote the name Triple-X next to Lara Gibson and Willem Boethe.

But Gillette stood – unsteadily thanks to his wounded shin – and walked to the board. He erased the name.

"What're you doing?" Bishop asked.

Gillette took a marker and wrote "Peter Grodsky." He said, "That's his real name. He was a programmer who lived in Sunnyvale." He looked at the team. "I just think we should remember that he was more than a screen name."

Bishop called Huerto Ramirez and Tim Morgan and told them to find Grodsky's address and run the crime scene.

Gillette noticed a pink phone message slip. He said to Bishop, "I took a message for you just before you got back from the hospital. Your wife called." He read the note. "Something about the test results coming back and it's good news. Uhm, I'm not sure I got this right – I thought she said she's got a serious infection. I'm not sure why that's *good* news."

But the look of immense joy in Bishop's face – a rare beaming smile – told him that, yes, the message was right.

He was happy for the detective but felt his own personal disappointment that Elana hadn't called him. He wondered where she was right now. Wondered it Ed was with her. Gillette's palms sweated with angry jealousy.

Agent Backle walked into the office from the parking lot.

His fastidiously tidy hair was mussed and he walked stiffly. He'd had his own medical treatment – but his had been administered by professionals with the Emergency Medical Services, whose ambulance was outside in the parking lot. He'd suffered a slight concussion when he'd been attacked in the coffee room. He now wore a large white bandage on the side of his head.

"How you feeling?" Gillette asked blithely.

The agent didn't respond. He noticed his gun sitting on a desk near Gillette and snatched up the weapon. He checked it with exaggerated care then slipped it into his belt holster.

"What the hell happened?" he asked.

Bishop said, "Phate broke in, blindsided you and got your weapon."

"And *you* took it away from him?" the agent asked Gillette skeptically.

"Yep."

"*You* knew I was in the coffee room," Backle snapped. "The perp didn't."

"But I guess he *did* know, didn't he?" Gillette responded. "Otherwise how could he blindside you and get your weapon?"

"It seems to me," the agent said slowly, "that you somehow got this idea he was going to come here. You wanted a weapon and helped yourself to mine."

"Well, that's not what happened," Gillette said then glanced at Bishop, who cocked an eyebrow in a way that suggested that it seemed this way to him too. The detective, though, said nothing.

"If I find out that it was you—"

Bishop said, "Hey, hey, hey . . . I think you ought to be a little more grateful, sir. There's a good argument to be made that Wyatt here saved your life."

The agent tried to stare down the cop but gave up and walked to a chair and sat down in it gingerly. "I'm still watching you, Gillette."

Bishop took a phone call. He hung up then reported, "That was Huerto again. He said they got a report from Harvard. There were no records of anybody named Shawn who was a student or working at the school around the same time Holloway was. He checked the other places Holloway worked too – Western Electric, Apple and the rest of them. Negative on an employee named Shawn." He glanced at Shelton. "He also said it's getting hot and heavy with the MARINKILL case. The perps were spotted in our backyard. Santa Clara, just off the 101."

Bob Shelton gave an uncharacteristic laugh. "Doesn't matter whether you wanted a piece of that case or not, Frank. Looks like it's dogging you."

Bishop shook his head. "Maybe, but I sure don't want it around here, not for the time being. It's going to pull off resources and we need all the help we can get." He looked at Patricia Nolan. "What'd you find at the hospital?"

She explained how she and Miller had looked through the medical center's network and, while they found signs that Phate had cracked into the system, she couldn't find any indication of where he'd been hacking in from.

"The sysadmin printed these out." She handed Gillette a large stack of printouts. "The log in and log out activity reports for the past week. I thought you might be able to find something."

Gillette began poring over the hundred or so pages.

Then Bishop looked around the dinosaur pen and frowned. "Say, where *is* Miller?"

Nolan said, "He left the hospital computer center before me. He said he was coming straight back here."

Without looking up from the printouts Gillette said, "I never saw him."

"He might've gone over to the computer center at Stanford," Mott said. "He books supercomputer time there a lot. Maybe he was going to check out a lead." He tried the cop's cell phone but there was no answer and he left a message on Miller's voice mail.

Gillette was scanning through the printouts when he came to a particular entry and his heart thudded with alarm. He read it again to make sure. "No . . ."

He'd spoken softly but everyone on the team stopped talking and looked toward him.

The hacker looked up. "Once he seized root at Stanford-Packard, Phate logged into other systems that were connected with the hospital's – that's how he shut the phone system off. But he also jumped from the hospital to an outside computer. It recognized Stanford-Packard as a trusted system so he waltzed right though the firewalls and seized root there too."

"What's the other system?" Bishop asked.

"Northern California University in Sunnyvale." Gillette looked up. "He got files on security procedures and personnel information on every security guard who works for the school." The hacker sighed. "He also downloaded the files of twenty-eight hundred students."

"So he's got his next pool of victims all lined up," Bishop said and dropped heavily into a shabby office chair.

Someone was following him . . .

Who was it?

Phate looked in his rearview mirror at the cars behind him on the 280 freeway as he fled from CCU headquarters. He was badly shaken that Valleyman had outmaneuvered him again and was desperate to get home.

He was already thinking of his next attack – on Northern California University. It was less challenging than some targets he might've picked but the security at the dorms was high and the school had a computer system that the chancellor of the school had once declared in an interview was hacker-proof. One of the more interesting features of this system was that it controlled the state-of-the-art fire alarm and sprinkler systems throughout the twenty-five dorms that provided the bulk of student housing.

An easy hack, not as challenging as either the Lara Gibson or St. Francis one. But at the moment Phate needed a victory. He was losing this level of the game and that was shaking his confidence.

And fueling his paranoia: Another glance in the rearview mirror.

Yes, someone was there! Two men in the front seat, staring at him.

Eyes back to the road, then he looked again.

But the car he'd seen – or *thought* he'd seen – was just a shadow or reflection.

No, wait! It was back. . . . But now it was being driven by a woman alone.

When he looked a third time there was no driver at all. My God, it was a creature of some sort!

A ghost.

A *demon*.

Yes, no . . .

You were right, Valleyman: When computers are the only life that sustains you, when they're the only totems that ward off the deadly curse of boredom, then sooner or later the borderline between the two dimensions vanishes and characters from the Blue Nowhere begin to appear in the Real World.

Sometimes those characters are your friends.

And sometimes not.

Sometimes you see them driving behind you, sometimes you see their shadows in alleyways you're approaching, you see them hiding in your garage, your bedroom, your closet. You see them in a stranger's gaze.

You see them in the reflection of your monitor as you sit in front of your machine at the witching hour.

Sometimes they're just your imagination.

Another glance in the rearview mirror.

But sometimes, of course, they really *are* there.

Bishop pushed END on his cell phone.

"The dorms on the Northern California U campus have typical university security, which means it's pretty easy to get through."

"I thought he wanted challenges," Mott said.

Gillette said, "I'd guess he's going for an easy kill this time. He's probably pissed off we've gotten so close to him the last few times and wants blood."

Nolan added, "This might also be another diversion."

Gillette agreed that that was a possibility.

Bishop said, "I told the chancellor they should cancel classes and send everybody home. But he wasn't inclined to – the students start finals in two weeks. So we'll have to blanket the campus with troopers and county police. But that'll just mean more strangers on campus – and more of a chance for Phate to social engineer his way into a dorm."

"What do we do?" Mott asked.

Bishop said, "Some more old-fashioned police work." He picked up Phate's CD player. The detective opened it up. Inside was a recording of a play – a performance of *Othello*. He turned the machine over and jotted down the serial number. "Maybe Phate bought it in the area. I'll call the company and see where this unit was shipped to."

Bishop started making phone calls to the Akisha Electronic Products Company's various sales and distribution centers around the country. He was transferred and put on hold for an interminable period of time and was having trouble getting through to someone who could – or was willing to – help.

As the detective argued with someone on the other end of the line Wyatt Gillette spun around in a swivel chair to a nearby computer terminal and began keyboarding. A moment later he stood and pulled a piece of paper from the printer.

As Bishop's irritated voice was saying into the phone, "We *can't* wait two days for that information," Gillette handed the sheet to the detective.

Akisha Electronic Products Shipped – First Quarter

Model: HB Heavy Bass Portable Compact Disc Player

Unit Serial Shipping		
Numbers	Date	Recipient
HB40032–	1/12	Mountain View Music & Electronics
HB40068		9456 Rio Verde, #4
		Mountain View, CA

The phone sagged in the detective's hand and he said into the receiver, "Never mind," and hung up. "How'd you get this?" Bishop asked Gillette. Then held up a hand. "On second thought, I'd rather not know." He chuckled. "Old-fashioned police work, like I said."

Bishop picked up the phone and called Huerto Ramirez

again. He told him to send somebody else to run the scene at Triple-X's house and then directed him and Tim Morgan to Mountain View Music with a picture of Phate to see if they could find out if he lived in the area. "Also, tell the clerk that our boy seems to like plays. He's got a recording of *Othello*. That might help jog their memories."

A trooper from the state police headquarters in San Jose dropped off an envelope for Bishop.

He opened it and summarized for the team, "FBI report on the details from the picture of Lara Gibson that Phate posted. They said it's a Tru-Heat gas furnace, model GST3000. The model was introduced three years ago and it's popular in new developments. Because of its BTU capacity that model is usually used in detached houses that're two or three stories high, not town houses or ranches. The techs also computer enhanced the information stamped on the Sheetrock in the basement and found a manufacturing date: January of last year."

"New house in a recently developed tract," Mott said and wrote these details on the evidence board. "Two to three stories high."

Bishop gave a faint laugh and raised an eyebrow in admiration. "Our federal tax dollars are being well spent, boys and girls. Those folks in Washington know what they're doing. Listen to this. The agents found significant irregularities in the grouting and placement of tiles on the floor and think that suggests the house was sold with an unfinished basement and the homeowner himself laid the tile."

Mott added on the board: "Sold with unfinished basement."

"We're not through yet," the detective continued. "They also enhanced a portion of a newspaper that was in the trash bin and found out that it was a giveaway shopper, *The Silicon Valley Marketeer.* It's home delivered and only goes to houses in Palo Alto, Cupertino, Mountain View, Los Altos, Los Altos Hills, Sunnyvale and Santa Clara."

Gillette asked, "Can we find out about new developments in those towns?"

Bishop nodded. "Just what I was about to do." He looked

at Bob Shelton. "You still have that buddy of yours at Santa Clara County P and Z?"

"Sure do." Shelton called the planning and zoning commission. He asked about permits for tract developments of two- and three-story single-family homes with unfinished basements built after January of last year in the towns on their list. After five minutes on hold Shelton cocked the phone under his chin, grabbed a pen and began writing. He kept at it for some time; the list of developments was discouragingly long. There must have been forty of them throughout those seven towns.

He hung up and muttered, "He said they can't build 'em fast enough to supply the demand. Dot-com, you know."

Bishop took the list of developments and walked to the map of Silicon Valley, circled those locations Shelton had written down. As he was doing this his phone rang and he answered. He listened and nodded. Then hung up. "That was Huerto and Tim. A clerk at the music store recognized Phate and said he's been in there a half-dozen times in the past few months – always buys plays. Never music. *Death of a Salesman* was the last one. But the guy has no idea where he lives."

He circled the location of the music store. He tapped this, then the circle around Ollie's costume shop on El Camino Real, where Phate had bought the theatrical glue and other disguises. These stores were about three quarters of a mile apart. The locations suggested that Phate was in the central and western part of Silicon Valley; still there were twenty-two new housing developments spread out over what must have been seven or eight square miles. "Way too big for a door-to-door search."

They stared at the map and the evidence board for a discouraging ten minutes or so, offering largely useless suggestions about narrowing down the search. Officers called from the apartment of Peter Grodsky in Sunnyvale. The young man had died from a stab wound to the heart – like the other victims in this real-life game of Access. The cops were running the scene but had not found any helpful leads.

"Hell," said Bob Shelton, as he kicked a chair aside, expressing the frustration they all felt.

There was silence for a long moment as the team stared at the white-board – silence that was interrupted unexpectedly by a timid voice behind them. "Excuse me."

A chubby teenage boy, wearing thick glasses, stood in the doorway, accompanied by a man in his twenties.

It was Jamie Turner, Gillette recalled, the student from St. Francis, and his brother, Mark.

"Hello, young man," Frank Bishop said, smiling at the boy. "How you doing?"

"Okay, I guess." He looked up at his brother, who nodded encouragement. Jamie walked up to Gillette. "I did what you wanted," he said, swallowing uneasily.

Gillette couldn't remember what the boy was talking about. But he nodded and said, "Go on."

Jamie continued. "Well, I was looking at the machines at school, down in the computer room? Like you asked? And I found something that might help you catch him – the man who killed Mr. Boethe, I mean."

CHAPTER 00100100 / THIRTY-SIX

"I keep this notebook when I'm online," Jamie Turner told Wyatt Gillette.

Usually disorganized and slovenly in many ways, all serious hackers kept pens and battered steno pads or Big Chief tablets – any type of dead-tree stuff – beside their machines every minute they were online. In these they recorded in precise detail the URLs – the universal resource locators, addresses – of Web sites they'd found, names of software, the handles of fellow hackers they wanted to track down and other resources that would help them hack. This is a necessity because most of the information floating about in the Blue Nowhere is so complicated that no one can remember the details correctly – and yet they *have* to be correct; a single typographic error would mean a failure in running a truly moby hack or connecting to the most awesome Web site or bulletin board ever created.

It was early afternoon and everyone on the CCU team was feeling relentless desperation – that Phate might be making his move against his next victim at Northern California at any moment. Still, Gillette let the boy talk at his own pace.

Jamie continued, "I was looking through what I'd written before Mr. Boethe . . . before what happened to him, you know."

"What'd you find?" Gillette encouraged. Frank Bishop sat down next to the boy and nodded, smiling. "Go on."

"Okay, see, the machine I was using in the library – the

one you guys took – was fine until about two or three weeks ago. And then something *really* weird started happening. I'd get these fatal conflict errors. And my machine'd, like, freeze."

"Fatal errors?" Gillette asked, surprised. He glanced at Nolan, who was shaking her head. She pulled a mass of hair away from her eye and twined it absently around her fingers.

Bishop looked from one to the other. "What's that mean?"

Nolan explained, "Usually you get errors like that when your machine tries to do a couple of different tasks at once and can't handle it. Like running a spreadsheet at the same time you're online reading e-mail."

Gillette nodded in confirmation. "But one of the reasons companies like Microsoft and Apple developed their operating systems is to let you run multiple programs at the same time. You hardly ever see fatal error crashes anymore."

"I know," the boy said. "That's why I thought it was so weird. Then I tried running the same programs on other machines at school. And I couldn't, you know, duplicate the errors."

Tony Mott said, "Well, well, well . . . Trapdoor has a bug."

Gillette nodded at the boy. "This's great, Jamie. I think it's the break we've been looking for."

"Why?" Bishop asked. "I don't get it."

"We needed the serial and phone numbers of Phate's Mobile America phone – in order to trace him."

"I remember."

"If we're lucky this's how we're going to get them." Gillette said to the boy, "You know the times and dates when some of the conflicts shut you down?"

The boy looked through his notebook. He showed a page to Gillette; the crashes were carefully noted. "Good." Gillette nodded and said to Tony Mott, "Call Garvy Hobbes. Get him on the speakerphone."

Mott did this and a moment later the security chief from Mobile America was connected.

"Howdy," Garvy Hobbes said. "You got a lead to our bad boy?"

Gillette looked at Bishop, who deferred to the hacker with a wave of his hand and said, "This's *new*-fashioned police work. It's all yours."

The hacker said, "Try this on, Garvy. If I give you four specific times and dates that one of your cell phones went down for about sixty seconds then went back on, calling the same number, could you identify that phone?"

"Hmmm. That's a new one but I'll give it a shot. Gimme the times and dates."

Gillette did and Hobbes said, "Stay on the line. I'll be back."

The hacker explained to the team what he was doing: When Jamie's computer froze, the boy would have to reboot the machine again to get back online. That'd take about a minute. This meant that Phate's cell phone call was interrupted for the same period of time while the killer also restarted his machine and reconnected. By cross-checking the exact times Jamie's computer froze and then went back online against the times a particular Mobile America cell phone disconnected and reconnected they'd know that cell phone was Phate's.

Five minutes later the security cowboy came back on the line. "This's fun," Hobbes said cheerfully. "I got it." Then he added with some troubled reverence in his voice, "But what's weird is the numbers of his phone are unassigned."

Gillette explained, "What Garvy's saying is that Phate hacked into a secure, nonpublic switch and stole the numbers."

"Nobody's ever cracked our main board yet. This boy is something else, I'll tell you."

"But we know that," muttered Frank Bishop.

"Is he still using the phone?" Shelton asked.

"Hasn't since yesterday. The typical profile for a call jacker is if they don't use a stolen unit for twenty-four hours that means they've switched numbers."

"So we can't trace him when he goes online again?" Bishop asked, discouraged.

"Right," Hobbes confirmed.

But Gillette shrugged and said, "Oh, I figured he'd changed the numbers. No serious phreak uses stolen numbers for more than eight hours. But we can still narrow down where he was calling from in the past couple of weeks. Right, Garvy?"

"You betcha," Hobbes offered. "We have records of what cells all of our calls originate from. Most of the calls on that phone came from our cell 879. That's Los Altos. And I narrowed it down further from the MITSO data."

"The what?"

Gillette said, "The mobile telephone switching office. They've got sector capability – that means they can tell what *part* of the cell he's located in. Down to about one square kilometer."

Hobbes laughed and asked warily, "Mr. Gillette, how is it you know as much about our system as we do?"

"I read a lot," Gillette said wryly. Then he asked, "Give me the coordinates of the location. Can you give us the information by street?" He walked to the map.

"Sure thing." Hobbes rattled off four intersections and Gillette connected the dots. It was a trapezoid covering a large portion of Los Altos. "He's in there someplace." The hacker tapped the map.

Within this perimeter were six new housing developments whose addresses Santa Clara planning and zoning had given them.

It was better than twenty-two but was still discouraging.

"Six?" asked a dismayed Linda Sanchez. "Must be three thousand people living there. Can we narrow it down any more?"

"I think so," Bishop said. "Because we know where he shops." On the map Bishop tapped the development that fell halfway between Ollie's costume store and Mountain View Music and Electronics. Its name was Stonecrest.

A flurry of activity ensued. Bishop told Garvy to meet them in Los Altos near the development then he called Captain Bernstein and briefed him. They decided to use plainclothes officers to canvass door-to-door throughout the development with Holloway's picture. Bishop came up with the idea of buying small plastic buckets and handing them out to the troopers, who'd pretend to be soliciting money for some children's cause, in case Holloway saw them on the street. He then alerted the tactical troopers. The CCU team got ready to roll. Bishop and Shelton checked their pistols. Gillette, his laptop. Tony Mott, of course, did both.

Patricia Nolan would remain here in case the team needed to access the CCU computer.

As they were leaving, the phone rang and Bishop took the call. He was quiet for a moment then glanced at Gillette and, with raised eyebrows, handed the receiver to him.

Frowning, the hacker lifted the receiver to his ear. "Hello?"

Silence for a moment. Then Elana Papandolos said, "It's me."

"Well, hi."

Gillette watched Bishop shepherd everyone out the door. "I didn't think you'd call."

"I didn't either," she said.

"Why did you?"

"Because I thought I owed it to you."

"Owed what to me?"

"To tell you that I'm still going to New York tomorrow."

"With Ed?"

"Yes."

The words struck him harder than Phate's knuckles had not long before. He'd really hoped that she'd delay her departure.

"Don't."

Another cumbersome silence followed. "Wyatt . . ."

"I love you. I don't want you to go."

"Well, we *are* going."

Gillette said, "Just do me one favor. Let me see you before you go."

"Why? What good will it do?"

"Please. Just for ten minutes."

"You can't change my mind."

He thought, Oh, yes, I can.

She said, "I have to go. Goodbye, Wyatt. I wish you luck whatever you do in life."

"No!"

Ellie hung up without saying anything else.

Gillette stared at the silent phone.

"Wyatt," Bishop called.

He closed his eyes.

"Wyatt," the detective repeated. "We have to go."

The hacker looked up and dropped the receiver in the cradle. Numb, he followed the cop down the corridor.

The detective muttered something to him.

Gillette looked at him vacantly. Then he asked what Bishop had just said.

"I said it's like what you and Patricia were saying before. About this being one of those MUD games."

"What about it?"

"I think we just hit the expert level."

El Monte Road connects El Camino Real to the parallel backbone of Silicon Valley, the 280 freeway, a few miles away.

As you make the trip south the view from El Monte changes from retail stores to the classic California ranch homes of the 1950s and 1960s and finally to newer residential developments, intended to harvest some of the abundant dot-com money being strewn throughout the neighborhood.

Not far from one of these developments, Stonecrest, were parked sixteen police cars and two California State Police Tactical Services vans. They were in the parking lot of the First Baptist Church of Los Altos, hidden from El Monte Road by a high stockade fence, which is why Bishop had chosen the lot beside this house of God as a staging area.

Wyatt Gillette was in the passenger seat of the Crown Victoria, beside Bishop. Shelton sat silently in the back, staring at a palm tree waving in the wet breeze. In the car beside them were Linda Sanchez and Tony Mott. Bishop seemed to have given up trying to rein in the aspiring Eliot Ness and Mott now hurried from the car to join a cluster of tactical and uniformed police who were suiting up in body armor. The head of the tactical team, Alonso Johnson, was back again. He stood by himself, head down, nodding as he listened to his radio.

Department of Defense agent Arthur Backle had trailed Bishop's car here and he was now standing beside it, under an umbrella, leaning against the car, picking at the bandage on his head.

Nearby, Stonecrest was being scoured by a number of troopers – the social-engineered fund-raisers, brandishing yellow buckets and flashing pictures of Jon Holloway.

The moments passed, however, and no one reported any success. Doubts crept in: Maybe Phate was in a different development. Maybe Mobile America's analysis of the phone numbers was wrong. Maybe the numbers *had* been his but after the run-in with Gillette he'd fled the state.

Then Bishop's cell phone buzzed and he answered. He nodded and smiled, then said to Shelton and Gillette, "Positive ID. A neighbor recognized him. He's at 34004 Alta Vista Drive."

"Yes!" Shelton said, making a joyous fist with his hand. He climbed out of the car. "I'll tell Alonso." The burly cop disappeared into the crowd of troopers.

Bishop called Garvy Hobbes and gave him the address. In his Jeep the security man had a Cellscope hooked up – a combination computer and radio direction finder. He would drive past Phate's house, scanning for Mobile America cell phone frequencies, and see if the man was transmitting.

A moment later he called Bishop back and reported, "He's inside on a mobile phone. It's a data transmission, not voice."

"He's online," Gillette said.

Bishop and Gillette climbed out of the car, found Shelton and Alonso Johnson and gave them this news.

Johnson sent a surveillance van, disguised as a courier truck, to the street in front of Phate's house. The officer reported that the blinds were down and the garage door was open. A beat-up Ford was in the driveway. There were no interior lights visible from outside. A second surveillance team, perched near a thick jacaranda, gave a second, similar report.

Both teams added that all exits and windows were covered; even if Phate happened to see the police he wouldn't be able to escape.

Johnson then opened a detailed map, encased in plastic, of the streets in Stonecrest. He circled Phate's house with a grease pencil and then examined a catalogue of model homes in the development. He looked up and said, "The house he's in is a Troubadour model." He flipped to the floor plan of this model in the catalogue and showed it to his second in command, a young crew-cut trooper with a humorless, military attitude.

Wyatt Gillette glanced at the catalogue and saw an advertising slogan printed beneath the diagram. *Troubadour. . . . The dream house that you and your family will enjoy for years to come. . . .*

Johnson's assistant summarized, "Okay, sir, we've got front and back doors at ground level. Another door opens onto a deck in back. No stairs but it's only ten feet high. He could jump it. No side entrance. The garage has two doors, one leading inside, to the kitchen, the other leading to the backyard. I'd say we go with a three-team dynamic entry."

Linda Sanchez said, "Separate him from his computer immediately. Don't let him type anything. He could destroy the contents of the disk in seconds. We'll need to look at it and see if he's targeted any other vics."

"Roger that," the assistant said.

Johnson said, "Team Able goes through the front, Baker in the back, Charlie through the garage. Hold back two from Charlie team and post them near the deck in case he goes for a dive." He looked up and tugged the gold earring in his left lobe. "All right. Let's go catch ourselves a beast."

Gillette, Shelton, Bishop and Sanchez jogged back to one of the Crown Victorias and drove into the development itself, parking just out of sight of Phate's house, next to the tactical vans. Their shadow, Agent Backle, followed. They all watched the troops deploy quickly, crouching low and moving under cover behind bushes.

Bishop turned to Gillette and surprised the hacker by reaching forward formally and shaking his hand. "Whatever happens, Wyatt, we couldn't've gotten this far without you. Not many people would've taken the risks you have and worked as hard as this."

"Yeah," Linda Sanchez said. "He's a keeper, boss." She turned her wide brown eyes on Gillette. "Hey, you want a job when you get out maybe you oughta apply to CCU."

Gillette tried to think of something to say by way of acknowledging this. He was embarrassed, though, and unable to think of anything. He nodded.

For once Bob Shelton seemed on the verge of echoing their sentiments but then he climbed out of the car and disappeared into a cluster of plainclothes troopers he seemed to know.

Alonso Johnson walked up to them. Bishop rolled down the window. "Surveillance still can't see inside and the subject's got his air conditioner on full tilt so the infrared scanners aren't picking up a thing. Is he still on his computer?"

Bishop called Garvy Hobbes and asked the question. "Yep," was the cowboy's response. "The Cellscope is still picking up his transmission."

"Good," Johnson said. "We want him nice and distracted when we come a-calling." He then spoke into his microphone. "Clear the street."

Officers turned back several cars driving along Alta Vista. They flagged down one of Phate's neighbors, a white-haired woman pulling out of her garage, and directed her Ford Explorer down the street, away from the killer's house. Three young boys were ignoring the rain and happily doing acrobatics on noisy skateboards. Two troopers disguised in shorts and Izod shirts casually walked up to them and ushered them out of sight.

The pleasant suburban street was clear.

"Looks good," Johnson said, then ran in a crouch toward the house.

"It all comes down to this. . . ." Bishop muttered.

Linda Sanchez overheard him and said, "Ain't that the truth, boss." Then she gave a thumbs-up to Tony Mott, who was kneeling, along with a half-dozen tactical troopers, behind a hedge bordering Phate's property. He nodded at her and turned back to Phate's house. She said in a soft voice, "That boy better not hurt himself."

Bob Shelton returned and dropped heavily into the seat of the Crown Victoria.

Gillette didn't hear any commands given but all at once the SWAT troopers emerged from their hiding places and raced toward the house.

Suddenly there were three loud bangs. Gillette jumped.

Bishop explained, "Special shotgun shells. They're shooting the locks out of the doors."

Gillette, his palms sweating, found himself holding his breath, waiting for gunshots, explosions, screaming, sirens. . . .

Bishop remained motionless, keen eyes on the house. If he was tense he didn't show it.

"Come on, come on," Linda Sanchez muttered. "What's happening?"

Long, long moments of silence, except for the hollow tapping of the rain on the car's roof.

When the car's radio cackled to life the sound was so abrupt that everyone jumped.

"Alpha team leader to Bishop. You there?"

Bishop grabbed the microphone. "Go ahead, Alonso."

"Frank," the voice reported. "He's not here."

"What?" the detective asked in dismay.

"We're scouring the place now but it looks like he's gone. Just like at the motel."

"Fucking hell," Shelton snapped.

Johnson continued. "I'm in the dining room – it's his office. There's a can of Mountain Dew that's still cold. And the body-heat detector shows he was in the chair in front of the computer as of five to ten minutes ago."

In a desperate voice Bishop said, "He's in there, Al. He's *got* to be. He's got a hidey-hole somewhere. Check in the *closets*. Check under the *bed*."

"Frank, the infrareds aren't picking up anything except his ghost in the chair."

"But he *can't've* gotten outside," Sanchez said.

"We'll keep at it."

Bishop's body sagged against the door as despair eased into his hawklike face.

Ten minutes later the tactical commander came back on the radio.

"The whole house is secure, Frank," Johnson said. "He's not here. If you want to run the scene, you can."

CHAPTER 00100101 / THIRTY-SEVEN

———◆———

Inside, the house was immaculate.

Completely different from what Gillette had expected. Most hacker lairs were filthy, impacted with computer parts, wires, books, tech manuals, tools, floppy disks, encrusted food containers, dirty glasses, books and just plain junk.

The living room of Phate's house looked as if Martha Stewart had just finished decorating. The CCU team looked around them. Gillette wondered at first if they had the wrong house but then he noticed the framed pictures and saw Holloway's face in many of them.

"Look," Linda Sanchez said, pointing at one framed snapshot. "That woman must be Shawn." Then she glanced at another. "And they've got *kids?*"

Shelton said, "We can send the pictures to the feds and—"

But Bishop shook his head.

"What's the matter?" Alonso Johnson asked.

"They're fake, aren't they?" Bishop glanced at Gillette with a raised eyebrow.

The hacker picked up one frame and slipped a picture out. They weren't on photo lab glossy paper but had been printed out on a color computer printer. "He downloaded 'em from the Net or scanned them from a magazine and added his face."

On the mantel, next to a picture of the happy couple sitting in beach chairs beside a pool, was an old-fashioned grandmother clock, showing the hour as 2:15. The swinging pendulum was a reminder that Phate's next victim, or victims, at the university might die at any minute.

Gillette looked over the room, which smacked of affluent suburban living.

Troubadour. . . . The dream house that you and your family will enjoy for years to come. . . .

Huerto Ramirez and Tim Morgan had canvassed the neighbors but nobody offered anything that suggested any leads to other locations he might have a connection to. Ramirez said, "According to the neighbor across the street, he was going by the name Warren Gregg and telling people that his family'd be moving out here to join him after his kids were out of school."

Bishop said to Alonso, "We know his next target's probably a student at Northern California University but we don't know who exactly. Make sure your people look for anything that might give us a clue about who he's going to hit."

Johnson shook his head and said, "But now we busted his hidey-hole don't you think he'll go to ground and forget about other victims for the time being?"

Bishop looked at Gillette and said, "That's not my take on him."

The hacker agreed. "Phate wants a win here. One way or another he's going to kill somebody today."

"I'll give them the word," the SWAT cop said and went off to do so.

The team examined the other rooms but found them virtually empty, hidden from the outside by drawn blinds. The bathroom contained minimal products – generic-brand razors and shaving cream, shampoo and soap. They also found a large box of pumice stones.

Bishop picked one up, frowning with curiosity.

"His fingers," Gillette reminded. "He uses the stones to sand down the callus so he can key better."

They walked into the dining room, where Phate's laptop was set up.

Gillette glanced at the screen, shook his head in disgust. "Look."

Bishop and Shelton read the words:

INSTANT MESSAGE FROM: SHAWN

CODE 10-87 ISSUED FOR 34004 ALTA VISTA DRIVE

"That's the tactical assault code – a ten eighty-seven. If he hadn't gotten that message we would've collared him," Bishop said. "We were *that* close."

"Fucking Shawn," Shelton snapped.

A trooper called from the basement. "I've got the escape route. It's down here."

Gillette went downstairs with the others. But on the last step he paused, recognizing the scene from the picture of Lara Gibson. The clumsy tiling job, the unpainted Sheetrock. And the swirls of blood on the floor. The sight was wrenching.

He joined Alonso Johnson, Frank Bishop and the other troopers who were examining a small door in the side wall. It opened into a three-foot-wide pipe, like a large storm drain. One of the troopers shone his flashlight into the pipe. "It leads to the house next door."

Gillette and Bishop stared at each other. The detective said, "No! The woman with the white hair – in the Explorer! The one who pulled out of the garage. It was him."

Johnson grabbed his radio and ordered troopers into the house. He then sent out an emergency vehicle locator for the four-by-four.

A moment later a trooper called in. "The house next door is completely empty. No furniture. Nothing."

"He owned both houses."

"God *damn* social engineering," Bishop snapped, uttering the first cuss word Gillette had heard leave the detective's mouth.

In five minutes the report came back that the Explorer had been found in a shopping center parking lot not a quarter of a mile away. A white wig and dress were in the back-seat. Nobody canvassed at the shopping center had seen anyone swap the Ford for another vehicle.

The state police crime scene unit went through both

houses thoroughly but found very little that was helpful. It turned out that Phate – as Warren Gregg – had actually bought both of these houses, using cash. They called the Realtor who'd sold them to him. She hadn't thought it strange that he'd paid cash for two houses; in the Valley of the Heart's Delight wealthy young computer executives often bought one house to live in and one for investment. She added, though, that there appeared to be one odd thing about this particular transaction: when she'd looked up the credit reports and application a few moments ago at the police's request all the records of sale were gone. "Isn't that curious? They were accidentally erased."

"Yeah, curious," Bishop said wryly.

"Yeah, accidentally," Gillette added.

Bishop then said to the hacker, "Let's get his machine back to CCU. If we're lucky there might be some reference to his victim at the college. Let's move on this fast."

Johnson and Bishop released the scene, then Linda Sanchez filled out the chain of custody cards and she bundled up Phate's computer and disks.

The team returned to their cars and sped back to CCU headquarters.

Gillette broke the news to Patricia Nolan that the arrest had been unsuccessful.

"Shawn tipped him off again?" she asked angrily.

Sanchez handed Phate's laptap to Gillette and Nolan and then took a phone call.

"How did he know we were assaulting the house?" Tony Mott asked. "I don't get it."

"I only want to know one thing," Shelton muttered. "Who the hell *is* Shawn?"

Though he undoubtedly didn't expect an answer just then, one was forthcoming.

"I know who," Linda Sanchez said in a horrified, choked voice. She stared at the team then hung up. The woman flicked her red-polished nails together then said, "That was the systems administrator in Sacramento. Ten minutes ago he found someone cracking into ISLEnet and using it as a trusted system to get into the U.S. State Department database. The user was Shawn. He was instructing the State

Department system to issue two predated passports in fake names. The sysadmin recognized the pictures Shawn was scanning into the system. One was Holloway's" – she took a deep breath – "The other was Stephen's."

"Stephen who?" Tony Mott asked, not understanding.

"Stephen Miller," Sanchez said, starting to cry. "*That's* who Shawn is."

Bishop, Mott and Sanchez were in Miller's cubicle, searching his desk.

"I don't believe it," Mott said defiantly. "It's Phate again. He's fucking with our minds."

"But then where *is* Miller?" Bishop asked. Patricia Nolan said she'd been at CCU the entire time the team had been at Phate's house and Miller hadn't called. She'd even tried to track him down at various local college computer departments but he hadn't been at any of them.

Mott booted up Miller's computer.

On the screen came the prompt to enter a password. Mott tried the hard way – a few guesses at the most obvious ones: birthday, middle name, and so on. But access was denied.

Gillette stepped into the cubicle and loaded his Crack-it program. In a few minutes the password was cracked and Gillette was inside Miller's machine. He soon found dozens of messages sent to Phate under Miller's screen name, Shawn, logged onto the Internet through the Monterey On-Line company. The messages themselves were encrypted but the headers left no doubt about Miller's true identity.

Patricia Nolan said, "But Shawn's brilliant – Stephen was an amateur next to him."

"Social engineering," Bishop said.

Gillette agreed. "He had to look stupid so we wouldn't suspect him. Meanwhile, he was feeding information to Phate."

Mott snapped, "He's the reason Andy Anderson's dead. He set him up."

Shelton muttered, "And every single time we got close to Phate, Miller'd warn him."

"Did the sysadmin get a sense of where Miller was hacking in from?" asked Bishop.

"Nope, boss," Sanchez said. "He was using a bulletproof anonymizer."

Bishop asked Mott, "Those schools he books computer time at – would Northern California be one of them?"

Mott replied, "I don't know. Probably."

"So he's been helping Phate set up the next victims." Bishop's phone rang. He listened and nodded. When he hung up he said, "That was Huerto." Bishop had sent Ramirez and Morgan over to Miller's house as soon as Linda Sanchez had gotten the call from the ISLEnet sysadmin. "Miller's car's gone. His den at home's empty except for a bunch of cables and spare computer parts – he's taken all his machines and disks with him." He asked Mott and Sanchez, "Does he have any summer houses? Family nearby?"

"No. His whole life was machines," Mott said. "Working here in the office and working at home."

Bishop said to Shelton, "Get Miller's picture out on the wire and send some troopers over to Northern California with copies of it." He glanced at Phate's computer and said to Gillette, "The data on there isn't encrypted anymore, is it?"

"No," Gillette said. He nodded at the screen, scrolling over which was Phate's screen saver – the motto of the Knights of Access.

Access is God. . . .

"I'll see what I can find." He sat down in front of the laptop.

"He still could have plenty of booby traps inside," Linda Sanchez warned.

"I'll go nice and slow. I'll just shut the screen saver off and we'll take it from there. I know the logical places where he'd plant trip wires." Gillette sat down in front of the computer. He reached for the most innocuous key on a computer keyboard – the shift key – to shut off the screen saver. Since the shift key alone doesn't issue commands or affect the programs or data stored on a machine, hackers never hook a trip wire to that key.

But of course Phate wasn't just any hacker.

The instant Gillette tapped the key the screen went blank then these words appeared:

BEGIN BATCH ENCRYPTION
ENCRYPTING – DEPARTMENT OF DEFENSE
STANDARD 12

"No!" Gillette cried and hit the off switch. But Phate had overridden the power controls and there was no response. He flipped the laptop over to remove the battery but the release button had been removed. Within three minutes the entire contents of the hard drive were encrypted.

"Damn, damn. . . ." Gillette slapped the tabletop in disgust. "It's all useless," he said.

Department of Defense agent Backle stood and walked slowly to the machine. He looked from Gillette to the screen, which was now a dense block of gibberish. Then the agent glanced again at the pictures of Lara Gibson and Willem Boethe taped to the white-board. He asked Gillette, "You think there's something on there that'll save some lives?" Nodding at the laptop.

"Probably."

"I meant what I said before. If you can crack the encryption I'll forget I saw you do it. All I'll ask is that you give us any disks you've got with the cracking program on it."

Gillette hesitated. Finally he asked, "You mean that?"

Backle gave a grim laugh and touched his head. "That prick gave me one hell of a headache. I want to add assaulting a federal agent to his list of charges."

Gillette glanced at Bishop, who nodded – his own acknowledgment that he'd back Gillette up. The hacker sat down at a workstation and went online. He returned to his account in Los Alamos, where he'd cached his hacker tools, and downloaded a file named Pac-Man.

Nolan laughed. "'Pac-Man'?"

Gillette shrugged. "I'd been up for twenty-two hours when I finished it. I couldn't think of a better name."

He copied it onto a floppy disk, which he inserted into Phate's laptop.

The screen came up:

Encryption/Decryption

Enter Username:

Gillette typed, *LukeSkywalker*

Enter Password:

The letters, numbers and symbols Gillette typed turned into a string of eighteen asterisks. Mott said, "That's one hell of a passcode."

This appeared on the screen:

Select Encryption Standard:

1. Privacy On-Line, Inc.
2. Defense Encryption Standard
3. Department of Defense Standard 12
4. NATO
5. International Computer Systems, Inc.

Patricia Nolan echoed Mott. "That's one hell of a *hack*. You wrote script that can crack all of those encryption standards?"

"Usually it'll decrypt about ninety percent of a file," Gillette said, hitting key 3. Then he began feeding the encrypted files through his program.

"How'd you do it?" Mott asked, fascinated.

Gillette couldn't keep the enthusiasm out of his voice – pride too – as he told them, "Basically I input enough samples of each standard so that the program begins to recognize patterns that the encryption algorithm used in encrypting them. Then it makes logical guesses about—"

Agent Backle suddenly reached past Bishop, grabbed Gillette by the collar and pulled him roughly to the ground. "Wyatt Edward Gillette, you're under arrest for violation of the Computer Fraud and Abuse Act, theft of classified government information and treason."

Bishop: "You can't do that!"

Tony Mott started toward him. "You son of a bitch!"

Backle pulled his jacket aside, revealing the butt of his pistol. "Careful there. I'd think long and hard about what you're doing, Officer."

Mott backed off. And Backle, almost leisurely, handcuffed his prisoner.

Bishop said heatedly, "Come on, Backle, you heard us: Phate's targeted somebody already. He could be on campus right now!"

Patricia Nolan said, "You told him it was okay!"

But the unflappable Backle ignored her, pulled Gillette to his feet and shoved him into a chair. The agent then pulled out a radio, clicked it on and said, "Backle to Unit 23. I have the suspect in custody. You can pick him up."

"Roger," came the clattering response.

"You set him up!" Nolan shouted, furious. "You assholes've been waiting all along for this."

"I'm calling my captain," Bishop snapped, pulling out his own phone and walking briskly the front door.

"Call whoever you want. He's going back to prison."

Shelton said heatedly, "We've got a killer who's after another victim right *now!* This could be our only chance to stop him."

Backle responded, nodding toward Gillette, "And the code *he* broke could mean a hundred other people might die."

Sanchez said, "You gave us your word. Doesn't that count for anything?"

"No. Catching people like him counts – for everything."

Gillette said desperately, "Just give me one hour." But Backle merely slipped that snide smile on his face and began to read Gillette his rights.

It was then that they heard gunshots from outside and the huge crash of falling glass as bullets shattered the CCU's outside door.

CHAPTER 00100110 / THIRTY-EIGHT

———◆◆◆◆———

Mott and Backle drew their weapons and looked toward the doorway. Sanchez dropped to her knees, digging in her purse for her weapon. Nolan crouched under a desk.

Frank Bishop, on the floor, crawled back from the outside door, down the short corridor that led to the dinosaur pen.

Sanchez called, "You hit, boss?"

"I'm okay!" The detective took cover against the wall and stood unsteadily. He drew his pistol and called, "He's outside – Phate! I was standing in the lobby. He took a couple of shots at me. He's still there!"

Backle ran past him, calling on his radio to alert his partners about the perp. He crouched by the door, glancing at the bullet holes in the wall and the shattered glass. Tony Mott joined the DoD agent.

"Where is he?" Backle called, taking a fast look outside and ducking back to cover.

"Behind that white van," the detective shouted. "Over to the left. He must've been coming back to kill Gillette. You two go right, keep him pinned down. I'm going to flank him from the back. Keep low. He's a good shot. He missed me by inches."

The agent and the young cop looked at each other and then nodded. Together they burst through the front door.

Bishop watched them go then stood up and holstered his gun. He tucked his shirt in, pulled out keys and undid Gillette's handcuffs. He slipped them into his pocket.

"What're you doing, boss?" Sanchez asked, picking herself up off the floor.

Patricia Nolan laughed, figuring out what had just happened. "It's a jailbreak, right?"

"Yep."

"But the shots?" Sanchez asked.

"That was me."

"You?" Gillette asked, astonished.

"I stepped outside and fired a couple of rounds through the front door." He grinned. "This social engineering stuff – I think I'm starting to get the hang of it." The detective then nodded at Phate's computer and said to Gillette, "Well, don't just stand there. Get his machine and let's get out of here."

Gillette rubbed his wrists. "Are you sure you want to do this?"

Bishop answered, "What I'm sure about is that Phate and Miller could be on the Northern California campus right now. And I am *not* going to let anyone else die. So let's *move.*"

The hacker scooped up the machine and started after the detective.

"Wait," Patricia Nolan called. "I'm parked in back. We can take my car."

Bishop hesitated.

She added, "We'll go to my hotel. I can help you with his machine."

The detective nodded. He started to say something to Linda Sanchez but she waved him quiet with a pudgy hand. "All *I* know is I turned around and saw Wyatt gone and you running after him. For all I know he's on his way up to Napa, with you hot on his trail. Good luck finding him, boss. Have a glass of wine for me. Good luck."

But it seemed that Bishop's heroics had been futile.

In Patricia Nolan's hotel room – by far the nicest suite Wyatt Gillette had ever seen – the hacker had quickly decrypted the data on Phate's computer. It turned out, however, that this was a different machine from the one Gillette had broken into earlier. It wasn't exactly a hot machine but it contained only the operating system, Trapdoor and some files of downloaded newspaper clippings Shawn had sent to Phate. Most of them were about Seattle, which would have been the location of Phate's next game. But now that he knew they had this machine, of course, he'd go elsewhere.

There were no references to Northern California University or any potential victims.

Bishop dropped into one of the plush armchairs and, hands together, stared at the floor, discouraged. "Not a thing."

"Can I try?" Nolan asked. She sat down next to Gillette then scrolled through the directory. "He might've erased some files. Did you try to recover anything with Restore8?"

"No, I didn't," Gillette said. "I figured he'd shred everything."

"He might not have bothered," she pointed out. "He was pretty confident that nobody'd get into his machine. And if they did then the encryption bomb would stop them."

She ran the Restore8 program and, in a moment, data that Phate had erased over the past few weeks appeared on the screen. She read through it. "Nothing on the school. Nothing about any attacks. All I can find are bits of receipts for some of the computer parts he sold. Most of the data're corrupted. But here's one you can kind of make out."

```
Ma%%%ch 27***200!!!++
55eerrx3^^shipped to:
San Jose Com434312 Produuu234aawe%%
2335 Winch4ster 00u46Ike^
San Jo^^44^^^^9^^^$$###
Attn: 97J**seph McGona%%gle
```

Bishop and Gillette read the screen.

The hacker said, "But that doesn't do us any good. That's a company that *bought* some of his parts. We need Phate's address, where they were shipped *from*."

Gillette took over for Nolan and scanned through the rest of the deleted files. They were just digital garbage. "Nothing."

But Bishop shook his head. "Wait a minute." He pointed to the screen. "Go back up."

Gillette scrolled back to the semilegible text of the receipt.

Bishop tapped the screen and said, "This company – San Jose Computer Products – they'd have to have some record of who sold them the parts and where they were shipped from."

"Unless they knew they were stolen," Patricia Nolan said. "Then they'd deny knowing anything about Phate."

Gillette said, "I'll bet when they find out Phate's been killing people they'll be a little more cooperative."

"Or less," Nolan said skeptically.

Bishop added, "Receiving stolen goods is a felony. Avoiding San Quentin's a pretty good reason to be cooperative."

The detective touched his sprayed hair as he leaned forward and picked up the phone. He called the CCU office, praying that one of the team – not Backle or one of the feds – would pick up. He was relieved when Tony Mott answered. The detective said, "Tony, it's Frank. Can you talk? . . . How bad is it there? . . . They have any leads? . . . No, I mean, leads to *us* . . . Okay, good. Listen, do me a favor, run San Jose Computer Products, 2335 Winchester in San Jose. . . . No, I'll hold on."

A moment later Bishop cocked his head. He nodded slowly. "Okay, got it. Thanks. We think Phate's been selling computer parts to them. We're going to have a talk with somebody there. I'll let you know if we find anything. Listen, call the chancellor and the head of security at Northern California U and tell them the killer might be on his way to the school now. And get more troopers over there."

He hung up and said to Nolan and Gillette, "The company's clean. It's been around for fifteen years, never any trouble with the IRS, EPA or state taxation department. Paid up on all its business licenses. If they've been buying anything from Phate they probably don't know it's hot. Let's go over there and have a talk with this McGonagle or somebody."

Gillette joined the detective. Nolan, though, said, "You go on. I'll keep looking through his machine for any other leads."

Pausing at the door, Wyatt Gillette glanced back and saw her sit down at the keyboard. She gave him a faint smile of encouragement. But it seemed to him that it was slightly wistful and that there might be another meaning in her expression – perhaps the inevitable recognition that there was little hope of a relationship blossoming between them.

But then, as had happened so often with the hacker himself, her smile vanished and Nolan turned back to the glowing monitor and began to key furiously. Instantly, with a look of utter concentration on her face, she slipped out of the Real World and into the Blue Nowhere.

The game was no longer fun.

Sweating, furious, desperate, Phate slouched at his desk and looked absently around him – at all of his precious computer antiquities. He knew that Gillette and the police were close on his trail and it was no longer possible to keep playing his game here in lush Santa Clara County.

This was a particularly painful admission because he considered this week – Univac Week – a very special version of his game. It was like the famous MUD game, the Crusades; Silicon Valley was the new holy land and he'd wanted to win big on every level.

But the police – and Valleyman – had proved to be a lot better than he'd expected.

So: no options. He now had yet another identity and would leave immediately, moving to a new city with Shawn. Seattle had been his planned destination but there was a chance that Gillette had been able to crack the Standard 12 encryption code and find the details about the Seattle game and potential targets there.

Maybe he'd try Chicago, the Silicon Prairie. Or Route 128, north of Boston.

He couldn't wait that long for a kill, though – he was consumed by the lust to keep playing. So he'd make a stop first and leave the gasoline bomb in a dorm at Northern California University. A farewell present. One of the dorms was named after a Silicon Valley pioneer but, because that made it the logical target, he'd decided that the students in the dorm across the street would die. It was named Yeats

Hall, after the poet, who undoubtedly would've had little time for machines and what they represented.

The dorm was also an old wooden structure, making it quite vulnerable to fire, especially now that the alarms and sprinkler system had been deactivated by the school's main computer.

There was, however, one more thing to do. If he'd been up against anybody else he wouldn't have bothered. But his adversary at this level of the game was Wyatt Gillette and so Phate needed to buy some time to give him a chance to plant the bomb and then escape east. He was so angry and agitated that he wanted to grab a machine gun and murder a dozen people to keep the police occupied. But that of course wasn't the weapon closest to his soul and so he now simply sat forward at his computer terminal and began quietly keyboarding a familiar incantation.

CHAPTER 00100111 / THIRTY-NINE

———◆•◆•◆———

In the Santa Clara County Department of Public Works command center, located in a barbed-wire-surrounded complex in southwest San Jose, was a large mainframe computer nicknamed Alanis, after the pop singer.

This machine handled thousands of tasks for the DPW – scheduling maintenance and repair of streets, regulating water allocation during dry spells, overseeing sewers and waste disposal and treatment, and coordinating the tens of thousands of stoplights throughout Silicon Valley.

Not far from Alanis was one of her main links to the outside world, a six-foot-high metal rack on which sat thirty-two high-speed modems. At the moment – 3:30 P.M. – a number of phone calls were coming into these modems. One call was a data message from a veteran public works repairman in Mountain View. He'd worked for the DPW for years and had only recently agreed, reluctantly, to start following the department policy of logging in from the field via a laptop computer to pick up new assignments, learn the location of trouble spots in the public works systems and report that his team had completed repairs. The chubby fifty-five-year-old, who used to think computers were a waste of time, was now addicted to machines and looked forward to logging on every chance he got.

The e-mail he now sent to Alanis was a brief one about a completed sewer repair.

The message that the computer had *received*, however, was slightly different. Embedded in the repairman's chunky, hunt-and-peck prose was a bit of extra code: a Trapdoor demon.

Now, inside unsuspecting Alanis, the demon leapt from the e-mail and burrowed deep into the machine's operating system.

Seven miles away, sitting at his own computer, Phate seized root then scrolled quickly through Alanis, locating the commands he needed. He jotted them down on a yellow pad and returned to the root prompt. He consulted the sheet of paper then typed "permit/g/segment-*" and hit ENTER. Like so many commands in technical computer operating systems, this one was cryptic but would have a very concrete consequence.

Phate then destroyed the manual override program and reset the root password to ZZY?a##9\%48?95, which no human being could ever guess and which a supercomputer would take, at best, days to crack.

Then he logged off.

By the time he rose to start packing his belongings for his escape from Silicon Valley he could already hear the faint sounds of his handiwork filling the afternoon sky.

The maroon Volvo went through an intersection on Stevens Creek Boulevard and began a howling skid straight toward Bishop's police car.

The driver stared in horror at the impending collision.

"Oh, man, look out!" Gillette cried, throwing up his arm instinctively for protection, turning his head to the left and closing his eyes as the famous diagonal chrome stripe on the grille of the car sped directly toward him.

"Got it," Bishop called calmly.

Maybe it was instinct or maybe it was his police tactical driving instruction but the detective chose not to brake. He jammed the accelerator to the floor and skidded the Crown Victoria *toward* the oncoming car. The maneuver worked. The vehicles missed by inches and the Volvo slammed into the front fender of the Porsche behind the police car with a huge bang. Bishop controlled his skid and braked to a stop.

"Idiot ran the light," Bishop muttered, pulling his radio off the dash to report the accident.

"No, he didn't," Gillette said, looking back. "Look, both lights're green."

A block ahead of them two more cars sat in the middle of the intersection, sideways, smoke pouring from their hoods.

The radio crackled, jammed with reports of accidents and traffic-light malfunctions. They listened for a moment.

"The lights're *all* green," the detective said. "All over the county. It's Phate, right? He did it."

Gillette gave a sour laugh. "He cracked public works. It's a smokescreen so he and Miller can get away."

Bishop started forward again but, because of the traffic, they'd slowed to a few miles an hour. The flashing light on the dash had no effect and Bishop shut it off. He shouted over the sound of the horns, "What can they do at public works to fix it?"

"He probably froze the system or put in an unbreakable passcode. They'll have to reload everything from the backup tapes. That'll take hours." The hacker shook his head. "But the traffic's going to keep him trapped too. What's the point?"

Bishop said, "No, *his* place'll be right on the freeway. Probably next to an entrance ramp. Northern California University is too. He'll kill the next victim, jump back on the freeway and head who knows where, smooth sailing."

Gillette nodded and added, "At least nobody at San Jose Computer Products is going anywhere either."

A quarter mile from their destination traffic was at a complete standstill and Bishop and Gillette had to abandon the car. They leapt out and began jogging, prodded forward by a sense of desperate urgency. Phate wouldn't have created the traffic jam until just before he was ready for his assault on the school. At best – even if someone at San Jose Computer could find the shipper's address – they might not get to Phate's place until after the victim was dead and Phate and Miller were gone.

They came to the building that housed the company and paused, leaning against a chain-link fence, gasping for breath.

The air was filled with a cacophony of horns and the

whump, whump, whump of a helicopter that hovered nearby, a local news station recording the evidence of Phate's prowess – and Santa Clara County's vulnerability – for the rest of the country to witness.

The men started forward again, hurrying toward an open doorway next to the company's loading dock. They climbed the steps to the dock and walked inside. A chubby, gray-haired worker stacking cartons on a pallet glanced up.

"Excuse me, sir, police," Bishop said, and showed his badge. "We need to ask you a few questions."

The man squinted through thick-rimmed glasses as he examined Bishop's ID. "Yessir, can I help you?"

"We're looking for Joe McGonagle."

"That's me," he said. "Is this about an accident or something? What's with all the horns?"

"Traffic lights're out."

"That's a mess. Near rush hour too."

Bishop asked, "You own the company?"

"With my brother-in-law. What exactly's the problem, Officer?"

"Last week you took delivery of some supercomputer parts."

"We do that *every* week. That's our business."

"We have reason to believe that somebody may've sold you some stolen parts."

"Stolen?"

"You're not under investigation, sir. But it's important that we find the man who sold them to you. Would you mind if we looked through your receiving records?"

"I swear I didn't know anything was stolen. Jim, he's my brother, wouldn't do that either. He's a good Christian."

"All we want is to find this man who sold them. We need the address or phone number of the company the parts were shipped from."

"All the shipping files're in here." He started down the hallway. "But if I needed a lawyer or anything 'fore I talk to you, you'd tell me."

"Yessir, I would," Bishop said sincerely. "We're only interested in tracking down this man."

"What's his name?" McGonagle asked.

"He was probably going by Warren Gregg."

"Doesn't ring a bell."

"He has a lot of aliases."

McGonagle stepped into a small office and walked to a filing cabinet, pulled it open. "You know the date? When this shipment came in?"

Bishop consulted his notebook. "We think it was March twenty-seventh."

"Let's see. . . ." McGonagle peered into the cabinet, began rummaging through it.

Wyatt Gillette couldn't help but smile to himself. It was pretty ironic that a computer supply company kept dead-tree records in file cabinets. He was about to whisper this to Bishop when he happened to glance at McGonagle's left hand, which rested on the handle of the file cabinet drawer as he dug inside with the other hand.

The fingers, very muscular, were blunt and tipped with thick yellow calluses.

A hacker's manicure. . . .

Gillette's smile vanished and he stiffened. Bishop noticed and glanced at him. The hacker pointed to his own fingers and then looked once again at McGonagle's hand. Bishop, too, saw.

McGonagle looked up, into Bishop's revealing eyes.

Only his name wasn't McGonagle, of course. Beneath the dyed gray hair, the fake wrinkles, the glasses, the body padding, this was Jon Patrick Holloway. The fragments scrolled through Gillette's mind like software script: Joe McGonagle was just another of his identities. This company was one of his fronts. He'd hacked into the state's business records and created a fifteen-year-old company and made himself and Stephen Miller co-owners of it. The receipt they'd found was for a computer part Phate had *bought,* not sold.

None of them moved.

Then:

Gillette ducked and Phate sprang back, pulling his gun from the filing cabinet drawer. Bishop had no time to draw his own gun; he simply leapt forward and slammed into the killer, who dropped his weapon. Bishop kicked it aside as

Phate grabbed the cop's shooting arm and seized a hammer, which rested on top of a wooden crate. He swung the tool hard into Bishop's head. It connected with a sickening thud.

The detective gasped and collapsed. Phate hit him again, in the back of the head, then dropped the hammer and made a grab for his pistol on the floor.

CHAPTER 000101000 / FORTY

G illette instinctively jumped forward, seizing Phate by the collar and arm before the man could snag the pistol.

The killer repeatedly swung his fist at Gillette's face and neck but the two men were so close that the blows didn't do any damage.

Together they tumbled through another door, out of the office and into an open area – another dinosaur pen, just like CCU headquarters.

The fingertip push-ups he'd done for the past two years let Gillette keep a fierce grip on Phate but the killer was very strong too and Gillette couldn't get any advantage. Like grappling wrestlers they stumbled over the raised floor. Gillette glanced around him, looking for a weapon. He was astonished at the collection of old computers and parts here. The entire history of computing was represented.

"We know everything, Jon," Gillette gasped. "We know Stephen Miller's Shawn. We know about your plans, the other targets. There's no way you're getting out of here."

But Phate didn't respond. Grunting, he shoved Gillette onto the floor, groping for a nearby crowbar. Groaning with the effort, Gillette managed to pull Phate away from the metal rod.

For five minutes the hackers traded sloppy blows, growing more and more tired. Then Phate broke free. He managed to get to the crowbar and snatched it up. He started toward Gillette, who looked desperately for a weapon. He noticed an old wooden box on a table nearby and ripped off the lid then pulled out the contents.

Phate froze.

Gillette held what looked like an antique glass lightbulb in his hand – it was an original audion tube, the precursor to the vacuum tube and, ultimately, the silicon computer chip itself.

"No!" Phate cried, holding up his hand. He whispered, "Be careful with it. Please!"

Gillette backed toward the office where Frank Bishop lay.

Phate came forward slowly, the crowbar held like a base-ball bat. He knew he should crush Gillette's arm or head – he could have done so easily – and yet he couldn't bring himself to endanger the delicate glass artifact.

To him, the machines themselves're more important than people. A human death is nothing; a crashed hard drive, well, that's a tragedy.

"Be careful," Phate whispered. "Please."

"Drop it!" Gillette snapped, gesturing at the crowbar.

The killer started to swing but at the last minute the thought of hurting the fragile glass bulb stopped him. Gillette paused, judged distances behind him then tossed the audion tube at Phate, who cried out in horror and dropped the crowbar, trying to catch the antique. But the tube hit the floor and shattered.

With a hollow cry Phate dropped to his knees.

Gillette stepped quickly into the office where Frank Bishop lay – breathing shallowly and very bloody – and grabbed his pistol. He stepped out and pointed it at Phate, who was looking over the remains of the tube the way a father would stare at the grave of a child. Gillette was shocked by the man's expression of mournful horror; it was far more chilling than his fury a moment ago.

"You shouldn't've done that," the killer muttered darkly, wiping his wet eyes with his sleeve and slowly standing up. He didn't even seem to notice that Gillette was armed.

Phate picked up the crowbar and started forward, howling madly.

Gillette cringed, lifted the gun and started to pull the trigger.

"No!" a woman's voice cried.

Startled, Gillette jumped at the sound. He looked behind him to see Patricia Nolan hurrying into the dinosaur pen, her laptop case over her shoulder and what looked like a black flashlight in her right hand. Phate too paused at her commanding entrance.

Gillette started to ask how she'd gotten here – and why – when she lifted the dark cylinder she held and touched his tattooed arm with the tip. The rod, it turned out, wasn't a flashlight. Gillette heard a crackle of electricity, saw a flash of yellow-gray light as astonishing pain swept from his jaw to his chest. Gasping, he dropped to his knees and the pistol fell to the floor.

Thinking: Shit, wrong again! Stephen Miller wasn't Shawn at all.

He groped for the pistol but Nolan touched the stun wand to his neck and pushed the trigger once more.

CHAPTER 00101001 / FORTY-ONE

———◆———

Unable to move more than his head and fingers, Wyatt Gillette returned to painful consciousness. He had no idea how long he'd been out.

He could see Bishop, still in the office. The bleeding seemed to have stopped but his breathing was very labored. Gillette also noticed that the old computer artifacts, which Phate had been packing up when he and Bishop had arrived, were still here. He was surprised they'd left them all behind, a million dollars' worth of computer memorabilia.

They'd be gone by now, of course. This warehouse was right next to the Winchester on-ramp to the 280 freeway. As he and Bishop had predicted, Phate and Shawn would have bypassed the traffic jams and were probably at Northern California University right now, killing the final victim in this level of the game. They—

But wait, Gillette considered through his fog of pain, why was *he* still alive? There was no reason for them not to kill him. What did they—

The man's scream came from behind him, very close. Gillette gasped in shock at the raw sound and managed to turn his head toward it.

Patricia Nolan was crouching over Phate, who was cringing in agony as he sat against a metal column that rose to the murky ceiling. Her hair was pulled back into a taut bun. The defensive geek-girl façade was gone. She gazed at Phate with the eyes of a coroner. He wasn't tied up either – his hands were at his side – and Gillette supposed she'd zapped him too with the stun wand. She'd exchanged the high-tech weaponry, though, for the hammer Phate had struck Bishop with.

So, she *wasn't* Shawn. Then who was she?

"You understand I'm serious now," she said to the killer, leveling the hammer at him like a professor holding a pointer. "I have no problem hurting you."

Phate nodded. Sweat poured down his face.

She must've seen Gillette's head move. She glanced at him but concluded he was no threat. She turned back to Phate. "I want the source code to Trapdoor. Where is it?"

He nodded toward a laptop computer on the table behind her. She glanced at the screen. The hammer rose and dropped viciously, with a soft, sickening thud, on his leg. He screamed again.

"You wouldn't carry around the source code on a laptop. That's fake, isn't it? The program named Trapdoor on that machine – what is it really?"

She drew back with the hammer.

"Shredder-4," he gasped.

A virus that would destroy all the data in any computer you loaded it onto.

"That's not helpful, Jon." She leaned closer to him, her misshapen sweater and knit dress stretched even further. "Now, listen. I know Bishop didn't call in a request for backup because he's on the run with Gillette. And even if he did, there's nobody coming here because – thanks to you – the roads are useless. I've got all the time in the world to make you tell me what I want to know. And, believe me, I'm the woman who can do it. This's old hat to me."

"Fuck you," he gasped.

Calmly, she gripped his wrist and slowly pulled his arm outward, resting his hand on the concrete. He tried to resist but he couldn't. He stared at his splayed fingers, the iron tool floating above them.

"I want the source code. I know you don't have it here. You've uploaded it into a hiding place – a passcode-protected FTP site. Right?"

An FTP site – file transfer protocol – was where many hackers cached their programs. It could be on any computer system anywhere in the world. Unless you had the exact FTP address, username and passcode, you'd be as likely to get the file as you'd be to find a dot of microfilm in a rain forest.

Phate hesitated.

Nolan said soothingly, "Look at these fingers. . . ." She caressed the blunt digits. After a moment she whispered, "Where is the code?"

He shook his head.

The hammer flashed downward toward Phate's little finger. Gillette didn't even hear it strike. He heard only Phate's ragged scream.

"I can do this all day," she said evenly. "It doesn't bother me and it's my job."

A sudden dark fury crossed Phate's face. A man used to control, a master MUD player, he was now completely helpless. "Why don't you go fuck yourself?" He gave a weak laugh. "You'll never find anybody *else* who'll want to. You're a luser. You're a geek spinster – you've got a pretty shitty life ahead of you."

The flicker of anger in her eyes vanished fast. She lifted the hammer again.

"No, no!" Phate cried. He took a deep breath. "All right . . ." He gave her the numbers of an Internet address, the username and the passcode.

Nolan pulled out a cell phone and hit one button. It seemed that the call connected immediately. She gave the details on Phate's site to the person on the other end of the phone then said, "I'll hold on. Check it out."

Phate's chest rose and fell. He squinted the tears of pain from his eyes. Then he looked toward Gillette. "Here we are, Valleyman, act three." He sat up slightly and his bloody hand moved an inch or two. He winced. "The game didn't quite work out the way I thought. We've got ourselves a surprise ending, looks like."

"Quiet," Nolan muttered.

But Phate ignored her and continued, speaking to Gillette in a gasping voice. "I've got something I want to tell you. Are you listening? 'To thine own self be true, and it must follow, as the night the day, thou canst not then be false to any man.'" He coughed for a moment. Then: "I love plays.

That's from *Hamlet*, one of my favorites. Remember that line, Valleyman. That's advice from a wizard. 'To thine own self be true.'"

Nolan's face curled into a frown as she listened to her phone. Her shoulders sagged and she said into the mouthpiece, "Stand by." She set the phone aside and gripped the hammer again, glaring at Phate, who – though he seemed consumed by the pain – was laughing faintly.

"They checked out the site you gave me," she said, "and it turned out to be an e-mail account. When they opened the files the communications program sent something to a university in Asia. Was it Trapdoor?"

"I don't know what it was," he whispered, staring at his bloody, shattered hand. A brief frown on his face gave way to a cold smile. "Maybe I gave you the wrong address."

"Well, give me the right one."

"What's the hurry?" he asked cruelly. "Got an important date with your cat at home? A TV show? A bottle of wine you'll share with . . . yourself?"

Again her anger broke through momentarily and she slammed the hammer down on his hand.

Phate screamed again.

Tell her, Gillette thought. For God's sake, tell her!

But he kept silent for an interminable five minutes of this torture, the hammer rising and falling, the finger bones snapping. Finally Phate could stand it no more. "All right, all right." He gave her another address, name and passcode.

Nolan picked up the phone and relayed this information to her colleague on the other end. Waited a few minutes. She listened, said, "Go through it line by line then run a compiler, make sure it's real."

While she waited she looked around the room at the old computers. Her eyes occasionally sparked with recognition – and sometimes affection and delight – as they settled on particular items.

Five minutes later her colleague came back on the line. "Good," she said into the phone, apparently satisfied the source code was real. "Now go back to the FTP site and grab root. Check the upload and download logs. See if he's transferred the code anywhere else."

Who was she speaking to? Gillette wondered. To review and compile a program as complicated as Trapdoor would normally take hours; Gillette supposed a number of people were working on this and using dedicated supercomputers for the analysis.

After a moment she cocked her head and listened. "Okay. Burn the FTP site and everything it's connected to. Use Infekt IV. . . . No, I mean the whole network. I don't care if it's linked to Norad and air traffic control. Burn it."

This virus was like an uncontrollable brushfire. It would methodically destroy the contents of every file in the FTP site where Phate had stored the source code and of any machine connected to it. Infekt would turn the data of thousands of machines into unrecognizable chains of random symbols so that it would be impossible to find even the slightest reference to Trapdoor, let alone the working source code.

Phate closed his eyes and leaned his head back against the column.

Nolan stood and, still holding the hammer, walked toward Gillette. He rolled onto his side and tried to crawl away. But his body still wouldn't work after the electric jolts and he collapsed to the floor again. Patricia leaned close. Gillette stared at the hammer. Then he looked more closely at her and observed that her hair roots were a slightly different color from the strands, that she wore green contact lenses. Looking beneath the blotchy makeup, which gave her face that thick, doughy appearance, he could see lean features. Which meant that perhaps she too was wearing body padding to add thirty pounds to what was undoubtedly a taut, muscular body.

Then he noticed her hands.

Her fingers . . . the pads glistened slightly and seemed opaque. And he understood: All that time she'd been putting on fingernail conditioner she was adding it to the pads as well – to obscure her fingerprints.

She's social engineered us too. From day one.

Gillette whispered, "You've been after him for a while, haven't you?"

Nolan nodded. "A year. Ever since we heard about Trapdoor."

"Who's 'we'?"

She didn't answer but she didn't need to. Gillette supposed that she'd been hired not by Horizon On-Line – or by Horizon alone – but by a consortium of Internet service providers to find the source code for Trapdoor, the ultimate voyeur's software, which gave complete access to the lives of the unsuspecting. Nolan's bosses wouldn't *use* Trapdoor but would write inoculations against it and then destroy or quarantine the program, which was a huge threat to the trillion-dollar online industry. Gillette could just imagine how fast subscribers to Internet providers would cancel their service and never go online again if they knew that hackers could roam freely through their computers and learn every detail about their lives. Steal from them. Expose them. Even destroy them.

And she'd used Andy Anderson, Bishop and the rest of the CCU, just as she'd probably used the police in Portland and northern Virginia, where Phate and Shawn had struck earlier.

Just as she'd used Gillette himself.

She asked, "Did he tell you anything about the source code? Anywhere else he cached it?"

"No."

It would have made no sense for Phate to do so and, after studying him carefully, she seemed to believe Gillette. Then she stood slowly and looked back at Phate. Gillette saw her eyes examine the hacker in a certain way and he felt a jolt of alarm. Like a programmer who knows how software moves from beginning to end with no deviation, no waste or digression, Gillette suddenly understood clearly what Nolan had to do next.

He pleaded urgently, "Don't."

"I have to."

"No, you don't. He'll never be out in public again. He'll be in prison for the rest of his life."

"You think prison would keep somebody like him offline? It didn't stop you."

"You can't do it!"

"Trapdoor's too dangerous," she explained. "And he's got the code in his head. Probably a dozen other programs, too, that're just as dangerous."

"No," Gillette whispered desperately. "There's never been a hacker as good as him. There may never be again. He can write code that most of us can't even imagine yet."

She walked back to Phate.

"Don't!" Gillette cried.

But he knew his protest was futile.

From her laptop bag she took a small leather case, extracted a hypodermic syringe and filled it from a bottle of clear liquid. Without hesitating, she leaned down and injected it into Phate's neck. He didn't struggle and for a moment Gillette had the impression that he knew exactly what was happening and was embracing his death. Phate focused on Gillette then on the wooden case of his Apple computer, which sat on a table nearby. The early Apples were truly hackers' computers – you bought only the guts of the machine and had to build the housing yourself. Phate continued to gaze at the unit as if he were trying to say something to it. He turned to Gillette. "'To . . .'" His words vanished into a whisper.

Gillette shook his head.

Phate coughed and continued in a feeble voice, "'To thine own self be true . . .'" Then his head dipped forward and his breathing stopped.

Gillette couldn't help but feel a sense of loss and sorrow. Sure, Jon Patrick Holloway deserved his death. He was evil and could take the life of a human being as easily as he'd lift a fictional character's digital heart from his body in a MUD game. Yet within the young man was another person: someone who wrote code as elegant as a symphony, in whose keystrokes could be heard the silent laughter of hackers and could be seen the brilliance of a unbound mind, which – had it been directed on a slightly different course years ago – could have made Jon Holloway a computer wizard admired around the world.

He'd also been someone with whom Gillette had carried out some, yes, truly moby hacks. Whatever direction life takes, you never quite lose the bond that develops among fellow explorers of the Blue Nowhere.

Then Patricia Nolan stood and looked at Gillette.

He thought, I'm dead.

She drew some more liquid into the needle, sighing. *This* murder, at least, was going to bother her.

"No," he whispered. Shaking his head. "I won't say anything."

He tried to scrabble away from her but his muscles were still haywire from the electrical charges. She crouched beside him, pulled his collar down and massaged his neck to find the artery.

Gillette looked across the room to where Bishop lay, still unconscious. The detective would be the next victim, he understood.

Nolan leaned forward with the needle.

"No," Gillette whispered. He closed his eyes, his thoughts on Ellie. "No! Don't do it!"

Then a man's voice shouted, "Hey, hold up there!"

Without a second's pause Nolan dropped the hypodermic, pulled a pistol from her laptop case and fired toward Tony Mott, who stood in the doorway.

"Jesus," the young cop cried, cringing. "What the hell're you doing?" He dropped to the floor.

Nolan lifted her gun once more but before she could fire, several huge explosions shook the air and she fell backward. Mott was firing at her with his glitzy silver automatic.

None of the bullets had struck her and Nolan rose fast again, firing her own pistol – a much smaller one – at Mott.

The CCU cop, wearing his biking shorts, a Nike shirt and with his Oakley sunglasses dangling from his neck, crawled farther into the warehouse. He fired again, keeping Nolan on the defensive. She fired several times but missed as well.

"What the hell's going on? What's she doing?"

"She killed Holloway. I was next."

Nolan fired again then eased toward the front of the warehouse.

Mott grabbed Gillette by the pants cuff and dragged him to cover then emptied the clip of the automatic in the woman's direction. For all his love of SWAT team operations the cop seemed panicked to be in a real shoot-out. He was also a really bad shot. As he reloaded, Nolan disappeared behind some cartons.

"Are you hit?" Mott's hands were shaking and he was breathless.

"No, she got me with a stun gun or something. I can't move."

"What about Frank?"

"He's not shot. But we've got to get him to a doctor. How did you know we were here?"

"Frank called and told me to check the records on this place."

Gillette remembered Bishop's making the call from Nolan's hotel room.

Scanning the warehouse for Nolan, the young cop continued, "That prick Backle knew Frank and you took off together. He had a tap on our phones. He heard the address and called some of his people to pick you up here. I came over here to warn you."

"But how'd you get through all the traffic?"

"My bike, remember?" Mott crawled to Bishop, who was starting to stir. Then, from across the dinosaur pen, Nolan rose and fired a half-dozen shots in their direction. She fled out the front door.

Mott reluctantly started after her.

Gillette called, "Be careful. *She* can't get away through the traffic either. She'll be outside, waiting. . . ."

But his voice faded as he heard a distinctive sound, growing closer. He realized that, like hackers, people with jobs like Patricia Nolan must be experts at improvising; a countywide traffic jam wasn't going to interfere with her plans. The noise was the roar of the helicopter, undoubtedly the one disguised as a press chopper that he'd seen before, the one that had delivered her here.

In less than thirty seconds the craft had picked her up and was in the air again, speeding away, the chunky sound of the rotors soon replaced by the curiously harmonic orchestra of car and truck horns filling the late-afternoon sky.

CHAPTER 00101010 / FORTY-TWO

———◆·◆·◆———

Gillette and Bishop were back at the Computer Crimes Unit.

The detective was out of the urgent-care facility. A concussion, a fierce headache and eight stitches were the only evidence of his ordeal – along with a new shirt to replace the bloody one. (This one fit somewhat better than its predecessor but it too seemed largely tuck-resistant.)

The time was 6:30 P.M. and public works had managed to reload the software that controlled the traffic lights. Much of the congestion in Santa Clara County was gone. A search of San Jose Computer Products turned up a gasoline bomb and some information about the fire alarm system of Northern California University. Aware of Phate's love of diversion, Bishop was concerned that the killer had planted a second device on the campus. But a thorough search of the dormitories and other school buildings revealed nothing.

To no one's surprise Horizon On-Line claimed they'd never heard of a Patricia Nolan. The company executives and the head of corporate security in Seattle said they'd never contacted California state police headquarters after the Lara Gibson killing – and no one had sent Andy Anderson any e-mails or faxes about Nolan's credentials. The Horizon On-Line number that Anderson had called to verify her employment was a working Horizon phone line but, according to the phone company in Seattle, all calls going into that number were forwarded – to a Mobile

America cell phone with unassigned numbers, which was no longer in use.

The security staff at Horizon knew of no one fitting her description either. The address under which she'd registered at her hotel in San Jose was fake and the credit card was phony too. All the phone calls she'd made from the hotel were to that same, hacked Mobile America number.

Not a soul at CCU believed Horizon's denial, of course. But proving a connection between HOL and Patricia Nolan was going to be difficult – as was finding her in the first place. A picture of the woman, lifted from a security tape in CCU headquarters, went out on ISLEnet to state police bureaus around the country and to the feds for posting to VICAP. Bishop, however, had to include the embarrassing disclaimer that even though the woman had spent several days in a state police facility they had no samples of her fingerprints and that her appearance was probably considerably different from what the tape showed.

At least the whereabouts of the other co-conspirator had been discovered. The body of Shawn – Stephen Miller – had been found in the woods behind his house; he'd shot himself with his service revolver after he learned that they'd caught on to his identity. His remorseful suicide note had, naturally, been in the form of an e-mail.

CCU's Linda Sanchez and Tony Mott were trying to piece together the extent of Miller's betrayal. The state police would have to issue a statement that one of their officers had been an accomplice in the hacker murder case in Silicon Valley, and Internal Affairs wanted to find out how much damage Miller had done and how long he'd been Phate's partner and lover.

Department of Defense agent Backle was still intent on collaring Wyatt Gillette for a laundry list of offenses involving the Standard 12 encryption program, and now wanted to arrest Frank Bishop as well – for breaking a federal prisoner out of custody.

As for the charges against Gillette for the Standard 12 hack, Bishop explained to Captain Bernstein, "It's pretty clear, sir, that Gillette either seized root at one of Holloway's FTP sites and downloaded a copy of the script or just telneted directly into Holloway's machine and got a copy that way."

"What the hell does that mean?" the grizzled, crew-cut cop had snapped.

"Sorry, sir." Bishop had said then had translated the techno-speak. "What I'm saying is I think it was *Holloway* who broke into the DoD and wrote the decryption program. Gillette stole it from him and used it because we asked him to."

"You *think*," Bernstein had muttered cynically. "Well, I don't understand all this computer crap that's been going around." But he picked up the phone and called the U.S. attorney, who agreed to review whatever evidence CCU could offer supporting Bishop's theory before proceeding with charges against either Gillette or Bishop (both of whose stock was pretty high at the moment for having nailed the "Silicon Valley Kracker," as the local TV stations were describing Phate).

Agent Backle grudgingly returned to his office in San Francisco's Presidio.

At the moment, however, the attention of all the law enforcers had turned from Phate and Stephen Miller to the MARINKILL case. Several bulletins reported that the killers had been spotted again – this time right next door, in San Jose – apparently staking out several other banks. Bishop and Shelton had been conscripted into the joint FBI/state police taskforce. They'd spend a few hours with their families for dinner and then report to the bureau's San Jose office later tonight.

Bob Shelton was home at the moment (his only farewell to Gillette had been a cryptic glance, whose meaning was completely lost on the hacker). Bishop, however, had delayed his own departure home and was sharing a Pop-Tart and coffee with the hacker while they waited for the troopers to arrive to transport him back to San Ho.

The phone rang. Bishop answered, "Computer Crimes."

He listened for a moment. "Hold on." He looked at Gillette, lifted an eyebrow. Handed the receiver to him. "It's for you."

He took it. "Hello?"

"Wyatt."

Elana's voice was so familiar to him that he could almost feel it beneath his compulsively keying fingers. The timbre of her voice alone had always revealed to him the entire range of her soul, and he needed to hear only a single word to know whether she was playful, angry, frightened, sentimental, passionate. Today he could tell from her greeting that she'd called very reluctantly and that her defenses were up like the shields on the spacecrafts of the sci-fi movies they'd watched together.

On the other hand, she *had* called.

She said, "I heard that he's dead. Jon Holloway. I heard it on the news."

"That's right."

"Are you all right?"

"Fine."

A long pause. As if looking for something to fill the silence, she added, "I'm still going to New York."

"With Ed."

"That's right."

He closed his eyes and sighed. Then, with an edge in his voice, he asked, "So why'd you call?"

"I guess just to say that if you wanted to come, you could."

Gillette wondered: Why bother? What was the point?

He said, "I'll be there in ten minutes."

They hung up. He turned to find Bishop looking at him. cautiously Gillette said, "Give me an hour. Please."

"I can't take you," the detective said.

"Let me borrow a car."

The detective debated, looked around the dinosaur pen, considering. He said to Linda Sanchez, "You have a CCU car he can use?"

Reluctantly she handed him the keys. "This isn't procedure, boss."

"I'll take responsibility."

Bishop tossed the keys to Gillette then pulled out his phone and called the troopers who'd be transporting him back to San Ho. He gave them Elana's address and said he'd okayed Gillette's being there. The prisoner would be returning to CCU in one hour. He hung up.

"I'll come back."

"I know you will."

The men faced each other for a moment. They shook hands. Gillette nodded and started for the door.

"Wait," Bishop asked, frowning. "You have a driver's license?"

Gillette laughed. "No, I don't have a driver's license."

Bishop shrugged and said, "Well, just don't get stopped."

The hacker nodded and said gravely, "Right. They might send me to jail."

The house smelled of lemons, as it always had.

This was thanks to the deft culinary touch of Irene Papandolos, Ellie's mother. She wasn't the traditional wary, silent Greek matron but a sharp businesswoman who owned a successful catering company and still managed to find the time to cook every meal for her family from scratch. It was now dinnertime and she wore a stained apron over a rose-colored business suit.

She greeted Gillette with a cool, unsmiling nod and gestured him into the den.

He sat on a couch, beneath a picture of the waterfront at Piraeus. Family being ever important in Greek households, two tables were filled with photographs in a variety of frames, some cheap, some heavy silver and gold. Gillette saw a picture of Elana in her wedding dress. He didn't recognize the shot and he wondered if it had originally shown the two of them and had been cropped to remove him.

Elana entered the room.

"You're here by yourself?" she asked, not smiling. No other greeting.

"How do you mean?"

"No police baby-sitters?"

"Honor system."

"I saw a couple of police cars go past. I wondered if they were with you." She nodded outside.

"No," Gillette said. Though he supposed that troopers might in fact be keeping tabs on him.

She sat and picked uneasily at the cuff of the Stanford sweatshirt she wore.

"I'm not going to say goodbye," he said. She frowned and he continued, "Because I want to talk you out of leaving. I want to keep seeing you."

"Seeing me? You're in *prison,* Wyatt."

"I'll be out in a year."

She laughed in surprise at his effrontery.

He said, "I want to try again."

"*You* want to try again. What about what I want?"

"I can give you what you want. I will. I've done a lot of thinking. I can make you love me again. I don't want you out of my life."

"You chose machines over me. You got what you wanted."

"That's in the past."

"My life's different now. I'm happy."

"Are you?"

"Yes," Elana said emphatically.

"Because of Ed."

"He's part of it. . . . Come on, Wyatt, what can you offer me? You're a felon. You're addicted to those goddamn computers of yours. You don't have a job and the judge said that even when you get out of jail you can't go online for a year."

"And Ed's got himself a good job? Is that it? I didn't know that a good income was important to you."

"It's not a question of support, Gillette. It's about responsibility. And you're not responsible."

"I *wasn't* responsible. I admit that. But I will be." He tried to take her hand but she eased away. He said, "Come on, Ellie. . . . I saw your e-mails. When you talk about Ed it doesn't exactly sound like he's perfect husband material."

She stiffened and he saw he'd touched a nerve here. "Leave Ed out of this. I'm talking about you and me."

"Me too. That's exactly who I'm talking about. I love you. I know I made your life hell. It won't be that way again. You wanted children, a normal life. I'll find a job. We'll have a family."

Another hesitation.

He pressed forward. "Why are you leaving *tomorrow?* What's the hurry?"

"I'm starting a new job next Monday."

"Why New York?"

"Because it's as far away from you as I can get."

"Wait a month. Just one month. I get two visits a week. Come see me." He smiled. "We can hang out. Eat pizza."

Her eyes swept the floor and he sensed that she was debating.

"Did your mother cut me out of that picture?" He grinned and nodded at the snapshot of her in her wedding gown.

She gave a faint smile. "No. That was the one Alexis took – on the lawn. It was just of me. Remember, the one where you can't see my feet."

He laughed. "How many brides lose their shoes at the wedding?"

She nodded. "We always wondered what happened to them."

"Oh, please, Ellie. Just postpone it for a month. That's all I'm asking."

Her eyes swept across some of the pictures. She began to say something but her mother stepped into the doorway suddenly. Her dark face was even darker than before. "There's a call for you."

"Me?" Gillette asked.

"It's somebody named Bishop. He says it's important."

"Frank, what's—"

The detective's voice was raw with urgency. "Listen to me carefully, Wyatt. We could lose the line any minute. Shawn isn't dead."

"What? But Miller—"

"No, we were wrong. Stephen Miller isn't Shawn. It's somebody *else*. I'm at CCU. Linda Sanchez found a message for me on the main CCU voice mail. Before he died Miller called and left it. Remember when Phate broke into CCU and went after you?"

"Right."

"Miller was just coming back from the medical center then. He was in the parking lot and saw Phate run out of the building and jump in a car. He followed him."

"Why?"

"To collar him."

"By himself?" Gillette asked.

"The message said he wanted to bring the killer in on his own. He said he'd screwed up so many times that he wanted to prove that he could do something right."

"Then he didn't kill himself?"

"Nope. They haven't done the autopsy yet but I had a medical examiner check for traces of powder burns on his hands. There weren't any – if he'd killed himself there would've been plenty of trace. Phate must've seen Miller following and then killed him. Then he pretended to be Miller and intentionally got caught cracking into the State Department. He hacked into Miller's workstation at CCU and planted those fake e-mails and took his machines and disks out of his house. We're sure the suicide note was false too. It was all to stop us from looking for the real Shawn."

"Well, who *is* he?"

"I don't have a clue. All I know is we've got a real problem. Tony Mott's here. Shawn hacked the FBI's tactical command computers in Washington and San Jose – he got in through ISLEnet – and he's got root access." In a low voice Bishop continued. "Now listen carefully. Shawn's issued arrest warrants and rules of engagement for the suspects in the MARINKILL case. We're looking at the screen right now."

"I don't understand," Gillette said.

"The warrants say that the suspects are at 3245 Abrego Avenue in Sunnyvale."

"But that's here! Elana's house."

"I know. He's ordered the tactical troops to attack the house in twenty-five minutes."

VI
ITS ALL IN THE SPELLING

———◆◆◆◆◆———

```
CODE SEGMENT
ASSUME DS:CODE,SS:CODE,CS:CODE,ES:CODE
ORG $+0100H
VCODE: JMP
                    ***
virus: PUSH CX
MOV DX,OFFSET vir_dat
CLD
MOV SI,DX
ADD SI,first_3
MOV CX,3
MOV DI,OFFSET 100H
REPZ MOVSB
MOV SI,DX
mov ah,30h
int 21h
cmp al,0
JnZ dos_ok
JMP quit
```

                     – Portions of the actual source code
                             of the virus Violator Strain II

CHAPTER 00101011 / FORTY-THREE

E lana stepped forward, seeing Gillette's alarmed expression. "What is it? What's going on?"

He ignored her and said to Bishop, "Call the FBI. Tell them what's happening. Call *Washington*."

"I tried," Bishop responded. "Bernstein did too. But the agents hung up on us. The rules of engagement that Shawn issued say that the perps will probably try to impersonate state cops and try to countermand or delay the attack order. Only computer codes are authorized. Nothing verbal. Not even from Washington."

"Jesus, Frank. . . ."

How had Shawn found out he was here? Then he realized that Bishop had called the troopers to say that Gillette would be at Elana's place for an hour. He remembered that Phate and Shawn had been monitoring radio and phone transmissions for keywords like Triple-X and Holloway and Gillette. Shawn must've heard Bishop's conversation.

Bishop said, "They're near the house now, at a staging area." The detective added, "I just don't understand why Shawn's doing this."

But Gillette did.

Hacker revenge is patient revenge.

Gillette had betrayed Phate years ago, destroyed the carefully socially engineered life he'd made for himself . . . and earlier today he'd helped end the hacker's life altogether. Now Shawn would destroy Gillette' and those he loved.

He looked out the window, thought he saw some motion.

"Wyatt?" Elana asked. "What's going on?" She started to look out the window but he pulled her back roughly. "What is it?" she cried.

"Stay back! Stay away from the windows!"

Bishop continued. "Shawn's issued Level 4 rules of engagement – that means that the SWAT teams don't make any surrender demands. They go in assuming they'll be met with suicidal resistance. They're the rules of engagement they use when they're up against terrorists willing to die."

"So they'll shoot tear gas inside," Gillette muttered, "kick the doors in and anybody who moves is going to get killed."

Bishop paused. "It could go like that."

"Wyatt?" Elana asked. "What's going on? Tell me!"

He turned, shouted, "Tell everybody to get down on the living room floor! You too! Now!"

Her black eyes burned with anger and fear. "What've you done?"

"I'm sorry, I'm sorry. . . . Just do it now. Get down!"

He turned back, looked out the window. He could see two large black vans easing through an alley fifty feet away. In the distance a helicopter fluttered a hundred feet in the air.

"Listen, Wyatt, the bureau won't go ahead with the assault if there's no final confirmation. That's part of the rules of engagement. Is there any way to shut down Shawn's machine?"

"Put Tony on."

"I'm here," Mott said.

"Are you in the FBI system?"

"Yeah, we can see the screen. Shawn's imping that he's the Tactical Operations Center in Washington, issuing codes. The tactical agent in the field's responding like it's business as usual."

"Can you trace the call back to where Shawn is?"

Mott said, "We don't have a warrant but I'll pull some strings at Pac Bell. Give me a minute or two."

Outside, the sound of heavy trucks. The helicopter was closer.

Gillette could hear the hysterical sobbing of Elana's mother and her brother's angry words coming from the living room. Elana herself said nothing. He saw her cross herself, glance once at him hopelessly and bury her head in the carpet beside her mother.

Oh, Jesus, what've I done?

A few minutes later Bishop came back on the line. "Pac Bell's running the trace. It's a landline. They've narrowed down the central office and exchange – he's somewhere in western San Jose, near Winchester Boulevard. Where Phate's warehouse was."

Gillette asked, "You think he's in the San Jose Computer Products building? Maybe he got back inside after you finished going through it."

"Or maybe he's someplace nearby – there're dozens of old warehouses around there. I'm ten minutes away," the detective said. "I'll go over there now. Brother, I wish we knew who Shawn was."

Something occurred to Gillette. As when he was writing code, he applied this hypothesis against the known facts and rules of logic. He came to a conclusion. He said, "I have a thought about that."

"Shawn?"

"Yeah. Where's Bob Shelton?"

"At home. Why're you asking?"

"Call and find out if he's really there."

"Okay. I'll call you back from the car."

A few minutes later the Papandolos phone rang and Gillette grabbed the receiver. Frank Bishop was calling back as he sped down San Carlos toward Winchester.

"Bob *should* be home," Bishop said, "but there's no answer. You're wrong if you're thinking Bob's Shawn, though."

Looking out the window, seeing another police car cruise by, followed by a military-type truck, Gillette said, "No, Frank, listen: Shelton claimed he hated computers, didn't know anything about them. But remember: he had that hard drive in his house."

"The what?"

"That disk we saw – it's the kind of hardware only people who did serious hacking or ran bulletin boards a few years ago would use."

"I don't know," Bishop said slowly. "Maybe it was evidence or something."

"Has he ever worked a computer case before this?"

"Well, no . . ."

Gillette continued, "And he disappeared for a while before they raided Phate's house in Los Altos. He had time to send that message about the assault code and give Phate a chance to get away. And, think about it – it was because of *him* that Phate got inside ISLEnet and got the FBI computer addresses and tactical codes. Shelton said he went online to check me out. But what he was really doing was leaving the password and address of the CCU computer for Phate – so he could crack ISLEnet."

"But Bob's not a computer person."

"He *says* he isn't. But do you know for sure? Do you go over to his house much?"

"No."

"What's he do at night?"

"Usually stays at home."

"Never goes out?"

Bishop reluctantly replied, "No."

"That's hacker behavior."

"But I've known him for three years."

"Social engineering."

Bishop said, "Impossible. . . . Hold on – there's another call coming in."

While he was on hold Gillette peeked through the curtain. He could see what looked like a military troop carrier parked not far away. There was motion in the bushes across the street. Policemen in camouflage clothing ran from one hedgerow to another. It seemed that there were a hundred officers outside.

Bishop came back on the line.

"Pac Bell's got the location where Shawn's cracking into the FBI from. He *is* in San Jose Computer Products. I'm almost there. I'll call you when I'm inside."

Frank Bishop called for backup and then parked the car out of sight in the lot across the street; San Jose Computer seemed to be windowless but he wasn't going to take the chance that Shawn would get a look at him.

Crouching, moving as fast as he could despite the terrible

pain in his temple and the back of his skull Bishop made his way to the warehouse.

He didn't believe Gillette's conclusion about Bob Shelton. And yet he couldn't help but consider it. Of all the partners Bishop had had, he knew the least about Shelton. The big cop *did* spend all his nights at home. He *didn't* socialize with other cops. And while Bishop himself, for instance, had a basic knowledge of ISLEnet *he* wouldn't have been able to get inside the system and track down that information about Gillette the way Shelton had done. He recalled too that Shelton had volunteered for this case; Bishop remembered wondering why he'd wanted to take this one rather than MARINKILL.

But none of this mattered at the moment. Whether Shawn was Bob Shelton or someone else, Bishop had only about fifteen minutes before the federal tactical team began their attack. Drawing his pistol, he flattened himself against the wall beside the loading dock and paused, listening. He could hear nothing inside.

Okay. . . . Go!

Ripping the door open, Bishop ran down the corridor, through the office and into the dank warehouse itself. It was dark and seemed unoccupied. He found a bank of overhead lights and flipped the switches on with his left hand, holding his pistol out in front of him. The stark illumination shone down on the entire space and he could see clearly that it was empty.

He ran outside again to look for another building that Shawn might be using. But there were no other structures connected to the warehouse. As he was about to turn back, though, he noticed that the warehouse looked considerably larger from the outside than it had on the inside.

Hurrying back into the building he saw that a wall appeared to have been added at one end of the warehouse; it was a more recent construction than the original building. Yes, Phate must've added a secret room. *That's* where Shawn would be. . . .

In a dim corner of the pen he found a door and tested the knob quietly. It was unlocked. He inhaled deeply, dried the sweat from his hand on his billowing shirt and gripped the knob again. Had his footsteps or flipping on the lights warned Shawn of the intrusion? Did the killer have a weapon trained on the doorway?

It all comes down to this. . . .

Frank Bishop pushed inside, gun up.

He dropped into a crouch, squinting for a target, scanning the dark room, chill from the air-conditioning. He saw no sign of Shawn, only machinery and equipment, packing crates and pallets, tools, a hand-operated hydraulic forklift.

Empty. There was—

Then he saw it.

Oh, no . . .

Bishop realized then that Wyatt Gillette and his wife and her family were doomed.

The room was only a telephone relay station. Shawn was hacking in from someplace else.

Reluctantly he called Gillette.

The hacker answered and said desperately, "I can see them, Frank. They've got machine guns. This's going to be bad. You found anything?"

"Wyatt, I'm at the warehouse. . . . But . . . I'm sorry. Shawn's not here. It's just a phone relay or something." He described the large black metal console.

"It's not a phone relay," Gillette muttered, his voice hollow with despair. "It's an Internet router. But it still won't do us any good. It'd take an hour to trace the signal back to Shawn. We'll never find him in time."

Bishop glanced at the box. "There're no switches on it and the wiring's under the floor – this is one of those dinosaur pens like at CCU. So I can't unplug it."

"Won't do any good anyway. Even if you shut that one down, Shawn's transmissions'll automatically find a different route to the FBI."

"Maybe there's something else here that'll tell us where he is." Desperately Bishop began searching through the desk and packing boxes. "There're lots of papers and books."

"What are they?" the hacker asked, but his voice was a monotone, filled with helplessness, his childlike curiosity long gone.

"Manuals, printouts, worksheets, computer disks. Mostly technical stuff. From Sun Microsystems, Apple, Harvard, Western Electric – all the places where Phate worked." Bishop ripped through boxes, scattering pages everywhere. "No, there's nothing here." Bishop looked around helplessly. "I'll try to make it to Ellie's house in time, convince the bureau to send a negotiator in before they start the assault."

"You're twenty minutes away, Frank," Gillette whispered. "You'll never make it."

"I'll try," the detective said softly. "Listen, Wyatt, get into the middle of the living room and get down. Keep your hands in plain sight. Pray for the best." He started for the door.

Then he heard Gillette shout, "Wait!"

"What is it?"

The hacker asked, "Those manuals that he was packing up. What were the companies again?"

Bishop looked over the documents. "The places Phate worked. Harvard, Sun, Apple, Western Electric. And—"

"NEC!" Gillette shouted.

"Right—."

"It's an acronym!"

"What do you mean?"

The hacker said, "Remember? All the acronyms hackers use? The initials of those places he worked – S for Sun. H for Harvard. A for Apple, Western Electric, NEC . . . S, H, A, W, N . . . The machine – there in the room with you. . . . It's not a router at all. The box – *that's* Shawn. He *created* it from the code and hardware he stole!"

Bishop scoffed. "Impossible."

"No, that's why the trace ended there. Shawn's a machine. He's . . . *it's* generating the signals. Before he died Phate must've programmed it to crack the bureau system and arrange the assault. And Phate knew about Ellie – he mentioned her by name when he broke into CCU. He seemed to think I betrayed him because of her."

Bishop, shivering fiercely from the raw cold, turned toward the black box. "There's no way a computer could've done all this—"

But Gillette interupted, "No, no, no . . . Why wasn't I

thinking better? A machine is the *only* way he could've done it. A supercomputer's the only thing that could crack scrambled signals and monitor *all* of the phone calls and radio transmissions in and out of CCU. A human being couldn't do it – there'd be way too much to listen to. Government computers do it everyday, listen for key words like 'president' and 'assassinate' in the same sentence. That's how Phate found out about Andy Anderson going to Hacker's Knoll and about me – Shawn must've heard Backle call the Department of Defense and sent Phate that portion of the transmission. And it heard the assault code when we were about to nail him in Los Altos and sent the message to Phate to warn him."

The detective said, "But Shawn's e-mails in Phate's computer . . . They sounded like a human actually wrote them."

"You can communicate with a machine any way you want – e-mails work just as well as anything else. Phate *programmed* them to sound like somebody'd written them. It probably made him feel better, seeing what looked like a human's words. Like I was telling you I did with my Trash-80."

S-H-A-W-N.

It's all in the spelling. . . .

"What can we do?" the detective asked.

"There's only one thing. You've got to—"

The line went dead.

"We took their phone out," a communications tech said to Special Agent Mark Little, the tactical commander for the bureau's MARINKILL operation. "And the cell's down. Nobody's mobiles'll work for a mile around."

"Good."

Little, along with his second in command, Special Agent George Steadman, was in a panel van that was serving as the command post, a half block from the subjects' house in Sunnyvale. The vehicle was parked around the corner from the house on Abrego where the perps in the MARINKILL case were reportedly hiding.

Taking the phones down was standard procedure. Five or

ten minutes before an assault you had the subject's phone service suspended. That way nobody could warn them of the impending attack.

Little had done a number of dynamic entries into barricaded sites – mostly drug busts in Oakland and San Jose – and he'd never lost an agent. But this operation was especially troubling to the thirty-one-year-old agent. He'd been working MARINKILL from day one and had read all the bulletins, including the one just received from an anonymous informant, which reported that the killers felt they were being persecuted by the FBI and police and planned to torture any law enforcement officers they captured. Appended to this was another report that they'd rather die fighting than be taken alive.

Man, it's never easy. But this . . .

"Everybody locked and loaded and in armor?" Little asked Steadman.

"Yeah. Three teams and snipers ready. The streets're secure. Medevacs from Travis are in the air. Fire trucks're around the corner."

Little nodded as he listened to the report. Well, everything *seemed* fine. But what the hell was bothering him so much?

He wasn't sure. Maybe it had been the desperation in that guy's voice – the one claiming to be from the state police. Bishop was his name, or something like that. Yammering on about somebody hacking into the bureau's computers and issuing phony assault codes against some innocents.

But the rules of engagement issued by Washington had warned that the perps would impersonate fellow officers and would claim that the whole operation was a misunderstanding. The perps might even pretend to be state police. Besides, Little reflected, hacking into the bureau's computers? Impossible. The public Web site was one thing, but the secure tactical computer? Never.

He looked at his watch.

Eight minutes to go.

He said to one of the techs sitting at a computer monitor, "Get the yellow confirmation."

The man keyed:

```
FROM: TACTICAL COMMANDER, DOJ NORTHERN
DISTRICT CALIFORNIA

TO: DOJ TAC OP CENTER, WASHINGTON, D.C.

RE: DOJ NORTHERN DISTRICT CALIFORNIA
OPERATION 139-01

YELLOW CODE CONFIRM?
```

He hit ENTER.

There were three levels of tactical operational codes: green, yellow and red. A go-ahead green code approved the agents' movement to the staging site of the operation. This had happened a half-hour ago. Yellow go-ahead meant for them to get ready for the assault and move into position around their target. Red controlled the actual assault itself.

A moment later this message came up on the screen:

```
FROM: DOJ TAC OP CENTER, WASHINGTON,
D.C.

TO: TACTICAL COMMANDER, DOJ NORTHERN
DISTRICT CALIFORNIA

RE: DOJ NORTHERN DISTRICT CALIFORNIA
OPERATION 139-01

YELLOW CODE: <OAKTREE>
```

"Print it out," Little commanded the communications tech.

"Yessir."

Little and Steadman checked the code word and found that oaktree was correct. The agents were approved to deploy around the house.

Still, he hesitated, hearing the voice of that guy claiming to be Frank Bishop over and over in his head. He thought of the children killed at Waco. Despite the Level 4 rules of engagement, which stated that negotiators were not appropriate for tactical operations involving perps like these,

Little wondered if he should call San Francisco, where the bureau had a top-notch siege negotiator he'd worked with before. Maybe—

"Agent Little?" the communications officer interrupted, nodding at his computer screen. "Message for you."

Little leaned forward and read.

```
URGENT URGENT URGENT

FROM: DOJ TAC OP CENTER, WASHINGTON,
D.C.

TO: TACTICAL COMMANDER, DOJ NORTHERN
DISTRICT CALIFORNIA

RE: DOJ NORTHERN DISTRICT CALIFORNIA
OPERATION 139-01

U.S. ARMY REPORTS MARINKILL SUSPECTS
BROKE INTO SAN PEDRO MILITARY RESERVE
AT 1540 HOURS TODAY AND STOLE LARGE
CACHE OF AUTOMATIC WEAPONS, HAND
GRENADES AND BODY ARMOR.

ADVISE TACTICAL AGENTS OF SAID
SITUATION.
```

Man alive, Little thought, his pulse skyrocketing. The message knocked any suggestion of a negotiator right out of his thoughts. He glanced at Agent Steadman and said calmly, nodding at the screen, "Pass the word on this, George. Then get everybody into position. We go in six minutes."

CHAPTER 00101100 / FORTY-FOUR

— ◆ ◆ —

F rank Bishop walked around Shawn.

The housing was about four-feet square and made of thick metal sheets. On the back was a series of ventilation slats from which hot air poured, the white wisps visible, like breath on a winter day. The front panel consisted of nothing except three green eyes – glowing indicator lights that flickered occasionally, revealing that Shawn was hard at work carrying out Phate's posthumous instructions.

The detective had tried to call Wyatt Gillette back but the phone was out of service. He called Tony Mott at the CCU. He told him and Linda Sanchez about the machine and then explained that Gillette seemed to think there was something specific he could do. But the hacker hadn't had time to tell him. "Any ideas?"

They debated. Bishop thought he should try to shut the machine down and stop the transmission of the confirmation code from Shawn to FBI tactical commander. Tony Mott, however, thought that if that happened there might be a second machine somewhere else that would take over for it, send the confirmation and, after learning that Shawn had been taken down, might be pre-programmed to do even more damage – like jam an FAA air traffic control computer somewhere. He thought it would be better to try to hack into Shawn and seize root.

Bishop didn't disagree with Mott but he explained there was no keyboard here to use to crack into Shawn. Besides, with only a few minutes to go until the assault there was no time to crunch passcodes and try to take control of the machine.

"I'm going to shut it down," he said.

But the detective could find no obvious way to do that. He searched again for a power switch and couldn't locate one. He looked for an access panel that would let him get to the power cables under the thick wooden floor but there was none.

He looked at his watch.

Two minutes until the assault. No time to go outside again and look for power company transformer boxes.

And so, just as he'd done six months ago in an alley in Oakland when Tremain Winters lifted a Remington twelve-gauge to his shoulder and aimed it at Bishop and two city cops, the detective calmly drew his service weapon and fired three well-grouped bullets into his adversary's torso.

But unlike the slugs that sent the gang leader to his death, these copper-jacketed rounds flattened into tiny pancakes and bounced to the floor; Shawn's skin was hardly dented.

Bishop walked closer, stood at an angle to avoid ricochets and emptied the clip at the indicator lights. One green light shattered but steam continued to pour from the vents into the cold air.

Bishop grabbed his cell phone and shouted to Mott, "I just emptied a clip at the machine. Is it still online?"

He had to cram the phone against his ear, half-deafened from the gunshots, to hear the young cop at CCU tell him that Shawn was still operational and on line.

Damn . . .

He reloaded and poked the gun into one of the back vents and emptied this clip as well. This time a ricochet – a bit of hot lead – struck the back of his hand and left a ragged stigmata in his skin. He wiped the blood on his slacks and grabbed the phone again.

"Sorry, Frank," Mott replied hopelessly. "It's still up and running."

The cop looked in frustration at the box. Well, if you're going to play God and create new life, he thought bitterly, you might as well make it invulnerable.

Sixty seconds.

Bishop was wracked with frustration. He thought of Wyatt Gillette, somebody whose only crime was stumbling slightly as he'd tried to escape an empty childhood. So many of the kids Bishop had collared – kids in the East Bay, in the Haight – were remorseless killers and were now walking around free. And Wyatt Gillette had simply followed the fairly harmless path that God and the young man's own brilliance had jointly directed him down and, as a result, he and the woman he loved, and her family, were going to suffer terribly.

No time left. Shawn would be sending the confirmation signal at any moment.

Was there *anything* he could do to stop Shawn?

Maybe burn the damn thing?

He could start a fire next to the vents. He ran to the desk and threw the contents of the drawers onto the floor, looking for matches or a cigarette lighter.

Nothing.

Then something clicked in his mind.

What?

He couldn't remember exactly, a thought from what seemed like ages ago – something Gillette had said when he'd walked into CCU for the first time.

The subject had been Fires in a computer room.

Do something with that.

He glanced at his watch. It was the deadline for the assault. Shawn's two remaining eyes flickered passionlessly.

Do something . . .

Fire.

. . . with that.

Yes! Bishop suddenly turned from Shawn and looked frantically around the room. There it was! He ran to a small gray box with a red button in the middle – the dinosaur pen's scram switch.

He slammed his palm against the button.

A braying alarm sounded from the ceiling and with a piercing hiss, streams of halon gas shot from pipes above and below the machine, enveloping the room's occupants – one human, one not – in a ghostly white fog.

* * *

Tactical agent Mark Little looked at the screen of the computer in the command van.

RED CODE: <Mapleleaf>

This was the go-ahead code for the assault.

"Print it out," Little said to the tech agent. Then he turned to George Steadman. "Confirm that Mapleleaf green-lights us for an assault with Level 4 rules of engagement."

The other agent consulted a small booklet with a Department of Justice seal on the front cover under the word CLASSIFIED written in large block letters.

"Confirmed."

Little radioed to the three snipers covering all the doors. "We're going in. Any targets presenting through the windows?"

They each reported that there were none.

"All right. If anyone comes through the door armed, take them out. Drop 'em with a head shot so they won't have time to push any detonator buttons. If they seem to be unarmed use your own judgment. But I'll remind you that rules of engagement've been set at Level 4. Understand what I'm saying?"

"Five by five," one of the snipers said and the others confirmed that they understood too.

Little and Steadman left the command van and ran through the hazy dusk to their teams. Little slipped into a side yard to join the eight officers he was leading – Alpha team. Steadman went to his, Bravo.

Little listened as the search and surveillance team reported in. "Alpha team leader, infrared shows body heat in the living room and parlor. The kitchen too – but that might just be cooking heat from the stove."

"Roger." Then Little announced into his radio, "I'm taking Alpha up the operation-side right of the house. We'll saturate with stun grenades – three in the parlor, three in the living room, three in the kitchen, thrown at five-second intervals. On the third bang Bravo goes in the front, Charlie in the back. We'll set up crossfire zones from the side windows."

Steadman and the leader of the other team confirmed they'd heard and understood.

Little pulled on his gloves, hood and helmet, thinking about the stolen cache of automatic weapons, hand grenades and body armor.

"Okay," he said. "Alpha team forward. Go slow. Use all available cover. Get ready to light the candles."

CHAPTER 00101101 / FORTY-FIVE

———◆◈◆———

Inside the Papandolos home – the house of lemons, the house of photographs, the house of family – Wyatt Gillette pressed his face against lace curtains that he remembered Elana's mother sewing together one autumn. From this nostalgic vantage point he saw the FBI agents start to move in.

A few feet at a time, crouching, cautious.

He glanced into the other room, behind him, and saw Elana lying on the floor, her arm around her mother. Christian, her brother, was nearby, but his head was up and he looked with bottomless anger into Gillette's eyes.

Nothing he could say to them by way of apology would even approach adequacy and he remained silent, turned back to the window.

He'd decided what he would do – decided some time before actually but he'd been content to savor these last few minutes of his life in proximity to the woman he loved.

Ironically the idea had come from Phate.

You're the hero with the flaw – the flaw that usually gets them into trouble. Oh, you'll do something heroic at the end and save some lives and the audience'll cry for you. . . .

He'd walk outside with his arms up. Bishop had said they wouldn't trust him and think that he was a suicide bomber or had a hidden gun. Phate and Shawn had seen to it that the police were expecting the worst. But the officers were human too; they might hesitate. And if they did they might trust him to call Elana and the others out.

But you'll still never make it to the final level of the game.

And even if he didn't – if they shot and killed him – they'd search his body and find that he was unarmed and might think that the others would be willing to surrender peaceably too. Then they'd discover that this was all just a terrible mistake.

He glanced at his wife. Even now, he thought, she's so very beautiful. She didn't look up and he was glad for that; he couldn't have borne the burden of her gaze.

Wait until they're close, he told himself, so they can see you're not a threat.

As he stepped into the hall to wait beside the door he noticed on a desk in the den an old IBM-clone computer. Wyatt Gillette reflected on the dozens of hours he'd spent online in the past few days. Thinking: If he couldn't take Elana's love to his death, at least he'd have those memories of his hours in the Blue Nowhere to accompany him.

The tactical agents of Alpha team crawled slowly toward the stuccoed suburban house – hardly a likely setting for an operation of this sort. Mark Little signaled the team to take cover behind a bed of spiny rhododendrons about twenty feet from the west side of the house.

He gave a hand signal to three of his agents from whose belts dangled the powerful stun grenades. They ran into position beneath the parlor, living room and kitchen windows then pulled the pins of the grenades. Three others joined them and gripped billy clubs, with which they'd shatter the glass so their partners could pitch the grenades inside.

The men looked back at Little, awaiting the go-ahead hand signal.

Then: A crackle in Little's headset.

"Alpha team leader one, we have an emergency patch from a landline. It's the SAC from San Francisco."

Special Agent in Charge Jaeger? What was *he* calling for?

"Go ahead," he whispered into the stalk mike.

There was a click.

"Agent Little," came the unfamiliar voice. "It's Frank Bishop. State police."

"Bishop?" It was that fucking cop who'd called before. "Put Henry Jaeger on."

"He's not here, sir. I lied. I had to get through to you. Don't disconnect. You *have* to listen to me."

Bishop was the one they'd decided might be a perp inside the house trying to distract them.

Except, Little now reflected, the phone lines to the house and the cell were down, which meant that the call *couldn't* be coming from the killers.

"Bishop. . . . What the hell do you want? You know what kind of trouble you're going to be in for impersonating an FBI agent? I'm hanging up."

"No! Don't! Ask for reconfirmation."

"I don't want to hear any of this hacker crap."

Little examined the house. Everything was still. Moments like this summoned a curious sensation – exhilarating and frightening and numbing all at the same time. You also had the queasy sense that one of the killers had itchy crosshairs on you, picking out a target of flesh two inches off the vest.

The cop said, "I just nailed the perp who did the hacking and shut his computer down. I guarantee you won't get a reconfirmation. Send the request."

"That's not procedure."

"Do it anyway. You'll regret it for the rest of your life if you go in there under Level 4 rules of engagement."

Little paused. How had Bishop known they were operating at Level 4? Only someone on the team or with access to the bureau computer could have known that.

The agent noticed his second in command, Steadman, tap his watch impatiently then nod toward the house.

Bishop's voice was pure desperation. "Please. I'll stake my job on it."

The agent hesitated then muttered, "You sure as hell just did, Bishop." He slung his machine gun over his shoulder and switched back to the tactical frequency. "All teams, stay in position. Repeat, stay in position. If you're fired upon full retaliation is authorized."

He sprinted back to the command post. The communications tech looked up in surprise. "What's up?"

On the screen Little could still see the confirmation code okaying the attack.

"Confirm the red code again."

"Why? We don't need to reconfirm if—"

"Now," Little snapped.

The man typed.

```
FROM: TACTICAL COMMANDER, DOJ NORTHERN
DISTRICT CALIFORNIA

TO: DOJ TAC OP CENTER, WASHINGTON, D.C.

RE: DOJ NORTHERN DISTRICT CALIFORNIA
OPERATION 139-01:

RED CODE CONFIRM?
```

A message popped up on the screen:

```
<Please Wait>
```

These few minutes could give the killers inside a chance to prepare for an assault or to rig the house with explosives for a group suicide that would take the lives of a dozen of his men.

```
<Please Wait>
```

This was taking too much time. He said to the communications officer, "Forget it. We're going in." He started toward the door.

"Hey, wait," the officer said. "Something's weird." He nodded at the screen. "Take a look."

```
FROM: DOJ TAC OP CENTER, WASHINGTON,
D.C.

TO: TACTICAL COMMANDER, DOJ NORTHERN
DISTRICT CALIFORNIA

RE: DOJ NORTHERN DISTRICT CALIFORNIA
OPERATION 139-01:
```

```
<NO INFORMATION. PLEASE CHECK OPERATION
NUMBER>
```

The man said, "It's the right number. I checked."

Little: "Send it again."

Once more the agent typed and hit ENTER.
Another delay. Then:

```
FROM: DOJ TAC OP CENTER, WASHINGTON,
D.C.

TO: TACTICAL COMMANDER, DOJ NORTHERN
DISTRICT CALIFORNIA

RE: DOJ NORTHERN DISTRICT CALIFORNIA
OPERATION 139-01

<NO INFORMATION. PLEASE CHECK OPERATION
NUMBER>
```

Little pulled his black hood off and wiped his face. Christ,
what *was* this?

He grabbed the phone and called the FBI agent who
handled the territory near the San Pedro military reserve,
thirty miles away. The agent told him that there'd been no
break-in or theft of weapons that afternoon. Little dropped
the receiver into the cradle, staring at the screen.

Steadman ran up to the door of the trailer. "What the
hell's going on, Mark? We've waited too long. If we're
going to hit them it's gotta be now."

Little continued to gaze at the screen.

```
<NO INFORMATION. PLEASE CHECK OPERATION
NUMBER>
```

"Mark, are we *going?*"

The commander glanced toward the house. By now there'd
been enough of a delay that the occupants might have grown
suspicious that the phones were out. Neighbors had probably
called the local police about the troops in the neighborhood
and reporters' police scanners would have picked up the calls.

Press helicopters might be on their way. There'd be live broadcasts from the choppers and the killers inside could be watching the accounts on TV in a few minutes.

Suddenly a voice in the radio: "Alpha team leader one, this's sniper three. One of the suspects's on the front steps. White male, late twenties. Hands in the air. I have a shot-to-kill. Should I take it?"

"Any weapons? Explosives?"

"None visible."

"What's he doing?"

"Walking forward slowly. He's turned around to show us his back. Still no weapons. But he could have something rigged under his shirt. I'll lose the shot to foliage in ten seconds. Sniper two, pick up target when he's past that bush."

"Roger that," came the voice of another sniper.

Steadman said, "He's got a device on him, Mark. All the bulletins've said that's what they're going to do – take out as many of us as they can. This guy'll set off the charge and the rest'll come out the back door, shooting."

⟨NO INFORMATION. PLEASE CHECK OPERATION NUMBER⟩

Mark Little said into his mike, "Bravo team leader two, order suspect onto the ground. Sniper two if he's not face-down in five seconds, take your shot."

"Yessir."

They heard the loudspeaker a moment later: "This is the FBI. Lie down face forward and extend your arms. Now, now, now!"

NO INFORMATION . . .

The agent then called in. "He's down, sir. Should we frisk and restrain?"

Little thought of his wife and two children and said, "No, I'll do it myself." He said into the mike: "All teams, pull back to cover."

He turned to the communications officer. "Get me the deputy director in Washington." Then he pointed a blunt finger at the conflicting messages – the go-ahead print-out and the "no information" message on the computer screen. "And let me know *exactly* how the hell this happened."

CHAPTER 00101110 / FORTY-SIX

L ying on the grass, smelling dirt, rain, and the faint scent of lilac, Wyatt Gillette blinked as the searing spotlights focused on him. He watched an edgy young agent move cautiously toward him, pointing a very large gun at his head.

The agent cuffed him and frisked him thoroughly, relaxing only when Gillette asked him to call a state trooper named Bishop, who could confirm that the FBI's computer system had been hacked and that the people in the house weren't the MARINKILL suspects.

The agent then ordered Elana's family out of the house. She, her mother and her brother walked slowly out onto the lawn, arms raised. They were searched and handcuffed and, though they weren't treated roughly, it was clear from their grim faces that they were suffering nearly as much from indignity and terror as if they'd been physically injured.

Gillette's ordeal, though, was the worst and that had nothing to do with his treatment at the hands of the FBI; it was that he knew that the woman he loved was now gone from him forever. She'd seemed to be wavering on her decision to move to New York with Ed but now the machines that had driven them apart years ago had almost killed her family and that was, of course, unforgivable. She would now flee to the East Coast with responsible, gainfully employed Ed, and Ellie would become to Gillette nothing more than a collection of memories, like .jpg and .wav files – visual and sound images that vanished when you powered down at night.

The FBI agents huddled and made a number of phone calls and then huddled some more. They concluded that the assault had indeed been illegally ordered. They released everyone – except Gillette, of course, though they helped him stand and loosened the cuffs a bit.

Elana strode up to her ex. He stood motionless in front of her, making not a sound as he took the full force of the powerful slap against his cheek. The woman, sensuous and beautiful even in her anger, turned away without a word and helped her mother up the stairs into the house. Her brother offered a twenty-two-year-old's inarticulate threat about a lawsuit and worse and followed them, slamming the door.

As the agents packed up, Bishop arrived and found Gillette being guarded by a large agent. He walked up to the hacker and said, "The scram switch."

"A halon dump." Gillette nodded. "That's what I was going to tell you to do when they cut the phone line."

Bishop nodded. "I remembered you mentioned it at CCU. When you first saw the dinosaur pen."

"Any other damage?" Gillette asked. "To Shawn?"

He hoped not. He was keenly curious about the machine – how it worked, what it could do, what operating system made up its heart and mind.

But the machine wasn't badly hurt, Bishop explained. "I emptied two full clips at the box but it didn't do much damage." He smiled. "Just a flesh wound."

A stocky man walked toward them through the blinding spotlights. When he got closer Gillette could see it was Bob Shelton. The pock-faced cop greeted his partner and glanced Gillette with his typical disdain.

Bishop told him what had happened but said nothing about suspecting Shelton himself as being Shawn.

The cop shook his head with a bitter laugh. "Shawn was a computer? Jesus, somebody oughta throw every fucking one of 'em into the ocean."

"Why do you keep saying that?" Gillette snapped. "I'm getting a little tired of it."

"Of what?" Shelton shot back.

No longer able to control his anger at the cop's harsh

treatment of him over the past few days, the hacker muttered, "You've been dumping on me and machines every chance you get. But it's a little hard to believe coming from somebody with a thousand-dollar Winchester drive sitting in his house."

"A what?"

"When we were over at your house I saw that server drive sitting in your living room."

The cop's eyes flared. "That was my son's," he growled. "I was throwing it out. I was finally cleaning out his room, getting rid of all that computer shit he had. My wife didn't want me to throw out any of his things. That's what we were fighting about."

"He was into computers, your son?" Gillette asked, recalling that the boy had died several years ago.

Another bitter laugh. "Oh, yeah, he was *into* computers. He'd spend hours online. All he wanted to do was hack. Only some cybergang found out he was a cop's kid and thought he was trying to snitch 'em out. They went after him. Posted all kinds of shit about him on the Internet – that he was gay, that he had a record, that he molested little kids . . . They broke into his school's computer and made it look like he changed his own grades. That got him suspended. Then they sent some girl he'd been dating this filthy e-mail in his name. She broke up with him because of it. The day that happened he got drunk and drove into a freeway abutment. Maybe it was an accident – maybe he killed himself. Either way it was computers that killed him."

"I'm sorry," Gillette said softly.

"The fuck you are." Shelton stepped closer to the hacker, his anger undiminished. "That's why I volunteered for this case. I thought the perp might be one of the kids in that gang. And that's why I went online that day – to see if *you* were one of 'em too."

"No, I wasn't. I wouldn't've done something like that to anybody. That's not why I hacked."

"Oh, you keep saying that. But you're as bad as any of them, making my boy believe that those goddamn plastic boxes're the whole world. Well, that's bullshit. That's not where life is." He grabbed Gillette's jacket. The hacker didn't resist, just stared at the enraged man's face. Shelton snapped, "Life is *here!* Flesh and blood . . . human beings . . . Your family, your children. . . ." His voice choked, tears filled his eyes. "*That's* what's real."

Shelton shoved the hacker back, wiped his eyes with his hands. Bishop stepped forward and touched his arm. But Shelton pulled away and disappeared into the crowd of police and agents.

Gillette's heart went out to the poor man but he couldn't help but think: Machines're real too, Shelton. They're becoming more and more a part of that flesh-and-blood life every day and that's never going to change. The question we have to ask ourselves isn't whether this transformation is in itself good or bad but simply this: Who do we become when we step through the monitor into the Blue Nowhere?

The detective and the hacker, alone now, stood facing each other. Bishop noticed his shirt was untucked. He shoved the tail into his slacks then nodded at the palm tree tattoo on Gillette's forearm. "You might want to get that removed, you know. I don't think it does a lot for you. The pigeon at least. The tree's not too bad."

"It's a seagull," the hacker replied. "But now that you bring it up, Frank . . . why don't *you* get one?"

"What?"

"A tattoo."

The detective started to say something then lifted an eyebrow. "You know, maybe I just will."

Then Gillette felt his arms being gripped from behind. The state troopers had arrived, right on schedule, to return him to San Ho.

CHAPTER 00101111 / FORTY-SEVEN

———◆———

A week after the hacker returned to prison Frank Bishop made good on Andy Anderson's promise and, over the warden's renewed objections, delivered to Wyatt Gillette a battered, secondhand Toshiba laptop computer.

When he booted it up the first thing he saw was a digitized picture of a fat, dark-complected baby, a few days old. The caption beneath it read "Greetings – from Linda Sanchez and her new granddaughter, Maria Andie Harmon." Gillette made a mental note to send her a letter of congratulations; a baby present would have to wait, federal prisons not having gift shops as such.

There was no modem included with the computer of course. Gillette could have gone online simply by building a modem out of Devon Franklin's Walkman (bartered to Gillette for some apricot preserves) but he chose not to. It was part of his deal with Bishop. Besides, all he wanted now was for the last year of his sentence to roll by and to get on with his life.

Which isn't to say that he was completely quarantined from the Net. He'd been allowed onto the library's dog-slow IBM PC to help with the analysis of Shawn, whose new foster home was Stanford University. Gillette was working with the school's computer scientists and with Tony Mott. (Frank Bishop had emphatically denied Mott's request to be transferred to Homicide and had placated the young cop by recommending that he be named acting head of the Computer Crimes Unit, which Sacramento agreed to.)

What Gillette had found within Shawn had astonished him. To give Phate access to as many computers as possible, via Trapdoor, he'd endowed his creation with its own operating system. It was unique, incorporating all existing operating systems: Windows, MS-DOS, Apple, Unix, Linux, VMS and a number of obscure systems for scientific and engineering applications. His operating system, which he called Protean 1.1, reminded Gillette of the elusive unified theory that explains the behavior of all matter and energy in the universe.

Only Phate, unlike Einstein and his progeny, had apparently succeeded in his quest.

One thing that Shawn didn't disgorge was the source code to Trapdoor or the location of any sites where it might be hidden. The woman calling herself Patricia Nolan had, it seemed, been successful in isolating and stealing the code and destroying all copies.

She hadn't been found either.

It used to be easy to disappear because there were no computers to trace you, Gillette had told Bishop when learning this news. Now, it was easy to disappear because computers can erase all the traces of your old identity and create brand-new ones.

Bishop reported that Stephen Miller had been given a full-dress policeman's funeral. Linda Sanchez and Tony Mott were still apparently troubled that they'd believed Miller was the traitor when in fact he was only a sad holdout from the elder days of computing, a has-been on a futile search for the Next Big Thing in Silicon Valley. Wyatt Gillette could have told the cops, though, that they needn't have felt any guilt; the Blue Nowhere tolerates deceit far more than it does incompetence.

The hacker had been given further dispensation to go online for another mission. To look into the charges against David Chambers, the suspended head of the Department of Defense's Criminal Investigation Division. Frank Bishop, Captain Bernstein and the U.S. attorney had concluded that the man's personal and business computers had been hacked by Phate to get Chambers removed and to have Kenyon or one of his lackeys appointed as his replacement to get Gillette off the case

It took the hacker only fifteen minutes to find and download proof that, indeed, the man's files had been cracked and brokerage trades and off-shore accounts had been faked by Phate. The charges against him were dropped and he was reinstated.

No charges were ever brought against Wyatt Gillette for his Standard 12 hack or against Frank Bishop for helping Gillette escape from the CCU. The U.S. attorney decided to drop the investigation – not because he believed the story that it had been Phate who'd hacked together the cracking program that busted Standard 12, but because of a Department of Defense audit committee investigation looking into why $35 million had been spent on an encryption program that was essentially unsecure.

Gillette was also being asked to help track down a particularly dangerous computer virus, known as Polonius, which had made its first appearance in the past few weeks. The virus was a demon that would make your computer go online by itself and transmit all of your past and current e-mails to everyone in your electronic address book. Not only did this create major Internet traffic jams around the world but it resulted in a lot of embarrassment when people received e-mails not intended for their eyes. Several people attempted suicide when affairs, cases of sexually transmitted diseases and shady business practices were revealed.

What was particularly frightening, though, was how the computers were infected. Aware that firewalls and virus shields will stop most viruses, the perpetrator had cracked into the networks of commercial software manufacturers and instructed their disk-making machines to insert the virus into the disks included in the software packages sold by retail stores and mail-order companies.

The feds were running the case and all they could determine was that the virus had originated from a university in Singapore about two weeks before. They had no other leads – until one of the FBI agents on the case wondered aloud, "Polonius – that's the character from *Hamlet,* right?"

Gillette had dug up a copy of Shakespeare's plays and

learned that, yes, it was Polonius who'd said, "To thine own self be true. . . ." Gillette had them check to find the time and date of the first occurrence of the virus; it was late on the afternoon of the day that Patricia Nolan killed Phate. When her colleagues had called the first FTP site he'd given her, they'd unwittingly unleashed the Polonius virus on the world – a farewell present from Phate.

The code was very elegant and proved to be extremely difficult to eradicate. Manufacturers would have to completely rewrite their disk manufacturing systems and users would have to wipe the entire contents of their hard drives and start over with virus-free programs.

Remember that line, Valleyman. That's advice from a wizard. 'To thine own self be true' . . .

On a Tuesday in late April, Gillette was sitting at his laptop in his cell, analyzing some of Shawn's operating system, when the guard came to the door.

"Visitor, Gillette."

It would be Bishop, he guessed. The detective was still working the MARINKILL case, spending a lot of time north of Napa, where the suspects were reportedly hiding out. (never been in Santa Clara County at all. Phate himself, it seemed, had sent most of the advisories about the killers to the press and to the police as more diversions.) Bishop, though, stopped by San Ho occasionally when he was in the area. Last time he'd brought Gillette some Pop-Tarts and some apricot preserves Jennie had made from Bishop's own orchard. (Not his favorite condiment but the jam made excellent prison currency – this batch, in fact, had been traded for the Walkman that *could* be turned into a modem but would not be. Most likely.)

The visitor, however, wasn't Frank Bishop.

He sat down in the cubicle and watched Elana Papandolos walk into the room. She was wearing a navy blue dress. Her dark, wiry hair was pulled back. It was so thick that the golden barrette holding it together seemed about to burst apart. Noticing her short nails, perfectly filed and colored lavender, he thought of something that'd never occurred to him. That Ellie, a piano teacher, made her way in the world with *her* hands too – just as he had done – yet her fingers were beautiful and unblemished by even a hint of callus.

She sat down, scooted the chair forward.

"You're still here," he said, lowering his head slightly to speak through the holes in the Plexiglas. "I never heard from you. I assumed you'd left a couple of weeks ago."

She said nothing in response. Looked at the divider. "They added that."

The last time she'd been to visit him, several years ago, they'd sat at a table without a divider, a guard hovering over them. With the new system there was no guard; you gained privacy but you lost proximity. He would rather have had her close, Gillette decided, remembering during her visits how he'd loved to brush fingertips with her or press his shoe against the side of her foot, the contact producing an electric frisson that was akin to making love.

Gillette now found as he sat forward that he was air-keying furiously. He stopped and slipped his hands into his pockets.

He asked, "Did you talk to somebody about the modem?"

Elana nodded. "I found a lawyer. She doesn't know if it'll sell or not. But if it does, the way I'm handling it is I'll pay myself back for your lawyer's bill and my half of the house we lost. The rest is yours."

"No, I want you to have—"

She interrupted him by saying, "I postponed my plans. To go to New York."

He was silent, processing this. Finally he asked her, "For how long?"

"I'm not sure."

"What about Ed?"

She glanced behind her. "He's outside."

This stung Gillette's heart. Nice of him to chauffeur her to see her ex, the hacker thought bitterly, inflamed by jealousy. "So why'd you come?" he asked.

"I've been thinking about you. About what you said to me the other day. Before the police showed up."

He nodded for her to continue.

"Would you give up machines for me?" she asked.

Gillette took a breath. He exhaled and then answered

evenly, "No. I'd never do that. Machines are what I'm meant to do in life."

He expected her to stand up and walk out. It would have killed a portion of him – maybe most of him – but he'd vowed that if he had a chance to talk to her again he'd never lie.

He added, "But I can promise you that they'll never come between us the way they did. Never again."

Elana nodded slowly. "I don't know, Wyatt. I don't know if I can trust you. My dad drinks a bottle of ouzo a night. He keeps swearing he's going to give up drinking. And he does – about six times a year."

"You'll have to take a chance," he said.

"That might've been the wrong thing to say."

"But it's the honest thing."

"Reassurances, Gillette. I need reassurances before I even begin to think about it."

Gillette didn't respond. He couldn't present her with much compelling evidence that he'd change. Here he was, in prison, having nearly gotten this woman and her family killed because of his passion for a world completely alien to the one that she inhabited and understood.

After a moment he said, "There's nothing more I can say except that I love you and I want to be with you, have a family with you."

"I'll be in town for a while at least," she said slowly. "Why don't we just see what happens?"

"What about Ed? What's he going to say?"

"Why don't you ask him?"

"Me?" Gillette asked, alarmed.

Elana rose and walked to the door.

What on earth was he going to say? Gillette wondered in panic. He was about to come face-to-face with the man who'd stolen his wife's heart.

She opened the door and gestured.

A moment later Elana's staunch, unsmiling mother walked into the room. She was leading a small boy, about eighteen months old, by the hand.

Jesus, Lord . . . Gillette was shocked. Elana and Ed had a baby!

His ex-wife sat down in the chair once again and hauled the youngster up on her lap. "This's Ed."

Gillette whispered, "Him?"

"That's right."

"But . . ."

"*You* assumed Ed was my boyfriend. But he's my son. . . . Actually, I should say he's *our* son. I named him after you. Your middle name. Edward isn't a hacker's name."

"*Ours?*" he whispered.

She nodded.

Gillette thought back to the last few nights they'd been together before he'd surrendered to the prison authorities to start his sentence, lying in bed with her, pulling her close . . .

He closed his eyes. Lord, Lord, Lord . . . He remembered the surveillance at Elana's house in Sunnyvale the night he escaped from CCU – he'd assumed that the children the police saw were her sister's. But one of them must have been this boy.

I saw your e-mails. When you talk about Ed it doesn't exactly sound like he's perfect husband material. . . .

He gave a faint laugh. "You never told me."

"I was so mad at you I didn't want you to know. Ever."

"But you don't feel that way now?"

"I'm not sure."

He gazed at the boy's thick, curly black hair. That was his mother's. He'd gotten her beautiful dark eyes and round face too. "Hold him up, would you?"

She helped her son stand on her lap. His quick eyes studied Gillette carefully. Then the boy became aware of the Plexiglas. He reached forward with his fat baby fingers and touched it, smiling, fascinated, trying to understand how he could see through it but not touch something on the other side.

He's curious, Gillette thought. *That*'s what he got from me.

Then a guard appeared and announced that visiting hours were over and Elana eased the boy to the floor and stood. Her mother took the child's hand and Ed and his grandmother walked out of the room.

Elana and Gillette faced each other across the Plexiglas divide.

"We'll see how it goes," she said. "How's that?"

"That's all I'm asking."

She nodded.

Then they turned in separate directions and, as Elana disappeared out the visitor's door, the guard led Wyatt Gillette back into the dim corridor toward his cell, where his machine awaited.

AUTHOR'S NOTE

In writing this book, I've taken some significant liberties with the structure and operation of federal and California state law enforcement agencies. I wish I could say the same for my depiction of computer hackers' ability to invade our private lives, but I've got bad news: It happens with alarming frequency. Some of the computer specialists I spoke with felt that a program like Trapdoor probably couldn't be written at this time. But I'm not completely convinced – upon hearing their opinions I couldn't help but think of the senior researcher for one of the world's biggest computer companies who in the 1950s recommended that his company stick with vacuum tubes because there was no future for the microchip, and of the head of another international hardware and software manufacturer who stated – in the 1980s – that there'd never be a market for a personal computer. For the moment we can assume that a Trapdoor-like program doesn't exist. Well, probably. And, oh, yes, the chapter numbers are in binary form. Don't feel bad, I had to look them up too.

ACKNOWLEDGEMENTS

As one's career in this business lengthens so does the list of those for whom a novelist feels undying gratitude for their herculean efforts on his behalf: David Rosenthal, Marysue Rucci, George Lucas and everyone at my top-notch U.S. publisher, Simon & Schuster/Pocket Books; Sue Fletcher, Carolyn Mays, and Georgina Moore, to name just a few at my superb U.K. publisher, Hodder & Stoughton; and my agents Deborah Schneider, Diana McKay, Vivienne Schuster, the other fine folks at Curtis Brown in London, and movie-wizard Ron Bernstein, as well as my many foreign agents, who've gotten my books into the hands of readers around the world. Thanks to my sister and fellow author, Julie Deaver, and – as always – my special, enduring gratitude to Madelyn Warcholik; if it weren't for her you would just have bought a book containing nothing but blank pages.

Among the resources I found invaluable (and thoroughly enjoyable) in writing this novel are the following books: *The Watchman* and *The Fugitive Game* by Jonathan Littman, *Masters of Deception* by Michelle Slatalla and Joshua Quittner; *The New Hacker's Dictionary* by Eric S. Raymond; *The Cuckoo's Egg* by Cliff Stoll, *The Hacker Crackdown* by Bruce Sterling, *Bots* by Andrew Leonard and *Fire In the Valley* by Paul Freiberger and Michael Swaine.